I0777260

a vine mess

AMANDA CHAPERON

before you read

A VINE MESS IS a steamy small town romance full of explicit language and sexual content. To avoid—or locate—the open door chapters, please flip to the Dicktionary I've provided in the back. For the complete list of content warnings, please visit my website at www.achaperonauthor.com/content-warnings.

*It's about damn time I dedicate one
to myself, don't y'all think?*

*So from me to me: if you're ever
worried you're not good enough,
you're not doing enough, or
you're failing miserably at this
whole thing, just remember you've
already made your dreams come
true several times over.
Even if you stopped writing tomorrow,
no one can ever take that away from you.*

FOUR YEARS BEFORE THE TRIP

THE PEOPLE OF THIS town really had to stop giving me dirty looks when I walked down the street.

I wasn't some big scary dude like the residents of Apple Blossom Bay tried to pretend. I was simply…reclusive. I kept my head down, lived on the fringes of town, and was content to spend the bulk of my time alone amid the rows of vines at Chateau Delatou where I worked.

But they judged me anyway. Because of my size—six-four and broad shouldered. Because of the tattoos taking up real estate on my arms. Because of my lumberjack beard and the flannels I frequently wore that really drove the whole image home.

I couldn't control the way I looked. I kept the beard both because I hated shaving and because I looked about ten years younger than my actual age of thirty without it. My hair was perpetually in need of a cut, and I kept it out of my face with ball caps. Flannels were a good way to ward off the chill of the cooler

Michigan months—though, at the moment, it was mid-July so I only had on a black cotton tee—as were the faded jeans and scuffed Wolverine work boots I favored. All of it was designed for practicality. I was an efficient man, and the last thing I needed was the chaos of trying to pick out what to wear in the morning or how to style my hair.

All that to say...I supposed I could see where the townspeople were coming from. But I wasn't a bad guy. I just enjoyed my solitude.

I came into town on very rare occasions, and today was one of my boss's birthdays, which warranted a trip to the flower shop. I'd been living in Apple Blossom Bay for over a year now and working for the Delatou family at their winery for nearly as long, but I'd never set foot in the place.

Upon pushing open the door, I was greeted with high, sweet notes of numerous florals, and I resisted the urge to sneeze. I scrunched my nose and rubbed at it with the back of my hand as I moved further onto the showroom floor, eyes scanning for the perfect gift for Lena.

The tinkling of the door bell alerted a worker to my arrival, because a moment later, a young woman appeared from the back.

Time slowed to a crawl as she breezed toward me, and I was struck speechless, my mouth gaping.

Without a doubt, she was the most beautiful woman I'd ever seen. Long, dark hair piled atop her head in a messy bun, little pink tendrils falling free and framing her face. She wore a little slip of a sundress in a pale yellow, decorated with vibrantly colored flowers that offset her olive skin beautifully. The dainty straps were tied into bows over her delicate shoulders, and tattoos randomly dotted her arms.

Instantly, I was intrigued. By the sudden rush of desire I experienced. By her soft, welcoming presence, startlingly gorgeous face, and the random assortment of ink decorating her skin. By the way everything around me seemed to click into place.

I hadn't wanted anyone that way in a long ass time.

"Hi," she said brightly. "What can I help you with?"

"Hi," I responded gruffly, then cleared my throat and tried again. "Hello. I'm hoping you could help me pick out a birthday gift for my boss."

The woman's brow raised toward her hairline. "Do you always buy flowers for your boss?"

"What?" I asked, instantly picking up on her meaning. "No. It's not like that. She's a happily married woman and about twice my age. I just...she and her husband have done a lot for me, and I wanted to thank her by getting her favorite flowers."

Her brow drooped and her face slackened, mouth popping open slightly. "You're Liam."

"I...yes?" It came out as more of a question. Despite the fact that it was a small town, as previously mentioned, I didn't get out much, and I'd definitely remember if I'd laid eyes on *her* before.

"You know...it's my mom's birthday today too. And *Lena*"—she emphasized the name with a knowing look, and I realized with a jolt that I was looking at one of my bosses' daughters—"loves peonies."

With a wink, the woman weaved through the display tables until she stood behind the counter, where the thirty-foot wall was lined with coolers holding various buckets of blooms. She approached one and slid the door open, reaching in and emerging with three separate flowers. One pink, one white, one purple. Then she turned to me again.

"These three would look great in a bouquet with some greenery. I can put them in one of the milk can vases," she said, gesturing to the row of tins modeled to look like old school milk cans.

"Great," I croaked, swallowing hard. I suddenly had no idea what to do with myself. This woman—whose name I had yet to learn—was my bosses' daughter, which meant I needed to stay as far away as possible lest I wanted to lose my job...or worse. Still, I couldn't ignore the way my skin prickled in her presence, like she was meant to be in my life. But maybe that's all I was experiencing. The knowledge that she was going to be in my life because I was employed by her family and nothing more.

So why was that thought so goddamn depressing?

Admittedly, I'd been floating through life for a while. Basically since I'd left Portland, my previous job, and my ill-fated relationship in favor of a new life away from the pressure, drama, and expectations of people who had known me forever.

And then this woman appeared like a goddamn magical garden fairy and turned my entire world upside down in a flash. For a moment there, I'd been...almost excited. Excited for the future, for exploring this impossible, inexplicable, and immediate connection I felt for her. But it was all doused by the realization that her parents were my bosses, and her father would murder me if I broke his cardinal rule.

I liked my head attached to my body. And breathing. Definitely enjoyed breathing.

The woman canted her head to the side, studying me, before

giving me a little nod and going about building the arrangement for her mom. I watched as she worked, rapt by the way her long, delicate fingers maneuvered the scissors to snip the stems just right, how they patiently stuck them in the vase until they were arranged to her satisfaction.

We didn't speak as she worked. In fact, I stood there like a statue with my clammy hands shoved deep in my pockets, shoulders bunched up around my ears like I'd suddenly forgotten how to speak to people and didn't know what to do with my body.

But this woman...she wasn't just anyone. Inherently, I knew that. And while I wanted to make a good impression, my awkwardness told me I was failing miserably.

Maybe I really did need to get out of my house more.

"I don't believe I got your name," I blurted as she began sifting large, deep green leaves in between the peony blooms.

"Oh!" she said with a little giggle before she turned to face me. "Ella. The second youngest Delatou, at your service."

She let go of the flowers long enough to extend a hand, and I captured it with my own. A jolt shot up my arm, and I once again experienced that same sense of time crawling, warping around us until it was only me and her. Everything narrowed to that single point of contact.

"Pleasure to meet you, Ella. I'm Liam Danvers."

"Mom and Dad's vintner," she said with a nod. "I know."

Time sped again, and with it, some of my old charm seemed to return.

"So you've heard about me."

Ella only lifted a shoulder. "Some."

"All good things, I hope."

Ella grinned, showing off a straight, bright smile that punched me in the gut. "My parents have done nothing but sing your praises. From what I hear, you're damn good at your job, an impressive feat for someone so young."

"I'm thirty," I grumbled. "That's hardly young."

"Still awfully young to be head vintner at a winery as old as my family's."

Well, she wasn't wrong there.

I'd always felt a kinship with nature. After shunning the expectations my father had placed on me to study business and join him at the family company, I'd gone to college for bio-agricultural engineering. Creating a top notch product was important to me, and I knew that started with providing the best growing environment for the grapes. I worked tirelessly year round—yes, even in the winter when several feet of snow blanketed the vineyards—to ensure Chateau Delatou maintained its liquid excellence. And I'd cut my teeth in the Willamette Valley near Portland, where I'd accepted a job fresh out of college and worked my way up the ladder.

In comparison, Chateau Delatou was actually relatively small, but only on the surface. We distributed across the country as well as the world, and business was booming. It was exactly where I wanted—and *needed*—to be at this stage of my life.

Had I considered moving onto something else now that I'd secured a position at the top of my field? Of course I had. But I wouldn't do that. Not now—maybe not ever.

Both because I loved my job, loved Leon and Lena for taking a chance on a kid who'd never headed his own operation before, and because I'd made a home and a family within the winery and

Apple Blossom Bay—despite all their misconceptions of me.

And now? Even if I'd had to content myself with being on the fringes of her life, I wouldn't leave.

As long as Ella Delatou remained, so would I.

Biding my time until it'd be safe to make my move.

I only had to hope she'd be ready for me when the time came.

FOURTEEN DAYS BEFORE THE TRIP

WALKING INTO THE GREENHOUSE at the winery was a breath of fresh air...literally. Everything in me settled with the first inhale of the plants that rested inside, waiting for the day when they'd be placed in their forever home on the vineyard.

"Hey, Ella," someone said from behind me, and I whirled to find Liam standing at the side entrance, smiling softly at me.

I grinned when I faced him. "Hey. Fancy seeing you here."

Liam paused for a beat, eyes wide and darting across my face. I lifted my hand to my cheek, wondering if there was something there, but he moved on before I could ask. With a snort and eyeroll, he said, "Please. I practically live here."

That wasn't a lie. As the winery's head vintner, his job was never done. He spent more time at the winery than anyone I knew—including my sister Amara, the CEO of the entire company.

"What're you working on today?" I asked him.

Liam inclined his head to the back left corner of the space. "Getting those new white wine grapes ready to be planted next week. They were looking a little dry when they arrived, so I'm trying to perk them back up."

"Want some help?"

He blinked, surprised, before his expression slid into the same cool mask I always saw it in. Sometimes, I wondered if I bothered him, being around constantly. But I never asked, and he never said. All he did was nod once and lead me to the new vines.

"I never like nurturing them in pots like this," he said when we approached the massive spread.

I knew from Amara that we'd received over a hundred new plants from her contact in California, and they took up the bulk of the greenhouse space. The rest was reserved for some of Ezra's fresh produce and a small plot I used for my personal flower experiments.

"Then why'd you agree to let Amara ship them early? Couldn't we have just waited until planting season?"

Liam shook his head. "The winery we got them from was going to sell them to someone else if we didn't take them when we did, and...well, you know your sister. When she sets her sights on something—"

"There's no changing her mind," I finished with a grin.

Liam spread his arms out, gesturing to the plants. "So here we are."

My eyes swept over the large terracotta pots with a large wooden post staked in the center, the vines snaking their way upward. But they were getting dangerously close to overgrowing their confinement, and I could tell by the tightness around Liam's eyes and mouth that he was stressed.

"What are we doing today then?"

"First," he said, heading toward the end of the first row where a wheelbarrow waited, filled with a dark substance I knew from the smell was some sort of manure-based mulch, "we're going to feed them. We're only about a week away from planting, and I need them to retain as much water as possible so they're ready for the transition. Adding this to the top soil will help that process along. Then"—he gestured to a pile of wood behind him—"we're going to extend these stakes so the vines have somewhere to grow before I'm ready for them to start twining together."

I withdrew my gardening gloves from the back pocket of my baggy denim overalls, slipped them on, and said, "Put me to work then."

I felt the way Liam looked at me then all the way to my bones, like his ocean eyes cut right to my core, flaying layers away until all that was left was my most vulnerable, soft underbelly. And if he could see that deeply into my heart, he could tell how badly I needed this distraction. I held my breath, waiting for his next move—more than a little grateful when he directed me to start crumbling the mulch into the pots, so I filled a five gallon bucket and moved to the far side to begin.

This kind of work was therapeutic for me, when I got my hands dirty and could let my mind wander. Over three months had passed since Alfie and I had broken up, and I truthfully was doing better than ever. I'd be lying if I said it didn't hurt, but it wasn't the loss of *him* that made my heart ache. *That* came from the fact that I'd wasted so much time on him, had allowed him to treat me like less than the woman I was, had changed into someone different to keep him, and that his presence had caused so many problems for my family.

The last one in particular was something I didn't think I could ever forgive myself for. I'd let him routinely talk shit about my sisters and parents, about our family businesses, about my sisters' partners. He'd gaslit me and isolated me to the point where instead of the vibrant woman I'd been before, I'd become sullen, my natural light dimmed.

I was slowly clawing my way back, and I had the dirt under my fingernails to prove it.

Several rows across from me, Liam had begun to extend the stakes shooting out of the pots by screwing the new pieces of wood to the old. The construction wasn't the prettiest thing I'd ever seen, but I knew it would accomplish what he wanted.

"How long do you think before we'll be able to get these in the ground?" I asked him conversationally, mostly to fill the silence.

Before Alfie, I'd clung to my solitude. But in the wake of his betrayal, my thoughts were too loud. The voices in my head constantly reminded me I wasn't good enough. Not smart or pretty or talented enough. After all, if a rat like him would cheat on me, what hope did I have of finding someone better?

So I spent my free time—when I wasn't at Blossom's—working at the winery, doing whatever menial tasks I could get my hands on to quell the cyclone of my thoughts.

I had to admit, Liam had been...surprising. I wasn't blind to the way he looked at me, like I was some fragile flower that needed to be handled with care lest my petals wilted and withered. But when I told him to put me to work, he gave me something to do, no questions asked. He didn't try to talk to me, didn't try to pry out how I was feeling like my sisters and parents had a habit of doing.

After all, it had been over three months since the breakup. I was *fine*, if a bit jaded. And the constant reminder of the epic implosion of my relationship certainly didn't help matters.

In answer to my question at last, Liam said, "I'm hoping next week. Soil conditions are improving rapidly thanks to the warmer weather we've been having, and I really want to get them in the ground before I leave on vacation."

"Your big road trip, right?"

I'd heard rumblings about it here and there, mostly from Amara, who was nervous about the thought of Liam being gone for two weeks. But in all the time I'd known him, the man had never taken more than a few days off here and there. He deserved a vacation.

"Yeah," Liam grinned. "I'm really excited, but I know I won't enjoy it as much if I have to leave the planting of these to someone else."

"Can't Victor handle it?" I asked, naming the older man who used to have Liam's job but has since stepped aside to take on a less-involved role.

"Haven't you heard?" Liam flicked his eyes up to me briefly before he straightened, gripping the plackets of his flannel, which he'd left unbuttoned, and flexing and rolling his arms and shoulders to peel it off. The white tee beneath clung to his torso in the most distracting way, his tattooed biceps truly testing the limits of the sleeves, the back and chest stretched over his broad shoulders and pecs.

The man was a fucking specimen, a goddamn lumberjack wet dream.

"Haven't I heard, what?" I asked absently, unable to tear my gaze away from the rippling of his abdomen through the thin cotton of his tee as he twisted to grab another piece of wood.

"Victor retired."

That got my attention. "Really?"

Liam nodded. "Last month."

"How..."

I'd been about to ask how the fuck I missed that, but Liam only smiled sympathetically.

"You've had your own shit going on," he said softly.

"Still," I protested weakly. "I'm part owner of the company. I should know when a long-time employee decides to retire."

"Well, you know Vic," Liam continued. "Didn't want to make a big deal out of it."

"Did he even give *you* a heads up?"

Liam shook his head. "Nope. Just walked up to me on his last day, stuck out his hand, and said, 'It's been nice working with you, kid. Good luck.'"

"Damn, that's cold," I said with a chuckle. Then again, Vic wasn't the friendliest man. In fact, my sisters and I had been terrified of him when we were younger. He reminded me of the old next door neighbor in the first *Home Alone* movie. But unlike that guy, Vic was *actually* mean. He used to chase us around with pruning shears when we dared run through the vineyards as kids, and no amount of scolding from my parents could get him to stop.

But he also knew his stuff, which is why my father never fired him because of his antics. Personally, I wasn't sad to see him go. Not when Liam was far...*younger*.

And, okay, a lot better looking. No grizzled beard, leathery skin, and ratty old shirts to be found with Liam Danvers. Simply...flannels, a well-maintained beard, tan skin, and a whole lot of muscles.

Fuck, and don't even get me started on the tattoos.

Liam's eyes narrowed on me a bit as I lost myself to those thoughts, so I gave my head a little shake and smiled brightly, mentally urging him to let it go.

If there was one thing I knew about Liam, it was that he, unlike the bulk of the other men around here, generally stayed out of other people's business. He kept to himself, which was something I greatly appreciated.

I had four sisters and two parents who were constantly pestering me about how I was doing in the wake of my breakup with Alfie. The last thing I needed was Liam joining the fray.

That was why I appreciated days like this so much, when he gave me a task and left me to it.

And on that note, I awkwardly pointed at the plant I'd been working on, half-filled with mulch, and said, "I'm just gonna..."

Liam cleared his throat, his hand coming up to scratch at the back of his neck. I quickly averted my gaze to avoid watching his biceps bunch deliciously beneath his shirt.

Fuck, I needed to get it together—or spend some quality time with my vibrator. Going for so long without sex was turning me into a real horndog.

But this bout of celibacy had also been incredibly healing. With Alfie, sex had always been transactional, where he was taking, taking, taking, and I was giving, giving, giving. Finding out he'd been cheating on me with multiple women only made me feel as though I'd lost more than what he'd already stolen from me. My trust was broken, self-esteem shattered, and this time alone had done wonders in helping me find myself again.

I just wished I could've done it without my family breathing down my neck, wondering when the "old me" was coming back.

In truth, I didn't think I'd ever be wholly that girl I was before Alfie again. He'd run off, into the arms of someone else, with pieces of me still stuck to his hands like the mulch on my gloves. And I didn't even *want* them back. Those were pieces of me that belonged to him because he'd created them. Nurtured me, took me from a little seedling to a withered old plant that, in those early days after the breakup, hadn't been sure how to survive without him. But being here, doing something I loved—helping my family and getting my hands dirty in the process—settled me in a way I hadn't experienced in a long time.

I must have been really lost in my thoughts because Liam startled me when he asked, "You okay over there?"

I canted my head to the side, my brows pinching together. "Yes?"

Liam chuckled. "You just let out the loudest sigh I've ever heard from another human."

"Really? I'm sorry." I swore softly. "I didn't realize—"

"It's okay," he said, gently cutting me off. "I think we've all been there, and you've been through a lot lately."

I grimaced but said, "Being here helps."

"Then you can stay as long as you want."

chapter 2
Liam

ELLA WAS STARTING TO make me look bad with how much time she spent at the winery, and I'd be worried about my job if I didn't know how indispensable I was around here.

Truthfully, I didn't mind having her around—secretly loved it, actually. And every day for the last few months, I found myself looking forward to walking into the greenhouse in the mornings and finding her already there, up to her elbows in dirt as she tended to the section in the corner that housed her flowers.

That morning, she hadn't noticed my arrival yet, so I took a moment to stand in the doorway, leaning my shoulder against it, arms crossed over my chest and a small smile on my lips as I watched her.

Her touch was gentle, reverent as she gently peeled the blooms apart and trimmed away a leaf that had begun to turn yellow at the edges. Then she set her tools down and cupped the fluffy snowball of a hydrangea, burying her face in the delicate petals as she deeply inhaled.

The smile—it couldn't be described as anything but pure bliss. And it was the kind of smile I hadn't seen on her in far too long.

Trust me, I'd been looking.

Not wanting to scare her but needing to announce my presence, I pushed off the door frame and cleared my throat loudly, letting my boots scuff on the concrete floor as I approached her.

That deep brown and bright purple hair went whipping around her head as she whipped it toward me, a hand to her chest. "Fuck, Liam."

"I'm sorry," I chuckled awkwardly. "I didn't want to startle you."

"It's okay," she said, waving a hand. "I get lost sometimes."

"Get you lost all you want," I assured her. "My greenhouse is yours whenever you want."

Ella quirked one of those perfect, dark brows. "*Your* greenhouse?"

I grinned. "Yeah, *mine*."

She pursed her lips. "Last I checked, it was *my* name on the walls of this place, but sure."

Fuck, I loved that fire. Missed the way her eyes flashed when she challenged someone. That side of her had been buried far too long under the large, stifling ego of her ex. I was happy to see it returning.

In truth, even since the last time I'd seen her just a few days ago, she was looking better. Her skin flushed healthily instead of looking sallow, the dark bags beneath her eyes brightened considerably.

Almost like she was coming back to life before my very eyes.

"What's your plan for today?" I asked her as I moved closer, bending to inspect the tulips growing along the edge of the planter box we'd constructed over here for her.

I'd never understand how she did it—turned something so ordinary, so common yet beautiful, into something so unique. It forever amazed me that a tiny seed could become something so incredible. Where they emerged from the stem, the petals were a vibrant pink, almost fluorescent, but as the color moved to the tips, it faded to a softer shade, like the inside of a seashell.

The flowers were works of art, and the entire planter was filled with similar masterpieces and experiments. The hydrangeas, for example, were a riot of colors from blue to purple to pink to white. Once, when I'd asked Ella about it, she told me she fertilized each with something different, weighing the outcomes so she could pass the information onto other florists and horticulturists.

Ella gave me a look that said it should've been obvious, but out loud told me, "This."

I barked out a laugh. "Fair enough. But how would you like to do something else?"

"Such as?"

"Such as...helping at the community garden?"

Ella perked up, shooting upright and wiping her hands on the legs of the white pinstriped denim overalls she favored while gardening. Either she had multiple pairs of the same ones, or she washed them daily, because I rarely saw her working in anything else.

"It's planting day?" she asked excitedly.

"It's planting day," I confirmed.

Personal project abandoned, she gestured toward the door.

"Lead the way."

The community garden was a new addition to Apple Blossom Bay, spearheaded by the winery's head chef, Ezra, and his now-fiancée, Brie, the youngest of the Delatou sisters. But as the resident agricultural engineer—yes, it was a thing, and an actual degree I held, hence securing my position as the head vintner at a winery so young—I'd helped Ezra and Brie with the construction and layout of the rows.

We were growing a plethora of things in the garden, which members of the community could come up and pick, use in their own kitchens, or sell at farm stands in Traverse City on the condition that a part of the proceeds came back to the garden as donations.

It was very much a farm to table operation, and I was honored to be a part of it.

Today, we were finally putting the plants we'd started in the on-site greenhouse into the ground. At last, that harsh Michigan winter had loosened its grip, and the string of warmer days had thawed the soil considerably. We'd constructed a temporary tent over the garden to keep it protected at night until we were safely out of the frost danger zone.

Ella bounced happily in the passenger seat of my truck the entire ten mile drive, and I smiled to myself, my own happiness uncontainable in the face of hers.

When we pulled into the gravel lot beside the garden, Ella was out of the truck like a shot, racing toward her sister, who hung out on the fringes, directing people who pushed carts full of starter plants.

I followed Ella, joining the two Delatou sisters.

Brie's head whipped toward me, blinking quickly as though she wasn't quite sure what she was looking at. Her green eyes—a few shades darker than Ella's—swung between the two of us like a pendulum.

"Liam, hi," she said. "Did you...come together?"

"I was at the winery working on my flowers, and he asked if I wanted to help."

Ella shot me a wide grin, and everything in me softened, yearning to reach for her.

Fuck. I had to get this silly little crush under control. She'd never looked at me in a way that made me think something was there between us—not once. And the last thing I need to be doing is thirsting after her when she was clearly still reeling from her breakup.

With a mental head shake and a strong desperation to change the subject, I blurted, "Where do you want me?"

It was a constant battle of wills—my body's desire to be near Ella in any capacity, and my brain's reminders that she wasn't mine to covet.

Brie pointed to the back corner, about as far from the sisters as I could get. "Will you help with the apple trees? They're small but mighty, so we could use your muscles over there."

With a salute, I sped off in that direction, reaching the area where the Granny Smith saplings would go into the ground right as Ezra exited the greenhouse.

"Liam!" Ezra greeted me happily. "Fuck, am I happy to see

you."

I snorted. "You sure about that?"

"Absolutely," Ezra grinned. "Your burly ass is a sight for sore eyes when I've been surrounded by women all morning."

"One of those women is your fiancée," I reminded him. "And the mother of your unborn child."

Ezra rolled his eyes. "I'm not talking about Brie, and you know it."

I barked out a laugh. Of course I knew that. Anyone with two eyes and a brain could see how much he worshiped his woman.

"I mean the rest of them." He swept a hand out at the women bobbing up and down rows, inspecting plants and arguing over the best use of the allotted space. "Who knew Fanny was such a tyrant?"

"*That* Fanny?" I asked, pointing at the owner of Blossom's Flower Shop. "That sweet old woman?"

"She may be sweet on the outside, but her chest holds the heart of a dictator. Just because she owns a flower shop doesn't mean she knows how to plant crops."

"Neither do you," I pointed out.

Ezra let go of the cart he wheeled over the uneven ground to shove me, and I chuckled. "You're an ass."

"Tell me something I don't know."

"You have icing in your beard."

My hand flew to my face, combing through the coarse hair in search of the food remnants from my breakfast. At last I found it, brushing it away and pulling up the collar of my flannel to be sure I got it all.

"That was actually nice of you, Ez," I said, clapping him on the back.

"One of Brie's, I hope?"

"That cranberry orange scone with the vanilla icing gets me every time."

In fact, Brie's Bakery was one of two reasons I ever ventured into downtown Apple Blossom Bay.

The other sat two storefronts away.

At last, we reached the space cordoned off with stakes and string where, with my help, Brie and Ezra had decided to plant the apple trees. Though the town was full of them, the bulk were located on winery grounds and used for Chateau Delatou recipes like their spiced apple wine and Brie's bakery treats. To give the community a piece of the pie, so to speak, they elected to plant a small grove of trees here at the garden as well.

Twenty trees would cross-pollinate year after year to ensure they remained ripe with fruit and adapted to their environments season after season.

Ezra and I worked in companionable silence, communicating mainly by grunts and clipped instructions.

It gave me too much time to think, too much time for my eyes to keep wandering toward the Delatou sisters.

To no one's surprise, Ella was already up to her elbows in dirt, on the far perimeter of the garden where the raised boxes that would hold the fresh herbs sat. From here, I couldn't tell what she was planting, but she stopped every so often to smell the leaves, or gently brush her fingers along the stem before carefully placing them in the earth and filling the hole.

I could watch her work all day like it was my favorite TV sitcom.

Unfortunately, Ezra noticed the way my gaze clung to her like a magnet.

"You've got it bad, my dude."

I scoffed. "No, I don't."

"Please." He pursed his lips and narrowed his eyes in a *get real* expression. "I know that look. It's the same one I gave Brie for months. So why don't you just, I don't know...man up and go for it?"

"She just got out of a relationship," I said quietly, seeing no point in refuting him. He had, after all, hit the nail on the head.

Ezra snorted. "That guy was a fuckhead. From what Brie says, Ella was less upset that it ended and more about the fact that she'd wasted so much time on him."

I cut him a look. "You shouldn't be telling me this. That's privileged information."

Ezra dusted his hands off and clapped me on the shoulder. "You need it more than I do."

I only hummed noncommittally.

"You want my advice?" Ezra asked.

"Not really."

He gave it anyway. "Feel her out. Dip a toe in the water and see what happens. She might surprise you."

I only glared at him and grumbled to get back to work.

Unfortunately, his words had taken root in my brain, and no amount of manual labor or reminding myself to stay away from Ella Delatou could shake them loose.

I CONTEMPLATED HANGING UP the phone no fewer than forty-seven times in the ten seconds it rang with an outgoing call. I couldn't tell if it was because I was afraid he'd actually answer...or because I was terrified he wouldn't. At least if he didn't, I could simply chalk it up to a butt dial, though I'd never been very good at lying.

Because, obviously, the truth—that he'd been the first person I thought to call—was out of the question.

Right when I was sure it'd go to voicemail, his deep timbre came over the line.

"Ella? Are you okay?"

"Hi, Liam," I croaked out. "I'm fine! I just...are you busy?"

"Just finishing up some last minute things around here before the weekend," he said, clearly still at the winery. "Why, what's up?"

"I really hate to bother you, and normally I'd call one of my sisters or one of the guys, but no one seems to be picking up the phone." *Okay, that was a lie.* I hadn't bothered to call anyone else. "And I just thought that maybe, if you weren't doing anything—not that I'm assuming you're just magically free, but—"

"Ella." His tone was so gentle, and I halted my rambling to suck in a breath. "What do you need?"

"Okay, well, you see, Fanny hurt her back. She's really too old to be doing any kind of manual labor anyway. But the Fawkes wedding is this weekend and the shipment of flowers arrived. If I try to unload them all myself, it's going to cost me double while the truck sits here. He's gotta have it back to the warehouse by a certain time, and since he drives so fucking slow, he just got here. He said he'd be back in an hour, and that was..." I checked my watch. "Twelve minutes ago. We're his last stop of the day," I added, explaining why he was delivering so late. It was nearly seven p.m., and I should've been back upstairs right now, curled up on my couch with a glass of wine and *Chicago Fire* on the TV.

"Where is the driver?"

I snorted. "That putz went to Granny's." Exactly like he did every time he made a delivery up here. Technically, it was in his contract to help me unload, but he'd never been very good at following directions. I'd damn near called his superiors to complain more times than I could count, but Fanny always told me it wasn't worth it to rock the boat and risk them not delivering to us at all.

"I'll be there in five."

Every muscle in my body relaxed. "Oh, thank god. You're a lifesaver."

"Anything for you," he rushed out, then hung up almost as fast.

Huh. Was Liam...?

No, I shook my head firmly. That was a silly notion. One I refused to entertain.

True to his word, Liam arrived five minutes later—an impressive feat given the winery was ten miles away down a winding backroad—pushing through the front door of the flower shop and purposefully striding toward me.

"Put me to work, boss," he said with a cheeky grin.

I relaxed further at his nearness, at having help to complete this task without having to pay the driver double because his lazy ass refused to do his job.

Deep breaths, El.

I offered Liam a grateful smile. "You have no idea how much this means," I said.

"It's the least I could do," he said, lifting a single shoulder in a half-shrug.

In truth, offering a helping hand when someone reached out was really the bare minimum for anyone, but something about Liam, about the way he rushed to my aid without a second thought...I don't know. It felt like more than that.

I wasn't going to question it.

So I jerked my chin toward the back of the shop and said, "This way."

He followed me down the two short hallways that led to the back door and followed me into the cool spring night. The days were thankfully getting longer, but as soon as the sun went down, there was still a bite to the air, and my breath fogged in front of my face. My boyfriend jeans kept the chill from my legs, but my skin exposed below the sleeves of my oversized tee shirt immediately pebbled with goosebumps.

Liam, in his standard thick flannel, appeared unperturbed. He simply rolled up his sleeves, exposing those strong, veiny forearms covered with tattoos and dark hair, and directed me to hop into the back of the box truck and line the buckets of flowers up at the edge so he could carry them inside.

We worked in easy tandem, the project that would've taken me over two hours—yes, there were that many flowers—accomplished in less than thirty minutes thanks to Liam's muscles.

As he hauled the final two buckets inside and placed them in the cooler, I couldn't help leaning against the doorway and watching him work, watching his ink flex and wave with each of his movements.

I was sure there was a story behind each of the marks, but I couldn't make sense of them. There was a blooming rose on the back of his left hand, a bright, blue butterfly on the inside of his left wrist—one that looked suspiciously like my own—and some peonies and dahlias on his right forearm, a snake wending its way through the petals. Letters across his knuckles. I knew from spending time with him in the muggy greenhouse, when he traded his signature uniform for a cutoff tee, that there was a topless mermaid with devil horns on the inside of his right bicep. Even now, as he lifted a bucket to place it on a higher shelf, I could just make out the tips of her fins. On that same deltoid, I'd seen a woman's lips with her tongue sticking out. I knew, like me, he had more covered by his clothing that I'd never seen and probably never would.

Why did that thought depress me so much?

"Enjoying the show?" he asked, his voice jerking me from my

optical exploration of his body.

Shit. My cheeks heated with embarrassment.

"Sorry," I said sheepishly. "I was just looking at your tattoos."

Liam extended his arms in front of him and twisted them side to side, examining them. "What about them?"

"Just...curious about their stories," I said, mimicking him with my own arms. "Obviously, tattoos fascinate me."

Liam studied me for a moment, and time seemed to slow and stretch when our gazes locked.

What the fuck was happening to me?

Awkwardly, he cleared his throat and said, "Maybe one day, I'll tell you about them. Now"—he gestured toward the exit, and I gratefully led the way into the warmer showroom—"what do you say to dinner at Granny's? We need to get you warmed up."

"Oh, you really don't have to—" I began to protest, but he cut me off.

"I want to," he assured me. "Plus, I want to give that driver of yours a piece of my mind."

I chuckled, not bothering to tell him no. Though he didn't intimidate me, Liam was...imposing. Maybe he'd scare the dweeb enough to never leave me high and dry again.

"On one condition," I said.

"What's that?"

"I'm buying."

"No."

"Liam," I warned.

"Ladies don't pay. I can't accept that."

I rolled my eyes. "It's not like this is a date. Consider it payback for helping me tonight."

"I'd do that for free."

I gaped at him. Fuck, he had to stop saying things like that to me. It was giving me all kinds of ideas, taking my mind down paths I wasn't allowed to walk where this man was concerned.

"*Liam.*"

Sensing he was on the receiving end of that signature Delatou stubbornness—and rightly so—he deflated slightly. "Fine."

I grinned widely, pleased I'd gotten my way. Then I stepped into the office to grab my coat and keys. With the cooler sealed tightly, I made quick work of my closing routine: powering down the POS system, flipping all the lights off and lowering the blinds on the bay windows out front, then ushering Liam onto the street before I set the alarm and locked up behind me.

There wasn't much crime to speak of in Apple Blossom Bay, but I'd just received a delivery of thousands of dollars worth of flowers, and I wasn't taking any chances.

I stuffed my hands deep in my pockets as he walked up to Granny's, the silence between me and Liam companionable. We knew that quiet would evaporate the second we pushed into the old tavern. The residents of Apple Blossom Bay happily and raucously enjoyed their Thursday night dinner, and I swore every set of eyes in the room was on us as Tanya, the owner, brought us to a booth in the back corner.

I couldn't decide if it was because Liam was notoriously reclusive, or because we'd shown up together.

Likely both.

"Drinks?" she asked, glancing curiously between us.

"I'll have the ale on tap," Liam said.

Tanya nodded, having been at her job so long she no longer

needed to even write it down. "And for you, El?"

"Can I have hot chocolate with a shot of Rumchata?" I asked, rubbing my hands up and down my arms. "I'm still freezing."

"Coming right up," she said, leaving us with menus as she sped away toward the bar.

I'd been here enough times over the years that I no longer needed to look to know what I'd order, but I liked to peruse anyway, simply to see if Tanya had changed anything up since I'd last been in. She rarely did, operating on the if-it-ain't-broke-don't-fix-it mentality, but I liked to check.

Then it occurred to me that Liam may not be nearly as familiar with the place as I was.

I leaned forward, resting my elbows on the table as I whispered, "Have you ever been here?"

He snorted, mirroring my position, and said in a normal tone, "Of course I have, you weirdo. I like to keep to myself, but I still have to eat. I've been here with Vic a few times, but mostly I get takeout."

"So what's your favorite thing on the menu?" I asked. "And choose wisely. This could make or break our friendship."

His brows shot up. "We're friends now, huh?"

"Duh," I said, flipping my hair over my shoulder. "We bonded over flowers and douchebag delivery drivers."

Liam sat up straighter, eyes scanning the bar. "Speaking of, where is that little shit?"

I pointed toward the bar and the guy at the end, nursing a dark soda, a plate piled high with onion rings and a burger in front of him.

Before I could protest, Liam was out of his seat, his long legs eating up the distance between us and the driver. I experienced a brief pang of guilt right before Liam reached him. After all, the kid couldn't have been older than his mid-twenties, scrawny, a Western Michigan University ball cap settled backward over his dark hair. I realized with a start that being in his mid-twenties meant he was only a few years younger than me, but...I felt so much older. Especially after the drama of the last few months.

Still, that didn't give him the right to be lazy.

When Liam reached the kid's side, he took the back of his bar stool and swung it so they faced each other. Liam began talking, his expression stern, the kid leaning as far away from him as the chair could possibly permit. Liam appeared to have asked a question, glancing quickly at me before returning his attention to the kid. With a look over his shoulder, dark eyes wide in fear, he looked at Liam and nodded.

A moment later, I watched in fascination as Liam stalked back to our table. The kid signaled Tanya for a to-go box, threw a couple bills onto the bartop, and hightailed it out of the restaurant.

When Liam slid back into his side of the booth, I asked, "What exactly did you say to him?"

"Just reminded him that, while you're perfectly capable of unloading those flowers yourself, the gentlemanly thing to do is help you. I also warned him that if I heard of this happening again, he'd be receiving another visit from me, and I won't be so friendly next time."

A giggle slipped free, and I clapped my hand over my mouth. "That poor kid is probably scared shitless," I said through my fingers. "I probably shouldn't be laughing at his pain."

Liam sat back and crossed his arms over his chest. "He'll be fine. Hopefully he doesn't give you any more trouble."

Before I could say anything else, Tanya reappeared with our drinks, and I gratefully wrapped my hands around my mug, bringing it to my mouth for a long sip, letting the warmth of the hot chocolate seep into my body from the inside out.

"What can I get you?" Tanya asked.

"My usual," I told her.

Tanya grinned. "One chicken parm sandwich—extra mushrooms—coming right up. You want onion rings today?"

"Nah," I said. "Let's make it sweet potato fries."

"Sure thing, kiddo." She turned to Liam. "And for you?"

His eyes never left mine as he said, "I'll have my favorite...the chicken parm sandwich. Extra mushrooms. *And* onion rings."

I gasped, and Tanya shot me a skeptical look before nodding at Liam and scurrying off.

"That is *not* your favorite meal here," I said, pointing an accusatory finger at him. "You only ordered that because I did."

Liam shook his head with a small laugh, reaching for the brim of his ball cap—a deep red, Chateau Delatou branded one, I noted with no small amount of satisfaction; I liked that he was wearing my last name—and flipped it backward.

Fuck.

I couldn't explain the reaction accurately except to say my insides went molten.

Liam Danvers, with his dark hair, bright blue eyes, thick beard; that big body and long, thick fingered hands; and those fucking tree trunk thighs, was an absolute snack on any given day. Even if I was out of the dating scene right now, I could recognize a good looking man when I saw one.

But Liam with that goddamn hat turned backward, locks of his raven hair flipping over the brim, giving him a boyish charm that only added to his overall attractiveness?

He was downright devastating.

Seemingly oblivious to the mental roadblock he'd conjured with that simple, innocent move, he laughed and said, "As adorable as that would be, it really is my favorite."

"What is?" I asked dumbly, the point of the conversation having completely vacated me.

I mean...*Liam Danvers in a backward ball cap.* Who could fucking blame me?

"The chicken parm sandwich?" he said, though he phrased it more like a question, his eyes narrowing on me. My face flamed, and he must've noticed because he added, "Are you okay?"

"Fine!" I said quickly, tone way too high to be believable. "That Rumchata is just working its magic."

The excuse was lame, and we both knew it, but he let it go.

Desperate for a subject change, I said, "So tell me about this road trip you're taking."

Liam's entire countenance lit up like I'd just flipped a switch on him, and I couldn't help grinning in response as he launched into his plan, his fingers tracing patterns on the table as though mapping his entire route from here to Portland.

"Your brother is getting married, right?" I asked when he paused his storytelling long enough for Tanya to deliver our food.

Like I'd flipped that earlier switch that lit him up in the opposite direction, Liam's body language shifted again, stress and tension now lining his shoulders, his jaw muscles jumping as he ground his teeth together.

Then he exhaled heavily and said, "Yeah."

That was it. That single syllable. But I could tell there was a lot he was holding back, and I could also see that pressing the issue would be equivalent to breaking a dam.

I had no desire to see what was on the other side, not when I was still dealing with my own shit.

But I hated the thought of him embarking on that journey alone, knowing he was racing toward something that clearly caused him so much distress.

So I did the only thing I could think of to provide him even a modicum of comfort and ease.

I blurted four words.

"Take me with you."

chapter 4
Liam

Take me with you.

Those words hung in the air between us.

Ella, horrified by her outburst, clapped a hand over her mouth, and I was doing everything I could to not immediately and vehemently agree.

"But why?" I blurted, then mentally punched myself in the face.

My dream girl—who was finally single for the first time in three years—wanted to take this two-week long vacation with me, and I was *questioning it*?

Christ, Danvers. Get your shit together.

I picked up my sandwich and took a massive bite to keep my mouth busy, lest I say something even dumber.

"I...need to get out of here," she said quietly, her tone toeing the line of pleading. Somehow, I sensed that wasn't all there was to it, but it was a solid reason nonetheless. She picked up a fry and popped it in her mouth, chewing and swallowing before continuing. "I've been doing better since the breakup. But I could really use the chance to regroup away from everything." She waved a hand in the air, as if to encompass her whole life in Apple Blossom Bay.

Her whole family.

I understood that sentiment well. Hell, isn't that exactly what I'd done when things with Mellie imploded? I ran away from home and found myself in the middle of nowhere, Michigan. Licking my wounds and making a new name for myself. I knew Ella would return home at the end of the trip. I wasn't in danger of losing her to some far flung locale like my family had lost me.

But I *was* in danger of losing her, period. If I let the space between us grow further, the chasm opening wider between where we were and where I wanted us to be. I couldn't explain it, but I knew I had to jump at this chance if I ever wanted things to change between us. If ever there was an opportunity to show this woman how fucking good I could be to her—how perfect we could be together—this was it.

Her calling me tonight had been a good sign, right? That she'd come to me for help when all of her family was busy? She'd been so frazzled when I arrived at the flower shop, and it gave me an extreme sense of pride to know I'd been the one to soothe her.

I'd come to her rescue every goddamn day if she'd let me.

I had to be careful, though. I couldn't appear too eager, because the last thing Ella needed was me forcing her into something she wasn't ready for. And I definitely wasn't the kind of guy to take advantage of her situation.

I wasn't privy to what exactly caused the end of their relationship, but I'd bet good money her twit of an ex was the one who fucked it all up. Ella wouldn't have spent those first couple months so devastated and withdrawn otherwise.

Ezra's words from a few days before came back to me then, reminding me that she'd been more devastated by the lost time than the lost love...so maybe I had it all wrong. Maybe she'd simply finally come to the realization that she could do better.

Whatever the reason, I was glad for it. Not that she'd been hurting, but that it was over. That I had a chance.

"Liam?" Ella prompted.

I blinked at her, realizing I had yet to give her a response. "Are you sure you want to do this?"

The words came out more skeptical than I intended, and I winced as I watched them land. As Ella's shoulders curved in just a bit.

Determined to not let me see her sweat, though, she straightened her spine and tipped her chin up. With a scoff, like she was damn tired of people questioning her, she said, "Look, I know you're a big, beefy man and can take care of yourself, but wouldn't it be nice to have some company?"

Inwardly, I preened. She *had* been checking me out as I hauled those buckets earlier, and I definitely hadn't imagined the way her eyes darkened when I'd flipped my hat backward.

Damn. It turned out that move really did work. For me, it was a force of habit, but I wasn't above performing it more often simply to see that color rise to her cheeks again.

Admittedly, I was a big dude, but Ella wasn't petite by any means. Each of the Delatou daughters was only two or three inches shy of six feet. Ella was on the curvier side, and I loved that about her.

In fact, she had an ass I wanted to sink my teeth into. I never thought I was an ass man until the first time I laid eyes on hers.

I raised an amused brow in response to her statement. "Beefy?"

Ella's cheeks turned pink again, and I found myself desperate to reach out and brush my fingertips over that warmth. Fuck, I bet her skin would be so smooth under my rough hands.

And not just the skin on her face.

There I was, thinking about her ass again.

Marching ahead despite my light teasing, she waved a hand at me, eyes scanning my body up and down.

"*Yeah*," she said, like *duh*. "Beefy. How tall are you anyway?"

"Six four."

"Fucking hell," she breathed as she stepped closer, close enough that we were basically sharing air. "I'm five ten and you make me feel tiny."

I reached up and tugged on a lock of her hair. "You *are* tiny. Like a little wildflower compared to all this lumber," I said with a grin, flexing my biceps. "But you're strong too."

"As weird as this is going to sound, 'lumber' kind of suits you."

"Oh?" I asked. I hadn't been serious; it'd simply been the best I could come up with. But I was interested to see why she thought so.

"You're...rough around the edges. Like tree bark. But you're solid and steady all the way through."

I blinked in surprise. "That is...one of the nicest things anyone has ever said about me."

Ella giggled, the sound music to my ears. "Plus you dress like a fucking lumberjack."

I tossed a piece of bread from my sandwich at her, but she batted it away, giggle morphing fully into a laugh.

"You're a lot like a wildflower too," I said quickly. "In fact, I think that's what I'm going to start calling you."

"And how is that, exactly?" she asked, sobering.

"Beautiful," I told her, eyes scanning her face. She was beautiful in all ways, but without all that heavy makeup and dark lipstick she used to wear, she was breathtaking. I remembered a week ago, showing up at the winery greenhouse, my breath literally leaving me when she turned to look at me. It was the first time in months I'd seen her face free from that shit. Clear, olive skin. Marking pen eyebrows. Those gorgeous green eyes I wanted to get lost in for hours. "Stronger than she looks. They're called *wild*flowers for a reason. Nothing can tame them. They keep popping up no matter the circumstances."

Ella appeared thoughtful for a moment, then said, "I like that." She mouthed the word *wildflower*, as though savoring it, turning it over in her mind and letting it soak in. Then her eyes clapped on mine again. "But you're still not giving me an answer. Can I come on this road trip with you or not?"

"Yes."

Ella's entire face lit up like a child's on Christmas morning. "Really?"

"Of course," I assured her. "You made a good point about keeping me company. Who else am I going to use as a human shield if a bear attacks?"

To demonstrate, I grabbed her hand and dragged her halfway across the table, angling myself behind her. Pretending to peek around the sides of her head as if avoiding one the surly creatures.

Ella's squealing filled the space between us, and she tipped her head back as she laughed.

I looked down at her, wide grin at her hysterics softening. God, she was stunning. Those bright green eyes like fresh flower stems, lined with long, sooty lashes. Her purple-streaked hair and the way it spilled past the tops of her creamy shoulders. The lines of her tattoos were stark against her skin, and I barely resisted the urge to lower my head and press my lips to the one at the cap of her shoulder.

As it was, my restraint was fraying rapidly with her rosebud mouth slightly parted, offered up to me with the angle of her head.

Reluctantly, I cleared my throat and let go of her.

I wasn't about to fuck this thing up before it even started.

Ella sat back, dropping her gaze to her plate and roughly shoving her hair behind her ears. "So when do we leave?"

"In a week."

Her head snapped up, eyes wide as she leveled me with them. "A *week*? That's not nearly enough time for me to prepare."

"I'll get you a list of everything you'll need to buy."

"That's not what I mean," she said. "I mean...I have to tell Fanny I'm leaving. I have to tell my *family*."

I sensed what she wasn't saying. "Are you worried they'll try to talk you out of it?"

She snorted. "Please. You've met them. You tell me."

I nodded in understanding. "I'll help you tell them if you want. Ease the blow a bit. Your parents love me."

"My *mother* loves you," she corrected me. "My father is wary of any man in the vicinity of any of his daughters."

My brows drew together. "All of your sisters are in deeply committed relationships."

"Exactly. The only one he actually likes, I think, is Logan."

"I'm failing to see the point."

"The point, my friend," she said with a mischievous grin, "is that my sisters have done whatever they wanted regardless of how our parents feel about it."

The lightbulb clicked on. "So you're going on this trip whether they like it or not."

She shot finger guns at me and made little clicking noises with her tongue, as if to say *bullseye*. "Precisely. But I will take you with as back up when I tell them."

"Which will be when?"

"Tomorrow," she said around a yawn. I flicked my wrist to check the time, fighting back a yawn of my own. It was well past eight p.m., and I'd been up since five.

"Are you going to warn them you're coming over?" I asked.

"No need. They're expecting me for dinner."

"Wait wait wait," I said, holding up my hands. "You want me to come to dinner with you? Just us four?"

"Yeah?" Ella said, though it sounded more like a question. "Is that going to be a problem?"

I swallowed hard. *You mean other than the fact that it feels an awful lot like a double date with your parents?* "No, of course not," I said aloud.

"Perfect."

We both glanced up as Tanya dropped off our check and cleared our plates. I'd been so caught up in this conversation that I'd somehow managed to eat my entire meal without remembering a bite.

Ella had that effect on me. Had the ability to wrap me so wholly in her presence that everything around me drifted away to nothingness.

Across the table, our gazes collided, and I knew what she was thinking. That she was buying, as some sort of misguided need for paying me back for the help earlier.

She had no idea I'd meant what I said: I'd do it for free.

Again. And again. And again.

So before she could move, before she could fully complete the thought and reach for the check, my hand snaked out and grabbed it.

Then I was out of my seat and running toward the register, Ella hot on my heels and swearing up a storm.

I grinned.

This road trip was going to be fun.

⁂

As I followed Ella into the Delatou home the next evening, I was practically shaking in my boots. I had to remind myself the stakes here weren't all that high given their daughter was only taking a road trip with me. But...I had high hopes it would become more than that.

"Mom? Dad?" Ella shouted into the ominously silent house.

"Back here, El!" Lena hollered from somewhere down the long hallway that served as the foyer and entrance into the house.

She glanced back at me, and I didn't miss the tightness around her eyes. For all her bravado yesterday about not caring what they

42

thought, it was obvious her parents' opinions mattered to her. The last thing I wanted to do was be responsible for some sort of rift within the family, but if they couldn't see how badly she needed this escape, then I was making it my job to help her in any way I could.

A few steps later, we passed through the archway into the main living spaces. To the left was the kitchen and formal dining room. To the right was the formal living room they never used, which I knew from attending several special occasions. Seated on the floral patterned sofa that belonged on the pages of a homestyle magazine were Leon and Lena.

Ella clocked them at the same moment I did because, with a tentative step in their direction, she asked, "Mom? Dad?" for the second time since arriving.

"Hi, honey," Lena said softly.

"Ella," Leon greeted his second youngest daughter. "Why is he with you?"

"Backup," Ella said as she sauntered deeper into the room, throwing herself unceremoniously onto one of the uncomfortable looking armchairs, accent pillows flying to the floor. Lena made a noise of protest, but Ella ignored her.

"And what exactly do you need backup for?" Lena questioned.

Ella, who had been tapping away at her phone, glanced up at me and gestured me into the chair at her side before saying, "You tell me. This is quite the little production. Very...*Godfather.*"

"We're worried about you," Leon said, reaching for his wife's hand and giving it a squeeze.

In that moment, I understood with stark clarity why Ella

wanted me here. She must have had a sense they were going to pull some shit like this, and for whatever reason, her sisters hadn't been brought up to speed.

I refused to examine too closely how deeply satisfied that made me—to know I was the one she was relying on when her parents were staging some sort of fucked up intervention.

"And why is that?"

"You're—" Lena cut herself off, clearly grasping at straws. She cleared her throat and tried again. "You're looking a little thin."

Ella, who had made herself comfortable in the hideously uncomfortable chair by slinging her legs over the arm, tipped her head back and laughed. A full body, throaty sound that had my skin tightening. I had to turn away, mentally urging my cock to stay where it was.

The last thing this evening needed was me popping a spontaneous boner because of this woman's *laugh*.

Fuck, I was down bad. But it was mesmerizing to watch her come to life before my very eyes. That flush of her skin, her throat working, her eyes squeezed shut with mirth. It was like watching the petals of a flower slowly unfurl beneath the light of the sun.

I was making it my personal mission to hear that sound at least once a day from now on, and to be the reason for it.

At last, Ella settled and looked her parents dead in the face as she said, "You two are insane."

"Ella," Leon warned.

Distantly, I heard a door slam, but I was too transfixed by Ella and the fire in her eyes to question it.

"What?" she asked, sitting up, spine ramrod straight. "If you're worried about me, do you really think *this*"—she gestured between them—"is the best way to go about it?"

"Really, parents," a voice said from behind us, and I whirled to find the cavalry filing in, Delia leading the charge. She stepped up beside Ella and gripped her shoulder reassuringly. "Got your SOS text."

"Thanks for coming," Ella said to her sisters as they fanned out around her. When she caught me gaping, she tossed me a wink, then faced her parents once again.

"Really, Ella?" Lena asked, crossing her arms over her chest and narrowing those peculiar golden eyes she shared with Amara and Delia. "You had to bring them into it?"

"You tried to ambush me," Ella reminded her. "Of course I called in reinforcements."

"What do you call Liam, then?" Leon glanced at me, his pine-green eyes colder than I'd ever seen them.

"A friend," Ella told him, this time grinning widely at me. That smile was so fucking contagious, I couldn't help but return it. "And my road trip buddy."

The room went terribly silent for a moment before the entire Delatou family erupted. I barely resisted the urge to cover my ears. As it was, I had difficulty picking out who was saying what—though from the expressions on faces as my gaze swept the room, it was obvious some of Ella's family was less enthused than others.

Namely Lena Delatou, who seemed to be pouting.

And, okay, definitely Leon, who glared daggers at me.

If looks could kill, I was a dead man.

POOR LIAM LOOKED LIKE a deer caught in the headlights of an oncoming semi, and I shot him an apologetic smile as he struggled to navigate the turn the evening had taken.

"I can't believe you guys still do this," Mom said, obviously pouting.

"Do what?" I asked innocently.

"Gang up on us."

Next to her, Dad snorted, and I fought back a grin at the death glare Mom leveled him with. "Oh, you think that's funny, do you?"

"I mean...yeah," Dad said. "Or are you forgetting that you gave me five children and not a single one of them is a son?"

My mother rolled her eyes in a gesture so like Delia, the chuckle I'd been choking down burst free. All heads in the room snapped to me, but I sobered quickly as I took in my sisters while Mom and Dad had a murmured argument.

"Excuse you," I said, glancing between Chloe and Amara.

"Where are my nieces?"

As if on cue, Calvin and Logan waltzed into the room, each with a baby bundled against their chests. Owen and Ezra followed closely behind, moving to stand next to Delia and Brie respectively. Cal paused in front of me long enough to hand off baby Cora while Logan beelined for Mom, who made grabby hands at Aleah.

"Hello, my beautiful girl," I cooed at Cora.

At barely a month old, she was the most alert I'd ever seen her, with her eyes wide open. She was so damn precious it nearly took my breath away.

Was I ready for kids myself? No. But with Chloe and Amara bringing these new additions to the family, and because Brie had one on the way, I could admit I was experiencing a bit of baby fever.

"Now that everyone is sufficiently calmed down with a baby in their arms," Dad said, "will someone tell me what the fuck you're talking about when you say 'road trip buddy'?"

I shrugged. "Exactly what it sounds like. I'm going out west with Liam."

"Over my dead body."

"That can be arranged," Delia said sweetly, and Dad made a low, menacing growling sound deep in his throat.

Of all my sisters, Delia was the one who most loved poking the bear, so to speak. Recognizing this about her, Owen, her boyfriend, bent and whispered something in her ear. Delia relaxed a fraction and nodded, smiling up at him. Happier than I'd ever seen her.

The same could be said for all of my sisters, and a stab of hurt panged in my chest. I'd had that—someone to share my life with. It may not have been perfect, and, okay, it definitely would've ended sooner rather than later, Alfie's infidelity notwithstanding, but I missed having someone by my side for moments like this.

I was grateful Liam had at least agreed to come with me, even knowing he'd be facing my father. Liam and I were friends, so it wasn't exactly the same, but I appreciated his presence nonetheless.

Dad pointed a finger at Delia. "Watch it, missy."

Delia simply stuck her tongue out, and Dad reclined on the couch, lifting his hands to grip his salt-and-pepper hair at the temples.

"These girls were raised by wolves," he grumbled.

"You love us," I quipped.

"Most days," he said, though his grin told me he was all bluster. That man would do anything for any of us, and we knew it. "Now let's circle back to the matter at hand. You're going on a road trip with Liam?"

I nodded emphatically. "I sort of invited myself, but he was gracious enough to allow it."

I shot Liam a wink, who returned it before sobering his expression and facing my parents.

"I know you're not exactly thrilled about this idea," he said, taking the words right out of my mouth, "but I promise I'll take good care of her. And while it's not my place to insert myself in what is clearly *family* business"—he pointedly looked around at the crowd of my sisters and their significant others—"I've spent considerable time with Ella over the last few months. I've watched her struggle when she thinks no one is watching. And if she says she needs this, then I'm inclined to give it to her."

No one in my family had dared to voice that thought before, that I wasn't doing as well in the wake of my breakup as I liked to pretend. While this intervention wasn't exactly my idea of a good time, it also wasn't entirely unwarranted. So for this man—who wasn't related to me and really had no personal stake in my welfare—to have been paying that close attention...it sparked something under my skin. Something long slumbering. Some intrinsic part of me I'd forgotten I'd been missing.

"She's not going with you," my dad said. "End of story."

Around me, my sisters' groans drowned out the sound of my own. "In case you forgot, Dad, I'm twenty-six years old. I'm fully capable of making my own decisions, and this is one I'm not backing down on."

One of my sisters cupped a hand around my shoulder and gave me a reassuring squeeze. With the contact, the reminder that they were behind me, I sat up straighter, steeling my spine, readying for what came next.

My parents shared a look, silently communicating in that way they always had. After nearly thirty-five years together, I supposed it made a lot of sense that they'd developed their own secret language. When I was younger, it used to freak me out.

Now, though? Now, it made me jealous.

At last, Dad looked straight at Liam and said, "You protect her with your life. If you don't, yours is over. Understood?"

Liam didn't balk, didn't even flinch. He only nodded. "Consider it done."

During dinner, everyone studiously avoided the topic of my impending departure, focusing instead on the babies who were growing like weeds and the apples of everyone's eyes.

I was terribly exhausted by the time the whole production was over, after I'd walked Liam to the door and seen him off.

When all the men left, my sisters and I convened in the den for a nightcap. Since opening the distillery with her boyfriend, Delia had been working on improving her bartending skills. She typically had a heavy hand with the liquor, but I had to admit, the old-fashioned she concocted was perfectly balanced. I snuggled into the oversized sectional, a fleece blanket draped over my lap and my sisters spread out around me.

Not one for beating around the bush, with an eyebrow wiggle, Delia said, "So you and Liam, huh?"

I threw a pillow at her.

"It's a fair question," Chloe pointed out. Logan and Cal had taken the girls home so Chloe and Amara could have sister time, and truthfully, I was grateful.

With them starting their own families outside of the people in this room, sometimes I felt a little left behind. And it wasn't through any fault of their own. I was ecstatic for each of them, that they'd all managed to find their person.

I simply wanted to find mine too.

"There's nothing going on there," I said, though the words tasted like a lie. Maybe, deep down, I wanted to be wrong. "We're just friends."

Brie snorted. "Yeah, you sure looked like it."

I whirled on her. "What's that supposed to mean?"

"Him coming to your defense like that with Dad? Hell, him coming with you to the house at all? That's not *friendly* behavior. Trust me, I would know."

And she would. She and Ezra had tried the "just friends" thing...and it landed them engaged with a baby on the way.

But our situations couldn't have been more different. Before I could open my mouth to protest, to say exactly that, Amara chimed in.

"You know that man has been half in love with you since he met you, right?"

"Please," I said, rolling my eyes, though the shiver of a thrill raced down my spine. "How could you possibly know that? The man doesn't speak."

"He speaks to you," Chloe said.

Yeah, I didn't want to examine too closely why that was. I had given three years to a man—no, *boy*—who had done nothing but string me along and get my hopes up only to repeatedly dash them. I wasn't about to make the same mistake again.

"We work together," Amara reminded me in answer to my question. "And...I can just tell."

Delia snorted. "One workplace romance under your belt and suddenly you're an expert?"

"That's a little pot-calling-the-kettle-black, don't you think?" my second eldest sister countered.

As the two got swept up in an argument, I tuned them out, turning my attention inward.

Over the course of the last few months, Liam had been there

for me in ways I'd never seen him be for anyone else. And I had been watching. His presence in any room, in any space, was magnetic. He was so goddamn hard to look away from.

But maybe I hadn't been looking close enough.

Maybe...Amara had a point.

Maybe...Liam really did feel something for me beyond some sort of white knight complex.

And maybe, just maybe...this road trip would be my chance to figure it out.

MY HOUSE WAS MORE spotless than it had ever been, including the day I moved in.

Ella was coming over, and I refused to let her think I lived in squalor.

Truth be told, I was fairly organized—I had to be for my job. But there were always a few things I let get out of hand before I mustered the energy to tackle them, namely dishes and laundry.

I did my laundry weekly, but I typically lived out of my dryer, my clothes often finding themselves spilling out onto my laundry room floor. As for the dishes...some days I was motivated to load the dishwashers, and some weeks I wasn't.

Now, my old log cabin on the fringes of Apple Blossom Bay was so clean you could eat off the floor.

And not a moment too soon, because tires crunched on the gravel just as I finished wiping down the counters in the kitchen, and a minute later, a light knock came at my door.

I took one last frantic scan around the living space, pleased to find everything in order. Then I wiped my damp palms on the thighs of my jeans and opened the door for Ella.

Every time I saw her, she took my goddamn breath away.

No one had the right to be as stunning as she in simple black leggings and an oversized Chateau Delatou sweatshirt, the hood cut off and draping over her torso to expose a single shoulder and the florals tattooed there. She'd braided her hair back, though a few wispy purple bangs fell free, framing her green eyes, which sparkled in the low lights from behind me.

"Hi," I said, stepping aside to admit her.

Not bothering with pleasantries, she simply walked past me, dropped her bag on the hardwood near my feet, and moved deeper into the space.

I did my best to stay still, to not word vomit all over the place, to not pick out tiny little details about my home and explain everything that was wrong with it.

I didn't know why the fuck I was so nervous.

Actually, I did, and it had everything to do with the woman turning a slow circle in the center of my living room, her feet making soft *shush*ing sounds on the thick rug.

"You know," she said at last, turning to face me with a soft smile on her lips, "I've lived in this area my entire life and never knew this place existed."

"Well, it was a shit hole when I bought it," I blurted.

A surprised laugh escaped her at my candor, and her eyes twinkled. "You'd never know it."

"That's kind of the point," I grinned. "I needed a project when I moved here. This property was the perfect canvas."

"How large is the lot?" she asked.

"Ten acres."

She whistled low, moving toward the back of the cavernous living space, where a wall of windows and sliding glass door captured the view of the field and forest beyond my house. This time of year, the deciduous trees were just beginning to bud with fresh leaves, turning my backyard into a springy wonderland that mixed with the darker hues of the coniferous trees. The field stretched quite a ways, and Ella turned to me once again.

"How far back do you mow?"

An odd question, but I said, "About halfway. Just enough to give me some room to work if I need it. There's actually a short fence back there, and that's where I stop."

"You should plant some wildflowers out there," she said, almost absentmindedly. "That'd be so dreamy in the summertime. The sun sets back there, right?"

"Sure does," I confirmed, nodding to the rocking chairs sitting on my back deck. It was still winterized, but once it warmed up some more—probably after we got back from our trip—I'd open it up again. "I sit out there with my coffee in the morning and bourbon at night."

Ella sighed audibly, her shoulders relaxing away from her ears as she hugged herself. "It's so quiet."

I wasn't sure if she meant it as a good or bad thing, but I said, "I like my solitude."

Her eyes darted to me and held as she asked, "Doesn't it get lonely?"

"Never," I replied with a headshake. "There's a reason I bought a place on the fringes of civilization, Wildflower. I like being alone. And after—" I choked on what I was going to say next, clearing my throat awkwardly and plowing ahead despite it. "I needed this space. This stillness."

"*Needed*? Or *need*?"

A great question. With her standing in front of me, I wasn't sure anymore.

Unwilling to expose that closely guarded secret, I ignored the question and turned from the window, moving away from her and into the kitchen.

Ella followed me, gasping in surprise. "You cooked?"

I snorted. "What, like it's hard?"

"Did you just...*Legally Blonde* me?"

"Maybe," I grinned. "But to answer your first question: yes, Ella. I cooked."

It wasn't anything fancy, certainly not an Ezra Wendt-worthy meal, but I knew my way around the kitchen enough to put together a fairly decent chicken marsala and salad.

"You are..." She gnawed on her bottom lip as she searched for something to say, and my eyes locked in on that spot. My entire body hummed with how badly I wanted to tug it free, to pass my tongue over the spot, soothing it before slipping into her mouth.

I hated how badly I wanted to taste her.

More so because I knew I'd likely never get the chance.

"You're not at all like I thought you were," she said, at last finishing her thought.

I chuckled. "I can assure you, Wildflower, I'm every bit who everyone else thinks I am."

I plated the food and walked it to my dining room table, erring on the side of caution and placing the dishes opposite each other. I didn't dare give myself the chance to sit next to her and spend the next however long breathing in her scent and experiencing her warmth. I needed a solid slab of wood between us.

As she trailed behind me, Ella vehemently shook her head. "I don't think that's true at all. Everyone in town says you're a reclusive, grumpy bastard, but I don't see it."

The words weren't anything I hadn't heard before, but they still needled. I knew it was my own fault the residents of Apple Blossom Bay viewed me that way, but it still smarted that they so callously went along with it instead of attempting to get to know me.

"What do you see then?" I asked, not entirely sure I wanted to know the answer.

"You're crazy smart," she said quickly. "Though I doubt that's ever been in question. But you're kind—way more so than anyone gives you credit for. I'm sure that has a lot to do with you," she added with a brow raise, easily pegging me. I loved and hated that in equal measure. Loved having her be the one to see right to my core, but hated that she so easily exposed my soft underbelly.

"When I came here, I was running," I said, recognizing that was the first time I admitted that out loud to anyone.

"From what?"

I exhaled deeply through my nose. "I'll tell you one day. It's not important now. What is important is that I dove headfirst into my job at the winery and fixing up this old place because I needed the distraction. It seemed like, before I could really blink, over a year had passed, and the people around here had already made up their minds about me. I've never had the energy nor desire to correct them."

"Sometimes, I wish for that."

"For what?"

"The anonymity you have. I've spent my entire life here, and my family settled this town. I've never known a single day of peace where its residents are concerned."

"It's great you have that sense of community, though. Right?"

"Yes, and no. Some days, I just want to disappear. To...feel my feelings without everything I do and say being examined under a microscope. And I know with my family, that will never go away. They care about me, as I do them, and I love them for it...but I would kill to go one week—hell, one *day*—without someone in town stopping me on the street to say how sorry they were to hear about my breakup. It makes my skin crawl to know these people are talking about me behind closed doors, you know? Or, sometimes, just right out in the open where anyone can hear and chime in. Sometimes, it just feels like my life isn't mine."

She glanced up at me then, those green eyes swimming with emotion, and added, "That's why I need this trip. Thank you for letting me tag along."

Breakups were like bruises. Eventually, they became nothing more than some discolored flesh and a memory of the ache you'd once felt. But in the thick of them, when your skin was still mottled black and blue, pressing on them meant only pain.

The last thing I wanted to do was cause this woman pain. It may have been several months past, but there was no timeline for healing.

Unbidden, my hand slid across the table to clasp hers.

"Anytime."

The mood between us was considerably lighter after that, as though we'd unburdened ourselves and could now move onto more exciting matters—the road trip.

Maybe it made me old fashioned, but I liked maps. In my home office, I had an older, sepia-toned map of the United States framed on the wall, and I liked sticking pins in the places I'd traveled. Recently, I hadn't added many, but I had taken the liberty of using a row of bright-blue-headed pins to map my route from here to Portland.

When we finished eating, I walked Ella back there, the trip taking twice as long as it should have because she stopped frequently to admire the craftsmanship of my home.

Her awe pleased me to no end, but I couldn't let it go to my head.

She wasn't admiring me, only my ability to use my hands.

I'd like to show her *all* the things I could do with them.

Fuck, Danvers. Snap out of it.

I turned the corner into the office ahead of her and mentally shook myself, but it was no use. My thoughts were clouded with *her* every time she was near.

I was a pathetic bastard.

But, I was a pathetic bastard who had the girl of his dreams in his home right then, so maybe I wasn't doing as bad as I thought.

When Ella entered the room, I swore all the clear air left it until only her floral scent remained. I wasn't complaining; I'd happily drown in it.

"Wow," she breathed, stepping closer to the wall to examine the map. "This is incredible."

Careful not to touch her, I also approached, tracing my fingers along the map's surface and the path I'd charted. "This is the route we'll take."

Ella leaned in and squinted. "Why are we going through the UP? Wouldn't it be faster to go south?"

"I want to make a stop at Pictured Rocks," I said. "It's been ages since I've been up there, so I figured now was a good time to fix that."

"I've never been up there," she told me. "Isn't that crazy?"

"Considering you've lived in Michigan your whole life? Yes. But also, not really. People tend to forget the Upper Peninsula is there."

That never made sense to me, that this whole piece of land just...didn't exist to some people. Arguably, it was the most beautiful and all the best parts of Michigan. From Tahquamenon Falls, Kitch-iti-kipi, Copper Harbor, to Black Rocks and our stop at Pictured Rocks National Lakeshore, there was so much natural wonder to enjoy. Being there, surrounded by so much undeveloped and protected land—it put a lot of things in perspective. Yoopers enjoyed a slower way of life, a lot like what we had here on Old Mission.

"That just wasn't the place we went for family vacations, you know?" she said, her delicate pointer finger and its bubblegum-pink tip following the same line of push pins I'd just traced.

I shrugged but didn't answer. Given her family had money, that wasn't surprising.

Then she whirled on me. "So what's the plan, exactly?"

"We'll leave from here on Wednesday and head straight for the UP," I started, dragging my finger from Old Mission up to Munising. Then I moved south, over Wisconsin to a spot along the eastern Minnesota border. "Then we'll head to Rochester for the night. It's a pit stop to sleep, basically. I want to avoid night driving as much as possible, so this is a safe place to rest for the night until we proceed to South Dakota." Again, I moved my finger along the route. "We'll spend one night camping in the Badlands National Park—"

"I've always wanted to visit there!" Ella exclaimed, cutting me off. "Those rock formations look so pretty in pictures."

"I hear the sunsets are spectacular."

"If we're camping, I'll bring stuff for s'mores."

"Deal. Now, where was I?" I squinted at the map, looking for the road I wanted. "Ah, here. We'll travel through the Badlands, taking some backroads until we reach Hermosa, South Dakota. It's about a half hour south of Rapid City, where Mount Rushmore is. There's a lot in that area we can do, so other than seeing the monument, we can play it by ear."

I had a few things I wanted to accomplish, personally—hiking, checking out Custer State Park and the local wildlife, a drive through the Black Hills—but I hadn't planned on Ella, and I wasn't going to force her into anything she didn't want to do.

"All of this sounds amazing so far," she gushed, dropping down into my desk chair and tucking her feet under her crisscross style. "What's next?"

I grinned. "The part of the trip I'm most looking forward to: Yellowstone."

Ella perked up. "Think we'll meet any of the Dutton family?"

I barked out a laugh. This girl continued to surprise me. "You watch that?"

She *tsk*ed at me. "Of course, I watch that. Haven't you seen Luke Grimes?" She made a *whew* sound, tipping her head back and fanning herself and though she was suddenly all hot and bothered.

"He's not really my type," I said. "But it's nice to know what yours is. I'm more of a Rip guy myself."

Ella flushed deeply, and I chuckled. I loved that I could elicit that sort of reaction from her.

Instead of acknowledging my comment, though she did make a show of looking me up and down, she plowed ahead. "Where to after Yellowstone?"

"Originally, I was going to head right to Portland for the wedding," I said, drawing a line through Montana and across northern Idaho until my finger came to rest over Portland. "But when we had that community garden meeting and Owen mentioned his hometown, I couldn't get it out of my head. I'd like to see where he grew up, and I've never spent any meaningful time in Idaho, so we'll be taking a few days in Dusk Valley before ending up in Portland."

"I love that," she said. "I mean, he'll be my brother-in-law one day, so I'd like to meet his family and see how he grew up."

My brows drew together in confusion. "Haven't you already met them at the distillery opening?"

Ella's shoulders slumped. "Alfie and I were in a bad place then, so I wasn't exactly putting my best foot forward."

My teeth ground together at the mention of that asshat. I vowed then and there to do everything in my power to return Ella's happiness—to remind her of the girl she'd been the day we met.

"I'm sure they don't fault you for that," I said, reaching out and giving her shoulder a squeeze. Touching her was a horrible idea, but I couldn't help myself. I needed the physical contact for both our sakes, to remind her she'd be okay, that I was here supporting her on that journey, and to remind myself that she was just...here. With me.

She sniffed and said, "I'm sure you're right." Then, like a switch flipping, she straightened and said, "So tell me about sleeping arrangements."

Sleeping arrangements? Oh hell.

I awkwardly cleared my throat and scratched at the back of my neck, eyes darting around the room, everywhere but in her direction.

"Well, there will be one night of camping in the Badlands," I started. "You can take the van and I'll sleep in my tent. But the night in Rochester...I tried, I really did, but they only had the one room available, so for that night...ahh..."

"Liam, spit it out."

"We have to share a room."

I squeezed my eyes shut, waiting for Ella's rebuttal.

It never came.

Instead, a small, light tinkle of laughter left her, growing in volume until she was practically in hysterics.

I frowned, confused.

"I'm sorry," she said when she'd regained some of her composure, swiping at her eyes. "It's just...you looked so fucking terrified about telling me that."

"I...wasn't sure how you'd react."

"As long as there's two beds, I don't see an issue."

I gaped at her, impressed by how well she was handling all of this.

"You sure? I can call and cancel, look for something else. We can pick a different city, or—"

Standing, she lifted her hand and slapped it over my mouth so quickly I stumbled back a step, breaking the contact before it fully settled. Which was probably the smartest thing I'd ever done.

"Liam, this is your adventure, okay? I'm just along for the ride. We'll be fine."

Then she breezed out of the room, leaving me staring after her like a putz.

I'll never be fine *where you're concerned.*

chapter 7
Ella

I SPENT THE NIGHT before we left with my sisters, who came over to *help* me pack.

By *help*, I really just meant they sat around my living room while I anxiously shoved as much as I could fit into my duffels. I'd spent all day Sunday driving around Traverse City, picking up the *essentials*, according to the list Liam had given me.

I'd managed to hit the jackpot at an Army surplus store, where I found these dark green canvas bags, a dark green sleeping bag, and some heavier sweats for the colder nights. I wasn't exactly sure what I'd need since Liam wasn't the most helpful in that arena, so I bought several thermal pajama sets, figuring I could wear them under baggier joggers and sweaters if it was particularly cold, and activewear sets for the warmer days exploring nature. This late in the spring, it was difficult to predict the weather, so I was erring on the side of caution. I'd thrown in some sundresses, shorts, jeans, my favorite little black dress, and some nicer tank tops. I'd also purchased three pairs of hiking boots that I'd taken to wearing around so I could break them in before we left.

The duffels were stuffed full, the seams damn near bursting, and I silently thanked the Army for taking the construction of their gear so seriously.

"Are you sure you're ready for this?" Amara asked skeptically, glancing at my stuff scattered around my apartment.

I stood in the center of it all, hands on my hips, glaring down at her. "It's not like I'm going off to war."

"Could've fooled me," Delia quipped.

I threw a balled up pair of socks at her head. "Oh, fuck off."

"I just mean...emotionally," Amara clarified.

My eyebrows pinched together in confusion. "Yeah? Why wouldn't I be?"

Amara sighed deeply, as though preparing to impart some deep wisdom upon me. "I just mean...you and Alfie—"

"Don't say his name," Brie said before I could.

"Sorry," Amara apologized. "You and *fuckface* were together for a long time. And I know it ended a while before it was truly over, but...are *you* truly over it?"

Instead of answering right away, I flopped onto my small couch next to her. Cora, who was sleeping soundly against my sister's chest, let out a small whimper of protest before setting again. I reached out and ran my hand over her soft little head.

While it annoyed me to no end that my sisters continued to ask me such questions four months after the breakup, she wasn't entirely off base.

I thought I was over it, but there were days when the crushing weight of the realization that I was alone yet again—that I had to start from scratch with someone new—suffocated me. It wasn't that I wanted to be with Alfie. Far from it, in fact. It was just that, despite the pitfalls of our relationship, we'd found a rhythm together. Maybe not an ease, but some weird, twisted sort of comfort in knowing we had each other at the end of the day.

Although...that hadn't been enough for Alfie.

Maybe that was the worst part, the hardest hurdle for me to jump over. Not the fact that we'd ended, but the fact that he hadn't ended it *before* he stepped out on me. Had I been the perfect girlfriend? Of course not. But I'd *tried*. I'd tried so fucking hard, had let him strip me down to my bones and rebuild me the way he wanted.

I supposed that made me young and naïve, to let a man control so much of who I was.

"Maybe I'm not," I whispered to my sisters at last. "And I can't explain it, but...I *need* this. Alfie took so much from me. I need to find myself again, and what better way to do that than a cross-country adventure?"

"Doesn't hurt that your tour guide is hot as fuck," Chloe added.

Though we all broke into fits of laughter, I couldn't disagree.

No, that certainly didn't hurt at all.

⚜

Liam pulled up behind my building the following morning, and I let out a delighted squeal of surprise.

"Oh. My. God," I gasped, rushing forward and running my hands all over the exterior. "We're really taking this?"

Liam only nodded, his normally composed expression breaking into a toothy smile at my excitement. "What do you think? This a chariot fit for a winery heiress?"

I rolled my eyes. "I'm not an heiress." Then I glanced over my shoulder at him and grinned. "But it's perfect. You're cool with driving a purple vehicle?"

And it *was*. The van wasn't just any vehicle—it was an old-school Volkswagen Crafter van, painted a beautiful pastel purple that inexplicably matched my hair. The top half was white, the accents chrome that shone brightly in the early morning sunlight. The seats were a sumptuous-looking dark purple cloth, the back windows tinted and covered by what appeared to be Roman blinds.

"My masculinity isn't threatened by the color of this van, Wildflower," he said, puffing out his chest for show. "I'm glad you like it. I would've gotten something different if you didn't, though."

"What'd I tell you the other day? This is your adventure. I'm just along for the ride," I said as we both strode toward the side of my building, where everything I'd need for this road trip waited.

Liam had told me to pack as light as possible, and I swear I'd tried. But from the way he glanced skeptically between me and my duffels, the sleeping bag, and the two canvas reusable grocery bags I'd stuffed full of nonperishable food items—and, okay, the bottoms of both were lined with extra clothes, plus a medium-sized paper grocery bag full of a special project I'd been curating for ages—I'd done the best I could under the circumstances.

We returned to the van and Liam popped open the back door, revealing the surprisingly spacious cargo space. Along one side was Liam's luggage, which filled all of one bag. *Men*, I thought wryly as we loaded my duffels. The other side was overtaken by some folded up mechanism.

"What is that?" I asked, gesturing to it.

"The bed."

"The *bed*?" I asked, incredulous. "This thing is outfitted with a mattress?"

Liam shrugged. "I mean, yeah. It can only sleep one, so on nights when we're really roughing it, I'll take the tent and you can sleep in here. I told you that the other day."

I tossed the duffel I carried unceremoniously in after the one he'd carefully placed and folded my arms over my chest, turning a glare on him. "Why can't I sleep in the tent too?"

My annoyance evaporated almost immediately as Liam gaped like a fish, grasping for something to say. "I just figured..." he finally settled on.

"Well, you figured wrong. You know—" I started then cut myself off with a rough shake of my head. "Nevermind."

He stepped closer and pushed a lock of purple hair that had clung to my lip balm off my face. His calloused fingertip scratched against the skin of my cheek, and a shiver raced down my spine. "No, tell me. If we're going to be stuck together for the next two weeks, we need to be honest with each other. Right?"

I nodded, swallowing hard. The poor guy kept stepping on landmines he didn't even know existed. I shuffled backward, dropping my gaze and scuffing my shoe through the gravel at my feet. "First, please don't say things like 'stuck together,'" I pleaded. "If you didn't want me to come with you, you could've just said so. And if you've changed your mind, you better let me know now so I can haul my stuff back upstairs."

"No, no," he said, holding his hands up placatingly. "I'm sorry. That was a poor choice of words. I just mean we're going to be spending basically every waking second for the next fourteen days together. It'll only make things uncomfortable if one of us does something that pisses the other one off. This"—he gestured between us—"is a good start."

I softened at that, at his willingness to make sure I was as relaxed as possible on this trip. And having an open line of communication with a man who wasn't my dad for the first time in my life felt...nice. Foreign, but nice.

"He—Alfie made a lot of comments like that. About being 'stuck' at family functions with me."

"He didn't like them, did he?"

I shook my head. "Not even a little bit. And that right there should've been reason enough to cut him loose but...it was all so fun and exciting in the beginning, you know? When everything was shiny and new and we were still discovering things about each other. Things lost their luster quickly. Thankfully, my family stuck with me, though I knew they cared for him even less than he did them. So that's just...kind of triggering for me."

Liam jerked his head in the approximation of a nod, gripping the back of his neck. "Understood. Now what's the other thing?"

"Other thing?"

"You said 'first' earlier, meaning there was more coming."

"Right," I said, snapping my fingers as I came back to myself. "I've already told you this, but...I *need* this, Liam. Need this adventure. Need this time away from the Apple Blossom Bay and Chateau Delatou bubble. All I'm asking from you is to not coddle me. I can handle sleeping in a tent, or on the ground, or in a fucking tree, okay? Just let me be the one to decide whether or not I want to."

Another nod. "Got it. Anything else?"

"No, I think that about covers it," I said, shooting him a cheeky grin.

Liam's own mouth spread into a smile, and I stilled, mesmerized by its appearance. Such a rarity, but with increasing frequency around me. Or maybe that was wishful thinking.

God, he was beautiful. Suddenly, I was gripped by a wave of anxiety so fierce I nearly stumbled as I moved to grab my backpack. Was I making a mistake? Was this about to be the worst idea I'd ever had—even worse than the three years I'd given Alfie?

Liam...he wasn't the kind of man you took for a ride one night and never thought about again. Liam Danvers was the kind of man who reeled you in slowly with those sexy tattooed forearms, wrapped you against that broad chest of his, and never let you go.

When I turned and faced him again, that smile still graced his lips, and I knew I was a goner.

Nothing could stop me as I closed the distance between us and flung my arms around him.

"Thank you," I whispered.

He stiffened almost imperceptibly before relaxing into my touch, his arms coming tentatively around my shoulders. "Anytime," he breathed.

Though I was reluctant to do so for reasons best not examined too closely, I let him go and moved around to the passenger side while he shut the back door and got behind the wheel.

Liam beamed at me as he inserted the key into the ignition and turned it over. The deep rumble vibrated the entire cab, settling along my bones in an exciting hum.

"You ready, Wildflower?"

"Take me away, Danvers."

❧❦

"Wait wait wait," I said, sitting up straighter in my seat as we rounded a corner on the freeway and the Mackinac Bridge came into view in the distance. "You mean to tell me we have to cross *that*?"

Liam glanced quickly at me out of the corner of his eye before returning his attention to the road. Without his gaze focused on me, I couldn't help but admire him—which I'd been unabashedly doing the entire drive so far. The stupid, sexy forearms, the flannel pushed to his elbows, the loose grip of his long, thick fingers of one hand wrapped around the leather of the wheel. He had to feel my gaze like a brand on his skin, but he never called me out on it. Secretly, I thought he enjoyed the attention.

And I enjoyed giving it.

Mentally, I shook my head. We were far too early into this road trip for me to be salivating over him. Actually, I wasn't sure that was appropriate behavior *ever*. I liked having him as a friend, and I'd hate to jeopardize that.

"It's really not as bad as it looks," Liam said with a chuckle.

"There's really no way around crossing it?"

He shook his head. "Sorry but no. I mean, short of driving all the way around Lake Michigan, which would take about three times as long as going this way. There's also a crossing over Lake Michigan from Ludington to Green Bay, or…"

"Okay, okay," I said. "I get the idea. This is the fastest way to get there." I shifted in my seat so I faced him. "Have you ever crossed the Bridge?"

"Loads of times."

"But you've only lived here for…"

"Five years," he supplied.

"Holy shit," I breathed. "That long already? Aren't you only like…"

"Thirty-four."

I whistled low. "Can't believe Dad hired someone so young for such an important role."

Liam snorted. "To be fair, I was under Vic's wing for a while. But the last year and a half or so, basically since Amara took over, it's really just been me running the show."

"And you're doing an amazing job," I assured him. "You're kind of a jack of all trades around the winery."

Color rose high on Liam's cheeks, and I bit back a grin. "Just doing my job."

"Right. Taking full responsibility for the grape yield and quality of each new vintage, helping Amara with the canned wine-based cocktail line, helping Delia and Owen craft the drink menu for the distillery, helping Brie and Ezra get the community garden up and running…" I theatrically sucked in a breath, blowing it out with a *whew*, even going so far as to pretend to wipe sweat off my forehead. "Yeah, sounds like you're 'just doing your job.'"

"Well, when you put it like that..."

I don't know what possessed me to do it, but before I could stop myself, I was reaching across the narrow center console and settled my palm on his arm. A jolt shot up mine at the contact, his skin throwing off massive amounts of heat.

What an interesting man Liam was proving to be, and more interesting still was my reaction to him. I found myself thrilled by the realization, enticed by the idea of continuing to peel back the layers, to learn who he was beneath the beard and the brawn and the obvious brains. To learn who he could be to me.

"Don't sell yourself short," I said at last, voice hoarse.

The air in the van had thickened, energized in a way I'd never experienced in Liam's presence before, but it wasn't entirely unwelcome.

"Your dad gave me a shot when probably no one else in the world would have...except maybe my old boss. But I definitely wasn't going back *there*."

His jaw was clenched so tightly, muscle fluttering so wildly, that I knew pressing the issue was a bad idea. So I let it drop.

And not a moment too soon because when I returned my attention out the windshield, I found we were rounding a final corner—and then the Mackinac Bridge stretched out before us.

"Oh fuck," I breathed, reaching for the oh shit handle and squeezing my eyes shut. "Just tell me when it's over."

"Absolutely not," Liam said, reaching out and pinching my thigh. My eyes and mouth popped open in protest, leveling him with a death glare. "It's really not that bad. The view is incredible."

I hazarded a glance around me. "It's literally just water."

"It's the Straits of Mackinac," he corrected, then pointed to our right. "Out there is Lake Huron." Gesturing to the left, he added, "And that's Lake Michigan. This is the spot where the two bodies of water collide."

"Thanks for the little geography lesson," I quipped. "But this thing still freaks me out."

Liam held his hand out, palm up. "Take my hand."

"What? No! You need both hands to drive."

"It's a clear day with absolutely no wind to speak of, Wildflower." He gripped the wheel with his left hand so the leather creaked. "I've got it under control. Now take my hand."

My fingers shook as I reached for him, but Liam didn't give me a chance to second guess myself before his warmth was enveloping me. He easily threaded our fingers together, as though this was something we did all the time and not the *first* time. With a light but reassuring squeeze, he asked, "You good?"

No, I thought. *I fear I'm worse off with us skin to skin than I was simply crossing this death trap of a bridge.*

But despite my nerve endings going haywire over this single, chaste point of contact, when I managed to tear my gaze away from Liam—this man who was becoming a bigger enigma by the minute—I realized we'd passed the halfway point, the highest part of the bridge, and were now making our way down to solid ground once again.

Liam swore quietly and suddenly. Without removing his hand from mine, he began glancing furtively around the front seat, grumbling, "Where the fuck is my wallet?"

I joined in on the search, finding it wedged between the center console and my seat. Extracting my hand from his grip, I reached for it and tried to hand it over, but he waved me off.

"Can you just get out four dollars?"

"For what?"

"Bridge toll," he said, indicating the line of booths ahead blocking our entrance into the Upper Peninsula.

Flipping the faded brown leather open, I rifled through until I found the compartment where he kept his cash. I withdrew four ones and handed them over as he pulled up to the toll booth, but his conversation with the attendant faded away as my curiosity got the better of me in the form of studying his driver's license.

"Oh my god," I yelped as the gate opened and we passed through.

I startled Liam, who accidentally jerked the van to the side, eliciting a honked horn and a few choice hand gestures from the driver of a nearby vehicle. "What the fuck?" he breathed.

"Sorry," I offered with a sheepish grin. "It's just...your name is William."

Liam released a deep sigh and shook his head disbelievingly. "I'm aware."

"But you go by Liam."

He cut his eyes to me then back to the road, navigating us onto an exit toward a town called St. Ignace. "Are you okay? Why are you stating the obvious?"

I let out a nervous giggle, surprised he wasn't mad I'd been rifling through his shit. "I've just never heard anyone named William go by Liam as a nickname before. It's always Will or Bill."

Liam shrugged but didn't respond as he turned into a gas station and pulled up to a pump. He got out, then turned to me.

"Are you done holding my wallet hostage, or can I have my credit card?"

Instead of answering, I withdrew my own credit card and handed it over.

"No," he said, crossing his arms over his chest. God, the stance should be illegal for him, all bulging biceps, black shirt clinging to his abs, chest puffed out and really testing the limits of that tee.

Secretly, I hoped one of our adventures on this trip would have an opportunity for swimming, because I needed to see this man shirtless like I needed to breathe, if only to add it to my mental spank bank.

"What do you mean, *no*?" I asked.

"I mean, *no*, you're not paying."

"What did I tell you about letting me make my own choices on this trip?"

"That was about fucking sleeping arrangements, not putting gas in the car."

"As far as I'm concerned, the two are one and the same."

"Ella."

"William."

A grumble emanated from his chest, and he uncrossed his arms to rest them in the upper door frame, leaning forward and staring me down.

I had to hand it to him, the man could be menacing when he wanted to be. His size alone was intimidating enough. But he was fucking with the wrong girl if he thought I'd fold that easily.

Delatou women were a stubborn breed; he should've known that by now.

Ultimately, I settled the stalemate—that Liam would have lost, obviously—by getting out of the car, rushing around to the pump, and sliding my card into the slot before Liam had time to react.

"You little shit."

I did the mature thing and stuck my tongue out before turning my attention to the prompts on the dirty screen. Once my card was safely back in my possession, I lifted the nozzle and put it in the tank.

"You're welcome," I said, giving him my most winning smile.

"That's the last time you're paying to gas this thing up," he replied. "Don't get used to it."

"How come you don't go by Will or Bill?" I asked, ignoring his comments altogether.

Liam's brow furrowed as he navigated my mental leap, then cleared as he once again shrugged. "My dad is Will Danvers. And honestly, Wildflower. Do I look like a 'Bill' to you?"

I giggled. "Absolutely not. The first Bill that comes to mind is Clinton, and you, my friend"—I scanned him from head to toe—"look nothing like him."

"I'll take that as a compliment."

"You definitely should. Bill Clinton is a dog, and not in a cute way."

Liam chuckled. "I think Monica Lewinsky would agree with you."

"I'm sure," I said, returning my attention to his ID. Even in that photo, he wore one of his signature flannels—this one white with alternating varying shades of grey squares. "So your birthday is March eighth. That makes you a Pisces."

"I guess?" Liam said, phrasing it more like a question as the car's automatic fuel valve *thunk*ed to let us know the tank was full. He reached for the nozzle and replaced it, and our conversation paused while we got back in the vehicle.

While my attention was elsewhere, Liam plucked his wallet from my hand and lifted his hips to put it in his back pocket.

"Says here that Pisces men are flirtatious, charming, and romantic, but they can also be introverted and highly emotional."

Liam snorted a laugh. "There's not a woman in the world that would call me *charming* or *romantic*."

"I would."

Fuck.

I regretted the words immediately, wishing I could suck them back in and pretend they weren't awkwardly hanging in the air between us like a giant elephant taking up space.

"You barely know me."

I scoffed. "I know enough. I know you came into the flower shop every week for years picking up a bouquet for someone special." I waggled my eyebrows at him, loving the way his cheeks flushed.

"That wasn't what you think."

"Then enlighten me."

"They..." He trailed off, eyes cutting furtively toward me before he blew out a breath. "Okay, fine. They were for someone special."

"Ha!" I shouted, pointing a finger at him. "I knew you had someone, I also told Fanny that. So who is she? Anyone I know?"

ANYONE I KNOW?

Fuck, what a loaded question.

I mentally scrambled, grappling for purchase on the walls of my mind, searching for a way out of this without spilling my guts all over the interior of this van.

"Ahh, no," I eventually choked out. "She's just...some girl from Traverse City. It fizzled out."

The words felt like glass on my throat, scraping their way out.

I fucking hated lying to her. But I couldn't admit the truth. Not yet at least.

We were a far cry from me letting Ella in on my deepest, darkest secret.

"Fair enough," she said, moving on as quickly as she'd picked up that thread of conversation. "I think I'm going to give *you* a nickname."

I scrunched my brows together in confusion. Her brain must work a thousand miles a minute. "*Liam* already is a nickname."

"Yeah, but it's the name everyone calls you. I don't want to be like everyone else."

"You're unlike anyone I've ever met, Wildflower," I assured her.

I glanced at her quickly, pleased to find her beaming at me. "Thank you. And just like you have a super special nickname for me, I'm giving you one."

I raised my hand and moved my fingers in a *bring it on* gesture. "Let's hear it then."

She tapped a finger to her chin thoughtfully, then said, "*Wills*."

I snorted. "Very original."

Ella hummed happily. "I think it's cute. Reminds me of the Prince."

I raised a brow, gesturing to my body. "I hate to break it to you, but I definitely don't give off princely vibes. I'm more like...Quasimodo."

Ella snorted right as she sipped her water, accidentally inhaling it into her windpipe if the wheezing, hacking sounds she made trying to clear it were any indication. She bent in half, gasping for air as I pounded on her back.

"Jesus, Wildflower. *Breathe*."

"I'm...trying," she croaked.

At last, she straightened, inhaled the first deep breath she'd managed in minutes, and let out a disbelieving chuckle. "Quasimodo," she said with a head shake. "You are so far from Quasimodo, it's not even funny."

"I never would've said it had I known it'd nearly send you to your death."

Ella waved me off. "I'm fine. But damn, Wills. Who knew you had a sense of humor?"

I shrugged. It existed—at least, it used to. Now, that part of me lay buried deep beneath the layers of a relationship that hadn't worked out and all of the ways I'd tried to forget about it.

Maybe the townsfolk of Apple Blossom Bay were onto something when they glared, whispered behind their hands, or outright avoided me when I walked down the street. I wasn't exactly the most friendly man.

But I used to be. Before...everything.

And now here I was, hurtling down the highway on a journey that would ultimately end with me right back where it all started—and fell apart.

At the very least, I was making it my personal mission to ensure Ella attended Sam's wedding with me, if only for emotional support. Showing up alone, and facing all of those people by myself wasn't high on my list of priorities. I knew if I asked, and explained the situation, Ella wouldn't hesitate to do me a solid. But I didn't want her to feel obligated, didn't want her to feel like some human shield I needed between me and my and Mellie's families.

I wanted her to *want* to be by my side, exactly like I wished for her to be since the day I met her.

Ella was quiet as she marveled at the scenery around us, which wasn't too different from where we lived, actually. That was until she realized how unreliable cell phone reception was between St. Ignace and Munising.

She held her phone up toward the ceiling and whined. "How do people live like this?"

"They get used to it," I deadpanned. "Now stop being a brat and just enjoy the ride."

Ella gasped theatrically. "Well, I never..." she said, affecting a horrible high-society accent.

I chuckled and spared her a quick glance, pleased to find she was grinning at me.

The rest of the trip passed quickly after that, and soon, we were driving through the small town of Munising.

"Oh my god," Ella said as we pulled into a parking space down by the city dock, where boats of various sizes were tied up, including the cruise ships that took tourists out for a view of Pictured Rocks National Lakeshore. "This is...dreamy."

I hummed in agreement. "It's truly one of my favorite places."

A lot of people knew about the area, of course; I'd spent enough time here on quick trips over the years to ingratiate myself with the locals. I liked to pretend I was one of them. And I'd heard the stories about how this small, sometimes sleepy town turned into a hotbed of activity between Memorial and Labor Days.

It was a lot like Old Mission in that regard, when our town of six hundred residents swelled with an influx of tourist activity from June to September and beyond.

But there were even more who had no idea such a natural gem existed on the shores of Lake Superior in this one-stoplight town.

"You've been here before?" Ella asked as we got out of the van and crossed into the grassy bayshore park.

Ella seemed content to follow my lead, her head on a constant swivel as she appreciated the scenery.

"Loads of times," I said. "It's my favorite weekend getaway."

"Reminds me of home," she murmured, tipping her face toward the sun, her large sunglasses blocking her eyes from my view.

"That's why I like it so much," I agreed. "I get that same sense of peace here as I do in Apple Blossom Bay."

I jerked my head in the direction of the massive, T-shaped dock, and she trailed behind me as I led us toward it, then pulled up to my side as I stepped on.

"There are two major boat cruises in town," I explained. "This is Pictured Rocks Cruises"—I hooked a thumb over my shoulder at the white and blue building behind us—"which takes guests on a tour of the hot spots along the Lakeshore." Then I pointed across the Bay to the west. "Over there is Shipwreck Tours. Munising Bay has a number of wrecks and one ship that was sunk intentionally for diving purposes. That tour has glass bottom boats, and the water is clear enough that you can see all the way to the wrecks."

Ella shivered, and I raised a brow at her.

"Shipwrecks freak me out," she explained.

"I think there's a name for that."

"Submechanophobia," she supplied quickly.

"What about them bothers you, exactly?" I asked. Not in a judgemental way, more out of curiosity.

"Drowning seems like a pretty terrible way to go, don't you think?" Another chill swept through her, and she wrapped her arms around herself. I felt bad enough that I nearly took her into my own arms to comfort her. "And it's...dark and cold down there. You could get trapped, and you never know what's hiding in those ruins."

I nodded. "That makes perfect sense."

We reached the end of the dock and the top of the T that branched off to our left and right. A smaller cruise ship docked to the right, *Miss Superior* emblazoned on her hull. Back at the shore on the other side, a large Catamaran waited while passengers loaded onto its decks, preparing to hit the open water.

Along the left side were smaller, wooden docks where vessels ranging from speed and fishing boats to pontoons and jet skis were tied up and bobbing on the smooth surface. People milled about, enjoying the unseasonably warm weather.

"What is that?" Ella asked, pointing out into the bay, where a landmass rose from the lake.

"Grand Island."

"So they get all of this"—she spread her arms out and gestured to the scene around us—"and their own little island too? Seems unfair."

I chuckled. "Ella, you grew up in a winery."

"I want to see the island," she said, ignoring my comment. "Can we check it out on our kayaking trip?"

I flicked my wrist to check my watch, realizing we needed to head out if we wanted to get to the other side of town in time to set off.

"I think that can be arranged."

❦

"Well, Liam Danvers, as I live and breathe."

A giant grin broke across my face as I took in the woman before me. It had been long enough since I'd last seen her that I easily clocked the newer, deeper lines creasing her face and the silver streaks glimmering under the sun in her otherwise chestnut hair. She was fit for a woman in her early fifties, though her body showed the softening signs of aging. Her spine remained ramrod straight as ever for her years in the service—though I forget which branch—and the top of her head came to somewhere around my collarbones.

"Dori," I replied, holding my arms wide for her to step into them. I swept her in a bear hug and spun her around. "It's been too damn long."

When I returned her to her feet, she swatted at me then placed her fists on the swells of her hips. "And whose fault is that?"

I grimaced. "Sorry, work has been crazy."

She waved a hand, ire instantly forgotten. "Trust me, I get it. I was more than a little pleased to see your name pop up for today's charter, though."

"You know I won't go anywhere else."

"And I'm grateful for it."

I gestured behind her to the boat that would haul us and the sea kayaks out into open water. "Let's get this show on the road then."

Dori pursed her lips and inclined her head toward something behind me. "Aren't you going to introduce me to your friend?"

"Oh!" I yelped, feeling like the biggest ass for having momentarily forgotten about Ella. "Ella, this is our captain, Dori. Dori, this is my friend Ella."

I practically choked on the word "friend," but neither of them pointed it out if they noticed.

Dori extended a hand, which Ella accepted and shook. "Pleasure to meet you, Ella. How'd you meet this one?" She turned to me then and added, "What're you even doing here? Aren't you guys about to head into busy season?"

"He works for my family's winery," Ella said, answering the first of Dori's questions.

"And we're taking a cross-country road trip," I added to clarify the second. "Had to get it in now before the tourists descend."

Dori chuckled. "Don't I know it. The fact that it's still slow is the only reason I can afford to take just the two of you out."

I scoffed. "I paid an arm and a leg for this private charter, thank you very much."

Ella's eyes swung to me. "Private charter?"

"I don't like crowds," I shrugged. Ella only nodded in understanding.

"Grumpy bastard," Dori mumbled, though loud enough for us all to hear.

"I'm not grumpy," I muttered as she led us onto the boat and immediately began directing us through security protocol. A boy who couldn't have been older than twenty waited on board, gesturing to life jacket storage and other safety instruments as Dori mentioned them.

"This is my son, Marshall," Dori said. "He's my first mate today."

I knew how old Dori was, yet I was still taken aback by the fact that she had adult children. To me, Dori was *life* personified: she wore a black bandana looped around her neck that she'd shove over her hair before the end of our trip, thick, polarized sunglasses, and no-nonsense khaki cargo shorts and a grey tank that exposed her brown arms and the sleeve of tattoos on her left one.

She was so fucking cool, and her energy instantly put me at ease the first time I'd met her. There was no bullshit, and she didn't tolerate drama or gossip.

"So where are we headed?" she asked as she stood at the wheel, flicking random controls. A moment later, the boat rumbled to life beneath our feet, the heavy vibration instantly soothing me.

"Ella wants to see the island," I told Dori. "And maybe we head out toward Miners?"

"Consider it done!" Dori agreed with a mock salute in my direction.

At last we backed away from the dock and set off into open water, picking up speed the further from the shore we got. Ella and I stood at the bow, the wind whipping her hair into a frenzy around her head, and I had to hold my hat onto mine. Her tattooed fingers casually gripped the railing, and I was mesmerized by the way she closed her eyes and sank into the sensation of the sunshine on her skin, the scents of the lake stirred up and wafted around us as we cut through the water. She looked so at peace.

We were only four hours from home and already she was coming out of her shell, like a flower blooming in the spring. I'd believed her when she said she needed this escape from her family and all the other people in town who refused to stay out of her business, but hearing it from her mouth and witnessing the near-immediate change first hand were two entirely different things.

Even if nothing happened with us, I was glad I could be the one to give her this.

chapter 9
Ella

I TRIED TO LISTEN to Dori as she pointed out landmarks along the way to the spot where we'd anchor and take the kayaks out, but I was having difficulty focusing over the blissful emptiness in my head.

All my thoughts seemed to have evaporated on the wind until there was nothing but the rush of the waves and the roar of the boat engine.

Liam stood next to me, content to let me enjoy the silence, and I was grateful for it. His hands, those broad palms and long, thick fingers, curled over the railing exactly as mine were, and I stole furtive glances at his tattoos.

Alfie didn't have any ink, and god, something about seeing Liam's skin marked—about recognizing how polar opposite he was from everything my ex stood for—awoke something positively feral in my chest.

That delicate rose on the back of his left hand.

The letters on each knuckle, spelling out "overcome."

The dark hair dusting over the lines etched into the tan skin of his arms.

Every inch of Liam Danvers was sexy as sin, what should've been a walking red flag wrapped in flannel and tight cotton tees.

But I'd be damned if I could find a single viable reason to stop myself from appreciating every single thing about him.

As though sensing my attention, he turned toward me, offering me a little smirk that did nothing to quell my body's reaction to him. To avoid him seeing my face heat, I turned away, and I swore I heard a faint chuckle on the wind.

In truth, I had no idea what I was doing here.

What *we* were doing.

I desperately wanted to find out.

We cruised past the shoreline of the island, and an old, weathered lighthouse came into view. The shoreline below it was heavily fortified with posts forming a break wall of sorts.

"That's the East Channel Light," Liam said, pointing at the structure. "It was once in danger of collapsing into the lake as the soil below it eroded, but a group of people constructed that seawall to save the structure. It's not operational anymore, but it's been fully restored and is one of the most recognizable landmarks in the area."

"It's beautiful."

"You should see it in the fall!" Dori shouted over the wind. "With the colors in the hills behind it? It's unlike anything else."

I looked at Liam. "Maybe we'll have to come back."

"Whatever you want," he said quickly.

The words were a caress, and inherently, I knew it was a promise he'd make good on if I asked. Why did that thrill me so much?

Eventually, after lapping around the entire perimeter, Dori puttered to a stop in a small bay, one side lined by rocky cliffs that sloped into a beach on the other side.

"This is Trout Bay," Dori said when the engine noise died down. "It's the larger of Grand Island's two bays and a popular spot for cliff jumping, swimming, and pulling up the pontoon onto the beach for some socialization."

I took in the shore, where the leaves on the trees were budding and the sand was almost blindingly light. I could easily imagine it filled with people, laughter, children squealing, good drinks, and good food.

I inhaled deeply yet again, branding the silence and peace on my memory.

"Do we want to paddle around here?" Liam asked.

I shook my head. "No. I want to see the actual rocks."

Dori gave me a salute, flipped the controls, and revved the engine out of there.

"We can explore the island next time," Liam said.

Next time.

Damn I liked the sound of that.

Dori once again stopped and dropped the anchor in open water probably a hundred yards off the cliff faces.

To be perfectly honest, I was terrified of being on such a large body of water in such a tiny vessel, but the surface was incredibly smooth, showing barely a ripple, waves gently lapping at the base of the rocks. Dori assured us these were perfect kayaking conditions, and I trusted her. Given her weathered face and relaxed but vigilant demeanor, I knew she'd been doing this a long time and wouldn't send us into any dangerous situations.

Plus, I had Liam nearby, and we wore lifejackets, so there was no reason to be afraid.

Once I got over the initial trembling in my hands as Marshall launched us off the boat, I marveled at how peaceful it was. The gentle sluicing of our paddles through the water, the birds cawing overhead, Dori's voice as she explained how Pictured Rocks had formed. I tipped my face to the sun, letting it warm me right down to my core, making a silent promise to myself.

I wanted—no, *needed*—to be better.

And not as a human, though I thought we could all use work in that arena. I meant to be better to myself. I needed to stop letting the circumstances of my breakup and the things that had happened in the past control so much of my future.

"I should exercise more," I said almost absently on the tail end of that train of thought, though I knew Liam could hear me.

"Why is that?" he asked, though his attention remained on the cliffs looming over us.

"My mind is...quiet."

"You seem a lot more settled since we got here," he mused. "Like maybe things aren't bothering you as much?"

I nodded in agreement.

I'd felt that way too, and I loved that he'd noticed. It was impossible to focus on the bad shit that often swirled in my brain when confronted with so much natural beauty. It was hard to remain sullen and withdrawn when reminded that there was so much goodness in the world and in this life. I simply had to look for it and accept it.

Liam had no idea what allowing me to come on this trip with

him meant to me—and *for* me—but I vowed to give him my gratitude at every possible opportunity.

❧ ❧

By the time we returned to shore, my arm muscles were deliciously sore, and my mind was blissfully calm. I never expected something as simple as rowing a paddle through the water to be so difficult, but it ended up being a killer workout. With the sun on my face, Liam nearby, and Dori giving us all sorts of fun facts and history about the area, I hadn't been so content in a long time.

But now, I was starving, and before I could say anything to Liam, my stomach made him aware of it.

He laughed and patted my tummy. "Don't worry, Wildflower. We'll get you filled up."

The touch was so unexpected that I didn't move, didn't dare breathe for a few moments. Liam went about his business, helping Dori unload stuff from the boat and carry it up the hill toward headquarters, completely unaware of my minor internal freak out.

By the time he finished helping Dori and Marshall, I'd managed to unglue my feet from the docks and trek toward the building, meeting Liam at the door.

"So what're you thinking for dinner?" he asked. "We could go to a sit-down restaurant, have some drinks and eat, or..."

He trailed off, eyes fixed on something over my shoulder, and I turned to find a white food truck fifty or so yards away, the words FRESH FISH emblazoned in blue on the side.

"Or...we could have fresh fish," I said excitedly.

"My kinda girl," he grinned, then gestured for me to lead the way.

There was a short line, and while we waited, I took the opportunity to just soak the day in. The sun was beginning to set, turning the sky a dusky pink and painting all the buildings golden.

When it was our turn to order, we went for a ten piece basket with fries, coleslaw, and beans. Before Liam could even reach for his, I'd already inserted my card into the reader, sticking my tongue out when he frowned at me.

"For today," I said when I removed it.

"I don't like it when you don't let me pay," he grumbled.

"That makes two of us," I quipped as we stepped to the side to let the next people in line order.

Our fish was ready in minutes, and I pretty much drooled all over the to-go containers on the short trip between there and our campsite.

Actually, *campsite* was a misnomer.

We were spending the night in *yurts*.

Truly, I didn't think people actually did that, but Liam informed me that, up here, there were a number of places that offered yurt accommodations, and I was wildly pleased.

So far, everything about this trip had been unlike anything I'd ever experienced before, and we were less than twelve hours into it. I couldn't wait to see what the rest of the journey would bring.

Liam checked us in while I waited in the van, nibbling on a piece of fish and groaning loudly at its deliciousness. Crispy breading that gave way to tender, perfectly seasoned meat beneath. The coleslaw added a nice fresh, acidic burst of flavor to the heavier textures of the fish.

I was in heaven.

In fact, when Liam returned to the van, just as he slid behind the wheel to direct us into a parking space closer to our accommodations, I let out a low, long moan around a particular bite that had his head whipping toward me.

"Ella," he warned.

"Yeah?" I asked, not bothering to look at him as I licked crumbs from my fingers.

"You can't make sounds like that."

My forehead creased as I turned to him. "Why not?"

He cleared his throat awkwardly, a flush appearing high on his sharp cheekbones. "I'm a man," he growled. "I can't—"

Helplessly, he gestured at his crotch, and it took everything in me not to allow my eyes to drift there. It all clicked anyway.

I was turning him on, and he was asking me to knock it off.

Putting the van in gear, he drove around the building and rolled us to a stop in a little lot along the tree line where a silty path disappeared into the woods.

The tension between us was so thick, you could cut it with a rusty spoon.

"Sorry," I murmured.

Liam huffed out a laugh. "It's okay. Just...part of the job description."

"Of being a guy?"

"Of being around you," he said quickly, then clapped a hand over his mouth, eyes wide. "Fuck, I'm sorry. I shouldn't have said that."

I gave him what I'd hoped was a reassuring smile but it felt forced and brittle. "It's okay."

Clearing his throat again, he unceremoniously opened his door and threw himself from the van in an effort to get away from me.

I met him at the back of the vehicle, which he'd already opened and began digging through in search of his things.

"What will you need for tonight?" he asked, his tone clipped.

I stared at the side of his face, equal parts annoyed and confused by his change in mood. I couldn't fucking control how people reacted to me, and the fact that he'd so quickly gone from...*flirting* with me—there was no other way to describe it—to this was disconcerting and disheartening.

When he didn't acknowledge me further, I surveyed my luggage and pointed at one of the duffels, my backpack, and the reusable shopping bag I knew was layered at the bottom with a sweat suit and my toiletries.

He raised a skeptical brow but still kept his eyes off my face. "That's it?"

I shrugged. "That's it."

Liam pulled the bags free and, arms laden with both my things and his, he jerked his head in the direction of the path, a sign pointing us toward Paddler's Village.

"Wow," I breathed when the wooded area opened up onto a large swath of sand, several yurts constructed sporadically along the water. They were a mix of red and green, draped in some sort of waterproofing material, and bigger than I expected.

Liam shot me a quick smile over his shoulder—though it was forced and brittle. "Pretty neat setup."

Neat wasn't the word I'd use.

Peaceful was more like it.

It was early enough in the season that no one was here but us, and I relished that fact. That we had this entire stretch of beach, with the cold Lake Superior waters gently lapping at the shore, a canopy of budding trees at our backs, and the soft sand between my toes.

"This one is yours," Liam said, walking up the steps to a yurt with an iron number two affixed beside the door.

I followed him, excitedly dancing on the balls of my feet while he unlocked it, then handed me the key before he pushed inside.

Truthfully, I had no idea what to expect. I wasn't exactly well-versed in the camping experience. But I was pleasantly surprised.

"This isn't so bad," I told him as I pushed past—careful not to come into contact with his body; he didn't need any more ammo to be a jackass—and into my home for the night.

First, I was most surprised by its spaciousness given its circular shape and how small it appeared from the outside. The walls were treated wood, stained lightly to let the natural grain shine through. The scent of fresh pine hung in the air, mixed with some sort of artificial freshener that reminded me of fall. It was clean, well lit, and both the bunk beds and sofa pushed to opposite sides looked plenty comfortable.

Liam snorted. "Don't get used to it, Wildflower. There are some points on this trip when we'll definitely be roughing it."

"I can handle rough," I quipped.

Liam's gaze dipped to my mouth before jerking back to my eyes. "I'm sure you can."

Fuck. I'd really stepped in it with that comment, and now my mind wouldn't stop conjuring images of Liam's strong, working-man's hands on my body. Throwing me around. Pulling my hair and leaving fingerprints on my thighs.

And he really had to stop replying so suggestively. In the same way he was a man, I was just a girl, and I could only handle so much. We'd only been together for eight hours and the constant back and forth was already giving me whiplash.

He scrubbed at the back of his neck, breaking the tense silence by saying, "Want to eat at a picnic table and watch the sunset?"

"Sure," I said, gesturing the way out.

He left well ahead of me, and when I was alone, I rifled through one of my bags until I came away with a small brown paper envelope that held a collection of wildflower seeds. Seeds I'd been carefully collecting and mixing into packets for the past few years, waiting for the perfect opportunity to start spreading them around.

And what better time than a cross-country road trip?

I still carried the food so, seeds stowed in my back pocket, I made my way toward a table up the beach a ways while Liam dropped his things in his own yurt—right next to mine.

I refused to let that knowledge burrow in, to consider the fact that we were alone on this trip, on this beach, and tonight only a few walls and a short walk would separate us. If we wanted to, we could easily say "fuck it" and let our errant words turn from mere ideas into the real deal.

But hopping into bed with a new guy wasn't what I'd been thinking when I vowed to be better to myself. I need to focus on *me* and *only me*, full stop.

Liam was doing me a solid here, letting me tag along on this trip. I could easily ignore the tension as well as admire him—the way he moved, how he filled out those jeans, his tattoos—from afar and not make it weird. I wasn't even trying to pretend I wouldn't ogle him. The man was fucking gorgeous, impossible to look away from.

But what I desperately needed right now was a friend. Someone who wasn't related to me but maybe wouldn't mind listening to me if I needed to get some things off my chest in order to heal on this journey. Someone who took me at face value, good days and bad, and didn't try to fix me like everyone else in my life seemed to want to.

Liam was a calming presence in that he made it okay for me to feel my feelings without hiding them behind a mask.

Even if my body was having other ideas about him. And even if he'd been acting like a bit of a dick for the last twenty minutes.

With him safely out of sight, I set the food on the table, then withdrew the packet of seeds, opened it up, and casually walked along the tree line, sprinkling them as I walked until they were all gone.

I had no idea if they'd be able to take root in this particular soil, but I figured if the trees could grow, so could flowers.

A few minutes later, Liam exited his yurt and, barefoot, padded down the beach toward the table I'd selected, dropping down next to me. Wordlessly, I handed him one of the takeout containers, which I'd split half of the fish into, and equally as silently, Liam tore into the meal.

My own was half-eaten, so I mostly picked at it while we sat there, not talking, watching the sun sink below the horizon, turning everything brilliant orange before the darkness descended.

A short while later, Liam cleared our trash and bid me good night, disappearing into his yurt without a backward glance.

I couldn't help feeling like I'd once again done something wrong, but instead of going after him and demanding an explanation for why he'd suddenly gone cold and mute around me, I tipped my head back to look at the sky.

chapter 10
Liam

THE NEXT MORNING, AFTER I'd tossed and turned all night, Ella and I woke, got ready, and hit the road again. By the time we pulled up to our lodgings for the night in Rochester, Minnesota—one of those inexpensive roadside motels that had certainly seen better days, probably in the seventies when it was built—I was glad I hadn't decided to drive further. By then, the sun was already going down, and I was nursing a massive headache from clenching my jaw, trying to keep all the words I wanted to say to Ella locked safely away until the right moment.

I was acting like a giant dick to her, and I couldn't quite figure out why.

Or maybe I knew *exactly* why, but thinking the words made me feel like an even bigger dick.

I'd expected this trip to be a turning point for us. The opportunity for me to show her I could be good for her—be good *to* her. Instead, I found myself saying stupid shit, reacting poorly when she did something that had my skin tightening like I would burst if I didn't do something about it.

Like the evening before, when I'd got back into the van and heard the moan she'd released over a bite of fish.

All I could think about was how I could be the one to get her to make those sounds, and my cock had risen to the occasion.

But me thirsting after her wasn't fair to either of us, especially not when it was obvious that she was still working through some shit. I'd been watching her so closely for so long that I could easily decipher her moods, and it was easy to see whenever the darkness passed back over her, like a cloud covering the sun.

And that's what Ella was—the sun. She deserved to be treated that way, deserved to be reminded that she shone brighter than anything around her. That she was better than some fucking twit who didn't know what a good thing he'd found in her.

She could do better than him. Better than *me*. I wasn't sure there was a man on Earth worthy of her.

But I'd be damned if I wouldn't kill myself trying.

Except she'd done her level best to ignore me all day, which made me feel even worse for being an asshole.

It was just...being around her was a lot harder than I expected it to be, and there were moments where I found myself questioning whether or not letting her tag along was truly in either of our best interests.

As soon as we arrived in Rochester and I checked us in, Ella disappeared straight into the bathroom while I brought in our luggage.

The shower turned on and soft humming filtered through the paper thin wall over the sound of rushing water. I glanced at the bags I'd set on Ella's bed, certain she didn't magically have a fresh change of clothes hidden somewhere on her person.

The leggings she'd been wearing were too goddamn tight for that.

Trust me, I'd noticed.

With a resigned sigh, I lifted her duffel and walked to the bathroom, lightly tapping on the door and saying, "Ella?"

"What?" she bit out.

"Do you need your bag?"

I swore I felt her softening toward me a little bit as she said, "Yes, please."

"I'm just going to leave it outside the door."

"Thank you."

The bag settled to the floor with a soft thump, and I quickly backed away, putting as much space as I possibly could between myself and the flimsy hollow core door separating me from her naked body.

I'd already fucked up enough in only two short days. Crossing that line and completely destroying that boundary would only make things worse.

We were only an hour away from Minneapolis, after all. With my luck, she'd hop on a plane home before I could figure out a way to apologize.

So instead, I went outside and called my grandfather.

My relationship with my family was...strained, to say the least. In the aftermath of me leaving Portland, I'd essentially cut ties with my dad and brother, much to their chagrin. Especially when they discovered I still spoke to my mom and grandfather almost daily.

My dad hadn't exactly been absent when Sammy and I were

growing up. He'd been there—but he'd been emotionally un-available. Our family owned a real estate development company that my grandfather founded in his twenties and spent years cultivating into the most successful company of its kind in the Pacific Northwest, servicing an area from Vancouver, B.C., to as far south as Sacramento and as far west as Edmonton and Calgary.

I'd grown up in Vancouver. When I started high school, my grandfather ultimately decided to move the business headquarters to Portland to be more centrally located, so I'd also spent a lot of time in the PNW.

The only thing my dad cared about was money and the company. As an only child, he'd taken over as CEO when Gramps retired, and as the oldest son, I should've taken up the mantle when it was time for him to step down.

I never wanted any part of it.

So now he had my brother in his back pocket, the spare becoming the heir apparent, and it caused a massive divide in our immediate family. Us versus them. Me and mom versus Sammy and Dad.

Gramps—and Gran when she'd still been alive—had thankfully been on my side, both frequently appalled by the way their son treated his children. I knew for a fact they hadn't raised him that way, but something had gone wrong with Dad, and there was just no fixing it.

Now, as an adult, I could handle my father, which I did mostly by removing myself entirely from the situation.

The phone rang and rang with the outgoing call to my grandpa, and I was a little crestfallen when it went to voicemail. I left him a brief message letting him know where I was and to call when he could.

Then I dropped onto the curb in front of our room and closed my eyes, taking a moment to collect myself before going back inside and facing all the ways I was failing where Ella was concerned.

So lost in my thoughts, I didn't hear the door creak open behind me until Ella softly called my name.

I whipped around, finding her dressed in a sage green sweatsuit, her wet hair darkening the fabric around her shoulders.

"What're you doing out here?" she asked, stepping with bare feet onto the concrete. "It's freezing."

"Just...thinking."

"About?"

I took my hat off, hooked it over my knee, and scrubbed a hand through my hair as I decided how to respond. I'd always operated on the belief that honesty was the best policy, so I said, "I'm sorry I've been such an asshole today."

Ella leaned against the wall and crossed her arms over her chest. Her sweatshirt rode up a bit, revealing a slice of her stomach, and I swallowed hard.

Fucking hell, I was down bad.

"You should be," she agreed, then sighed. "Look, we've both said things we shouldn't have. But...there's no harm in flirting as long as it doesn't go beyond that, and as long as we don't make a habit of it. We're friends, right?"

"You tell me." If I couldn't have her in every way that mattered—every way I *wanted* her—friends was the next best thing, and more than I'd ever had from her before.

Ella nodded. "I could really use a friend, Liam."

I stood and faced her, extending my hand for a shake. "Friends it is, then."

Ella's grin lit me up from the inside. Then she turned away from me. "Now get in here before you catch a cold or something."

I chuckled and gave her a mock salute. "Yes, ma'am."

When we were safely back inside, I followed Ella's lead and decided to take a shower. There was something about spending all day in the car that made me feel grimy, and I was, admittedly, chilled to the bone after sitting outside for so long with nothing more but a thin, long-sleeved shirt on.

I turned the water on, keeping my hand under the spray until it reached the perfect temperature—just this side of burning my skin. Then I stripped off my clothes and stepped in, tipping my head back and letting the water pound against my scalp.

For a roadside motel, the water pressure was impressive, and I let the steady thrum of it attempt to drill some sense into me.

Unfortunately, as it always did, my mind traveled to thoughts of Ella. Knowing she was just on the other side of the door. That we would be alone for the majority of this trip, and anything could happen.

My cock stiffened until it was throbbing so insistently I couldn't ignore it.

I could be quiet, right? She'd never have to know.

Tentatively, I curled my hand around my shaft, hissing at the pressure, then slowly worked it up and down. Thinking about her in here was torture, imagining her standing right here, completely bare, water sluicing over the planes and curves of her body. My imagination was vivid in conjuring up what her body looked like naked.

Working myself slowly up and down, I imagined it was her hand instead of mine, those delicate fingers, so adept at coaxing plants to life instead coaxing an orgasm out of me. I wondered what she'd look like on her knees before me, her mouth open, ready to take me deep into her throat.

Most of all, I thought about how she'd feel if I finally got to sink into her cunt, to bury myself there and never leave.

My hand flew faster as my imagination ran away with all the ways I'd take her, all the time I'd spend learning her body until I knew exactly what it took to make her scream, my balls drawing up tighter and tighter, until the pressure at the base of my spine was damn near unbearable.

With a groan I hoped was too low for her to hear through the walls, I came all over the tile, leaning on an arm over my head, face tilted down as the water continued to pound against my side. Once I caught my breath, I rinsed my cum down the drain and got out.

When I exited the bathroom, Ella's eyes darted my way quickly before she said quickly to whoever was on the other end, "Okay, gotta go. Love you, bye."

Despite her rush to hang up the phone, the tension between us had eased considerably since my apology outside, and I didn't think anything of it when she disappeared into the bathroom to brush her teeth, then returned and crawled under the covers, whispering "good night" before she turned her back to me and promptly fell asleep.

I could tell she was out because the soft snuffles of her breath filled the otherwise silent room.

It had been a long ass time since I'd shared a space with anyone like this, and while I was having difficulty falling asleep simply because it was *her*, letting her into my personal bubble had actually been as easy as breathing. Because, in that same vein, I hadn't let anyone close enough to see the less pleasant sides of me in forever—probably since I left Portland—and the fact that I felt safe enough with her to do so spoke wonders.

"Shhhhhh!"

The loud hiss came from Ella's bed, and I sat up in a flash, squinting into the darkness, trying to figure out if I'd accidentally said any of that out loud. But she still faced away from me, her body not moving save for the gentle rise and fall of her shoulders with each breath.

I chuckled silently as realization dawned: Ella Delatou talked in her sleep.

I laid back down, curling on my side facing her, imagining I was wrapped around her instead, and closed my eyes.

As I was hovering on that precipice between awake and asleep, Ella whispered one more word, so faint I couldn't be sure I didn't imagine it.

"*Liam.*"

Finally, I fell into a deep sleep with a smile on my face.

⁂

"What is that?" Ella yelped excitedly as we crossed the city limits into Sioux Falls, South Dakota about four hours after we'd left the motel the next morning.

On one street corner was an abstract bronze sculpture, the next a statue that appeared to have been carved out of wood. All the way down the main drag, regular art installations popped up.

"Must be some sort of festival," I mused as I drove us deeper into the city.

After some quick tapping on her phone, Ella nodded and said, "The Sioux Falls Sculpture Walk. Apparently, there are over eighty sculptures placed all around town, and we're encouraged to walk around and enjoy them."

I knew the words that would come out of her mouth next before she could even speak them, and as she asked if we could stop, I already had my blinker on and was digging my wallet out of my pocket to pay for parking.

With no real destination in mind, we got out of the car and wandered in the direction we'd driven in from, Ella stopping every so often to marvel at the creations.

"Artists are incredible, aren't they?" she asked me as she canted her head to the side to get a better angle on the sculpture in front of us. It was some sort of optical illusion that presented a new facet with each movement around it.

The sculpture was impressive, but I really only had eyes for her.

"Yeah, they are."

Her cheeks turned that pretty pink color as she said, "You can't possibly mean me."

"Why not? Art evokes emotion, right? Isn't that what you're doing every time you put together a fresh arrangement of flowers?"

"I mean, yeah, but it's not—"

"Don't you dare say it's not the same," I warned, wagging a finger in her face. "Because it is. You bring people happiness every time they get a delivery from Blossom's. And you're insanely talented, Wildflower. Your arrangements are the best I've ever seen."

"You're a man," she grumbled. "What do you know about it?"

More than I cared to admit.

I didn't particularly appreciate her stereotyping me either. I made my living growing grapes and producing high quality wines. And wasn't that a form of artistry in and of itself? While growing conditions varied considerably from region to region, winemakers across the world were given the same tools when starting out. It was how they were nurtured and fermented that determined whether the wine would win awards or be considered bottom shelf. As a daughter of an impressive winery legacy, Ella should know that better than anyone. Not being part of the family business directly didn't give her an excuse to ignore that.

"Vinting is an artform too, Wildflower. A less aesthetic one, based in chemistry and a slave to the weather more than anything else, but an artform nonetheless." She opened her mouth to protest, or to explain herself. I didn't know, and I wasn't about to find out. Because unfortunately, my mouth decided to run away without me, dropping a bomb between us in the middle of the sunny street. "And I'm a man who came into the shop once a week every week for the last four years to buy flowers just so I could see your face. So someone reminded you how amazing you are. Because I'd bet all the money I have that your tool of a boyfriend wasn't doing it."

There it was. My deepest secret laid bare. The secret crush I'd been harboring was no longer locked away but out in the open at last.

"You..." she sputtered. Then, barely above a whisper: "There was no one else."

I shook my head. There was no going back now, and I wasn't even going to try. "You've always been the someone special, Wildflower."

"You mean to tell me...*four years*?"

I nodded, surprised to find there wasn't a hint of embarrassment to be found anywhere within me. Truthfully, it felt *good*, cathartic, even, to finally be admitting this.

Fuck being friends. I wanted to show her there was an alternative to the relationship she'd been broken by.

Maybe, with all of my cards on the table now, things could become something more between us.

Maybe, she'd stop pretending she didn't feel this spark too.

We continued to wander for another hour or so, slowly making our way back to the van and hitting the road farther west into South Dakota.

"So where exactly are we staying tonight?" Ella asked an hour or so from the Badlands.

"There's this campground on the edge of the Badlands where I have a site reserved."

Ella glanced behind her, at the retrofitted back of the van where the single bed folded against one side.

"Are you sure two people can't fit on that thing?"

"Not unless we want to cuddle," I said, flicking a glance her way and wiggling my brows. "You offering?"

Ella choked on her tongue in her haste to respond, and I

chuckled at her discomfort. Eventually, she forced out, "No."

"I was joking anyway. But trust me. Lumberjack Wills can handle himself." To prove my point, I lifted my free arm and curled my forearm toward my shoulder, my biceps popping up into a mountain of muscle.

It felt good to be acting this way, to drop the moody bastard act and flirt with her the way I'd been dying to for years.

A giggle slipped free from Ella, and she shook her head. "You're ridiculous."

"You love it."

I could feel her gaze on the side of my face for a long time before she spoke again. "You're different than I thought."

"How so?"

It wasn't the first time someone told me that, but I was more curious than ever because it was *her*. Was it a good different? Bad different? Somewhere in the middle?

"You have this really gruff exterior that has everyone in town thinking you're a serial killer—"

"Well, I hadn't heard *that* particular rumor," I grumbled, though I wasn't entirely surprised. I hadn't done anything to dispel the notion, after all.

"—but you're soft underneath."

I patted my abdomen. "Nothing soft here."

"I don't mean physically," she said with an eye roll, though I didn't miss the way her eyes dipped to my stomach, could read everything though flashing across those green depths.

She clearly liked what she saw.

And maybe, just maybe, I'd get the chance to show her everything one day.

Clearing my throat, I said, "Then what did you mean?"

"I mean like...emotionally. Personality wise. You're silly and funny and incredibly kind. You should let more people see that side of you."

"As long as you know it exists, I don't care about anyone else."

I'D DONE A LOT of research before making definitive plans for this trip, and when I ultimately decided I wanted to see the Badlands, I really wanted to immerse myself in the experience. So when I came across this campground tucked among the rock formations, I knew it was the perfect stopping point for this leg of the trip.

Our site was nestled between two towers, the layers varying degrees of grey, beige, and that signature clay color. It felt protected somehow, like no harm would befall us with the rocks standing sentinel at our sides.

I also knew, thanks to my research, that the campground was spread out across a few square miles, the sites mainly situated like this one, with enough separation for privacy but close enough that someone would hopefully come running if you screamed for help.

Once we got settled, Ella and I changed into sturdier shoes and clothes and set off on a winding path through the formations.

The land was mostly flat, but both of us were having the time of our lives scrambling up the sides of the towers, perching as high as we could while the other one captured our toothy, carefree smiles in photographs.

Before we headed back—I didn't want to be caught out there in the dark—we paused for a moment, content to bask in the stillness and quiet.

"This is...breathtaking," Ella said.

She stood on a narrow patch of grass that had inexplicably sprouted up between the rocks, a hand shielding her eyes as the sun began to dip below the tops of the formations. It set everything in a bright, fiery orange, deepening the color of the clay to a rich red.

But I only had eyes for Ella, her hair pulled back into two French braids, shorter purple locks falling free around her face. She wore a blue athletic top, so dark it was nearly black, and matching leggings with her hiking boots. Her expression was completely relaxed, arm hanging loosely at her side while the other shaded those gorgeous green orbs. I couldn't resist lifting my phone to take a picture, wanting to remember this moment forever.

When I didn't respond right away, she glanced at me over her shoulder, a soft, serene smile on her face that didn't fade when she noticed my phone held aloft.

I snapped another shot.

My eyes never left hers as I said, "Yeah, Wildflower. It is."

We both knew I wasn't talking about the scenery.

"Howdy, neighbors!" a jovial male voice greeted us when we trekked back into our campsite.

Ella and I turned toward it to find a man and a woman perched on a nearby picnic table. Both had long, frizzy hair, some indeterminate shade between grey and white, their skin tanned and rough, eyes sharp. The woman's fingers were decorated with silver jewelry, and charms dangled from her bracelets. His long, Gandalf-esque beard reached nearly to his waistband, was braided, and tied off with a piece of pale purple ribbon. They were dressed similarly in simple, well-worn pants, boots, and layers of shirts and sweaters.

"Hello," Ella said warmly, walking toward them and extending her hand. "I'm Ella, and this is my friend Liam."

I followed her over and accepted handshakes, surprised by the heartiness despite their apparent frailty.

"We're Gertie and Corm," the woman said.

"Nice to meet you," I told them.

"Would you care to join us for dinner? We're having hot dogs and potato salad, and we picked up fixins for s'mores and a pan of my special brownies for dessert."

Gertie winked at us, and I could easily imagine what exactly was in those *special brownies*.

"That sounds amazing," Ella breathed, dropping heavily onto one of the picnic table benches, her stainless steel water bottle clinking loudly on the surface in front of her. "I'm starving."

Gertie and Corm seemed to be the community grandparents

of sorts, and they must've made the rounds to other campsites in our vicinity earlier, because as soon as Ella set herself up at the table, chatting animatedly with Gertie while Corm fired up the little camp stove, more campers began appearing until a group of ten of us were gathered around.

Conversation was fairly surface level as dinner was prepared, each of us getting the lay of the land and each other with softball questions about where we'd come from and where we were headed.

When Corm finished grilling up a mountain of hot dogs, and plates were loaded with buns, salad, and chips that Ella and I contributed to the feast, we pulled up chairs and gathered about the fire.

I found myself seated between Ella and a woman traveling on her own from Texas on her way to Winnipeg. When Ella was roped immediately into conversation with the man on her other side—D'mitri, he said his name was—I silently ate my meal and listened to the conversation floating around me.

I loved traveling for a number of reasons, but one the biggest was the people I got to meet along the way. This group was ragtag, Gertie and Corm certainly hardened from what I now knew was years traveling around the country, never staying in one place for longer than a few weeks, but they all had interesting stories to tell.

Except for D'mitri, who was getting on my last nerve with the way he was making Ella giggle like a schoolgirl.

"If you get cold later, you can crawl into my tent with me," he told her, and I darted my gaze in his direction in time to see him waggle his eyebrows at her. "I have a solar powered space heater to keep us warm."

I barely withheld a gag at his words.

Surely, Ella could see through this guy and his smarm, right?

Wrong.

After stuffing a whole brownie in her mouth—a bold move, if you asked me; I'd savored mine—and chewing before washing it down with a swig of the Bitburger Radler Corm had produced for her, she said saucily, "I might just take you up on that."

This time, I couldn't hold back my noise of disgust as I rose from my chair, dropped my empty plate in the fire, and went in search of some alcohol of my own.

"You're letting that girl slip away," someone said from behind me.

I shot it straight from where I'd been rifling through a cooler and whirled to find Gertie.

"What girl?"

Gertie rolled her eyes in a move that made her look decades younger. "Don't play dumb, boy."

"Sorry," I mumbled.

"I've been watching you two all night. You're orbiting each other now, both on slightly different planes. But I can sense these things, and your paths are about to align. Remind me where you're headed and how long you've been on the road."

"We're on day three of a two week trip to Portland."

Gertie nodded sagely and reached for my hand, rubbing it between her palms. "You'll figure it out well before your destination."

"Not if she keeps flirting with that tool," I mumbled under my breath.

Gertie's tinkling laugh filtered into the night around us. "Do not worry about D'mitri, dear boy. He is not a threat to you or her."

With that, she walked away, and her movements were so graceful despite the uneven ground that she appeared to be floating.

Was she right? I didn't typically put stock in witchy woo-woo shit, so maybe I was only latching onto Gertie's words because they were ones I desperately wanted to hear. I wanted to believe Gertie sensed something between me and Ella, that crackling energy I'd felt in the air around us since the day we'd met.

But as I watched D'mitri pull her chair closer to his and sling an arm around her shoulders, tucking her against his side as they laughed about something, I was having difficulty imagining Ella felt it too.

Later, after what felt like a few interminable hours of listening to Ella and D'mitri flirt, I'd had enough. The pot brownies combined with the two shots of tequila I'd taken earlier had settled warmly on my limbs, loosening them, and I could feel my tongue and my control loosening along with them. So I rose from my chair, folded it up and slid it back into its bag, then slung it over my shoulder and bid everyone around the fire good night.

My footfalls were heavy and heated as I weaved around smaller outcroppings toward our campsite, thankful I'd remembered to set my tent up earlier—and grateful I wouldn't have to spend the night in her proximity.

I sensed shuffling footsteps behind me, and glanced over my shoulder to find Ella toddling after me. With the moonlight illuminating her face, I could see her eyes were glassy, and I was glad she'd at least remembered to bring her own chair back with her.

"Where are you going?"

"To bed."

"But it's early yet."

I flicked my wrist to check my watch, the face lighting up to show me the time.

"It's actually almost two a.m.," I said flatly. We'd reached our campsite, and I crossed to the van, wrenching the door open and throwing my chair across the passenger seat.

"Fucking hell," she breathed, and I heard her stumble to a stop. When I turned to check on her, I saw she had her phone out, squinting at the screen. She murmured, "How did this happen?"

"You were busy flirting with *D'mitri*." I spat his name. "I'm surprised you didn't follow him back to his tent."

Ella gasped and yielded a step, her phone slipping from her hands and clattering to the ground.

"I'm sorry, I shouldn't have said that."

"What is wrong with you?" she asked.

I drove my hand through my hair, pulling on the ends and willing the stinging in my scalp to shock some sense into my brain.

"Earlier, I told you I've had a crush on you for *years*, and you responded by openly flirting with some random guy right in front of me? That feels like a slap in the face."

Ella reared back like I'd slapped *her*, hand coming up to cover her mouth.

"Sorry," I said again.

"No, you're absolutely right," she said quickly. "I shouldn't have done that. I guess…"

"What?" I prompted.

"I guess I just missed flirting with someone."

A growl left me, and I moved fully into her space, grasping her chin in my hand and forcing her to look at me. Those glossy green orbs latched onto mine, pupils wide in the darkness.

"You wanna flirt with someone? You flirt with *me*."

"I don't know if I can," she whispered.

I croaked out a laugh. "What do you think we've been doing this entire trip?"

"I don't know!" she shouted, seeming to momentarily sober up as she stamped her foot against the hard packed dirt beneath her boots. It would've been cute if I wasn't so goddamn irritated.

"I'm flattered, Wills," she continued. "Truly. But maybe I'm not ready to accept what you're offering. And maybe I can't give you what you deserve in return."

"Then I'll wait."

All the fight seemed to leave her, her shoulders dropping as she deflated. "I can't ask you to do that."

I gave her a soft smile as I stepped backward, treading carefully until I reached my tent.

"Don't worry about me, Wildflower. I've been doing it for years."

With a mock salute, I told her good night and disappeared inside.

THE LONGER I LAID there in the silence, the more my anxiety rose. I had no idea why. Maybe because I was all alone in a new place. Maybe it was Liam's parting words. Whatever it was, my chest felt painfully tight. Not to mention the fact that my stomach roiled from that beer Corm had given me. I needed to recall the name simply so I could stay the fuck away from it in the future.

And when some sort of animal howled in the distance, I was throwing open the door to the van before I could think better of it, wrapping my sleeping bag around me, and shuffling across the dirt between there and Liam's tent.

Without a door to knock on, I scratched at the fabric and whispered, "Liam?"

"Ella?" His response was instantaneous, and after some rustling, the zipper on the tent lifted to reveal him.

Holy fuck.

The man should *never* wear a shirt.

With only the light of the moon to guide me, my gaze raked over his exposed torso and the tattoos there that I'd never been privy to before.

The massive floral piece on his left shoulder which trailed into a skeleton hand holding a long-stemmed rose on his left pec, the petals floating off of it and morphing into the feathers of a bird in a cage on the opposite one.

I didn't have a hope of inspecting them all tonight, not when my eyes finally returned to his, their blue depths seeming to glow in the moonlight.

"Are you okay?" he asked, standing and meeting me outside. Clad in only a pair of boxers, revealing more tattoos on his thick thighs, he had to be freezing, but he didn't seem to notice.

He only cared about me, and when his hands came up to grip my upper arms, I shivered.

"I heard howling," I said lamely.

"They're not going to hurt you."

"You don't know that!" I protested, a little too loudly, and he shushed me with a finger over my lips.

Liam nodded, as if coming to a realization. "So you get paranoid when you're high," he mused. "Good to know."

"What? No! I'm not high. What would make you say such a thing?"

Although, I had been feeling a little off since the campfire earlier. Had our new friends laced the smoke with something?

"Ella," Liam said gently. "You ate a brownie."

"And?"

"And those were Gertie's *special* brownies."

I clapped a hand over my mouth. "Oh my god! I've been

drugged!"

"Wildflower," Liam groaned, and my nickname soothed the panic creeping up my throat. "You haven't been drugged. It's just weed."

"I've never done weed in my life!" I hissed.

The laugh he'd clearly been holding back burst free, and he said, "I thought you knew!"

"Well, I didn't," I pouted, crossing my arms over my chest, willing myself not to cry.

I didn't like being high, and I definitely didn't like coming to this state unknowingly. We were in an unfamiliar place, surrounded by nothing but these rock-and-clay deposits for miles. It would take ages for any sort of help to reach us.

My panic swirled higher, coiling around my heart and lungs, making it difficult to breathe. My breaths came in short gasps. With a whispered curse, Liam pulled me to him, one hand anchoring in my hair while the other rubbed soothing circles up and down my back.

"Shh," he murmured. "It's okay. Nothing is going to happen to you. I promise I'll keep you safe. Just take deep breaths."

With his heartbeat beneath my ear, his warmth wrapped around me, and his gentle words slicing through my hysteria, my heart rate gradually slowed. As it did, I noticed he was swaying us side to side, his arms tight and unyielding around me.

He must've felt me coming back to myself because he pulled away slightly, swept aside the tent flap, and said, "C'mon. We can share."

The adrenaline crash was coming, and I didn't have it in me to protest, to remind him that this was a terrible idea. Instead, I nodded and ducked inside.

The space was barely tall enough for me to stand upright, the flyaways atop my head brushing against the ceiling, which meant Liam had to hunch to get in here. Along one side were his bags, and the rest was dominated by a blowup mattress with a pile of blankets atop it.

Still cocooned in my sleeping bag, I merely shifted his blankets to the side and curled into a ball on one side, attempting to make myself as small as possible.

Liam loomed over me for a moment, making some sound I couldn't decipher the meaning behind before he laid down next to me.

The silence was deafening.

As soon as I'd settled, my anxiety rose again when I realized what a bad idea this had been. I was a grown woman; I should've been able to sleep in a locked vehicle by myself. Instead I'd made a scene like some damsel in distress.

I trembled in my sleeping bag, the fabric doing nothing to ward off the midnight chill, as I waited—and waited and waited—for Liam's breaths to even out. Once he was asleep, I could sneak back over to the van and forget this ever happened.

But then Liam did something that made it impossible to move.

He rolled toward me and sat up, head hovering just over my left shoulder as he said, "You're freezing."

"No shit, Sherlock," I quipped through chattering teeth.

"We could…cuddle," he whispered. "You know, for body heat."

I thought back to him appearing in the tent opening, how he

was wearing nothing but boxers, and how fucking warm I'd been when he held me. He clearly wasn't cold. Meanwhile my toes were minutes from falling off, and my jaw was starting to hurt from clenching it against my shivering.

He was hot—in more ways than one—and while I knew I'd probably hate myself for it in the morning, I scooted back in acceptance.

"For...body heat..." I stuttered out, unzipping my sleeping bag and shifting out of it.

The damn thing clearly wasn't doing its job anyway.

Liam wasted no time in gathering me to his chest and tucking the blankets around us. They were warm from his body and smelled like him, some heady mixture of pine and a masculine scent I couldn't name. I shifted around so I faced him, pressing my cold nose against his pecs and sliding my icicle toes between his calves.

He tensed only briefly before saying with a chuckle, "Make yourself comfortable."

I responded by pressing my hands flat against his abs, the muscles there jumping against my touch. Liam's free hand, the one not resting under my head, brushed up and down my arm, back and forth in a hypnotic rhythm, then slipped it over my shoulder, his fingertips dancing along the bumps of my spine. Lower still it traveled, over the gentle swell of my hip until it came to rest on the curve of my behind.

"You do realize that's my ass, right?"

"Really?" He flexed his fingers in an exploratory squeeze, a hum of satisfaction rumbling through his chest. "I hadn't noticed."

Then he pulled me even closer, hooking my thigh over his hip.

"I thought you were mad at me," I whispered.

"Wildflower, it's impossible to be mad at you with this perfect ass in my hands."

"God," I breathed, willing myself not to react to his words. "Are you high too?"

"Duh," he said, and I couldn't help but giggle.

"So I get paranoid, and you get…"

"Horny," he supplied. Then, with a soft kiss to the top of my head, he said, "Where weed apparently makes you anxious and paranoid, it mellows me out. Lowers my inhibitions. With you in my arms right now, an unfortunate side effect of that is I want to fuck you. But don't worry, Wildflower. I'll keep my dick where it belongs."

While I reeled from that pronouncement, Liam appeared entirely unburdened. A moment later, his soft snores filled the space between us, leaving me with a throbbing clit and no idea how I'd gotten myself into this mess.

While Liam had passed out quickly, sleep did not find me easily. I was comfortable, and thanks to Liam's heat, had warmed up quickly. Even with our bodies pressed tightly together, I'd managed to relax in a way I never had before when sharing a bed with a guy.

Alfie wasn't a cuddler.

But the thought of Alfie reminded me why I was having difficulty sleeping in the first place.

As silly as it was, I felt guilty.

To be wrapped in another man's arms when I obviously still wasn't entirely over the shit Alfie had put me through felt…icky somehow.

I realized that sounded insane given he'd cheated on me, and I was a free woman to do what I wanted with my time, but the last thing I wanted to do was hurt Liam. I'd never forgive myself for dragging him into my mess, but I couldn't ignore that...something was brewing between us.

He hadn't minced words when he told me he'd wait for me. Was that something I wanted?

Honestly, it felt good to *be* wanted. To be reminded that I was desirable for who I was. For a man to be interested in what I had to offer the world without trying to change me.

I could do a lot worse than Liam Danvers.

In fact, he was one of the best men I'd ever known.

With that thought, I burrowed deeper into his embrace, his arms tightening around me in his sleep, and drifted off at last.

⁂

We took what Liam referred to as "the back roads" from our campsite in the Badlands to Hermosa, South Dakota, which was about an hour south of Rapid City and where we'd be staying for the next two nights.

The KOA campground Liam selected was full of amenities, including a restaurant within walking distance of our cabin, a corral where people could feed and pet horses—or take them out on a trail ride for the more adventurous guests—a playground, and a massive outdoor swimming pool.

Once again, Liam had encountered a minor snag in that he couldn't secure us two separate cabins as they were fully booked, but thankfully the one he'd already booked had two bedrooms.

Although, us sleeping separately seemed to be a moot point after we'd spent the night before tangled together in the name of *body heat*.

My body was heated, alright, and it had nothing to do with the balmy temperature outside and everything to do with the man in the driver's seat of our van.

I'd woken this morning with his hand still firmly gripping my ass and the other tangled in my hair, his morning wood pressing insistently between us.

I didn't acknowledge it when I extricated myself from his embrace, merely hopped to my feet, wrapped my sleeping bag back around me, and rushed out of the tent in search of the bathroom before he could rouse himself from sleep.

And we'd barely spoken since then.

God, we needed to do something to break this awkwardness. We were only four days into the trip, and I wasn't sure I could survive another minute of this.

"What do you say we get our stuff unloaded, take a quick grocery run, then spend the rest of the day at the pool?"

"Deal," I grinned, feeling a bit of that tension bleed away.

Our cabin wasn't very large, probably less than five hundred square feet total, but it did have a small kitchenette, bathroom, living area, and two bedrooms. Despite the close quarters, it was clean, bright, and comfortably furnished.

"Which room do you want?" he asked after we'd hauled in the last load of our stuff.

I moved deeper into the cabin and peeked into each. They were roughly the same size, but one seemed to have more space around the bed, which I was sure Liam would appreciate with that big body of his. Ultimately, I pointed to the slightly smaller one and grabbed one of my bags, hauling it in and dropping it on the bed.

Liam followed me in with my other luggage then disappeared to settle in his room.

After changing my shirt and swiping on some deodorant, I walked back into the shared space to find Liam standing there waiting for me with his hands on his hips.

"You gave me the bigger one," he said.

Slinging my purse over my shoulder, I breezed past him and back outside, blowing him a kiss along the way.

"The big boy gets the bigger room," I shrugged. "It's science."

Though I couldn't be sure, he grumbled something lowly that sounded an awful lot like, "I'll show you a big boy."

Nope. I wasn't going within a hundred miles of *that.*

Later, after stocking up on groceries, we found ourselves at the pool. According to Liam, the campground was booked solid, but only a few souls had ventured out to swim. It was still the first week of May, but whereas back home it was chilly, the weather here was in the low seventies, the sun hot enough to make laying out poolside comfortable.

I took that as an opportunity to work on my tan. The problem with dating an aspiring musician was that he spent a lot of time inside, and his controlling nature meant I was always with him. My naturally olive skin had washed out and faded to a creamy shade, and I was desperate for some color once again.

I always felt better with a tan, and it made my tattoos look even better.

Liam, meanwhile, took the chance to actually get in the pool, diving under with a splash and surfacing moments later, wiping away the water dripping out of his hair and down his face.

I was grateful my sunglasses hid my eyes and allowed me to ogle him in peace.

Although, he seemed to have this sixth sense about me, and even from fifty or so feet apart, I swore I saw the corner of his full mouth kick up in a smirk.

The man was gorgeous in any situation, but in nothing but board shorts, water sluicing down his heavily inked and muscled skin?

He was damn near godlike.

In the darkness the night before, I hadn't been able to fully appreciate his tattoos, and in the light of day, I couldn't tear my eyes away. The ones on his chest and abdomen were even more beautiful now, especially the floral piece that dominated his right shoulder and deltoid. The colors were vibrant against his skin, the flowers incredibly lifelike. Then there were the thigh tats which, especially paired with his shorter swim trunks, had always been a weakness of mine. One leg had words scrawled across it that I couldn't read from here, the other a detailed lion's head with a set of roman numerals above and below it.

And when he turned around? Snakes started at the base of his spine, dipping just below the waistband of his shorts, and coiled upward, twining around each other until the massive cobra heads rested on his shoulder blades. I wanted to trace them with my fingers—and my tongue.

His chest was lightly dusted with dark hair that disappeared before the trail picked up again below his belly button and disappeared into the waistband of his shorts. I imagined running my mouth over his lower abdomen, following that line of hair and tasting the surprise that waited for me at the end.

And thanks to the way his bright blue shorts suctioned to his body when he rose out of the water like a goddamn tattooed Poseidon, not to mention the boner pressing into my stomach this morning, I knew exactly how big he was.

Long and thick.

Would likely break me in half.

I'd probably thank him for it—and beg for more.

At least I'd go happily. Because a man with hands like his and a cock like that? He knew what to do with them.

Peals of laughter snapped me out of my haze, and I came back to myself in time to watch a group of five little girls—all blonde and gangly-limbed—tossing themselves into the water, their towels and shoes carelessly abandoned on the deck.

"Be careful!" a woman who could only be their mother called after them as she selected a round table in the corner, dropped an oversized bag on the chair, then reclined in one of the chaise lounges nearby.

Liam stood at the edge of the pool, a speculative look on his face as he watched the girls splash around the deep end.

And then he did the last thing I expected him to.

With a wink over his shoulder at me and a finger to his lips urging me to be quiet, he slipped back into the water unnoticed, inhaled deeply, and disappeared under the surface.

The little girls were so caught up in their game of Marco Polo, they didn't notice a shark was in their midst until Liam breached the surface with a playful roar that sent them all screaming and splashing away.

Across the way, their mother tipped her head back and laughed, and a moment later, a man who probably wasn't much older than Liam appeared at the gate, towing pool noodles, goggles, and a small cooler that I assumed held snacks and drinks.

"What's so funny?" he asked the woman.

She pointed at Liam, who was now carefully lifting the girls out of the water and tossing them in different directions, their giggles turning to sputters as they went under and resurfaced. "He popped up in the middle of their little circle and scared the shit out of them."

"And now he's playing with them," the man, who I guessed was her husband and the father of the girls, said disbelievingly.

The woman smiled widely, then flipped the brim of her sunhat over her face and reclined, closing her eyes, fully trusting a stranger to care for her children.

Then again, her husband was right there.

But Liam...at first glance, he wasn't the kind of man you expected to be good with kids. Everything about him screamed *danger*—or maybe that was just to me. Some invisible red flag waving over his head, warning me off.

Unfortunately, like I was a goddamn bull, it only urged me closer.

The father set down his things and splashed into the water as well, joining Liam and his daughters.

I hadn't realized the mom noticed my presence until she said, "You lucked out with that one."

"I'm sorry?"

Her eyes popped open and leveled me. "Your guy"—she nodded in Liam's direction—"you lucked out with him. Having a partner who is good with kids is *so* important," she stressed, nodding at her husband, whose girls circled him like he was the sun, giant, toothy smiles on their faces as he played with them.

"Oh, we're not—" I cut myself off, searching for some way to explain. "It's not like that. We're...just friends."

The woman's brows rose, her eyes darting between me and Liam.

"Could've fooled me."

chapter 13
Ella

THAT NIGHT, THE TODD family invited me and Liam to their campsite for dinner. The people we were meeting was slowly becoming my favorite part of the trip—Gertie and Corm feeding me pot brownies notwithstanding. But as I watched Jon and Laura with their daughters, and as those five little girls swirled around us all evening, making their demands, laughing at the silliest things, and having conversations in a language only they understood, I realized how deeply I missed my own family.

It had been years since I spent any meaningful time away from my sisters, parents, and Apple Blossom Bay. As much as I groused about the busybody townsfolk, I knew what a rarity it was to be part of a community that cared so much. I had a large blood family, but I had an even bigger found family, and I was grateful for that. People who took care of us when we were down on our luck, who checked in when tragedy struck, who simply said hello when you walked down the street.

I'd taken those things for granted the past few years, when I was so wrapped up in keeping Alfie happy that I stopped focusing on my own happiness. I found reasons to be irritated by my neighbors' care and concern instead of accepting it for the gift it was.

And my sisters and parents—god, I couldn't survive without them. A long time ago, my sisters and I had developed the emergency text system. Whenever one of us sent "SOS" to the group chat, we dropped everything and came running. They were there for me in ways no one else had ever been or likely ever could be.

Fuck, I missed them.

So I excused myself early and headed back to our cabin, the phone ringing with an outgoing FaceTime call in the group chat before I'd fully settled on my bed.

"Ellaaaaaaaaaa," Delia shouted when she answered, her grinning face instantly soothing my melancholy. "We miss you."

"Fuck, I miss you guys too," I sighed. "That's why I called."

Delia turned the phone slightly so I could see Owen in bed next to her, shirtless with a book propped on his chest. He was far away, the screen too small, but the color of that cover was unmistakable—a bright, flaming orange.

"He's been reading *ACOTAR*," Delia supplied, confirming it for me a moment later. "He's all the way up to *Silver Flames*, and I'm just waiting for him to get to the dining room scene so we can reenact it." She wiggled her eyebrows suggestively, and I barked out a laugh just as Amara and Chloe's faces popped up on the screen simultaneously, followed closely by Brie.

"What are we laughing at?" Chloe asked. Aleah rested on her chest, her little lips parted and cheeks squished up as she dozed.

"Apparently, Owen is reading *ACOTAR*," I told them.

My younger sister fanned herself. "That dining room scene gets me every time."

"Exactly!" Delia exclaimed proudly.

Amara, as the only one of my sisters to not have read the series, groaned, albeit good-naturedly. And before we could dive deep into a bookish discussion, she promptly changed the subject.

"Sooooo, El. Tell us how it's going!"

"Seriously," Delia said. "We haven't heard from you in days."

"I literally texted the group chat like an hour ago."

"It's not the same as face-to-face," she pouted.

"We're hardly face-to-face now," I pointed out.

"Whatever," my middle sister said with a wave of her hand. "Tell us *everything*."

I chewed on my bottom lip, debating exactly how much I should share. I'd been intentionally keeping my status messages vague, mostly because I wasn't sure what the fuck I was doing anymore.

But if anyone could help me figure it out, it would be them.

"I think I like him," I blurted.

Two of them snorted, though I couldn't be sure which two, and Chloe held up her free hand, saying, "What's not to like?"

"No, I mean like…" I trailed off, unsure how to phrase it.

"You want to fuck him."

I rolled my eyes but huffed out a laugh. Leave it to Delia to cut right to the chase.

"Yeah," I agreed. "Badly. But that's not all."

"*Oh*," Amara said in realization. "You *actually* like him."

"That's what I just said."

"So what's the problem?" Brie asked.

And that was the crux of it all, wasn't it? I didn't actually *know* what the problem was. Was it that I felt it was too soon after the end of such a long relationship to move on? No, it couldn't be that. While I still had some things to work through personally as far as the scars Alfie left on me were concerned, I'd emotionally moved on. I'd let go of the embarrassment that I'd given him so much time.

Without a doubt, it had nothing to do with concern that he didn't feel the same. He'd been showing me for literal *years*, although not overtly, that he was into me. And he hadn't minced words in Sioux Falls.

That left only one thing.

"What if it doesn't work out?" I whispered.

Through the phone, even from hundreds of miles apart, I could feel my sisters softening toward me.

"But El..." Delia said. "What if it *does*?"

It really should've been that simple.

"Start at the beginning," Chloe said. "Tell us exactly what has happened so far."

So I did. I walked them through the trip to the UP, about kayaking and the fresh fish and watching the sunset together. I told them about the banter and suggestive comments, about how he'd become distant that evening, and the whole next day he was practically mute, not stringing more than a handful of words together every time he spoke to me.

"The mood swings are giving me whiplash," I admitted.

He'd been better since we crossed into South Dakota—basically since that impromptu stop in Sioux Falls, when he'd admitted his feelings. Unburdening himself had seemingly done wonders for his attitude.

"Maybe he's PMSing," Delia supplied.

From the background, I heard Owen say, "Men don't PMS, Whiskey."

"The fuck they don't," she said to her boyfriend. "You're a moody bastard at *least* one week a month."

He rumbled something in response, too low for us to hear, and whatever it was had Delia tipping her head back and cackling maniacally.

"It's honestly a wonder I put up with you," Owen groused.

"You love me," Delia told him, then returned her attention to us.

God, I wanted what they had—what all of my sisters had. The easy camaraderie. The support, the safety they'd found in the arms of their one true love. Building a home and a life together. Eventually welcoming children into the world.

"The point," I said, "is after Sioux Falls...things changed, and he was back to normal. Well, not normal, because nothing about that man is normal, but..."

"You are down so bad," Chloe giggled.

I didn't even try to deny it, found myself instead saying, "His body is...unreal."

"*Reeeeeeallly*?" Delia drawled.

Amara merely shrugged. "Makes sense, actually. He spends all of his free time outside working."

"And he's got big hands," Brie supplied.

"Huge," I agreed absently, though my mind was lingering on an entirely different appendage.

"Oh shit," Delia said, eyes widening. "You've seen his cock."

"Whiskey!" Owen shouted. "Fucking hell, woman."

"You don't have to be here for this," she told him, dropping the phone so we were treated to a lovely view of her bedroom ceiling. In the background, there was some rustling, Delia making *shoo*ing noises, and Owen's heavy footfalls as he left the room. Delia picked the phone back up and said, "I sent him out to my office so he won't bother us until I tell him he can come back. Now where were we?"

"Ella saw Liam's cock," Amara said with a wicked grin.

"I have not!" I shrieked. "Well, not exactly."

My sisters erupted, each of them trying to speak over the other. At last, Chloe calmed everyone enough for me to hear her say, "Explain, El."

"We went swimming today," I started, hitching a shoulder up in a half shrug. "I saw some things when his trunks got wet."

"Please tell me he wears those short shorts," Delia breathed. "I'm begging you."

I giggled, but nodded. "Short shorts and tattoos on *both* thighs."

"Fucking hell," she said. "You found a unicorn. If you don't fuck that man, I'll never forgive you."

I sighed, the lightness of the conversation leaving me in an instant. "I don't think Liam is the kind of guy you just...fuck."

"And why the hell not?" Delia protested.

"No, she's right," Amara said. "Liam is the kind of guy you lock down."

"And he told me he likes me. That he's been into me for *years*."

The silence was so complete, I could've heard a pin drop from halfway across the world.

Then they erupted, yet again speaking and screeching and shouting over each other. As usual, it was pure chaos, and made me grin so widely my cheeks hurt.

I loved being around Liam—truly. Not only was he eye candy, but he was just such a good dude that it was impossible not to be happy in his presence.

But damn, I missed girl talk. I missed these crazy women.

"Explain!" Amara yelled over the din, and I did. Succinctly, I told them about Sioux Falls, the impromptu stop, the conversation about artists—which still gave me the warm fuzzies, that he saw me that way—and him dropping that bomb on me.

"He said, and I quote, 'you've always been the someone special, Wildflower.'"

"Fuck," Chloe breathed. "That's going in my next book."

"Told you," Amara smirked. "Liam is one thousand percent husband material."

"How could you possibly know that?" Chloe said, surprising me. As a romance novelist who recently published her first book, she was surely the most optimistic of us when it came to matters of the heart. Normally, she'd be the first one to give credence to that kind of statement.

"I'm in a deeply committed relationship," she said. "I think that gives me some insider knowledge on the subject."

"Except you're not married," Delia helpfully pointed out.

"Didn't even really like the guy until about a year ago, actually," Brie quipped.

"Fuck you guys," Amara said, though there was no heat behind the words.

"We love Cal, for what it's worth," Chloe told Amara, placating her. "But *I* am the only one of us that's married, and here's what I think."

"Here we go," Delia said under her breath, accompanying it with an eye roll. I bit back a laugh.

In truth, I really wanted to hear what Chloe had to say. Both because she was right—she was the only one of us who was married, had been for over a year now—and because she was a best-selling romance author. Her words on the subject clearly resonated with the masses, and I could definitely benefit from her insights.

"I don't think we know enough about Liam to gauge whether or not he's marriage material," Chloe continued, ignoring Delia's statement. "*But* I do know that I'll forever be grateful to him for letting you tag along on that trip. You needed this time away, sissy," she told me. "And that right there is enough to show me he's a good man. What I do think is that Alfie fucked you over, and that fucked you up for a while. There's nothing wrong with taking time to heal, to find yourself again before you can begin giving pieces of yourself to other people again. We're by your side no matter what." Amara, Delia, and Brie nodded in agreement. "But it seems to me like you need someone to tell you it's okay to feel an attraction toward him so you stop beating yourself up over it. And that it's okay to take the leap, encouraged even, despite the slim chance it may not work out. Because I have a good feeling about this," she said, holding up a hand when I opened my mouth to protest. "But if that's what it takes, then listen to me very carefully little sister: it's okay to move on. And there are worse guys in the world to move on with than Liam Danvers."

Though I was seconds away from bursting into tears, deeply grateful for these four women who I was not only lucky enough to call my sisters but also my best friends, I tried to play it off. I'd cried enough the last few months.

"I think you guys will say just about anything to pair me off now that I'm the only lone wolf in our pack," I said, sniffing loudly.

"No," Chloe stated firmly. "We only want you to be happy, just like we are."

I could only nod, my throat clogged with emotion.

I wanted that too. Badly, with every fiber of my being. I just wasn't sure I knew what that looked like anymore.

But...it seemed like this road trip was as good a place as any to start figuring it out.

"What do we want to do today?" I asked Ella over coffee.

The stuff was the terrible instant kind, and I grimaced as it hit my tongue. That was the one thing we'd forgotten when we'd gone grocery shopping the day before, and these packets were all I'd managed to locate in the cupboards when I stumbled, bleary-eyed, into the kitchenette this morning after too many bourbon and Cokes at the fire last night with Jon.

What a vastly different experience last night had been compared to the night before. Ella had disappeared earlier than me, whispering that she wanted to call her family and urging me to stay put. I wasn't complaining. I liked Jon and Laura a great deal, and their girls were a chaotic bunch that passed the time before their parents put them to bed making up scary stories and disputing the best way to construct a s'more.

I hadn't laughed that much in a long time, and I was happy and relaxed by the time I returned to our cabin, deliciously fuzzy-brained.

But that fog cleared away quickly when I stepped inside, the liquor coursing through my veins the only reason I'd managed to convince myself I'd imagined the tail end of Ella's conversation with her sisters.

Because there was no fucking way Ella was feeling this attraction between us the same way I did. That simply wasn't possible. I was trying and fucking up every step of the way, so there was no reason for her to be interested in me.

Then again, I had poured my heart out to her. She was aware of my feelings, and maybe that had her seeing me in a new, more favorable light.

There are worse guys in the world to move on with than Liam Danvers.

Obviously, I agreed, but those were just pretty words from one of her sisters. Whether or not Ella acted on them remained to be seen.

We stood side by side on the little porch of our cabin, and each sip of coffee went down my esophagus like acid.

Ella took a sip of hers, swirled it around in her mouth briefly before turning and spitting in the ground beside the porch, dumping the whole mug out after it.

"I vote we go somewhere with real coffee," she announced. "And stop at the store for some too."

I tipped my head back and laughed. "Deal."

"How are your sisters?" I asked once we were seated at a hole-in-the-wall diner that had been listed on the KOA's website for local eateries. I practically moaned in appreciation when the waitress set a pot of coffee between us, a similar sound breaking free from Ella when she swallowed her first sip.

I stilled and, realizing what she'd done, Ella whispered, "Sorry" with a sheepish grin.

"But to answer your question," she continued, "my sisters are good. Dying to know what we've been up to."

"Did you tell them...everything?"

Ella grimaced but nodded, hitching up a shoulder in a half-shrug. "They're my sisters."

"You guys are really close," I said, stating the obvious, my voice surprisingly steady given the realization that my boss now knew what a jackass I'd been to her younger sister so far on this trip.

Ella grinned. "Yeah we are."

"Must be nice."

The waitress reappeared then, quickly taking our orders before once again leaving us to continue our conversation.

"You and Sam aren't close?" Ella asked.

"No." I swallowed hard, unsure of how much I wanted to reveal.

My childhood hadn't been idyllic like hers. Ella and I...we were a study in contrasts. The different ways rich families raised their children. What it was like to be nurtured versus being treated as nothing more than another employee to manage. "We—my dad had a habit of pitting us against each other growing up. Made it hard to be friends when he always felt like my enemy."

In the end, Sammy got everything he wanted anyway. The title, the money, the status. Everything that, as the first born son, rightfully had been mine first.

But I'd spit on that tradition.

Then pissed on it and set it on fire.

Leaving for college and finally getting a taste of life out from under my father's thumb made me realize how little I wanted that life. And I never would've gotten out had it not been for Gramps. He was the paternal figure I'd always longed for, he and Gran giving me the love I'd so desperately craved but lacked in my own home. And Mom too. She did what she could under the circumstances, and I loved her for it. They'd all tried with Sammy, but he was our father's son through and through.

Simply to placate my dad, I'd originally gone to school for architectural engineering and business. I had always been a great student, and while the work stimulated me to an extent, I felt the much larger, creative side of my brain dying a little bit more every day.

When I'd gone home for Christmas break my sophomore year, my grandfather sensed something wasn't right with me and offered to help.

Up to that point, Dad had been paying for college, only doing so on the condition that I majored in what he wanted.

By supplying me with an early loan from my trust, which I wouldn't have been able to access until I was twenty-five otherwise, Gramps made it possible for me to quietly switch from architectural to bio-engineering and drop business altogether. Thanks to my summers working at a winery, I'd become fascinated with the process of wine production, and loved the idea of making a career out of it. I got a job locally at a bar to supplement my spending money, and that fostered my love of mixology. When I moved to Michigan and into the Traverse City area, I completed a certification, making me sort of an authority on the subject.

"What does your family do?" Ella asked. "I don't think you've ever told me."

I hadn't, and for good reason.

"They're in construction," I said, though that was putting it mildly.

What she didn't know wouldn't hurt her.

"I can't imagine that," she said quietly. "Not being close with my family."

"I'm still close with my mom," I told her, my heart warming at the thought of seeing her at the end of this trip. It had been too goddamn long. "And my grandpa."

"Tell me about him."

So I did. While we waited for our food to arrive—and even after the fact—I told Ella about William Preston Danvers the first.

"He's been more of a father to me than my dad ever has," I started. "It's honestly a wonder people as incredible as my grandparents created such a monster."

"I'm sure it wasn't intentional," Ella piped in.

"No, it definitely wasn't. They were both busy when my dad was growing up, and he developed that classic rich kid, single child mentality thanks to nannies and years of boarding school. By the time Gran and Gramps realized he'd gone bad, it was just too late."

I'd never understood how my mother, my sweet, kind, nurturing mother, ended up with an asshole like him.

"But Gramps...they vowed not to let him turn us into the same kind of man. It worked on me, not so much on Sammy."

"Aren't you Canadian?" she blurted.

I barked out a laugh at her outburst, grinning widely as I nodded. "I have dual citizenship. Right before I started high school, Gramps decided he wanted to move the company to somewhere more centrally located so we could service a larger area. The board ultimately settled on Portland, and that first summer, he got me a job at a winery that the company had recently done a major renovation on."

I'd been a glorified errand boy that summer, spending more time pushing paper than working out in the vineyard. Being cooped up hadn't suited me, and I'd been damn near coming out of my skin by mid-July.

Then I met Mellie, and everything changed. We'd met one day when I'd dropped by her father's office to deliver some reports from the CFO, and she'd been waiting to go to lunch with him. I quickly realized she had no idea who I was, thinking I was some middle class summer hire and not the heir to the Danvers Architecture empire.

I hadn't bothered to correct her.

Sneaking around proved thrilling for both of us. Those early kisses snuck when one of us pulled the other into a supply closet when no one else was looking.

The picnics deep in the rolling hills of the vineyard where no one would ever find us.

The first time we had sex, right there on a blanket between the vines.

When she eventually learned who I was, she wasn't even mad. She reacted by finally introducing me to her family—as William Preston Danvers, III, which to this day still grated; I'd change my last name if it wasn't also my grandfather's. For years after that, we were on again, off again, a truly chaotic love story better suited for television teen dramas than real life.

And then, it all came crashing down, and I ran away to Michigan.

I didn't tell Ella any of that, though, and she didn't press me about my momentary silence while my mind was a thousand miles away.

She only said, "We never really got to know our grandparents." She chuckled softly and gently shook her head. "Although Great-Grandpa Andreas is such a legend in our family, I *feel* like I know *him*."

"Why is that?"

"Oh, he was a bootlegger during prohibition."

I inhaled so sharply a piece of egg lodged itself in my throat. Once I'd cleared it and chugged my entire glass of water to soothe my burning throat, I implored Ella to start at the beginning.

"They started construction on the main building, which now holds the restaurant and offices, in the summer of 1917. Thanks to those wonderful Michigan winters, it took ages to finish. They'd been planning to open in the spring of 1920, but Prohibition went into effect that January, so they never got the chance.

"But while the winery was being constructed, Andreas had been tending to the vineyards in preparation for opening the doors," she continued. "Despite Prohibition, they opened the doors anyway. With Great-Grandma's help, they sold grape jam, juice, and other grape-based products out of what should've been the tasting room, using that legitimate business as a front for the smuggling." She leaned closer, and I mirrored her so I could hear when she dropped her voice and whispered, "There's a smuggler's tunnel below the winery that leads right to the Villa, which Andreas built for the family before construction on the winery started."

I sat back in my seat, scrubbing a hand over my beard, absolutely floored by this knowledge.

Ella chuckled at what I'm sure was a gobsmacked expression on my face. "Who knew, right? The Chateau Delatou legacy was built on a criminal enterprise."

"Your family history is so cool," I told her. "It must be amazing to live in the place your ancestors actually settled."

"It has its perks...but also its downfalls. Everyone knows you, for starters."

"Good or bad?"

"Bad," she breathed out on a laugh. "At least recently. But most of the time, it's good. The history part of it is cool though. To look at old drawings and schematics of the vineyards and see how much it's grown. To realize how much the area has changed in the last hundred plus years."

"But you didn't want to be part of the family business?"

"Hell no." She vehemently shook her head. "That's all Amara's domain. And Chloe would've done what was expected of her, but thankfully for her—for all of us, really—Amara was more than willing and equipped to step up to the plate. And the beautiful thing is, especially for me and Brie, who found our passions outside of the winery, our parents didn't care what we wanted to do as long as we were happy doing it."

"That's a gift, Wildflower. One not all kids are afforded. You and your sisters...you're really lucky."

Before she could respond, the waitress returned to clear our plates and drop the check off, telling us we could pay at the counter on our way out. A quick glance at my watch alerted me to the fact that we'd been sitting there talking for nearly two hours.

It had been so goddamn easy, I hadn't paid attention to how much time was passing.

"You ready to go?" I asked her.

"Sure am," she grinned.

And before I could react, the little shit swiped the check from the table and ran toward the counter, cackling maniacally the whole way.

With a muttered curse through my smile, I took off after her.

chapter 15
Ella

OUR FIRST STOP OF the day was Mount Rushmore, and pictures truly couldn't have prepared me for the sheer majesty of the monument.

The cliffs were towering, the faces intricately rendered in the rock in a feat of mankind I had difficulty grasping fully. The walkway to enter was lined with flags from each of the states, and I gave a cheesy grin as Liam made me stop in front of the Michigan one for a photo.

When we approached the end of the walkway and leaned against the concrete half wall that prevented us from falling to great bodily harm on the trees and rocks below, I said to Liam, "Why these four?"

His forehead was creased when he turned to me. "What do you mean?"

"I mean, why did they pick these four to memorialize?"

"Well, I think Washington and Lincoln are obvious," he said, gesturing to the two giant heads of our first and sixteenth presidents. "First president of our country, and the man who led our country through the Civil War."

"Okay, fair enough," I conceded. "But what about the other two?"

Liam held up a finger, said, "Hold that thought," and darted away. I brought my attention back to the faces of those four long-dead presidents as I waited for him.

"Okay," he said, a *whoosh* of air stirring my hair with his return. "Thomas Jefferson represents the expansion of our country, both as the signer of the *Louisiana Purchase* and author of the *Declaration of Independence*. Roosevelt represents conservation and the industrial boom of the country."

I hummed, greatly appreciating the history lesson. "Do you want to walk down there?" I asked him, pointing at the pathways that cut through the hillside and brought visitors closer to the monument.

"Sure," he said, gesturing for me to lead the way.

We chatted about nothing important as we moved down the paths, stopping every so often to take photos, both of the monument and each other.

"You know what we should do," Liam said as we stepped off the path back onto the main walkway that would take us to the parking lot.

"Huh?" I asked, turning toward Mount Rushmore to get one last shot.

His grin was mischievous as he said, "I was thinking...we should go hunting for Cíbola while we're here."

The comment was so off handed, I stopped dead in my tracks, tipped my head back, and let loose a full belly laugh that seemed to go on forever.

Damn, it felt good.

"Oh my god," I said, swiping at my eyes when I calmed down enough to speak. "You're a *National Treasure* fan?"

"Duh," he replied, like it should've been obvious. "Isn't everyone?"

I chuckled as we continued our trek back to the van.

"No," I assured him. "My sisters hate when it's my turn to pick for movie night because we end up watching those a lot. They're classics, you know. I don't understand why people don't like them."

"I'm not disagreeing with you. But Nick Cage is a divisive man."

"He definitely has some duds," I agreed. "But those aren't it."

"Preach, sis," he said with a wink as we loaded into the van.

I chuckled as we pulled out and headed for Deadwood.

There was so much more to this man than I thought, and I was loving peeling back his layers, excited by the prospect of what I'd uncover next.

⁂

Deadwood, South Dakota, was one of my new favorite places. The buildings had that old western vibe that made me feel like we'd stepped back in time. There were frequent shootout demonstrations and music in the streets, the people were friendly as hell, and it was a gorgeous day to simply wander around without any destination in mind.

I'd been terrible so far on this trip about buying my family souvenirs, so I forced Liam to stop in no fewer than twenty shops with me. Much to his chagrin, we spent nearly an hour in a cobbler's store while I tried on several pairs of cowboy boots, FaceTiming my sisters to get their opinions on which ones I should buy.

I had an ulterior motive, though. I wasn't even remotely surprised when they each chose different pairs as their favorites, and they were all coming home with me as presents. Would they be mad at me for spoiling them? Of course. But what good was my money if I didn't spend it on the people I loved most?

For myself, I settled on a pair of classic tawny brown ones with beautiful detailing along the vamp and shaft in black thread. Combined with my outfit that day of ripped skinny jeans, tank top, and my tattoos fully on display, I felt like a bit of a bad ass.

I didn't feel even a little bit bad when Liam offered to carry the bags of boots down the street and I let him. The whole thing seemed very...domestic. Like he was my boyfriend, and man enough to carry the spoils of my shopping adventures.

My head was on a swivel as we stepped back into the sun, seeking our next stop, when we were halted on the sidewalk by a man pointing a toy gun in my face and saying, "Hand over your wallet."

He looked haggard, his black cowboy hat dusty and well loved, his chaps soft and buttery over blue jeans that had faded—purposely or from use, I had no idea.

Though I knew he was an actor, he had perfected the lawless cowboy persona, a sneer on his lips, his dark eyes narrowed in anger.

Before I could react—a laugh had gone as far as bubbling in

my throat, never to be released—Liam stepped between me and the man. "I don't fucking think so, pal."

The man blinked, clearly confused, and I'd bet good money no one had ever challenged him like that before.

As he lowered the gun, the man said, "I'm just messing around."

"Pick another target."

I knew it was all an act, that the man truly didn't mean me any harm, but Liam stepping in front of me and protecting me? Fuck. My panties might've gotten a little wet at the sudden rush of desire I experienced. I could take care of myself, but it was ridiculously sexy that he wanted to do it for me.

With his hands raised in surrender, the man stepped around us and disappeared down the street. Not long after, I heard laughter coming from behind us as he claimed his next victim.

"You didn't have to do that," I told him as we stepped into the street, his hand looped around my elbow to steer me around an oncoming carriage towed by a massive horse.

Liam chuckled softly, almost disbelievingly, to himself. "I know. That was an overreaction. But I saw a gun and...just moved."

"So what you're saying is you'd take a bullet for me," I joked.

When he glanced down at me, his expression was serious as he said, "Of course I would."

Fucking hell. This man and his proclamations. If he kept saying shit like that, I'd wind up as nothing more than a puddle at his feet.

Desperate for a subject change, I said, "What do you say we take these bags to the van and pay a visit to the cemetery?"

"Sure."

After dropping my shopping spoils off, we headed up the hill, away from town and to the ridge that overlooked it where Mount Moriah Cemetery was. Cemeteries had always given me the creeps—it was why I rarely went to visit my grandparents in Traverse City—but there was something particularly sinister hanging over this one. Maybe it was because it was the final resting place of outlaws like Wild Bill Hickok and Calamity Jane.

People meandered along the pathways, but a number of them seemed to be heading straight toward the monument to Wild Bill then taking their leave immediately after.

I could see the draw. The armless bronze bust was an incredible likeness—I assumed anyway; I'd never actually seen his photo. But the artist had paid great attention to detail, at the very least. Face intricately rendered, shaggy hair blowing on a phantom wind, almost as if he lived on in spirit.

"Did you know most of Wild Bill's notoriety came from fictitious stories he told about himself?"

I turned to Liam, who had stepped up beside me to admire the monument. "Really? I thought he was like a super bad guy."

Liam shook his head. "He was actually a lawman, and he fought and spied for the Union during the Civil War."

My eyes widened. "So he was actually...a good guy?"

"Seems that way."

Damn. Incredible, the way time could twist the truth until it became something unrecognizable.

Isn't that exactly what had happened to me by the end of my relationship with Alfie? He'd stripped away everything I'd been, the woman I was growing into, until I was the girl *he* wanted.

And even then, it hadn't been enough to make him stay.

"Calamity Jane was apparently a mostly upstanding citizen too," he continued, unaware of the negative turn my thoughts had taken. "Although, she was an alleged prostitute, so maybe not *that* upstanding."

His comment was wild enough to pull me out of the funk that threatened me, and a laugh bubbled out. "Where did you learn all this shit?"

He shrugged. "Google."

That only made me laugh harder, and I clapped a hand over my mouth to quell it. We were in a cemetery, for fuck's sake. I needed to show some respect.

Eventually, after taking a few turns along the paths, studying the old monuments and headstones, seeing who could find the oldest one with a legible date, we meandered back down into town in search of some food.

"Bet you feel a kinship with these wild westerns," Liam said, jostling me with his elbow as we walked down the sidewalk. Twenty or so feet ahead of us, the fake robber from earlier held up another couple.

With a chuckle, I slapped him playfully in response to his comment. "Ahh yes, criminals. My kinda folk."

"Your entire family enterprise *was* built on illegal activity," he reminded me.

"Be careful how loud you say that!" I hissed jokingly, pulling him into an alcove and furtively glancing up and down the street, pretending like the lawmen were after me. "People could get the wrong idea!"

Liam boomed out a laugh, and I pinched him to shut him up.

"You're ridiculous. Maybe I should shorten your nickname to 'Wild.'"

"Shhhh," I whispered. "There are eyes everywhere."

But there weren't. Definitely not here in this small, shaded space.

I moved my hand to his cheek, loving the rough stubble against my delicate palm.

Liam's eyes fluttered closed briefly as he sighed, then opened again. That ocean blue stare fucking leveled me.

"There aren't any eyes on us, Wildflower," he said quietly. "Just mine on you."

I inhaled sharply, the movement sending the tips of my breasts brushing against Liam's upper abdomen. Fuck, he was tall. And so broad he could turn us sideways and entirely block my body from view. He could cocoon us in here so no one would ever see what was happening between us.

That was enough to get my heart rate pumping, but it was only when his palms settled on my hips, his fingers flexing into the sides of my ass, reminding me of our night in the tent, that I realized what a truly grave error I had made.

Slowly, I dropped my hand from his face, only to lower it to his chest, copping a feel of a single ridiculously firm and meaty pec, and Liam licked his lips.

"W-what're you doing?" I asked.

"Touching you. Is that okay?"

"Depends what you're going to do next."

"I'm not sure," he answered honestly, his voice a low rumble that sent goosebumps skittering across my skin. "Every nerve ending in my body is demanding I pull you closer, but my mind is screaming at me that that's a bad idea. So we're going to let you decide."

I lifted my other hand so both were on his chest. Like this, I could push him away—or curl my fingers into the soft material of his tee and pull him closer. Fuse our mouths together and give into this attraction sparking to life between us.

But...I wasn't ready for that, and he must've been watching me closely enough to understand the second I made the decision, must've seen it in my eyes because he only nodded, yielded a step but took my hand, and pulled me from the alcove.

"Are we okay?" I dared ask as he dropped my hand once we were back out in the open and set a brisk pace up the street in the direction of the old timey saloon we'd passed earlier.

"Of course," he said. "Just...need a drink."

That made two of us.

chapter 16
Liam

THE NEXT DAY, ELLA and I decided to take our first big hike of the trip. In truth, I needed the fresh air and physical exertion. I was damn near coming out of my skin being so close to her all the time, and after our *moment* in Deadwood the day before, I needed to push myself and hopefully be so tired by the time we returned to the campground that I'd forget how badly I wanted her.

Still, a little voice in the back of my mind sought to remind me that it seemed like Ella was coming around to the idea of us, and I wasn't entirely sure what to do with the knowledge. I knew I needed to tread lightly, but my hands itched to pull her against me every time I looked at her, and I could feel my self-control rapidly fraying.

Since she had virtually no knowledge of the area and I had personally spent weeks preparing for this trip, she was more than okay with letting me choose the trail, and I selected Black Elk Peak.

Located in Custer State Park, I selected Black Elk Peak for a number of reasons, the main one being that, at over seventy-two thousand feet, it was the highest point of elevation between the Rocky Mountains and the Pyrenees Mountains in France. When I told Ella this, she hadn't been nearly as impressed or excited as I was.

"Are you sure you want to do this?" I asked as we loaded some gear into the van. "You can stay here and relax. I don't mind going alone."

In fact, despite knowing there'd be no way in hell she took me up on my offer, I almost wished she would, simply so I could have some time to myself in order to get my head back on straight.

She glared at me in response. "I'm not letting you go alone."

I didn't bother to fight her. I knew exactly how deep that Delatou stubborn streak ran, and I had zero desire to go up against it.

Once the van was fully stocked with water and snacks for the trip—it was a seven mile loop that could take us anywhere from two to four hours, and with Ella's lack of experience, I was betting on the latter—we set off.

Custer State Park was beautiful, named so because it was where General Custer led an expedition that discovered gold in the late 1800s.

I was a bit of a history nerd, and I'd spent hours reading up on each of the areas I wanted to explore before I began booking places to stay for this trip. There was just so much to be seen and so little time to do so. I wanted to get the most bang for my buck, and I liked being able to come into a place like this park and know the history behind it.

Especially when I spouted those facts and impressed the dark-haired beauty next to me. Well...mostly impressed.

We parked in the lot at the trailhead, loaded up our packs, and set off.

It was relatively easy going at first, a gentle incline that allowed us to get used to moving our bodies in new ways.

At least, it was for me.

Ella, on the other hand, was huffing and puffing barely a hundred yards down the trail.

"We can turn around now," I assured her. "Do something easier."

She paused to gulp down some water before answering me. "No, Wills. I'm doing this. The views at the top are supposed to be incredible, right?"

I nodded. "Supposedly, you can see Wyoming, Montana, Nebraska, and North Dakota as well as South Dakota from up there."

"Then let's go. We're losing daylight."

I chuckled, though she wasn't wrong. We'd bummed around the Park for a while before taking this hike, hoping to catch the sun going down as we made our descent.

She stomped past me, and I decided I didn't quite mind the view from back here.

The day had heated up quickly, burning off the fog and dew clinging to the grass outside our cabin when we'd woken up. We'd swung through a store and grabbed a can of coffee the day before, and I was grateful I didn't have to suffer through another cup of that disgusting instant shit. And I'd been even more so when Ella stepped outside with a mug in hand, like taking our morning caffeine on the porch was part of our routine. Her hair had been mussed from sleep, and she'd been dressed in a silky pajama set, clearly braless, the top of which had done nothing to hide her peaked nipples—or the small balls resting on either side of them.

My mouth dried out at the memory, at the knowledge that she had her tits pierced, and I guzzled down some water to combat it.

The sight of her ass in her tight little workout leggings didn't help matters, either, nor did the skimpy little workout tank she revealed when she slipped off her quarter-zip, tying it around her waist and tying her hair back in a ponytail. The damn thing suctioned to her chest, leaving nothing to the imagination, almost like she *wanted* to torture me.

I was completely obsessed with every part of this woman's physical appearance, but especially her tattoos, which were truly works of art, and I was desperate to know who her artist was. They were an odd collection, exactly like mine were, and it made me feel connected to her in a weird way. There were tiny, scrawled phrases, butterflies and bees, a hummingbird, sparrow, and blue jay. And, of course, the flowers.

My personal favorite was the rose on the cap of her left shoulder, mostly because it reminded me so much of the one on my hand.

Of course, it wasn't *only* her physical appearance I was attracted to. The brains, the heart, and the soul underneath? They were even more stunning than the exterior packaging. I'd considered myself lucky that she even gave me the time of day.

Ella paused for a moment ahead of me, so abruptly I accidentally slammed into her back, an *oof* leaving me as her pack dug into my stomach. Still, I put my arms around her to steady us both.

She spun toward me, standing close enough that I could pick out each individual freckle on her perfect face, could see the gold flecks in her green eyes. Her skin was flushed, plump lips parted, harsh exhales filtering through my beard.

"What're you doing?" she asked.

"I got distracted," I answered honestly, stepping away.

Her brow furrowed. "Distracted by what?"

"An eagle," I said, waving my hand at the sky in an approximation of where the bird that didn't exist had been. "It's gone now." Roughly clearing my throat, I added, "Sorry for bumping into you."

"It's okay," she replied, giving me a reassuring smile, then hooking her thumb over her shoulder. "Shall we continue?"

I swung my arms out in a gentlemanly gesture, though that was so far from the places my mind had wandered it might as well be on another planet. "After you, Wildflower."

With a smirk, as though she could read my mind—understood that I wanted further opportunities to look at her ass—she took off up the trail, leaving me alone to adjust my cock before racing after her.

Even though we'd barely made it half a mile up the hill, the views were already incredible. We'd cleared the treetops, and below I could see fields where wildlife grazed and numerous rock outcroppings that gave the Black Hills their name.

We made it another two hundred yards or so before bad luck struck, and it was almost as if I watched the whole thing play out in slow motion.

Ella had her phone out, presumably recording a video as she walked, completely unaware of what was happening beneath her feet. I saw the root before she did, but was too slow to call out to her before it caught the toe of her hiking book.

Her arms pinwheeled wildly as she fought to keep her balance, stumbling to the side, closer and closer to the edge—where the trail dropped into a jagged cliff face.

I pumped my arms and legs as hard as I could, rushing to her side, reaching my hand out for her, screaming her name.

Time resumed its normal speed as my palm wrapped around her wrist. I tugged her to me, and we both fell to the ground. After rolling a few times, we stopped, Ella on top of me, all the air rushing from my lungs with the impact.

"Oh my god!" Ella screamed, sitting up enough to run her hands all over me while I fought to regain my breath. "Oh my god, Wills. Are you okay?"

All I could do was hold up a finger before gripping her wrists and pulling her hands away, silently asking her to stop touching me; it was only making things worse. I felt like I was living in that J. Holiday song.

Ella kept her hands to herself after that, but she remained straddling me, her face hovering over mine.

And okay, that was almost worse.

As my bronchioles once again expanded, allowing me to breathe, the lightheadedness I'd been experiencing a moment before could no longer be attributed to lack of oxygen.

Now, it was all Ella's fault. Her proximity had the ability to take the wind completely out of my sails.

"I'm okay," I croaked at last, after interminable minutes of us staring at each other, her forehead creased with worry while she watched me.

"Are you sure?"

"Positive," I said. "Here, let me sit up."

She scrambled off me, though didn't go any further than kneeling at my side while I sat up and took slow, measured breaths. My lungs still burned, but I was able to almost fully inhale.

Finally, I got to my feet, Ella rising with me, both of us dusting ourselves off.

Then, without warning, Ella threw herself into my arms.

I clutched her tightly to me, one hand at the small of her back, the other anchored at the nape of her neck.

God, I'd almost lost her thanks to a tree root.

I didn't know which of us was shaking—likely both—as we held each other, Ella softly sniffling against the crook of my neck.

When she pulled away, I mourned the loss of her warmth and vitality instantly. But she was alive, and that was the most important thing to remember.

"You saved my life."

I shrugged. "Your dad would've killed me if I hadn't."

Ella tipped her head back and laughed at the sky, though the adrenaline coursing through her veins had tears continuing to cut paths through the dust on her cheeks.

Somber mood broken when she calmed again, she grabbed my hand, lacing our fingers together and saying, "Thank you."

"Anytime, Wildflower," I said hoarsely. I glanced up to the trail, then back to her. "I'm assuming you don't want to finish this hike."

Ella shook her head vehemently. "I want to eat my weight in pasta, then maybe get drunk later—in the comfort of our cabin."

I chuckled, letting her hand go to hook my arm around her shoulders, steering us back down the hill. "Your wish is my command."

A quick Google search located a highly rated Italian joint nearby, and when Ella said she wanted to eat her weight in pasta, she wasn't being figurative. We arrived back at the cabin with several paper bags of food, having ordered several of Ella's favorite dishes. I wasn't a big pasta guy, but after the near miss earlier, I *was* the kind of guy to give the girl whatever she wanted as long as it made her happy.

And when we spread the food out on the small coffee table—containers of spaghetti and meatballs, chicken alfredo, penne alla vodka, macaroni and cheese in a thick, creamy white sauce, plus a mountain of cheesy bread and a large bowl of salad to balance out all the carbs—Ella's face lit with glee. Like a kid in a candy store, she dug into the meal with gusto, eating so quickly I wasn't entirely sure she actually tasted any of it.

Though, when she caught me staring at her, dumbfounded, she offered me a close-lipped smile around her mouthful of food and slowed down.

"Thank you," I said with a laugh. "Can't have you choking after I saved your life once today."

She swallowed audibly and said, "God, that was fucking scary.

I still have no idea how you got to me so quickly."

I sat up straighter and placed my hands on my hips. "I'm Superman."

A cackle burst free from her, and she clapped a hand over her mouth, devolving into giggles behind it.

"Whatever it was, thank you."

"You don't have to thank me, Wildflower."

"You saved my life," she reminded me.

I shrugged. "You probably wouldn't have died. Just been maimed or seriously injured."

Next thing I knew, a pillow was smacking me in the side of the head, knocking the piece of bread I'd just bitten off clean out of my mouth.

I turned to her slowly, a feral smile twisting my lips.

"Oh, you're in for it now."

Ella's eyes widened a moment before I lunged. She barely managed to set her plate down before I was on top of her, pressing her into the couch cushions and digging my fingers into her ribs.

"Please, stop!" she gasped between bouts of laughter. "Please, I'll do anything!"

"Anything?" I grinned wider, not letting up in my assault.

"Anything!"

God, there were so many directions I could go with that. But I decided to be a good boy and said, "Stop thanking me."

"Okay, okay!"

I pulled my hands away, though I remained hovering over her as she caught her breath.

"I'm glad you're okay, Wildflower."

Ella nodded. "Me too, Wills."

Reluctantly, I returned to my side of the couch and lifted the remote off the table, turning the TV on and flipping through streaming services.

"Now, what do you want to watch while we get drunk?"

An hour later, we were deep in a variety pack of beers from a local brewery, and Nicolas Cage was running from the FBI on the TV.

"Riley is such an underrated character," Ella said with a sigh, propping her chin on her fist and staring at the man on the screen. She'd just taken a sip of her beer, an errant drop clinging to the curve of her bottom lip, and I leaned deeper into my end of the couch to avoid leaning into her and licking it off. Fuck, I was in trouble. "Like...you could argue he's solely responsible for Ben being able to steal the *Declaration*."

"I'm not disagreeing with you," I told her. "But I've only got eyes for Abigail."

She turned to me, brows drawn together. "So you're into blondes?"

Dodging the question, I said, "You can't deny she's hot."

Ella faced the screen again, watching Diane Kruger playing Abigail Chase as she and Nicolas Cage bent over his father's dining room table, lemons and blow dryers in hand.

"Okay, fine," Ella huffed. "She's hot."

"Thank you," I grinned. Then, daring to lean closer, I added, "For the record, brunettes with green eyes are more my type."

Ella sucked in a sharp breath but didn't look at me, and I chuckled lowly as we continued the movie.

As it progressed, and as we transitioned into the second, she shifted on the couch, turning herself from upright to laying down, stretching her legs over the arm and her head resting on my shoulder.

"Comfortable?" I asked.

Ella hummed and sleepily said, "Very."

And there was no fucking chance in hell I was moving her. Not when she felt comfortable enough with me to use me as a pillow.

We were barely twenty minutes into *Book of Secrets* when she snuffled faintly, and I knew she was out cold.

I remained there, wholly content, and allowed the movie to play out before I moved us. I wanted this time with her, even when it was something as simple and innocent as us sort of cuddling during a movie until she fell asleep.

Before I lifted her off the couch, I took a beat to study her. How long her hair had gotten, the bright purple streaks faded to lavender, most likely thanks in large part to all of the time she'd been spending outside. Her sooty lashes fanned out over the freckles high on her cheeks, her skin flushed slightly in sleep.

And that mouth. My god, that mouth.

Plush, the bottom lip slightly fuller than the top, giving her a pouty expression. I wondered what they'd feel like beneath my own, and narrowly held myself back from brushing my thumb along the bottom one, pulling it to the side and imagining them wrapped around my—

No.

Vigorously, I shook my head, deciding that was the moment I needed to get up and bring her to bed before I did something stupid, crossed some line I could never come back from.

Gently, I shifted out from under her then lifted her into my arms. She tensed only slightly before relaxing into me, her head lolling against my shoulder. She wasn't heavy in the slightest, but she was incredibly long-limbed, even with her tucked against my body the way she was, so I had to shuffle through the doorway and narrow space between her bed and the wall in order to peel the covers back and lay her across it properly.

When I released her, she shifted only to curl herself tighter into a ball, and I pulled the blankets up over her.

Fuck, she was stunning. Faint strains of moonlight filtered into the room through the window, illuminating her skin until it practically glowed.

I had to get out of this room, but I couldn't resist bending over her, planting a soft, lingering kiss on her forehead, and whispering, "Good night, Wildflower," before I went to bed alone.

Ella

I BLINKED MY EYES open to bright sunlight streaming through the window. I expected to find myself on the couch in the living room, so I was shocked to be in my room, wrapped up in my blankets, still in the comfy clothes I'd thrown on when we got back from hiking the day before.

Wracking my brain, I tried to latch onto the last thing I remembered before apparently passing out for—I lifted my phone to check the time—somewhere about twelve hours.

Holy shit.

And then it came back to me.

Watching *National Treasure* with Liam. The way he'd loomed over me as he tickled me. That flare of desire that heated his eyes before he retreated to his side of the couch, turning their ocean depths the same color of a blue flame.

He must have carried me to bed.

My cheeks flamed. I had a habit of talking in my sleep, and I hoped like hell I hadn't said anything weird when I'd been unconscious.

After scrolling through social media and texting my sisters to check in, I shuffled out into the kitchenette, where Liam had been making noises for the last twenty minutes—trying, and failing, to be quiet.

"Morning, Wildflower," he said brightly, handing me a steaming mug of coffee.

"Morning, Wills," I responded, inhaling the scent of the beans deep into my lungs. I glanced into the liquid before I took a sip, pleased to find it was exactly the way I liked.

My heart swelled at the realization that he knew how I took my coffee.

I took a seat at the narrow counter, clutching the mug between my hands while Liam turned back to the small stove where something that smelled like bacon sizzled.

"How'd you sleep?"

"Great," I told him. "How did I get to bed anyway?"

Liam shot me a wink over his shoulder. "I carried you."

I balked at that, my face blanching.

"Liam, I'm not exactly light."

And I wasn't. I was curvy, and had the ass to prove it.

Although...he didn't seem to mind.

He scoffed. "You weigh basically nothing. The problem was you're so fucking tall. I had to go sideways through the door to get you in bed."

I was deeply pleased that he didn't think I was heavy.

And I realized then that was yet another lie Alfie had made me believe about myself. I wasn't skinny like other girls. In fact, none of my sisters except maybe Delia were. We had big butts and big boobs, and I actually liked that about myself. I was tall, yes—a few inches shy of six feet—but I wasn't model thin. I had meat on my bones, and I liked to eat. I continued to do so when I was with Alfie, even when he complained about it, even when he made snide remarks about my appearance.

My girlfriend should be skinny, Ella.

Why aren't you skinny, Ella?

You should skip a few meals, Ella.

But here I was with the hottest man I'd ever laid eyes on, who was fiercely masculine but sweet and gentle with an undercurrent of sexuality running through everything he did, who hadn't batted a single eyelash last night when I told him I wanted to eat my weight in pasta. He simply found a place that offered takeout and demolished platefuls alongside me while we laughed and joked at theorized about the *National Treasure* movies.

Shame on me, for taking so long to recognize what a catch he was.

Double shame on me for allowing Alfie's shitty words to wriggle so deep into my brain that I was excited when a man told me I weighed nothing to him.

Looking at Liam, at the way *he* looked at me, the way his plush lips parted in a grin to reveal those straight white teeth through the tangle of his beard as he set a plate of eggs, bacon, and the random assortment of diced fruit we had left in the fridge in front of me...I rolled my shoulders back, exhaled slowly, and let those words go.

Let *Alfie* go.

It was about goddamn time.

After breakfast, Liam and I quickly packed up and loaded the van, ready to set off on the next leg of our trip, which would take us to Grand Teton Park and the Yellowstone area.

Before we drove away, I stood on our tiny lawn, surveying our cabin.

"I'm gonna miss this place," I said wistfully.

Liam stepped up next to me, laughing softly. "I'm looking forward to not banging my elbows and knees off the walls when I shower."

"Oh please," I said with an eye roll. "You're going to miss it too. Admit it."

I looked up at him, and our gazes snagged for one heartbeat—then two, then three.

Finally, he said, "Fine, Wildflower. You're right. I'll miss this place too."

Somehow, I didn't think he meant only the cabin.

Somehow, like me, I thought he meant the memories we'd made there.

But those memories proved to be the very reason I was squirming in my seat a couple hours down the road. The energy in the van was charged with electricity, being in such close proximity after all the revelations of South Dakota sending a current across my skin.

Liam wasn't doing anything wrong. In fact, he was being his typical self. Mostly quiet, content to listen to the Steve Cavanagh legal thriller audiobook we'd started on the trip from Rochester to the Badlands. But unlike him, I couldn't focus on anything the narrator was saying, damn near going out of my mind with whatever was crawling through my veins.

Unable to stand it anymore, I slammed my finger into the pause button on his phone, sat up and turned in my seat to face him, saying, "Let's play twenty questions."

His left brow rose as he cut his eyes to me. "Alright..." he said slowly.

"I'll go first!" I tapped my finger to my chin, trying to conjure a really good one from the depths of my mind. There were so many things I wanted to know about him—like...everything—and I had no idea where to begin.

So I started with a softball. "What's your favorite gas station snack?"

"I don't eat gas station snacks."

I groaned. "Don't be a spoil sport, Wills."

The corner of his mouth twitched, but he sighed and scrubbed a hand over his beard. "Okay fine. I have a weakness for gas station hot dogs."

I wrinkled my nose. "Gross."

"They're not like a foundational part of my diet," he said, chuckling at my expression. "But every now and then, I get a hankering."

"A *hankering*?" I parroted. "What are you, fifty?"

He reached out and flicked my nose. "Thirty-four, thank you very much."

"Could've fooled me."

"Brat."

"Old man."

Mouths stretched wide in matching grins, mine so big my cheeks hurt, Liam and I simply stared at each other for so long that he drifted toward the shoulder, the rumble strips vibrating under our tires finally snapping us out of it.

Fuck, I was in so much trouble where he was concerned.

"My turn," he said roughly.

I shifted myself so I faced the road, deciding looking at him dead-on was too dangerous—for both of us.

"Shoot."

"Which of your sisters is your favorite?"

"Liam!" I squeaked, turning to smack him on the arm. "You can't ask me that!"

"Why not?" he said, a mischievous twinkle in his eye.

"I love each of my sisters equally," I said with a huff, crossing my arms and throwing myself back against my seat.

"C'mon, Wildflower. You can tell me."

"There's nothing to tell. I love each of my sisters equally," I repeated. "Though I love them for different reasons."

He lifted his arm and folded his fingers over his palm repeatedly in an *out with it* gesture.

That I could handle.

So I told him how I loved Chloe both for being the one to lead the charge with all of us growing up, and also for her ability to romanticize everything. How easy it was for her to find beauty in the mundanity of life and turn those moments into these incredible words on a page that resonated with people around the world.

I loved Amara for her fierceness and intelligence. How, even when Cal was doing everything he could to get her removed from head of the company, she slotted so effortlessly into her new position. Her first year as CEO and President of Delatou, Inc. had proved to be the company's best, and that was all thanks to her ingenuity.

"And yours, of course," I told Liam. "The canned cocktails were a huge part of that."

He shrugged. "Mixology is a passion of mine."

"And you're damn good at it."

Without taking his eyes off the road, he reached out and gave my knee a squeeze. "Thanks, Wildflower. Now what about Delia and Brie?"

"I love how Brie is such a gentle soul. She's easily the most selfless of us, and when we were growing up, I think we all thought that would come back to bite her in the ass one day. That, as the baby of us, we'd somehow used up all the steel spines and stubbornness. But just because she's also the quietest of us doesn't mean she won't hesitate to go to bat for any one of us in a heartbeat. She's so fierce, but in this subtle way that makes you forget it exists sometimes.

"And as for Delia...well, Delia is a badass." He nodded in agreement as I plowed ahead. "Did you know that when she and Owen were getting started on the distillery, the architect he'd hired insulted her, so she basically told him and Owen to go fuck themselves and walked right out? I've always admired that about her."

"Her stubbornness? I'd say you've got some of that going on too."

"Her confidence," I corrected him. "How she refuses to take shit from anyone because she knows exactly who she is and exactly what she's worth. And the fact that she has a backbone," I added, quietly and wryly.

He heard me anyway. "You dropped the dead weight, Ella. You just have to find your way back to yourself."

"I'm working on it," I assured him. "And I hope you know how helpful you've been."

Liam only nodded, clearly unsure what to say, and the conversation moved on.

"I've got another one for you," I said.

"Shoot."

"How come you're always wearing Chateau Delatou merch?"

One corner of Liam's mouth kicked up, but he was silent for long enough that I thought he wouldn't answer me. When he did, it wasn't at all what I was expecting.

"I like having your last name on me."

Something feral and long slumbering within me opened its eyes, sights set wholly on him. Emboldened by his admission, I glanced pointedly at his tattoos and said, "Maybe you should make it permanent."

A grumble emanated from him, and I giggled.

"Don't tempt me, Wildflower."

He would too. I knew he would.

After that, we chatted about benign things—favorite color; his was blue, mine was purple; what artists we currently had on repeat; favorite flower. I burst out laughing when Liam told me his was the Venus Flytrap, loving the grin that bloomed on his face when he got the reaction he wanted. He'd said it so calmly, so seriously, that I had to wonder for a moment if he actually meant it. That smile told me he was messing with me, and I loved it. Love that this conversation was something that would surely become an inside joke between us down the road.

Which had me wondering how we'd be when we got home from this trip. Would we hang out? Would we be…more than friends?

Suddenly, I couldn't wait to find out.

But I needed to be present in this moment, wanted to enjoy this adventure with him at my side.

"For what it's worth," I said, "my favorite flower is African violets."

"Those are pretty," he mused. "And purple."

I giggled. "I'm nothing if not predictable."

He hummed noncommittally in response, then said, "Okay, I've got one for you."

"Lay it on me, Wills."

"What's your biggest regret?"

The joviality from a moment before dissipated instantly, and my entire body stilled.

"What a loaded question," I choked out.

Liam cursed softly under his breath and said, "Sorry. You don't have to answer."

I waved him off. "No, I want to. It's just…I never really believed in regret, you know? We all make our own choices. Sometimes they work out great, and sometimes they backfire. When I met him, I thought Alfie was the best idea I'd ever had."

I remembered that day like it was yesterday. My sisters and I had gone to Detroit for a little girls' weekend, and we'd been at this small music venue where indie artists performed. Chloe was looking for inspiration for her next novel, still searching for that hook that would be the thing to finally make all her dreams come true, and she got a bug up her ass about writing a rockstar romance.

I suggested we go see *actual* rockstars, like The 1975, but my sisters quickly vetoed that idea.

At that time, I'd been feeling a little restless, watching my sisters accomplish all of these big things while I worked at a flower shop. I loved my job, and adored Fanny, who was like a grandmother to me and my sisters, but...I'd been craving more.

And then Alfie came on the stage, his low, smoky voice ringing out over the crowd, and I was a goner. I'd been mesmerized by him, by how at odds his singing voice was with his whole vibe—the skinny jeans, the stupid studded collar he wore routinely for the first year of our relationship, the artfully distressed Metallica tee.

His voice was meant for cigar lounges and intimate gatherings, for velvet jackets and wing-tip shoes, not the grungy ass club we'd been standing in, nor the clothes that looked like they came from a dumpster.

Still, afterward, I couldn't resist the pull to introduce myself.

In the early days, everything had been great. The first six months had been some of the best of my life.

But then Delia shared a video on her TikTok, a two minute clip of one of his shows. He blew up overnight, and everything changed. I didn't blame my sister. Had she known what would happen, she likely wouldn't have done it, and I would've remained blissfully unaware of the kind of man I'd shackled myself to.

It had started as little things: backhanded comments about

my outfits, jokes about "more cushion for the pushing" when we had sex, especially when he took me from behind. Then he started traveling more, insisting I join him only to get pissed off when I couldn't because I had to work.

Fanny would've let me go too, but I never told Alfie that. My job was the one thing I'd refused to let him take from me when every other thing I'd loved had been slowly stripped away or turned against me.

Except my sisters. Through the worst of it, despite how much they hated him, they were there for me.

That final month had been almost blissful in the sense that he'd pulled away considerably until we only spoke once every few days. I hadn't minded—in fact, I'd relished the distance, savored the silence in my mind where his shitty words normally cycled constantly.

I could almost see the hit coming before it punched me in the face, that first "hey girlie" DM sending me into a spiral of shame and anger.

I didn't tell Liam any of that, though. I wasn't ready to fully air out that dirty laundry in front of him, knowing he'd never look at me the same again.

Finally, I said, "I regret that I wasted so much fucking time on him. Time I could've given to someone who deserved it."

I gave him a wry smile as his thoughts flickered across his blue eyes, broadcasting them between us, mirroring my own.

Someone like him.

THE DRIVE FROM SOUTH Dakota to the edge of Grand Teton had been...informative, to say the least. I loved getting to know more about Ella outside of the things I'd observed over the years, and her genuine curiosity about me pleased me deeply.

I was also excited to realize there was no pain in her voice when she spoke about her ex anymore. No darkness flashed across her eyes. That relationship was simply a part of her past now, and while I still had no idea what exactly had led to their downfall, I was just grateful it led her—and us—to the here and now.

For our time in Wyoming, I'd rented a secluded Airbnb in a small town on the southern side of the park. The cabin, which was far more spacious than the one we'd just left, had three bedrooms, two bathrooms, a large living area consisting of kitchen, living, and dining area, presided over by vaulted, dark-beamed ceilings and a massive stone fireplace.

Through the entire wall of windows, two of which opened like sliding doors, along the backside was a deck with a few chairs, grill, and picnic table. Beyond was a field that slowly rose up into a mountain range.

There were no other homes for miles around. No one to interrupt us. No one to steal Ella's attention.

Maybe I was crazy, but I had a good feeling about Wyoming—about this cabin, about what would happen between us here. Now that she'd seemed to fully let go of Alfie, I was holding out hope that maybe, just maybe, she was ready to give us a shot.

"This place is incredible," Ella breathed when I unlocked the door and we stepped inside. Her bags fell unceremoniously to her feet just inside the entrance as she moved deeper into the space, reaching the center of the cavernous great room and turning in a slow circle. "Although I could do without the mounts."

I chuckled, my eyes straying up to the deer, elk, and fish mounted on the walls.

"Just pretend they aren't there," I told her, walking past her to peek my head into the first of the bedrooms. "See, there aren't any mounts in here. You want this one?"

"Is it the biggest?"

I rolled my eyes. "I have no idea, Wildflower. It's literally the only one I've seen."

She gestured for me to move down the short hall, where, from photos, I guessed the master, other bedroom, and second bath were located. "Let's have a look then."

All of the rooms were painted a warm, mocha color, the carpets beige and thick beneath our feet, decorated with pops of red and dark blue. Ella walked into the second bedroom and bent over, pressing her hands into the mattress, and I had to force my eyes away, lest I get any ideas about her in that position, both of us wearing a lot less clothing and her screaming my name as I made her come.

I shook my head to dispel the thought, and Ella said, "I'll take this one."

"You don't want to see the master first?"

She sighed heavily, like I was greatly testing her patience. "Haven't we had this conversation before, Wills? Big boy gets the big room."

I frowned. "That hardly seems fair to you though."

"You're the one that booked and paid for all of this," she reminded me. "You wouldn't even let me pay you back! The least you can do for me is take the goddamn master and be happy about it."

I shot her a grin, which was more teeth than anything, and she laughed. She *had* tried to pay me back for half by sending it through Venmo, but I'd sent it right back. I didn't need her money.

I only needed *her*.

"Fine," I huffed, turning from the smaller room, her feet padding softly behind me as we moved toward the master.

Before we even entered, Ella gasped.

"Well, I'm regretting my little tirade now," she said.

I didn't blame her. The view from here was incredible, the wall of the windows immediately drawing your eye outside. The glass was so crystal clear, it felt as though you were a part of nature. The four-poster, king-sized bed was positioned in a way that you woke up with the perfect view of the gently swaying grasses and snowy mountain peaks every morning, and so they were the last thing you saw at night before falling asleep.

There were things I wanted—*needed*—to say to her, but the immediate thought was to invite her to share this room with me. And *that* would've been crossing so many fucking lines. If the last four years watching her from afar had taught me anything, it was that I was a patient man, and I could wait for her to come to me.

She pulled me out of my thoughts by saying, "So what's the plan for today?"

I checked my watch, noting it was barely five p.m. We'd gotten on the road early enough, and with the days steadily growing longer, we'd reached Wyoming in plenty of time to do some sight-seeing this evening if we wanted.

"What do you say we give our sunset hike another shot?"

I half expected her to shoot down my idea instantly, but I should've known better because she only grinned, throwing a, "Deal!" over her shoulder as she disappeared to get changed.

⚬⚬⚬⚬⚬ ⚬⚬⚬⚬⚬

We'd opted for a more moderate trail, but one that would provide us with amazing views of the park. The website I'd looked at claimed this was a fairly popular hike, and I believed it considering it brought people up to the observation point for Old Faithful. I was surprised, however, when we didn't encounter a single other soul on the entire ascent.

Almost like some invisible higher power wanted us to have this moment all to ourselves.

We didn't reach the summit in time to catch the geyser go off, but we stopped in the middle of the trail on the way up, watching it through the trees.

And when we did reach the top, the sun had just kissed the tops of the hills in the distance, turning everything bright orange, making the flat area around Old Faithful look like some giant had spilled gold in the valley.

"Holy fuck!" Ella squealed as the trail plateaued. "Holy fuck, we did it!"

"You're stronger than you think you are," I said, my grin matching hers.

Her smile slipped just a bit, and she looked to her feet, dragging her toe through the dirt in senseless patterns as she said, "Sometimes, I don't think so."

I stepped closer to her, tucking my pointer finger under her chin and tilting her head up until she met my eyes once again.

"I promise, you are. The way you carried yourself after the breakup. All those times in the flower shop when someone made a backhanded comment about how they admired you taking a quaint little job instead of working for the family business. Every single holiday where Alfie quietly talked shit about your family and you put him in his place every day. Over the course of the last year, watching your sisters find their happily ever afters when your own relationship was slowly falling apart, and being happy for them despite it all. You're *so* fucking strong. More so than you even realize, I think. But if I have to remind you every day, I'll do so happily."

Ella blinked slowly, seemingly at a loss for words. Her mouth opened and closed a few times before she swallowed hard and finally spoke.

"You've been watching me?" she whispered.

I exhaled slowly, my breath sending the tendrils of hair around her face fluttering. "For years, Wildflower." I tipped my forehead against hers and closed my eyes. "The real question is, what're you going to do about it?"

Without warning, she threw herself into my arms and captured my lips with hers.

I was so stunned, my entire body went rigid, my lungs burning as I held my breath. I'd asked the question that led us here, had forced her hand, but my brain had no time to catch up with reality before she was pulling away, slapping a hand over her mouth.

"Oh my god," she breathed through her fingers. "Fuck, Wills. I'm so sorry. I don't know what got into me. That was a mist—"

I didn't give her the chance to finish that word, didn't allow her to take it back. I simply wrapped her in my arms, my eyes locked on hers to make sure she was okay with this. Her breath hitched slightly, but she didn't push me away. With one hand anchored at her hip and the other coming up to cup the back of her head, I pulled her to me and slanted my mouth over hers.

My mind was blissfully empty as we sank into the kiss, at first a slow, tentative slide of our lips that became hungrier and hungrier by the second.

Even now that I'd made the first move, I was having difficulty recognizing this as anything other than a fantasy. I'd wanted this for so long, had spent so many hours over the last four years daydreaming about this very moment, that I couldn't believe it was finally happening.

Her body was soft and warm against all of my hard planes, her hair tickling my forearm as she angled her head a certain way, getting closer, licking her way into my mouth until our tongues tangled.

She tasted like fresh air and freedom.

A drop of moisture hit my cheek, and I jerked back, confused, eyes darting across Ella's face, searching for any sign that she was, inexplicably, crying.

All I found there was a sated expression, her eyes still closed, mouth open slightly.

"More," she breathed.

As though we timed it that way, right as I leaned in to give her what she wanted...the fucking sky opened up.

Ella pulled away from me and squealed, throwing her hands up to shield herself, but it was no use. We were soaked in seconds. All we could do was stand there in the downpour and stare at each other.

She tipped her head back and laughed, water sluicing down the delicate column of her neck and turning her white tank sheer so the bright purple sports bra she had on beneath it practically glowed.

I reached for her hand and shouted, "Let's get out of here!"

We raced back down the trail toward the parking lot at its base, mindful of the mud and rivers forming beneath our feet. We slipped and slid our way, holding onto each other for dear life, both of us cackling the entire way.

Finally, we approached the parking lot and threw ourselves into the van. I immediately turned it over, kicking the heaters up into high gear to hopefully slice through some of the chill settling on our bones.

I glanced down at myself, at the puddles forming on the carpet floor mats beneath my feet, at the moisture seeping into the seat beneath our asses, and grinned at Ella.

"I'm never getting my deposit back."

Ella, who had barely calmed from her hysterical laughter from before, once again broke into a fit of giggles, swiping at her face as she did so. I couldn't help laughing alongside her. The last half hour had been surreal, like a fever dream I wasn't sure I ever wanted to wake up from.

"We're a mess," she said when she regained her composure sometime later.

Reaching out, I twirled a damp lock of her hair around my finger. "You're kinda sexy like this."

She looked down at herself, at her bra and her nipples pointed against the fabric, then pointedly back up at me. "You *would* think so."

I chuckled but didn't disagree. Beyond the van, the rain had let up from a deluge to a trickle, so I backed out of the space and set off for the cabin.

When we pulled up to hour rental an hour later, the sun had completely set and, despite the heat in the van cranked all the way up, both Ella and I shivered in our wet clothing.

"I d-don't know about y-you," she said through chattering teeth, "but I-I'm going to t-take a s-shower to warm up."

"S-sounds good," I stuttered in response. "I'll throw s-some d-dinner in then do the s-same."

Without a backward glance, Ella power-walked down the hall in the direction of the guest bath, and though my limbs were stiff and shaking, I quickly cobbled together a chicken and broccoli bake thanks to years of experience prepping that particular meal, then I disappeared into the master suite and the massive, glass-enclosed, walk-in shower that had more nozzles and spouts and heads than I knew what to do with.

I found the knob for the rain shower head and turned it on until the water was warm enough to prickle my skin. I was so fucking cold, all the way down to my bones, my balls damn near shriveled up inside my body for protection, that I wanted to fry myself alive in this shower just to get some warmth back into my limbs.

My wet clothes clung to me as I stripped out of them, and I was breathing a little hard—mostly in frustration—by the time I was free and stepping under the spray.

Everything melted away the moment that hot water hit my skin, though, my entire body coming back to life. And then I was frustrated for a whole new reason.

Our first kiss had been cut short, and I wasn't sure when we'd get the chance again. But god, seeing her soaking wet, those nipples and the little barbells passing through them like beacons attempting to guide me into her body...I was a man with a finite amount of self-control, and this trip had drained ninety-nine percent of it.

I didn't think twice when my cock stiffened, blood flow returning to my body full force. I took myself in my hand and squeezed almost too tightly, my vision going a little hazy at how fucking good it felt. And once again, I imagined it was her as I worked myself over.

A little gasp from the doorway had my head jerking upright, my hand stalling on my shaft, and I found Ella standing in the doorway in an oversized shirt—*my* shirt, I realized with no small amount of satisfaction—miles-long legs on full display.

"Hey, Wildflower," I said, my voice like gravel.

"I'm sorry," she said, though she made no move to look away or retreat. "You're just so...everything."

The final word was a soft exhale, and I choked on a laugh.

"I don't mind," I replied hoarsely. "You can look."

In fact, I *loved* that she was looking; my cock had grown impossibly harder under those hypnotic green eyes.

Emboldened by the intimacy of the moment, I added, "You could even touch if you wanted."

After over a week on the road with her constant companionship, I was barely leashed. I wanted her so badly I couldn't fucking think straight, and that kiss on the trail had done nothing to quell my desire. While she made up her mind, I fought against an onslaught of filthy images, of wondering what her cunt would feel like wrapped around my fingers, my cock. How she'd taste. The sounds she'd make.

Looking was...safe. *Touching* was dangerous. Touching this girl would be my undoing.

But I was ready to unravel us—if only so we could come together as something better and stronger.

Ella continued to stare, her fingers toying with the frayed hem of my tee.

I braced myself for her rejection, but once again, this girl surprised me.

With a swift movement, she gripped the tee and pulled it off, leaving her standing at the entrance to the bathroom in nothing but a pale pink thong, a barely-there scrap of lace that was sheer enough for me to see the spot where her pussy lips met at her pubic bone.

I felt like one of those cartoon characters whose eyes bugged out of its head when presented with something it liked. Because Ella Delatou, half-naked, her perky, pierced tits and curves on display for me? I liked that *a lot*.

She toyed with the thin straps at her hips, brazenly staring at me, waiting for my next move.

"What do you want, Wildflower?"

She shook her head. "You first."

The words flew from my mouth with zero hesitation. "I want to know how good your lips taste."

A single finger traced along her bottom lip as she said, "You've already tasted me."

"I don't mean those ones."

"And what about what I want?" she asked, shuffling a few steps closer, though still not close enough.

"What about it?"

"Ask me again."

"What do you want, Wildflower?"

"You," she breathed. "And I think...maybe, I finally deserve you."

I softened at that. "You've always deserved me."

She shook her head. "I didn't, not for a long time. But—" She paused, and neither her voice nor her gaze wavered when she continued. "I'm finally ready."

Fuck yes.

"Lose the panties, Wildflower, and come here."

Her thong hit the floor and she was in my arms in a flash, the water spraying around us as I backed her against the tile wall and stuck my thigh between her legs.

Fuck, I didn't even know where to begin.

I smoothed my hands over her hair, still slightly damp from her own shower and becoming soaked once again. She shifted, grinding against my quad, and twin groans escaped us.

"Is this what you want?" I asked, leaning in to place a soft kiss beneath her ear, then nipping at the spot. "You want to use me for a quickie? Or do you want more? I'll give you anything, Ella. You just have to ask."

"I want..." She trailed off, reaching up to drag a finger across my collarbone, at the flowers inked there. "I want you to kiss me. And then I want you to fuck me."

"If I take you right now, there's no going back for either of us." I cupped her chin, brushing my rough thumb along her smooth bottom lip. "You're mine and *only* mine."

"Yes," she whimpered, driving herself harder down onto my thigh. "That's exactly what I want. As long as you're mine."

I pressed a soft, slow kiss to her lips, lingering there, savoring her wildness and strength. "I've always been yours."

chapter 19
Liam

"Prove it," Ella said, the word punctuated by a gasp as I dragged my hand down her neck to her breast, tugging at the tip.

Then I bent my head, cupping her tit to bring it to my mouth. "You have no fucking idea how sexy these are," I said, my tongue darting out to trace over the cool metal and her warm nipple. "Did they hurt?"

"Less than my tattoos," she breathed, arching into me as I sealed my mouth around her.

The juxtaposition of the biting metal against her soft flesh was so incredibly hot that I moaned against her, moving to the other side to repeat the process.

Ella's hand came up to grip the back of my head, and I let her direct me where she wanted—for now.

"I need you."

Pressing open mouthed kisses to the valley of her chest, I sank to my knees as I peppered her stomach with more until I stopped at eye level with her pussy.

I leaned forward and brushed my nose against her, inhaling. "Fuck, Wildflower. I hope you taste as good as you smell."

Ella's hand tightened in my hair. "You should find out."

With a wicked grin up at her, I lifted one of her feet off the floor and placed it on my shoulder, kissing my way up her calf and thigh until I reached her sex, then hooked her leg so her foot dangled against my back. Ella inhaled in anticipation which quickly morphed into a frustrated exhale as I moved to the other side.

"Hold on," I said.

"What're you—"

Her words were cut off as I grasped her other ankle and slung that leg over my shoulder. One of my hands found the tile behind her, using my forearm as a shelf for her ass, while the other snaked around her hip, using two fingers to spread her pussy open.

My scalp stung as she yanked on me until I looked at her.

"I'm too fucking heavy for this."

"You're perfect, Ella. The most goddamn beautiful woman I've ever seen in my life. Now please, baby," I said, brushing my lips over her thigh and grinning when goosebumps erupted in my wake. "Stop worrying and let me make you feel good."

Ella's head dropped back against the tile with a *thunk*, and I chuckled darkly as I dove into my feast.

That first lick from back to front nearly undid me, my cock painfully hard as I savored her. She was so smooth, so sweet. Her hips bucked in response, pressing her pussy closer to me. I dragged my tongue in a reverse path, driving the tip gently in and out of her entrance while my thumb settled over her clit.

"Fucking delicious," I mused when I pulled away briefly.

Ella only whimpered and wriggled closer.

"I've had four long years to think about what I want to do to this pussy, Wildflower."

"*Liam*," she said insistently, but I merely chuckled.

"Patience, my sweet girl. We've got all night, and all the ones after that. I'm going to ruin you for anyone but me."

"*Please.*"

"Since you asked so nicely..."

I was done toying with her anyway, needed to finally learn the sweet sounds she made when she came.

I sealed my mouth around her clit, fluttering my tongue against it as she writhed above me, desperate to get closer, seeking friction.

"That's it, Wildflower," I murmured against her slick flesh. "Ride my face. Get yourself there."

"Fingers."

"What's the magic word?"

"*Please.*"

It was a growl of frustration that she combined with a sharp tug on my hair. The sting in my scalp was fucking perfect, keeping me anchored in this reality.

Roughly, I shoved two fingers inside her, and she gasped, her entire torso bowing away from the wall at the intrusion.

"Fuck," she breathed.

"Feel good?"

"Gimme one more. Please," she added, almost as an afterthought.

I grinned. "My filthy, needy girl. Needing three fingers to fill you up. Just wait until you get my cock, baby. You'll be so full nothing else will ever do it for you."

Ella merely moaned, and I returned my mouth to her clit as I pumped my fingers in and out of her, curling them against her walls, knowing I hit the right spot when her thighs began shaking.

"That's it, Wildflower," I praised, continuing my oral assault.

Her legs shook harder, her heels digging into my back as she held on the only way she could, her walls clamping tighter and tighter around me until—

"Wills!" she screamed as she shattered, her thighs boxing my head in as I slowly licked her through it, lapping at her clit while she quivered as she came down, slumping against the wall above me.

I kissed her sex softly once more and slowly removed my fingers, then shifted back so my legs were tucked under me and slid her legs off my shoulders, sliding her down my torso until she straddled me.

Eyes on me, growing wider by the second, the irises turned a deep green and pupils blown with desire, she watched raptly as I stuffed my fingers into my mouth and licked myself clean.

"Fuck, you taste good."

Her mouth was on mine a moment later, her tongue tangling with mine as though she wanted to consume every morsel of her arousal from mine.

When she pulled away, her eyes had gone a little hazy, and she said, "Now I want to taste you."

We hurried from the shower, drying off quickly but not bothering to dress as she dragged me into the bedroom. There was a small dresser off to the side, and Ella unceremoniously pushed me against it, dropping to her knees before me.

God, how many times had I imagined her like this? Supplicant before me, her mouth open and waiting for me?

More times than I'd ever admit to her, that was for damn sure.

I braced myself on my palms, my chest heaving as everything within me coiled tightly from the simple act of her staring at my cock like she wanted to devour it.

At last, she leaned forward, resting a palm on my thigh, tracing her fingers of the scrawl of words there as her other hand reached for me, her long, delicate fingers wrapping around my base and giving me a tug.

Tentatively, she darted her tongue out, sweeping it along the slit at my crown and collecting the precum beaded there. She glanced up at me before those green eyes fluttered closed as she savored me. A small hum left her throat, and I echoed it.

Then she leaned in again, closing her mouth around me, surprising me by taking me all the way in until my head bumped against her throat, those delicate muscles closing around me as she swallowed, making me groan.

I tipped my head back and closed my eyes.

"Fuck, Wildflower. Your mouth is heaven."

"I don't think so, Wills," she said, and my head rose. "Eyes on me."

I lifted a hand to trace a finger over her cheek, down to the soft flesh of her lower lip. "You want me to watch you suck my cock, pretty girl?"

Ella shook her head, eyes glinting with mischief. "I want you to watch me *enjoy* every single second of sucking your cock."

I huffed out a low, husky laugh. "Then by all means, do your worst."

She did as I asked, once again sealing that perfect fucking mouth around me, swirling her tongue along the broad crown and gently scraping my shaft with her teeth. I had no idea how she knew I'd like that—that I preferred it a little rough and unhinged. My hips bucked forward, shoving me deeper down her throat, and a small gag left her.

"Damn, Wills," she gasped when she pulled off.

I growled in protest. Gripping her jaw, I directed her head my way, waiting until those gorgeous green eyes snapped to mine before I spoke.

"No, Ella. *Liam*. In here, like this, you call me by my chosen name. You understand?"

Ella only nodded, and I let her go.

"Good girl. Now spit on it and put it back in that slutty little mouth."

"Better idea," she said, and before I could question her, her hand dipped between her thighs. When she pulled it free, her fingertips were coated in her arousal—which she then wrapped around my cock and tugged, spreading it up and down my length.

"Fucking hell, woman. That's the hottest thing I've ever seen."

Satisfied with her work, she ignored me, opening up and taking me deep, deeper than before, her moan vibrating against my flesh, shooting straight to my balls.

Fuck, I wasn't going to last. She'd barely touched me and already, I was coming undone.

"That's it, Wildflower. Make all the noise you want," I said to distract myself. "And as soon as I'm done letting you have your fun, I'm going to destroy that pretty little pussy."

Chasing her mouth with her fist as she pulled away, she squeezed just the way I liked it. My hands white-knuckle gripped the edge of the flimsy dresser, and I couldn't give a fuck less if I broke it. Not with that little string of spit and cum connecting us, not with her staring at my cock like it was her new favorite meal.

She repeated the process of lubing me up with her desire, her fist working at my base as her mouth sealed around my tip. I felt more than heard her noise of approval this time.

"So fucking sexy taking my cock like this," I said, tracing her lips with the tip of my finger. "Tell me, baby. How do we taste?"

With a soft *pop*, she let me go and said, "Fucking incredible."

Fuck, this woman was going to ruin me.

"That's my girl," I praised. "But playtime is over."

I was wound so tightly, I thought I might come out of my skin if I didn't bury myself in her cunt immediately. In one swift move, before she even had time to fully process, I lifted her off the floor, crossed the room in three long strides, and tossed her onto the bed.

Ella yelped in protest. "I wasn't done!"

I grinned wickedly down at her. "Yes you were."

"Greedy, aren't we?"

I dropped to my knees before her, eye level with her sex, and said, "For this gorgeous cunt? Fuck yeah, I am."

I punctuated my words with a long, slow lick from back to front. Needing to taste her once more before I made a mess of us. Collecting all her cum, savoring how fucking wet she was from me fingering her and the simple act of sucking me off.

God*damn*, she was heaven on my tongue.

Then I stood, shifted her higher on the bed, and crawled between her thighs. Gripping myself at the base, I swiped the head of my cock through her slit, and we both moaned.

"Fuck," I hissed. "Condom."

Ella shook her head. "Birth control."

"You're sure?" I asked, surprised.

Ella only nodded, nibbling on her lower lip. I reached down and pulled it free with my thumb, and she nipped at me.

"I'm done for," I told her. "Haven't even got inside you and I'm already fucking *gone* for you, Ella."

"Please, baby."

I gave her a soft small, notching my head at her entrance. "You're so fucking pretty when you beg."

Despite the animal in my chest urging me to take her hard and fast, I slowly inched in, giving us both time to adjust.

Fucking hell, she was tight. A hot, wet glove gripping my cock.

What felt like a lifetime later, I was fully seated, and I curved myself over Ella's body, our mouths a breath away. Ella craned her neck to kiss me.

I expected it to be a hot, wet kiss full of unspent desire and urgency.

I hadn't prepared myself for the slow, gentle glide of her lips against mine, of the way her hands brushed up my arms and came to rest at the nape of my neck, fingers sifting through my hair.

"It's okay, baby," she said against my mouth. "You can move. You won't hurt me."

chapter 20
Ella

ALONGSIDE MY HEAD, LIAM'S palms pressed deep into the mattress, his muscles quivering as he leashed himself. I could practically hear that basic, feral thing in his chest screaming at him to fuck me like our lives depended on it. But he held himself back.

I wasn't timid or a prude, but in comparison to my fuckboy ex? I'd had partners before him, but I'd never really got to explore the more adventurous side of myself. By the end, Alfie and I weren't even having sex at all.

Liam, though, was a *man*, one who knew how to use those veiny, calloused hands for pleasure—the kind of pleasure I'd never experienced before. The kind I never thought I could.

It had been so hard for me to get off with Alfie, often requiring time and attention he didn't have the patience for. With him, *all* that mattered was *his* baser needs.

Which meant, all too frequently, I found myself taking matters into my own hands.

I knew now the reason we'd stopped having sex was because he'd begun seeking his pleasure elsewhere, but also because I couldn't fucking stomach the thought of him touching me. For a long time, it was impossible for me not to blame myself for that. I hated the exasperation that clouded his eyes every time we fucked and it ended with me silently frustrated and unsatisfied. Even before we broke up, I'd done a fantastic job at convincing myself I was the broken one.

In reality, it was Alfie who was broken, who was such a small-minded man that he couldn't take the time to figure out what I liked and make sure he got me there every single time. He'd never once stopped to consider *he* was the problem.

Liam was not Alfie.

He still hadn't moved, his eyes squeezed tightly shut, his breath sawing in and out of him, so I whispered his name.

Those baby blues popped open, and a blissful smile overtook his face like the sun coming out on a cloudy day.

"I want to remember this," he said softly in answer to a question I hadn't asked. "The first time I got to take you. The day I made you mine."

I placed a palm on his cheek, his beard scratching at my skin, and he leaned into my touch.

"Not sure what I did to deserve you."

"You didn't have to do anything, baby," he said, bending to give me a lingering kiss. He shifted so he could place a hand over my heart, and it thumped wildly against his touch. "I fell for the woman you are in here. The last three years haven't changed that."

Unable to hold them back anymore, my emotions from

this whole day—hell, this whole trip and the last four months—boiled over, and tears slipped from my eyes and down the sides of my face.

Liam merely brushed them away. "I hope those are happy tears," he murmured.

"They're a lot of things," I answered honestly, "but happiness is the main one."

He leaned in and gently brushed his lips over the tracks of moisture, cleaning me up. Taking care of me, like he'd always done.

"I'm going to move now, okay?"

I nodded, sniffling loudly, instantly reminded that his cock was nestled deep inside my body. Experimentally, I clenched my inner walls around him, and he hissed.

"Wicked woman," he gritted out, then shifted his hips backward, pulling his cock free to the tip before plunging back in.

"Fuck," I breathed. The combination of the intimate words we'd just shared and the rough way he slammed into my body had pressure coiling low, my clit throbbing almost painfully, desperate for attention.

So I snaked my hand between us and passed my fingers over it lightly, hips jumping against Liam's as I did.

His strokes were slow and measured to begin, his jaw clenched so tightly I swore he'd crack a tooth if he didn't let go. I needed him undone, fucking me recklessly. I needed him here with me, not trapped in the past or somewhere deep inside his head where he thought he'd hurt me if he was any rougher. I didn't use my words to urge him on, only lifted my hands from his nape and raked my fingernails down his back, pausing and digging them into his ass.

Like I'd hoped, he bucked against me, some of his restraint fraying.

"I don't want to hurt you, Ella," he ground out. "I don't know what he did, but it wasn't enough, and I don't want you to think less of me for giving you too much."

This fucking man. His heart was so incredibly big, it was a wonder his chest could contain it.

And he wanted to give it to me.

Goddamn, I was a lucky girl.

"Sex with…him," I started, narrowly avoiding bringing my ex's name into bed with us, "was very vanilla. And never about me. I'm not made of glass, Liam. I can take it."

"You want it rough, Wildflower?" he asked, driving a little bit harder into me with his next thrust. My back bowed a bit, hips angling impossibly closer.

"I *need* it rough."

The way he looked at me in the wake of those four words sent fire licking at my skin and coursing through my veins. I watched that leash snap, and he straightened, gripping my legs behind my knees and shifting them back so they were damn near at my ears, bending me in half. His eyes flared, their bright blue fading to something darker and stormier as he watched where we connected.

"Hold on, baby."

I anchored my hands around his wrists as he gave me what I wanted at last.

There was no mercy in his thrusts, nothing I could do but take everything he gave me, my moans growing in volume until I was practically screaming for him, begging in nonsensical ways for him to get me there faster. Having him uncaged and feral like this was delicious, knowing I was the only one who got to witness it.

Even through my delirious, desire-induced haze, I was mesmerized by the way his muscles bunched as he flexed his hips into me over and over, branding that spot so fucking deep, the one no one else had ever been able to find let alone reach.

It was a claiming, the way he took me, and he confirmed it with his next words.

"Fuck, Wildflower," he grumbled. "I knew you'd feel good, but I didn't expect this. I was made for you. You hear me? My cock was made specifically for your perfect cunt."

And I'd be damned if he wasn't right, if the way he slotted inside me, filling me better than anyone—or any toy—ever had before, wasn't the most exquisite, perfect fit. The kind predestined. All of our mistakes and missteps lead us right here, to the time when we finally came together.

"A little bit more, baby," he huffed out, both of our chests heaving, both of us sticky with sweat, some even trailing along Liam's hairline and dripping into his beard. "You're so close."

He moved one hand to my clit, ghosting over my swollen flesh, and I reached for his other with mine, lacing our fingers tightly, almost painfully, together. Like he was my harbor in the storm brewing beneath my skin.

"Come with me," I begged. My orgasm was so close, shimmering at the surface. A few swipes against my clit would send me flying off the cliff—but I wanted him by my side.

Our gazes snagged, and I couldn't look away. The world could've been ending outside the windows, and I wouldn't have noticed, couldn't have torn my eyes from his if I tried.

His hips pistoned impossibly faster, the entire bed shifting and creaking with the movement, and he groaned.

"Fuck, okay, I'm gonna come," he said, then pressed the pads of three of his fingers to my clit.

I detonated.

My back arched off the bed as I screamed his name, pieces of myself scattering into the room around us as I broke apart. I was vaguely aware of him pulsing and spilling inside me. His murmured praises barely reached my ears as my entire body shook, goosebumps rising on my skin. I wasn't aware of anything but the sheer amount of pleasure coursing through me.

By the time I came back to myself—days, weeks, months later—Liam had collapsed at my side, pulling me to his chest and holding me tightly.

We were silent for a beat before he chuckled softly, which quickly grew into full on laughter. Though my limbs were deliciously wrung out and it took every ounce of strength I had, I lifted my head to glare down at him.

"What's so funny?"

He grinned at me, and his smile was so fucking beautiful it took my breath away. "Has it ever been like that for you?"

I shook my head. "I've never come that hard in my life," I confirmed.

"You're goddamn right," he said, lightly tapping my nose, and I dropped my head to burrow deeper into his side. "I've had a thing for you from the very first moment I saw you."

"The day you came in to buy flowers for my mom's birthday."

He lightly pinched my side. "Don't interrupt."

I only giggled but remained quiet so he could continue.

"Watching you with another guy was...torture, to say the least. But some part of me always knew that we'd end up here. And now here I am, falling deeper for you by the day, having just had my brain scrambled by the best sex I've ever had in my life, and...it's nice to know I was right. It's funny because it's such a fucking *relief*." He rolled us so I was once again on my back beneath him, his expression earnest as he said, "Promise me, Ella. Promise me this is real."

I softened, my heart melting straight into my stomach. Cupping his cheeks, I brought my face closer to his, our lips brushing as I said, "It's real, Liam. It's the realest thing I've ever felt."

I had no idea how or when it happened. Somewhere along the way—honestly, probably in the months leading up to this moment where he sat by my side while I worked through my grief—I'd fallen for this man. For his giant heart, his kindness, his support and ferocity. How closely he paid attention to the little things that made me happy and never let me go a day without one of them.

How he held me. His filthy words and gentle touches. The way he said my name and called me Wildflower.

The ease I felt when I was with him, like I didn't need to be anyone but me. With him at my side, I was free to be the Ella Delatou I was always meant to be. The best, most authentic version of myself.

That was the woman he wanted, and it was the woman I vowed to be from now on.

For the rest of the night, Liam took the time to map every inch of my body with his hands and mouth, willingly put in the time and effort to discover what I liked and didn't, and took great care to make sure everything he did felt good for me. Each and every time, it was enough to coax my release.

Maybe I'd just never been fully comfortable with Alfie. Liam was so quick to have my body singing with pleasure multiple times over before ever seeking his own.

Hours later, as the sky beyond the windows began to shift from black to grey, we at last collapsed into a sweaty mess of tangled limbs and fell asleep.

It was the best sleep I'd had in years.

chapter 21
Liam

THE SUNLIGHT WAS DAMN near blinding when I cracked my eyes open the next morning. My abs were sore as hell, and my quads felt like I'd run a marathon.

Nope, I reminded myself. *Just had marathon sex.*

I stretched out, arm sweeping across the bed to find the space next to me cold and empty. Sitting up, I looked around the room, but the bathroom was dark, and there was no sign of Ella.

Then I heard humming from somewhere else in the cabin.

Sliding out of bed, I threw on a pair of boxer briefs and padded down the hallway.

At the entrance to the great room, I paused, leaning against the wall and watching my girl move around the kitchen.

Yeah, she was *my girl* now.

Music filtered softly through the space from somewhere, low enough that I knew she hadn't wanted to wake me with its volume, and she hummed along. With one of my shirts—the one she'd abandoned last night when she got in the shower with

213

me—hanging to her knees, her hair piled atop her head in a messy bun, she was every inch my idea of heaven.

Seeing her in my tee, a Delatou & Danvers branded one that Amara and I had designed and offered in PR packages when we launched the canned cocktails, did something to me. Maybe it was the simple act of seeing our last names together, and the hope that one day, mine would be hers.

"Smells good in here," I said as I walked toward her.

Ella turned to me with a wide grin, a spatula in her hand, which she waved in the air like a wand and said, "Just making some magic."

Coming up behind her, I wrapped my arms tightly around her and pressed a kiss to the side of her neck, lingering there, deeply inhaling her scent and branding it on my memory. Even with the smells of bacon, eggs, and pancakes mingling in the air, I could easily pick out the floral blend that was all her. Like night blooming jasmine and something earthy.

"Good morning, Wildflower."

"Good morning to you too," she giggled as I flexed my hips against her, my fully erect cock pressing into her backside. It didn't take much for this woman to turn me on, especially not when I snaked my hand under the hem of the tee and discovered she wasn't wearing panties.

"How'd you sleep?" I asked as my fingers tiptoed higher, closer and closer to the apex of her thighs.

Ella turned in my arms so I was left grabbing a handful of her ass—not that I minded—and slanted her mouth over mine in a long, slow kiss. Only the bacon sizzling insistently in the pan behind her hand me drawing back before we took things too far and burnt the place down.

"Better than I have in months," she admitted. "Actually, no. Better than I have in *years*."

"Fucked you that good, huh?" I teased, bending to nip at her earlobe.

Ella leaned back in my arms, trying to break free, and swatted at me with the spatula, leaving behind a streak of grease on my left shoulder, right over the lips tattooed there. Pressing her own lips to my skin, she licked away the mess she'd made, then pulled from my hold before I could react.

"You're a brat," she told me, returning her attention to our breakfast.

"You love it."

She winked at me over her shoulder in response.

"This looks amazing," I added, peering over her shoulder. "I didn't know you could cook."

"I've picked up quite a few things from Brie over the years," she said. "We only live two buildings apart, so I've spent a lot of time over there cooking dinner with her. Not so much lately, though..."

I frowned, catching onto the sadness in her tone. "How come?"

"Well, she's all happy in a committed relationship with a baby on the way," she said with a frown. "Doesn't really have a lot of time to devote to me anymore."

Once again, I wrapped my arms around her and pulled her back against my chest. Her head dropped to my shoulder, those green eyes bright as she stared up at me.

"Your sisters—all of them—love you, El. That's never going

to change." I pressed a kiss to her cheek. "Besides, I have every intention of monopolizing your time from here on out."

Ella smirked. "Oh really?"

I nodded. "If you'll have me."

"In all the ways you'll let me," she promised.

"All of them. Everything I am is yours."

After breakfast, we lost ourselves in each other's bodies for another few hours before we decided to do some exploring. We spent most of the day wandering the foothills around our rental, content not to share our attention with anyone or anything but each other and the vast expanse of nature. We had a picnic out in the fields, where numerous wildlife, including bison, deer, and too many rabbits to count, roamed nearby.

That evening, I booked us a hot springs excursion, which sounded romantic in theory and felt even more so now that Ella and I were...doing whatever we were doing. We hadn't slapped labels on anything, but I knew I belonged to her on a soul-deep level, in a way no one else would ever have me. I hoped, and was fairly confident, she felt the same.

When we arrived, I was surprised to find the lot in front of the rustic lodge empty. The hot springs were part of some sort of spa retreat, and inside were rooms for massages, facials and other self-care treatments, plus an indoor pool and hot tub, a restaurant, and gift shop. The second and third floors held the guest suites that offered beautiful views of Grand Teton National Park beyond the windows.

"Hello!" the woman behind the check-in counter said brightly when Ella and I entered the lobby, the ceilings soaring high above us. The entire place was decorated in muted, neutral tones, and soft, instrumental music filtered through some unseen sound system. "Welcome to Grand Lodge and Spa! How can we help you today?"

"Hello, Marcie," I said, squinting at her name tag. "I'm Liam Danvers. I called yesterday to book a soak in the hot springs."

"Ahh, yes, yes," she said, her long-nailed fingers tapping away at her keyboard. "Two of you, correct?"

I smiled down at Ella. "Yep, just the two of us."

She squeezed my hand tighter in response.

With a flourish, Marcie tapped the keyboard a final time and stepped out from behind the desk, motioning for us to follow. Her steps were extra peppy as she led us down a long hallway. At the end, Marcie pushed through a door. Three doors branched off each side of the small alcove, one marked *men*, one *women*, and the third *unisex*. I appreciated the inclusivity.

"The locker rooms beyond these doors are the only way to access the hot springs," Marcie said, gesturing at the fogged window on the far wall, beyond which I assumed were the springs. "All we ask is you rinse off when you get out."

"I think we can handle that," I said, and Ella nodded in agreement.

"Then I'll leave you to it!" Marcie crowed with a clap. She retreated to the door we'd entered through, but just as she pulled it open, she turned back to us.

"By the way, I don't have anyone scheduled for the rest of the day. You'll have the place entirely to yourselves for as long as you want." She winked suggestively, and I nearly choked on my tongue at the implication. "Have fun."

And then she was gone, leaving me and Ella staring dumbfoundedly after her.

"Well, what do you say, Wildflower?"

Ella grinned as she grabbed my hand, towing me toward the door to the unisex locker room.

"I don't think—"

"Shh, Wills. Just go with it."

And who was I to deny this woman anything?

The locker room was as spacious and well-appointed as the parts of the lodge we'd seen so far, with sturdy wooden cubbies, a row of toilets, and individual shower stalls. The wall next to the door outside was lined with hooks draped with fluffy white robes and a cabinet filled to the brim with towels and toiletries.

We quickly changed into our swimsuits, and I barely kept my hands to myself when Ella was naked before me, only doing so by reminding myself I could play later. Before we stepped outside, we donned robes and grabbed a couple of towels.

The wind nipped at my exposed skin the second we left the building, and I gave into a shiver, tucking Ella into my side as we made our way toward the water.

The rocks surrounding it were worn smooth, whether by some feat of man or from natural wear, I couldn't tell. The water itself bubbled gently and steamed the air around us, enticing us closer, wrapping around us invitingly.

Ella's phone beeped, and she dropped my hand to check the notification while I remained rooted in place, closing my eyes and inhaling a lungful of mountain air.

"God, this place is incredible. I never want to leave."

When she didn't respond, I popped my eyes open and sought her out. She stood about ten feet away with her back to me. I knew something was wrong instantly from the way her shoulders were tense and curved inward, from how she was practically vibrating in a way that had nothing to do with the slight chill in the air.

"Ella?" I asked gently, moving closer. I came around her front and peered down at her.

Her phone was gripped tightly in her hand, bleaching her knuckles white, and shaking violently.

"Wildflower," I tried again. Slowly, her head raised, eyes swimming with tears colliding with mine. "Baby? What's wrong? Is everyone okay?"

"Everyone except me," she whispered. Then, slightly louder: "Alfie texted me. I should've known it wouldn't be that easy."

"What'd he say?" I asked, my teeth gritted.

"Nothing," she replied, turning and attempting to give me a bright smile. But I knew what her real smiles looked like, and this one was strained at the edges, her lips quivering as she attempted to hold it in place. Fake as fuck.

"What. Did. He. Say?"

Wordlessly and with a resigned sigh, Ella held out the phone, and I read her douchebag ex's message.

In fact, I realized as I scrolled backward, the entire thread was a stream of grey bubbles, each one having gone unanswered. The last text she'd sent was in early January, telling him if he didn't give her things back, she was sending Owen after him. I wanted to chuckle at that—I knew Owen wouldn't hesitate to put that little shit in his place—but was too overcome with fury to spare any other emotion.

Despite her silence, he'd continued to bother her for *months*, saying some incredibly shitty things that had me questioning how quickly I could get back to Michigan and beat his ass to a pulp. Finally, I scanned the most recent, and my vision went red.

You're such a slut. Spreading your legs for the first guy that shows you some attention. And of course it's one of your family's employees. You're no better than your whore sisters.

"I'll fucking kill him," I ground out. "How fast do you think we can get back to Apple Blossom Bay?"

Ella's lips twitched, a real—though small—smile appearing there. But it fell quickly, eyes going glassy with unshed tears.

Stepping into her space, I pulled her against me. I notched my thumb under her chin and tilted her head back until our gazes collided. "How did he even find out where you were?"

Instead of answering me, Ella took her phone back and tapped around, then flipped it toward me, showing her Instagram feed.

The most recently posted photo was so benign, it irritated me further that the douchebag saw fit to even message her about it. After that near-kiss in that alcove in Deadwood, we'd gone to a little bar for drinks and food. The picture wasn't anything special—an aerial view of the table, my arm splayed across it, hand gripping my pint, Ella's more delicate one doing the same across from me. There was a basket of fries, chicken tenders, fried mushrooms, jalapeno poppers, and onion rings in the middle between us, her BLT on one side, my burger on the other.

Completely innocent and absolutely nothing to get up in arms over.

God, I fucking hated this guy.

"I'll fucking kill him," I repeated.

Ella shook her head. "He's not worth it, Wills."

"I don't need to remind you, but that pissant never deserved you, Ella. Because *you* are worth *everything*. You *are* everything."

"I know you're right, but when you've been gaslit into thinking the opposite for so many years...it's hard to forget that. Hard to rewire my brain to the person I was before."

"Maybe you don't have to go back to her. Maybe you become someone new. Someone stronger. Someone who knows her worth and won't settle for anything less."

"Are you offering?"

I swallowed hard around the lump of emotion suddenly lodged in my throat. "If you'll have me."

"Selfishly, I want you. I want us to keep going on like we have been. But..." She trailed off, expression so stricken I feared what would come out of her mouth next. "You deserve to have all my cards on the table, and I understand if you change your mind afterward."

"Trust me when I tell you there is *nothing* you could do that'll drive me away at this point. And for what it's worth," I added, bending to press a kiss to her forehead, "you don't owe me anything. But if you want to tell me, I'm always here to listen."

She heaved a deep breath, holding it in for a few beats before she said, "He cheated on me."

I blinked slowly, trying to get my brain to process those words. That little shit had the most stunning woman I've ever known—inside and out—and he stepped out in her? Fucking hell, the rage I'd felt for him before was nothing compared to the hot, insistent anger coursing through me now, demanding I seek retribution for all the ways she'd been wronged.

"Fuck, Wildflower," I said, the softness of my tone completely belying my inner turmoil. "I'm so sorry."

And I was. For the way she'd been hurt, for having her trust broken. And because I knew all too well what it felt like to be on the receiving end of that level of unfaithfulness.

She waved me off, clearly not wanting my sympathy. "I thought I was over it, but that kind of thing sticks with you. Like a bone deep bruise that takes a lot longer than you hoped to completely heal." I only nodded, not wanting to interrupt her when she was on a roll. And anyway, I was more than a little familiar with that particular phenomenon.

"I think I knew something like that was happening, and I just didn't want to admit it," she continued. "He was on the road pretty frequently after Delia accidentally put him on the map, and I was content to live my life in Apple Blossom Bay and let him do his thing." Pausing, she shook her head with a disbelieving laugh. "God, I should've ended it years ago. I'm not sure I ever even loved him, you know? I think…maybe I just didn't want to be alone, and I secretly liked the attention he gave me. At least at the beginning."

"How did you find out?"

"A few girls DMed me on Instagram to let me know. They were friends of girls he'd cheated with, and it didn't sit right with them that I was oblivious to the whole thing."

"Girls' girls, then," I said, grinning.

"Yeah, I guess so," Ella said, one side of her mouth twitching up. "These months since the breakup haven't been hard in the sense that I miss what we had, because I really don't. They've been hard because I'm so fucking mad at myself for wasting so much time on him, and for turning a blind eye, burying my head in the sand when I knew something was off. And the people in town bring it up *every fucking time* they see me," she seethed. "How am I supposed to move on if they won't let me forget about it?"

"You need to be honest with them."

Ella only barreled ahead, apparently not having heard me. "It doesn't help that I can still hear his voice ringing in my head, telling me all the things that are wrong with me. I'm not pretty and skinny like Alix Earle, I'm not—"

"Alix who?"

"—talented like he is," she proceeded without missing a beat, ignoring my interruption. "I ruined myself with my tattoos." She held her arms out and shoved the sleeves of her robe up, revealing her ink. "They were my silent rebellion, you know. I mean, I had quite a few when we started dating, but I just kept getting more while we were together because I knew how much he hated them."

"I love them," I assured her, exposing my own forearms. "I-I love *you*. You're the most beautiful woman I've ever seen, Ella. I've been mesmerized by you since the first time I met you. And I love you for telling me this. The fact that you trusted me enough to let me shoulder some of the burden...I promise you're always safe with me."

I was surprised by the evenness of my tone, of how steady and sure I felt giving her the truth of those three words—giving her *my* truth at last.

Her entire face lit up, expression softening, and looked like she wanted to say she loved me in return, but honestly? I didn't want to hear it right then. Not on the heels of such an exhausting emotional purge. I wanted her to be happy when she said them, not crying because another man had broken her and her trust so thoroughly.

"In the end, he was the one who threw it all away. Spit on the years I'd given him, all the fights with my family, all the time with them I'd missed for him. But all that wasted time just led me right here, to this trip with you."

I folded her into an embrace and held her there, feeling her entire body go lax against me. I knew she was long past crying—she'd had a lot of time to come to terms with the shit he'd put her through, but sharing with me seemed to take the wind out of her.

I wanted to bring her back to herself—back to *me*, so I made a crazy declaration.

"What do you say we give him a taste of his own medicine?"

Ella pulled back, eyes flashing. "What'd you have in mind?"

I grinned mischievously down at her.

"Take off your clothes, Wildflower."

chapter 22
Ella

"LIAM!" I PROTESTED. "I'M not sending him a naked photo."

"You're not. It'll be very tasteful," he said with a wink.

Though I glared at him skeptically, I did as he asked, putting on a show for him as I slowly slipped from my robe, then my swimsuit top and bottoms and laid it all on a bench off to the side.

The way his eyes darkened with desire, how he licked his lips when he stared at me made my skin tingle and my core tighten deliciously, desperate for him to fill it. I'd never had anyone look at me the way he does, like he's never seen anything quite as perfect as me. Like he could look forever and never get his fill.

"Like what you see, Wills?" I asked cheekily.

"I fucking love your body. Your skin is perfection, and I didn't spend nearly enough time last night mapping those sexy tattoos with my mouth. But don't worry, baby," he said with a grin. "I'm going to reward you tonight for being such a good girl."

I glanced down at myself, at my previously creamy skin now

turned golden thanks to so many hours outside, my tattoos seeming even more vibrant against the new backdrop. At my full breasts, the dip and curve of my waist and hips, my long, shapely legs.

"You're my goddamn dream girl, Ella Delatou," Liam added when I met his gaze again.

"You're not so bad yourself, Wills." I gestured to him. "And now it's your turn. Let me see the goods."

He shed his own robe and trunks far quicker than I had, and I couldn't help but laugh delightedly at his haste to get naked. In that moment, I rediscovered how much I loved that sound, how much I'd missed it, and how thankful I was to Liam for bringing it back. Mostly, I loved that I'd been able to move past the dark cloud that had shifted over me with Alfie's text.

Liam moved to the bench where my suit was and picked up my phone.

"Wade into the water," he instructed me. I was having difficulty focusing on anything when his entire perfect body was on display, that glorious cock engorged and begging for attention. "Waist deep, Wildflower. You can play later."

With a mock salute, I did as he asked, hissing as the heat of the spring caressed my skin, which had pebbled in the cool air.

"Now turn away from me but reach back your hand, and don't move."

I faced away from him but stretched out my arm, and he clasped my hand in his. I could see the vision—it would be one of those "follow me" type trends I always saw couples participating in on social media. He continued to direct me, subtly shifting my body this way and that until I was right where he wanted me.

"Hold still," he said softly, and a moment later, I heard the shutter of my phone going off, taking several photos in quick succession.

When he was finished, he tugged me to him and held out my phone.

"I'll let you pick which one to send."

I gasped as I swiped through my camera roll. Taken from the waist up, only my back was visible in the photos, showing off the scrawl of words that decorated my left shoulder blade and the floral piece that covered my right rib cage and wrapped around my back. My hair had grown longer in the months since the breakup, tickling the tops of my breasts, and the slight sideways angle of my body offered a tantalizing glimpse of the side of one. The sun was a paid actor, giving my skin a healthy, beautiful glow and silhouetting my body. It was obvious I was naked, but it was tasteful. Sexy. Powerful.

Liam's hand and forearm appeared in the bottom left corner, showing the viewer I wasn't alone.

I wanted to frame it, to always remember this moment with him.

"Go ahead," I directed Liam after I'd settled on one. "Send it."

After a few taps of the screen, he turned it to face me, showing the message he'd tapped out to my ex.

You don't speak to her anymore. You don't even think about her. Lose this number. I'm the only one that gets her like this from now on.

My phone made that little beeping sound as the text flew off into the ether, and I took it from Liam, turned it completely off, and handed it back.

"Put that away and come here," I said, crooking a finger at him as I sank deeper into the water, until it lapped gently at the upper curves of my breasts.

The temperature was pure heaven, doing wonders to soothe the irritation Alfie had elicited, and I dropped lower until my entire body save my head was submerged, watching Liam as he stalked toward me and slowly descended into the spring.

"For what it's worth," I told him as he approached, "I fucking love your body too. The tattoos, the muscles...you're incredibly sexy, you know."

When he stood scant inches away from me, looming in a way that probably would've been intimidating had I not gotten to know the soft-hearted man beneath the bearded brawn, he tucked a finger under my chin and tipped my head back. Our gazes collided, and I swear I lived a thousand lifetimes in that look. Seeing my future stretched out before me in his depthless, clear blue eyes was disconcerting, to say the least. Something deep within me clicked into place in that moment, like I'd finally found this missing piece of my genetic makeup that I'd been searching for my entire life.

Liam.

Wills.

William Preston Danvers, III.

He was that missing piece.

So I whispered the three words that would change every-thing—but, somehow, not change anything at all.

"I love you."

Liam's entire face lit up like that was the best thing he'd ever heard, and a heartbeat later, his mouth was on mine. I rose out of the water to eagerly greet him, twining my legs around his waist and his arms cupping the backs of my thighs to support me. The kiss was insistent and claiming, nothing gentle about it as he nipped at my lips and drove his tongue into my mouth, exploring every inch, marking me wholly as his. And I met him with equal fervor, unable to press myself close enough, breathing harshly through my nose so I didn't have to be separated from him for even a second.

Liam was the one to break the kiss, only so he could rest his forehead against mine and whisper, "You mean it?"

I angled my head so our lips brushed and said, "Always. I love you, Liam Danvers."

"And I love you, Ella Delatou."

His hand rose from the water, fingertips tracing my lips, my cheekbone, tucking my hair behind my ear before burying at the nape of my neck. Thumb under my jaw, he pressed against my pulse, and I could feel it thumping against him, fluttering rapidly. Then he dragged his palm along my neck, along my collarbone, until it came to rest over my heart.

"This heart is mine now," he said. "And I promise I'll take good care of it."

"I know you will," I said. "That's why I'm trusting you with it."

"And you get mine in return." Almost absently, his hand slid lower, the rough pad of his thumb arcing across my nipple in a way that had me gasping and arching into him. "Actually, I think you've always had it."

"Liam?" I breathed.

"Yeah, baby?"

"Kiss me."

He straightened to look into my eyes, smiling softly before he did as I asked.

The kiss was tender in that I could feel him pouring all of his love and adoration into it, reminding me not only with his words but with his body how deeply he cherished me, and how safe I was with him. I responded in kind, looping my arms around his neck and pressing myself flush against him until there was absolutely no space to be found between us.

"Think we'll get in trouble if I fuck you right here, Wildflower?" he murmured against my mouth, moving his lips away to press them to my cheek, jaw, throat, pausing at the crook of my neck and scraping his teeth over that sensitive spot just above my collarbone. Like he wanted to be gentle with me but couldn't help let a little bit of ferality slip through.

"I think *you*'ll get in trouble if you don't."

"My girl," he breathed. "Fuck, what did I do to deserve you?"

I didn't answer, and he didn't seem to expect one as he moved us deeper into the hot spring, walking me backward until he was setting me down on the natural stone ledge on the far side. Brazenly, I leaned back on my hands and spread my legs wide, hooking my heels on the edge, baring myself fully to him.

"Fuck."

I chuckled, which quickly morphed into a low moan as he reached out and swiped his thumb through my slit.

"Tell me I can have you like this," he said, his eyes never leaving that exposed apex. "Tell me you don't give a fuck if someone walks out here and sees you getting off on my tongue."

"It's yours, Liam. All of it. But especially my pussy."

"Fucking right it is," he told me, grinning as his eyes flicked up to mine as he drifted closer and sank lower so his face was level with my sex.

Using two fingers to spread me open, he licked from back to front, agonizingly slow, and I canted my head to the side as another moan slipped free. I wanted to pay attention, couldn't think of anything hotter than watching how much this man enjoyed unraveling me, so I rested my head on my shoulder, eyes heavily-lidded as he dove into his meal.

The only way to describe his expression was pure bliss as he ate me, lapping at my pussy like I was a treat he couldn't get enough of, passing that pleasure onto me until my limbs were singing with it. I'd never felt like this with another man before, and that simply heightened every sensation until I was acutely aware of each wave of ecstasy zipping through my veins.

"Fuck, you're delicious," he murmured against me, tongue tracing a path around my clit, toying with me. My hand went to his hair, yanking, and he chuckled darkly. "Patience, Wildflower. You want my fingers too?"

"*Please.*"

He inserted two painstakingly slowly until I was bucking against him, desperate for him to fill me completely.

"My needy fucking girl," he praised. "Never happy until your cunt is completely full. So be a good girl and come on my tongue so I can give you the cock you so desperately want."

"You want it too," I snapped, though the words lacked any heat behind them, especially when they were cut off by the moan he dragged from me as he pumped his fingers in and out and scraped his teeth at my clit. "Fuck, Liam. I love when you're rough."

"You like me unhinged?"

"I fucking need it. Need to know you feel as unglued as me when I remember I'm the only one who gets to see you like this. That every part of you belongs to me."

I reached between my thighs and gripped his chin in my hand, and he made a noise of protest as I forced him to look at me. I was walking a razor wire, my orgasm *right fucking there* as his hand continued to work me, but I said, "Promise me, Liam. Promise me you're not like him."

Liam rose up until we were eye level, capturing my mouth savagely, both of us panting as he continued to fuck me with his fingers. His thumb swept softly over my clit, and my hips twitched, eager for more pressure. I knew it wouldn't take much to set me off.

"I promise, Ella. Your body, your heart and mind, your fucking soul—they are the greatest gifts I've ever been given. Now," he whispered after dragging his tongue along my bottom lip and burying his fingers as deep as they could go, then crooking them in a come hither gesture that had my thighs quaking wildly, "come for me, Wildflower."

As soon as his thumb pressed down on my clit and stroked it once, twice, three times—I came apart, screaming his name at the clouds.

chapter 23
Liam

Fuck, my name on her lips was the most beautiful sound.

And the way she arched backward, her tits pressed forward and those studs glinting in the low light of the waning day, her eyes squeezed shut in ecstasy? *She* was the most beautiful thing I'd ever laid eyes on, her orgasms the most stunning thing I'd ever witnessed.

I wasn't a religious man by any stretch, but Ella's body was an altar I'd happily worship at every day.

When she calmed, her arms the only thing still quivering with the effort of keeping herself upright, I slowly withdrew my fingers from her pussy and held them in front of my face. They were coated in her desire, and Ella watched me closely as I licked them clean, groaning at her perfect taste.

"Gonna need more of that," I said, once again sinking into the water.

"What—" Ella started, cutting off with a yelp as I dragged my tongue through her pussy. She twitched against me, hissing, and said, "Fuck, Liam. Give a girl a break."

"Shh, baby. Let a man enjoy his treat."

"But I want your cock," she whined, and I looked up through my lashes to find her bottom lip jutted out in a pout.

"So fucking needy," I grumbled without menace as I stood up. In a flash, I lifted her off the ledge, spun us in the water, and sank onto the bench built into the rock wall beneath the water.

With my back against the wall, Ella settled on my lap, straddling my thighs, her breasts right above the surface of the water—and within reach of my mouth. Leaning forward, I captured one tight peak between my lips, cupping the other one in my hand. I swirled my tongue around the tip and tugged at her piercing with my teeth before moving over.

Ella's hands dug into my hair—one of her favorite things to do, I was quickly learning—and yanked hard until I was forced to peel my mouth from those fucking perfect tits.

"I know," she said with a smile as though she could read my mind. "The tits are great. But"—she leaned closer to kiss me, and we lost ourselves in that connection for too brief a moment before she backed away—"I have an emptiness only you can fill."

I dove my hand into the water, the time spent in the elevated temp making sweat break out on both our temples, and grabbed my cock, brushing it against her. "You mean this? This gonna fill you up?"

"The only thing that can," she agreed, rising onto her knees slightly so I could line myself up. I pushed in only as far as the head, letting my girl take me as fast or as slow as she wanted.

I should've known it'd be the former.

Ella impaled herself on me, forehead falling against my shoulder. "So deep like this, holy shit."

I rubbed my hand up and down her back, letting my fingers settle in the groove of her spine and trail over the bumps. I could feel that she held herself back, clearly needing a moment to adjust, like some unseen barrier prevented her from taking me completely.

But when she finally relaxed, and I sank that final inch into that tight, wet heat?

"Fuck," I breathed.

"Yeah," Ella said with a disbelieving laugh. "I see what you meant now, about being made for me." Experimentally, she lifted a bit and swiveled her hips around, lowering again, taking me impossibly deeper. "I don't think—"

Beneath the water, my hands gripped her thighs, waiting her out. Just being with her like this, neither of us moving, completely content to just breathe each other in and bask in this unreal connection—it was enough for me. Honestly, it was all I'd ever need.

"This scares me," she admitted, peeling back from me far enough to look into my eyes. "How much I care about you, how hard and fast I fell, and how quickly it all happened. But I'm ready to take this leap if you are. I'm all in, so long as *we*'re all in, together."

I gathered her hands in mine and brought them out of the water, pressing my lips gently to her fingertips, to every bit of exposed skin I could reach.

"Hate to break it to you, Delatou," I started, grinning up at her, "but you're stuck with me now."

Ella slumped against me, throwing her arms around my neck

and ducking so our mouths touched. "You're stuck with me too, Danvers."

"Thank fuck," I said. "Now I think I might die if you don't move."

With a laugh that was quickly becoming my favorite sound, Ella lifted herself almost completely off me and sank back down, all thoughts but her, but this moment, but the fucking vise-like grip of her pussy around me vacated my brain.

Her hands gripped my shoulders, nails digging sharply into my skin as she leveraged herself up and down, and I'd be damned if I didn't love the sting, didn't fucking revel in the way her tits bounced in my face. There wasn't anything else in the world as good as this—as good as *her*.

The water sloshed around us, mingling with our heavy breaths and our moans of pleasure.

"Nothing has ever felt as good as you," she said as I filled her again, as she wriggled her hips atop my lap to get closer. Then she circled them slowly, saying, "Oh, yes, right there," as her clit rubbed against the trail of hair at my lower abdomen.

"That's it, Wildflower," I said, grabbing a fistful of hair at her nape and holding her to me. "Take what you need."

"I'm close," she whimpered, though I already knew from the way her walls pulsed and clamped around me.

"Let go."

"Need a hand," she breathed.

I was far too happy to oblige, reaching between us and deftly finding her clit, angling my hand so I could circle it with three fingers. I fucking relished the way her hips moved faster as she bucked against me, how her thighs quaked like her clit was some on switch for her vibration setting. Her hands at my shoulders gripped me tighter, fingernails surely puncturing my skin, but I didn't give a fuck. Not as long as she got there.

I met every one of her downward thrusts with an upward one of my own, the water stirred up violently around our bodies like we were caught in the center of a tempest.

My balls drew up tight to my body, that pressure at the base of my spine nearly unbearable as I held myself off, refusing to go down unless she went with me.

"C'mon, Wildflower," I said through gritted teeth, punctuating my words by circling her clit faster. "Come for me."

A low, almost keening sound left Ella as I used my free hand to grip her tit, roughly pulling at the piercing, giving her so much sensation, forcing her orgasm to surface.

I was rewarded a moment later when she fell apart, that low sound building into a full-volume screaming of unintelligible words as she climaxed, the pulsing of her cunt triggering my own. I unloaded inside of her, hoarsely shouting her name, murmuring praises as I worked us through it, forcing her to feel every ounce I could wring out of her.

Exactly like the first time, fucking her—coming with her—was a goddamn out of body experience where I felt like I was floating, my flesh and bones unable to contain the sheer amount of ecstasy we made together.

What felt like hours later, I returned to myself, my limbs deliciously limp in the water and Ella collapsed against me. We merely embraced each other and the silence, neither of us willing to burst our blissful little bubble.

It was Ella who spoke first.

"You think it'll always be like this?" she asked, turning her head to look up at me.

"I fucking hope so."

She laughed then, the sound vibrating her entire body and reminding me I was still buried inside her but rapidly softening. Shifting us slightly, I slipped free, and Ella reclined across my lap rather than straddling it.

"Sex isn't everything," she began, cutting me off with a sharp look when I opened my mouth to retort. "But I'm fucking glad you blow my mind every time." Leaning in, she gave me a gentle kiss, then two more in quick succession. "Thank you."

"For what?"

"For taking the time to learn what I do and don't like. For your patience with me. For...just being you." Her shoulders twitched in a little shrug.

Before answering, I rose to my feet, Ella still cradled in my arms, and began wading toward the steps leading back up to the deck.

"You never have to thank me for that," I told her. "But what do you say we go back to the cabin and I spend a few more hours doing it anyway?"

Ella grinned. "Deal."

⁂

Several hours later, after doing exactly what I promised and learning new ways to get Ella off, we were a spent and sweaty mess. She was at my side, a leg hooked over my thigh, head resting on my chest with my arm around her, tracing the raised lines of the tattoo on her side. I was surprised that most of the skin of her back was free from ink.

"How come you haven't filled this in yet?" I asked, brushing my broad palm down her spine.

"Haven't found anything I loved enough to put there yet," she said, almost sleepily.

And I knew I should let us get some rest, but as I followed the line of one of the flower petals along her ribcage, I decided I needed to know the stories behind each of them—or if some of them didn't have a story at all. I had a feeling Ella was more sentimental about what she put on her body than I was, though.

"What do they all mean?" I whispered.

She was quiet for long enough that I thought she'd fallen asleep. Instead, she shifted out of my hold and sat up, tucking her legs under her, her torso and sexy thighs naked and on display.

Pointing to one of those thighs and the fine-line bouquet of five flowers there, she said, "My and my sisters' birth flowers." Right below that was four words inked in an old typewriter style. "A quote from one of my favorite fantasy book series."

Then she grabbed my hand and positioned it at her other knee, below the female bust, arm raised as she watered the flowers blooming from her head, covering the bulk of her face save her nose and lips. "I think this one is obvious," she said with a grin, sliding my hand upward toward her hip and that floral piece I'd just been tracing. "And again, obvious."

"You do have a lot of floral tattoos," I gently ribbed her.

"You don't call me 'Wildflower' for nothing." She paused to ponder it for a moment, though, dragging my palm across her stomach to the other hip, where another collection of sunflow ers, daisies, and what looked like strawberry blossoms stretched the length of her torso.

"We all need something to worship, right? For me, that's flowers. I seek my religion in the garden, or building arrangements for special occasions. My body is just a shrine to the thing that brings me joy and gives me purpose."

Our hands moved again, my fingertips dragging across the vines and blooms curving under her boob, mirroring the other side and meeting in the center, topped by a bee.

"That's beautiful," I murmured as she continued to map her flesh with our hands. I tiptoed my fingers up her arms as she told me about the other flowers decorating her skin. I hadn't realized how many she had until I had her naked like this and finally took the time to study them all.

"And what about those words on your back?" I asked when she was done showing me the vines twining around her fingers.

Ella reached across her body and tapped the words on her left. "It says 'I love you as big as the sky,' or as close as we could get in Greek, in my dad's handwriting."

"Do you have one for your mom too?"

I couldn't imagine, knowing how close all six of the Delatou women were, that Ella would get a tattoo for her dad and not her mom as well.

She shifted and extended her right leg, turning it to the side so I could see the heart on the side of her heel. I leaned closer for a better look.

"Are those...fingerprints?"

"Her thumbs," Ella confirmed.

I sat back and whistled low, shaking my head. "I was right.

You're way more sentimental than me."

Ella reached out and tapped the mermaid on my right deltoid. "I don't know. I'm sure the story behind this one is close to your heart."

Growling in warning, I lunged, tackling her so she was flat on her back, then peppered her face and neck with kisses.

"A lot of them are the result of being eighteen and on my own for the first time during my freshman year of college. A silent act of rebellion against my father that I could cover up for the holidays. Not that it mattered, anyway. They're a part of me, and despite the absolute meltdown he had when he first saw them, there was no erasing them. And believe me, he tried."

"He *what*?"

I couldn't help but laugh at her expression. We'd both heard the horror stories that removal is more painful than getting them in the first place.

"Scheduled the removal consultation behind my back," I confirmed, "then tried to bribe me into going. By then, Gramps had already given me access to my trust, so I didn't need his money—not that I would've taken it anyway."

I shook my head, tossing away the memories. I didn't want to think about my dad or those days. Not now, not ever.

Instead, I told her how I had a habit of walking into my favorite studio in Portland, flipping through the books of flash tattoos, and picking one at random to get done that day. Or I'd just let the tattoo artist do whatever he wanted—within reason, of course.

"There are only three that are truly meaningful," I said at last, looking down at her from where my head rested on my palm, the length of my body stretched out at her side. I didn't need to map my tattoos with her—she'd already spent enough time doing so herself, with her eyes, hands, and mouth. And they were mostly stupid little things that needed no explanation.

"Which ones?"

I sank back to sitting, hauling her up with me.

First, I pointed to the letters across my knuckles.

"This was the first tattoo I got in Michigan," I said. "I left Oregon in a hurry, brokenhearted, and needed a reminder that I'd get through it. Now...I think it's just a good mantra in general."

"Will you tell me about her one day?"

God, I hadn't thought about Mellie in *days*, nor had I paused for a second to remind myself I had my brother's wedding and my entire family to contend with at the end of this trip.

Ella had shared so much with me, had trusted me with so much, and I knew I owed her that in return. But not right now.

"Soon," I promised. "I just don't want to ruin this moment."

Ella nodded in understanding, urging me to continue.

I tapped the back of my left hand. "This one is for my late grandmother. Her name was Rose, and she was one of my absolute favorite people."

It had been several years and her loss still stung, still had the ability to punch me in the gut and knock the wind out of me. I breathed deeply, trying to quell the stinging behind my eyes.

"You miss her."

"Very much," I managed to choke out.

Ella didn't offer me any condolences or platitudes. She merely crawled onto my lap and held me tightly while I collected myself.

"What's the last one?" she whispered.

I swallowed hard, the momentary wave of grief quickly replaced by that of nervousness.

I stretched my right arm out in front of us, showing off the small blue butterfly inked on the inside of my wrist.

"This one...is for you."

"*Me*?" she gasped, then twisted enough to extend her same arm, displaying the similar creature tattooed in the same spot. "I always thought it looked a lot like mine."

"It was silly, getting it when I couldn't guarantee we'd end up here. But...that first time I saw you was the first time I felt like a small piece of the old me—the man I'd been before everything had gone to shit—had returned to me at last."

"How did I not know?" she whispered, gaze still fixed on our arms, though they had that glazed quality that told me she was somewhere far away. "How the hell could I have missed it?"

"Hey, no," I said, grasping her chin and turning her head until those green eyes met mine, clearing as they did. "You didn't know because I was too afraid to make a move. That's not your fault, Wildflower. And it doesn't matter. What's important is that we're here together now. That we're finally getting our chance."

"I'm sorry," she said quietly. "We could've had so much longer."

I gathered her closer and moved to recline against the headboard, pressing a kiss to her temple.

"It's okay, baby. We've got forever to make up for it."

chapter 24
Ella

"I'M SAD TO LEAVE this place," I told Liam as I stood on the front lawn, staring up at the cabin while he loaded our things into the van.

Gravel crunched beneath his boots as he approached me, and a moment later, he slid an arm around my waist and tugged me into his side.

"Me too," he said. "But the good news is we get to take our memories with us, and we get to keep making new ones."

I looked up at him, returning his wide grin. "I like the way you think, Wills."

He ducked his head to press a kiss to my nose. "Ready to hit the road?"

"Let's take a picture first!" I blurted, desperate to remain in this place, in this bubble, for a little while longer.

Though he grumbled, I knew he'd indulge me, and a second later, we had turned our backs to the building. Liam's long arm stretched in front of us, angling the phone to capture our smiling faces and the breathtaking landscape behind us. He snapped a few pictures in quick succession, then handed the phone to me for my approval.

My heart grew almost painfully in my chest as I studied them, as I took in how fucking *happy* we were, and how good we looked together.

We'd only been here for three days, but it felt like so much longer. I felt like a totally different woman now than the one who had first walked inside the gorgeous cabin before us. And I supposed, in a lot of ways, I was. Thanks to the man beside me, who I inexplicably got to call *mine* now, I felt...lighter. And genuinely content with myself and my life for the first time in years.

After applying a filter to my favorite picture, I shared it to my Instagram with the caption: *Gonna miss this place, but at least we get to take on our next adventure together.*

Liam chuckled when I showed him, then kissed me lightly. "You're cute."

I beamed. "I know."

The chuckle turned to all out laughter as he pinched my ass and said, "C'mon, cutie. Get your fine ass in the car so we can head out."

I didn't need any further encouragement. As amazing as this leg of the trip had been, I was even more excited for our next stop.

I threw myself into the passenger seat and buckled up before Liam could even open his door, grinning somewhat maniacally at him as he settled behind the wheel.

"Eager, aren't we?"

"Come on, Wills," I said, sliding my shades on. "You can't tell me you're not excited."

"Oh, I am. I've never ridden a horse before, and pictures I've seen of the ranch look stunning."

"I, for one, can't wait to see you in a cowboy hat."

He cut his eyes to me, and I giggled. "Don't press your luck, Wildflower."

"I think you'll change your tune when you hear the rule."

"What rule?" he asked as he turned the engine over and put the van in drive.

"There's this cowboy rule. *Wear the hat, ride the cowboy.* So what do you think? Will you wear a cowboy hat if only so I can take it from you?"

"Baby, you don't need some silly cowboy rule to ride me. All you have to do is ask."

I folded my arms over my chest and pouted. "You ruin all my fun."

His brow raised, and his eyes darted my way. "You're really into that shit?"

I shrugged noncommittally. "It always sounds super hot in books. Think about it: we're in some smokey, low-lit bar. You're at a table with the guys, drinking beer and shooting the shit, and I'm on the dance floor. Some cowboy comes up to me and wants to dance. You get all jealous, stomp over and slam your hat on my head, shoot the guy and death glare and say, 'Mine.'"

Liam's hand shot out, gripping my thigh and sliding higher, his voice lowering as he asked, "Then what happens?"

I laced my fingers through his and brought our hands to my mouth, pressing a kiss to the rose tattooed on the back of his. "There's only one way to find out."

His answering groan was a low rumble that sent shivers across my body. "Wicked woman."

I didn't respond as he navigated us out of the mountains and onto the main road, which would connect us to the highway leading straight to our next destination.

"Dusk Valley, here we come."

***

"Liam!" I yelped as my eyes popped open. I was only half-awake, but we were speeding down a two-lane road with wide open fields spreading out along the sides. For some reason, my mind instantly jumped to the packets of seeds in my bag, and how this would be the perfect place to sprinkle a few of them.

"What?" he asked, the wheel jerking to the side as he jumped. "Are you okay?"

"I'm fine. Just pull over!"

"What? Why?"

"Because I asked you to!"

He frowned but pressed the brake, turning his blinker on to indicate to the people behind us that we were pulling off to the side. A moment later we were parked, the flashers on, and I got out of the van.

Liam's door opened and slammed closed a moment later, his footfalls heavy as he met me at the back, where I was already rifling through my stuff, trying to locate the bundles of wildflower seeds.

"What in the fresh hell are you doing?" he asked.

I looked over at him, and I couldn't help the chuckle that es caped me at the picture he presented—hands on hips, legs spread in a steady, fighting stance, brows drawn low in annoyance.

I found what I was looking for and moved away from him without answering. I wore my only sundress—something about today felt magical, made me want to revisit that free-spirited girl I'd been...*before*—and the tall field grasses tickled my calves as I waded through them, deeper into the field but still close enough to the road that the flowers could be seen when they started to bloom.

"Ella!" Liam shouted as he crashed along behind me. "What're you doing?"

I held up one of the packets of flowers and handed it to him. "Spreading wildflower seeds."

The skin between his brows bunched in confusion. "I don't understand."

I opened the packet and shook some out into my hand, holding it up for examination. They were all shapes and sizes, some long and conical, others small and round, barely larger than a grain of sand.

"I've been collecting these for years," I said, closing my fist and turning my hand so some of the seeds funneled to the ground. "Just waiting for the perfect opportunity to spread some beauty. I've dropped a few packets here and there on the peninsula and on our travels through Michigan, but this trip has been my first real chance to drop these in new places."

"But why?"

I shrugged. "I guess it's my way of leaving my mark on the world in a way that doesn't hurt anyone and could potentially bring joy to people passing through here." I swept my arms out at the field, flinging some more seeds out as I did. "And we're turning this small space of this dry, boring field into something beautiful and magical."

When I faced him again, Liam had opened the seeds and was carefully sprinkling them on the ground around his feet, careful not to step on any.

"Have you been spreading these all along?" he asked when he'd finished.

I nodded. "I started in Munising, right on the tree line of the campground where the grasses met the sand. We'll have to go back next year and see how well they came in."

"Whatever you want, Wildflower." He gave me a soft smile. "That nickname feels even more appropriate now."

"It's not much," I said, dipping my head, suddenly shy. "But...it's something."

His hand found my face, cupping my cheek, and I raised my head to look at him. "You're incredible. You know that, right?"

I wanted to believe him, but...something always held me back from thinking so.

"Can I tell you a secret?" I whispered.

"Always."

"I haven't even told my family this, but...Fanny offered to let me buy the flower shop from her."

"Ella! That's amazing. You're going to do it, right? You have to."

"I don't know," I told him honestly. "I'm...what if I fuck it up?"

It was my greatest shame, to be so unsure of myself in the face of something I knew I was good at. Well, at the very least, I was good at creating beautiful bouquets and arrangements.

But that didn't exactly translate to being a business owner.

"My sisters are so talented and secure, you know?" I continued before Liam could say anything. "Chloe, the best-selling author. Amara, the CEO. Delia, the distillery owner, marketing whiz, and hella popular influencer. Brie, the bakery owner and incredibly talented pastry chef. They've all always known how they fit into the world—and into our family. I just...I've never felt that pull to anything. Not until I started working at the flower shop. I went to college because it was what was expected of me, but I didn't take it seriously. Not when I felt so fucking listless the entire time. It's silly—" I started, but cut myself off.

Not missing anything, Liam tilted his head to the side, regarding me in that quiet way of his. From anyone else, the assessment would've had my skin prickling with unease, but with him...he was on my side, one thousand percent, no matter what I wanted to do. And for the first time in months—hell, *years*—I felt safe enough to dream.

"What were you going to say?" he prompted, exactly as I knew he would.

"I love the flower shop. I'm good at it. I love working with different textures and colors and stem heights and bloom sizes. I love creating those beautiful arrangements and knowing my hard work is going to make someone feel special and loved. *I* get to do that. But...it also feels kind of silly, compared to my sisters, to want to spend my life playing with flowers."

"It's not silly at all," he said. "A lot of people never find their calling, Ella. Your sisters did, but so have you."

I leaned my face into his palm, closing my eyes and letting

his warmth seep into me, bolstering my confidence, letting his words sink deeper still until I believed them.

"Fanny wants to retire," I said, returning to the whole point of this conversation. "Her kids live in Arizona, and she wants to move south to be near them and her grandkids. So I can buy it if I want. The building. The entire business."

"And do you? Want to, I mean."

"If you would've asked me three weeks ago, or even three days ago, the answer would've been a resounding *no*. But now? After all this?" I waved my arm at the vast expanse of endless blue sky and the tall, country grasses swaying around our legs. "Now, I want it so badly I can barely breathe."

Liam stepped closer to me and dipped his head, planting a featherlight but lingering kiss on my lips, whispering, "So take it."

"What?" I asked dumbly, pulling away to look quizzically at him.

"Take it," he said again, the corners of his eyes crinkling in a smile. "What are you waiting for? You don't need someone to hold your hand, or give you permission. If you want to buy the business, *buy it*."

He was right, of course. What *was* I waiting for? In the last week and a half, since we'd embarked on this trip, the fear that gripped me whenever I considered my future had vanished, leaving only a sense of purpose in its wake.

And that purpose was Blossom's.

Without another word to Liam, I withdrew my phone from my dress pocket and dialed Fanny.

"Hello, dear!" she said brightly upon answering. "How's your trip?"

"It's been amazing," I breathed, a smile tipping up my lips as I stole a glance at Liam. He was, after all, largely responsible for my happiness. "Thank you so much for giving me time off to do this."

Fanny made a dismissive sound. "You deserved a break," she said. "And nothing heals a broken heart faster than fresh air."

Liam couldn't hear Fanny's end of the conversation, but his eyes remained glued to mine, and the emotion I found there nearly took my breath away.

Yeah, fresh air, I thought. *And the quiet, steadfast man staring at me with no small amount of pride shining in his gaze.*

"I appreciate you more than you know," I told her. "But look, there's a reason I'm calling."

"Yes?" she asked hopefully.

"I'll take it. The business, the building. I want to buy it."

"Oh, Ella!" Fanny crowed. "That's wonderful news. I just know you're going to do amazing things here."

Tears filled my eyes at her belief in me. "Thank you, Fanny. Couldn't have done it without you."

She scoffed, ignoring my comment by saying, "We'll get all the particulars worked out when you get home. Just enjoy the rest of your trip, and we'll talk soon."

"Sounds good. Bye, Fanny."

The sound of a disconnected call rang in my ear, and I barely pulled the phone away from my ear when Liam let out a *whoop* of excitement and hauled me into his arms, my feet coming off the ground as he spun me around.

"I'm so fucking proud of you," he said into my hair.

I could do nothing but laugh gleefully as we twirled around in that field, him whispering words of encouragement and praise in my ear.

This, I said to myself.

This is what I should've had all along.

This is what I fucking deserved.

And I was going to hold onto it with all my might.

"How excited are you right now?" Liam asked, nodding his chin at the sign that said *Welcome to Dusk Valley*.

I shot him a glare, though it was difficult given my grin. I was practically bouncing in my seat, buzzing with excitement over finally being here.

I'd heard plenty about Owen's hometown since he and Delia got together, but even more since they'd taken a trip out here this winter to visit. As we traveled the two lane road in, the mountains we faced scraped against the sky, the sun backlighting the peaks as it set behind them, turning everything pink and orange and purple.

"It'll be nice to see the Lawlesses again. I wasn't very...sociable when they were in town for the distillery opening," I reminded him.

"You were going through a lot."

I waved him off. I didn't want to talk about my life six months ago. I'd barely recognize it if I did. "Plus they're Delia's future in-laws."

"You really think so?" Liam asked.

"You don't?" I asked, quirking a brow at him.

"Okay, fair. They are...ridiculously obsessed with each other."

I know *obsessed* was putting it mildly, but also didn't do Delia and Owen's relationship justice. They were equals, two halves of a whole, predestined to find each other and spend their lives together.

Without making it obvious, I studied Liam out of the corner of my eye as he drove, his fingers drumming on the steering wheel, full mouth moving as he silently sang along to the Brooks & Dunn song on the radio. He was utter perfection, and I still had a hard time wrapping my brain around the fact that he'd harbored such a crush on me for so many years. That he'd waited for me. Little old Ella Delatou.

That right there was worth its weight in gold, the realization that someone saw something so beautiful and *worthy* in me that they recognized what we could have long before I did.

And as we drove deeper into town, on our way to meet my sister's future in-laws, I wondered if, maybe, our trip to Portland would be the first time I met my own.

It was far too early in our relationship for those kinds of thoughts. We hadn't even defined exactly who or what we were to one another beyond knowing we loved each other. But maybe we didn't need the labels. All I knew was I couldn't ignore the fact that being with Liam was as easy as breathing, and I could just as easily envision a lifetime of it.

chapter 25
Liam

Dusk Valley had been a late addition to the trip itinerary, but I couldn't pass up the opportunity to check out where Owen had grown up after he mentioned it a few months ago. Surprisingly—or maybe not—all rentals in the area, including hotels, were fully booked, but one of his twin brothers owned a dude ranch and had agreed to put us up in one of the cabins for the time we were in town.

For free, I might add, despite my insistence that we pay him.

I'd find a way to return the favor one day.

The heart of downtown was, for lack of a better word, charming. Ella *ooh*ed and *ahh*ed over the buildings, which were a mixture of craftsman and brick, each business sporting a different theme, and the signs and awnings out front gently flapping in the breeze. It was obvious the town took great pride in cleanliness and overall appearance, as everything was well-kept and inviting.

When we neared the end of the main drag—a street called Cassia—I had Ella pull up the GPS on her phone to get us to the ranch.

"*Turn right onto Spruce,*" the disembodied robot voice directed me. "*Then, in two hundred feet, take a right onto Balsam.*"

"That's so cute," Ella grinned. "All the streets are named after trees!"

I only shook my head and smiled indulgently, intent on getting us to our destination before the light from the day was completely gone.

Fifteen minutes later, once we'd made another turn onto a gravel road, Siri said, "*In two-tenths of a mile, your destination will be on your right.*"

Driving slowly to avoid blowing a tire on the rougher terrain, I turned my head back and forth. There was nothing out here for miles save flatlands broken up by gently rolling hills and cattle. In the distance, mountains rose up, standing sentinel over the land.

Up ahead, I could see a break in the fence where a gateway stood, and as we neared and turned down the dirt road, I grinned at the sign overhead.

LAWLESS RESCUE & DUDE RANCH

"Okay so which one of the twins owns which half of the business?" I asked Ella as we bumped down the dirt two track.

"If I'm remembering correctly, Finn has the rescue ranch, and West owns the dude ranch."

"How the fuck are we supposed to tell them apart?"

"From what Delia has told me, West is the wild child, and Finn is more laid back. Plus—and again, if I remember correctly—West has longer hair."

We rounded a bend where a large log outbuilding sat, the doors locked up tight, and the ranch opened up before us. To the left were barns and paddocks, with numerous farm animals roaming around. Chickens clucked around a nearby coop, and stable hands walked horses in and out as they came and went. To the right was a gorgeous log farmhouse that reminded me of something I couldn't quite put my finger on.

"Wow," Ella breathed as she stared up at the home. "Delia wasn't lying."

"About what?" I asked as I pulled to a stop out front next to a few other vehicles.

"About the distillery looking just like Owen's family home."

And then it clicked—the buildings were spitting images of each other, though the farmhouse was slightly more rambling with what appeared to be two additions added onto each side, the logs less weathered than that of the main, original structure.

A woman who couldn't be older than her late-sixties came out of the house, apron on, dish towel slung over her shoulder, grey-blonde hair piled atop her head in a bun.

"Ella!" Birdie exclaimed as we exited the van, rushing down the steps to greet my girl. Ella allowed Birdie to wrap her in a hug, and I watched as Ella's entire body relaxed. She must've been more nervous about facing these people again than she'd let on.

"And Liam!" Birdie crowed, rushing over to me and pulling me against her. Though she was small enough that there were several inches between the top of her head and the underside of my chin, the woman gave a fierce hug.

"Hi, Mrs. Lawless," I said when she pulled away. "It's so good to see you again."

Birdie snagged the towel from her shoulder and whipped it at me so quickly I didn't have time to react. "Call me Birdie," she admonished.

I chuckled. "Yes, ma'am."

"Just like my boys," she grumbled as she hooked her arm through mine, crossed the space between us to collect Ella, then dragged us up the steps and into the house.

Ella audibly gasped from Birdie's other side as we strode into the foyer, and I had to agree with that reaction though I didn't make a sound.

The ceilings soared, and a floating walkway connected one half of the upstairs to the other. I'd bet good money Owen and his brothers had a hell of a lot of fun playing around on that growing up, scaring the shit out of their parents.

Through an opening to the right, there appeared to be a living space and a set of ascending stairs. In the opposite direction, something positively mouthwatering scented the air, and Birdie directed us that way. We walked through a formal dining room with a table long enough to seat twenty easily, the vaulted ceilings continuing in there to make the room feel spacious.

Past that was an impressive kitchen, and we walked in to find two men arguing about which pie flavor was superior: apple or pecan.

"The fact that I'm related to you is disgusting," the one with shorter hair said, wrinkling his nose at the other. From where I stood, I could only see their profiles, which was disconcerting to say the least as they matched perfectly.

The twins, then.

"I've been saying the same thing for thirty-one years," the one with longer hair quipped. "I can't believe I have to walk around with a face that looks just like yours, and with the knowledge that you think pecans are even edible, much less better than apples."

The other—Finn, I now realized—shook his head. "You're a fucking moron."

"Boys," Birdie scolded, and they both turned abruptly to look at their mother, offering her sheepish smiles when they realized she wasn't alone.

In a flash, both twins were across the room, offering me handshakes and Ella hugs. Then Birdie ushered them both back into the kitchen where, still arguing, they each picked up a platter of food and disappeared through a different doorway. We followed behind Birdie, my hand on the small of Ella's back, and entered what appeared to be a more casual dining space. The long table had bench seating instead of chairs, and was nicked and scarred and even scorched in places. The length of it was laden with food—everything from mashed potatoes and gravy, diced and fried potatoes, green beans and corn on the cob, a bowl of salad I could swim in, burgers, dogs, and barbecue chicken legs, plus the aforementioned apple and pecan pies for dessert.

Birdie settled her hands on Ella's shoulders and grinned up at me. "Welcome to Dusk Valley."

Ella stepped out of her hold and whipped her head in Birdie's direction. "You did all of this for *us*?"

Birdie shrugged. "I've got a million children running around here, and at least half of them are here for dinner on any given night, but I never pass up the opportunity to put a feast together. Besides," Birdie said, clasping one of Ella's hands between her own, "you're family now."

I could see the tears welling in Ella's eyes by the way they took on a glassiness when she looked up at me.

Jumping in to save her lest she start crying, I ushered Birdie away from her and said, "Thank you. This is...wonderful."

"And I've got the cabin all fixed up for you too," West offered. "Best one I've got. Had to shuffle around a few reservations to make it work, but we got it squared away."

"You really didn't have to do that for us," Ella told him.

West only grinned, removing his hat and hooking it over a knee as he sat at one end of a bench. "It's like Mama said...you're family now too."

Considering I didn't have a big family of my own, I wasn't in a position to be turning down offers like that, so I merely nodded and dropped down next to Ella, who had slid onto the bench beside Finn, opposite West.

"Hello?" a man shouted from somewhere far away.

"That'll be another one," Birdie said, leaving the room to go greet one of her sons.

"Which one is that?" Ella asked, jerking her head in that general direction.

"Crew," West told her. He flicked his wrist to check his watch, and I couldn't help notice the ink stretching up into his shirt. "Which means Trey will be here any second."

"How many of my shithead baby brothers are already here?" another voice asked from the kitchen, and West smirked as if to say, *told ya*.

I nodded at West's arms. "You've got ink?" I asked, rolling up my own sleeves.

West pushed his long-sleeved tee to his elbows, and I whistled low at the tattoos covering both of them, cutting off abruptly at his wrists, which told me they likely went all the way to his shoulders in full sleeves.

"We all do," Finn said, following suit. "Except Aria, our sister. And Owen only has a few, but...well, you'll see."

Two more men shuffled into the room behind their mother, and it was obvious they were all related. The same dirty blond hair, exact same shade of blue eyes.

I knew I'd met them at the distillery opening briefly, but there were so many it was hard to keep track. I was grateful when the shorter of the two—which wasn't saying much since they were all over six feet tall—extended a hand and introduced himself as Crew. His hair was buzzed on the sides but long and floppy on the top, still wet from a recent shower, his tattoos stretching all the way to his fingers. The smell of something burnt followed in his wake.

"Sorry I couldn't help cook," he told his mom as he skirted the table to sit beside West. "I got a call out right before shift ended, and it took nearly six hours to knock it down."

"Crew is a firefighter," Birdie explained to us.

"Explains the smoke smell," Ella said, then clapped her hand over her mouth. "Shit, sorry."

Crew only barked out a laugh and waved her off. "It's fine. That shit clings to you. It's just part of my DNA now."

"A real smoke-eater," West said, clapping his brother on the shoulder.

Birdie whirled on Trey. "And what do you have to say for yourself?"

"Surveillance."

"You're the cop?" I asked.

Trey shook his head, grabbing the seat next to Crew. "Nah, that's Lane. I own a small private security company, and I was keeping an eye on a client's property. He's been out of town and having some issues with vandals."

"You catch the little shits?" a new voice asked from the doorway, and we all whirled to find a tall, broad man in a black sheriff's uniform standing there.

"Nope," Trey told him. "You'll be the first call when I do."

"I damn well better be. I'd hate to have to arrest you for obstruction."

Trey rolled his eyes, muttering, "Wouldn't be the first time."

The Lawless men burst into laughter, "remember when" stories immediately flying through the air. Under the table, Ella grabbed my hand as we silently watched the commotion.

"What set them off this time?" a feminine voice asked from next to me.

As though she'd appeared out of nowhere, a young girl who couldn't have been more than her early twenties sat next to me.

Ella leaned forward, peering around me, and said, "Hi, Aria."

The girl grinned. "How's my big bro doing?"

"He's good," Ella replied. "Things are picking up at the distillery now that Memorial Day is getting closer, so he and Delia are busy."

Aria's smile flattened a little. "Explains why he hasn't called in a week."

Ella grimaced. "Sorry, kid. But you've got me and Liam to keep you company!"

Aria turned those blue eyes, exactly like each of her brothers', on me and said, "Better than all this riff-raff."

"Who you callin' riff raff?" West asked, tossing a roll at his sister. Unfortunately, his aim was off, and it smacked me in the face instead. "Shit, man. I'm sorry. Don't beat me up, please."

I huffed out a laugh. "Why would I beat you up?"

"I don't know. You've got that look in your eye like you could kill a man if provoked."

"I hardly think taking a soft bread roll to the face is grounds for murder."

Lane, who had dropped into the bench across from us and straddled it, stuck his fingers in his ears. "How many times do I have to tell you idiots not to talk about killing people in front of me?"

Finn snorted, joining the conversation for the first time since his other brothers started appearing. "You say that like you don't know exactly the shit West and I got up to in the service."

"What branch?" I asked.

"Army," West supplied. "Rangers, to be exact."

"Impressive."

The twins shared a look before Finn said, "It was...something."

A hauntedness passed over both of their expressions, and I knew they'd seen shit they'd never talk about with anyone as long as they drew breath.

Before I graduated high school, I'd briefly considered entering the service. Senior year had been particularly hellish, my dad on my ass constantly about making sure my grades were tip-top so I could get into a good school, get my MBA, and come back to work with him.

Obviously, that was the absolute last thing I wanted to do with my life, had zero desire to walk any path that placed me under my father's control. The military sounded like an ideal way to make a clean break from him in a way he couldn't weasel me out of by throwing money at the problem until it went away.

Ultimately, I chose not to enlist, deciding facing college and finding a way out of the other shit down the line was the lesser of two evils, but I had a fuckton of respect for anyone who did.

Before the conversation could take another turn, Birdie returned with a stack of plates, silverware, and napkins, passing them out as she moved around the table.

"You staying, Lane?" she asked, not waiting for a response before she set a plate in front of him anyway.

"I'm on duty, so I'm not getting comfortable, but I won't say no to a meal."

"Good boy," Birdie said, patting him on the shoulder before taking the spot next to him. "Nice of you to join us, Aria."

"Whatever," she said, rolling her eyes.

Birdie released an exasperated sigh, and Trey grumbled his sister's name low in warning.

Aria merely glared in response.

"Let's eat," Birdie said, and all conversation ceased, the tension evaporating as we dug in.

Despite the gentle ribbing and petulance, there was a lot of love and respect to be found at that table. Conversation resumed as we piled our plates high, Ella and I content to watch and listen as the Lawlesses shared stories about the town and the ranch and their family. I knew from Ella that their father had passed away some years ago, and took care not to mention anything that would stir up bad feelings.

I was just happy to be there, surrounded by these people who clearly cared deeply for one another, but I'd be lying if the whole experience wasn't a little bittersweet.

Bitter, because I hadn't grown up around people like this, hadn't had a nuclear family that acted like a *family*.

But sweet because I was here now, because I got to live nights like these, with the Lawlesses here and with the Delatous back in Michigan.

When Birdie stood to serve dessert and the boys jumped up to clear dirty dishes, I turned to Ella and pressed a kiss to her temple.

"What was that for?" she asked, though she hummed happily and burrowed into my side.

"Just grateful to be here with you."

She tipped her head back, offering her mouth to me, and I gave her a quick kiss.

"I have a feeling there will be a lot more nights like this for us back home," she said.

I didn't need to tell her I was thinking the exact same thing.

This family, and all the times I'd spent around Ella's, made me long for one of my own. I desperately craved this kind of life, with lots of kids running around, big family gatherings where nothing exceptional happened save the time spent with the people you loved most in the world.

I wanted all of that for myself. A brood of children, and for the woman at my side to remain there forever.

I needed to ask her to stay, to extend her trip just a little longer. But we were still so new that I wasn't sure how she'd feel about meeting my entire family, especially knowing how strained my relationships with half of them were.

And, of course, there was the Mellie of it all. A story I'd definitely have to tell before the two came face to face.

Before, I'd been terrified to share that with her, but now that I knew *her* story, knew that she'd understand what I'd gone through, I thought maybe finally sharing my truth wouldn't be so bad after all.

chapter 26
Liam

AFTER DINNER, WEST HOPPED in his truck, and we followed him in the van to his side of the ranch and the cabin where we'd be sleeping for the next few nights. Essentially, it was a miniature version of the main house, constructed of logs with lots of windows to let in as much natural light as possible. A small porch jutted off the front, and it was shaded on one side by a massive, towering oak tree.

"This is so cute!" Ella said as we got out of the car.

"Thanks," West replied wryly. "I was going for rustic, but *cute* works too."

Ella gave him a middle finger, and we both snorted, shaking our heads.

West came around the back of the van to help me unload our things while Ella walked up the steps and disappeared inside.

"Speaking of cute," West said conversationally, "you two look great together."

I gave him a half smile. "Thanks. It's still really new, but...I'm crazy about her."

"That much is obvious. And she seems great."

"She's the best," I confirmed. "All the Delatou women are."

"Yeah…" West trailed off. "My big brother got a good one."

"What about the rest of you?"

West shook his head with a deep chuckle. "Fuck no. At least not for me. The other ones might fall in line after O, but…nah. Not in the cards for this cowboy."

I laughed softly. "You know, I thought the same thing after my ex fucked me up. Then I met Ella and everything changed."

While West stared at me, I had a feeling he was looking more through me, his eyes slightly unfocused as though he was a million miles away. I wondered if there was someone on his mind, someone in his life that he was imagining a future with.

But it wasn't my place to pry, so when he said, "Yeah, maybe," I let the subject drop in favor of hauling our luggage inside.

The rustic vibe West had been going for was carried indoors with exposed beams and stained shiplap walls, dark wood floors, oversized leather furniture in the living space, and plenty of dark green, burnt orange, and umber accents. Ella appeared from down the hallway, where two bedrooms and the bathroom branched off.

"This place is amazing, West," she said, leaning against the wall and watching us. "Thank you for accommodating us."

West waved her off. "It's no problem, really."

"Still," I said, reaching out my hand for a shake. Surprising me, he pulled me into a back-slapping bro hug, and when we parted, I continued. "I'll get you back one day."

West only winked, said, "We'll talk," and disappeared.

Ella was in front of me in a flash, running her hands up my torso and pushing my flannel from my shoulders.

"God, I thought he'd never leave." Rising onto her tiptoes, she pressed open mouthed kisses from the collar of my shirt and along my neck to my jaw.

"Fuck, Wildflower. Greedy, aren't we?"

"For you? Always," she said a moment before capturing my mouth. She was ravenous, her lips meeting mine eagerly, tongue sweeping along my bottom lip, seeking entrance, and I gave it to her. Everything in me settled when our tongues tangled, like she was breathing life into me.

But before things got too far, we needed to have a conversation.

"As badly as I'd like to fuck you into next week," I said when I pulled away, resting my forehead against hers and gripping her upper arms, our heavy breaths mingling between us, "there's something we need to talk about first."

Ella backed up further to meet my eyes, hers swimming with worry and confusion.

"Okay..."

"I know it's really soon and everything, but...well, I've already met your family so maybe it's not *that* soon, but I was hoping maybe you'd want to extend your trip and come to Sammy's wedding with me?"

I said the words in such a rush that I was breathing even harder by the time I'd gotten them all out.

"Your rambling is cute," Ella said with a giggle.

"That's not an answer."

"I thought it was obvious." She shrugged out of my hold and

reached down to lace our fingers together. "Of course I'll go with you."

"Think it'd be alright if I introduced you to my family as my girlfriend?"

Ella grinned. "As long as I can introduce you to mine as my boyfriend when we get home."

Home. Hell, I couldn't wait to return to Apple Blossom Bay with her, to start our normal lives together. To plant roots deep in the land her family settled and watch them grow.

"You can call me whatever you want, as long as one of those things is *'mine'.*"

"Deal," she said, humming happily and leaning into me. But she straightened abruptly. "Can I ask you something though?"

"Anything."

"When I told you about A—" I made a noise of protest, and she cut herself off before uttering the devil's name, then started again. "When I told you about douchebag cheating, you said you understood. And ages ago, you promised to tell me the story of why you left Portland. Are they related?"

Internally, I swore. This wasn't ever a conversation I wanted to have with her, mostly because Mellie meant nothing to me now, but she deserved to know anyway.

So as succinctly as I could, mostly because it was ancient history, I told her the story of Mellie. How we'd met during my first summer working at her family's winery. How we fucked around for years after that, breaking up and getting back together more times than I could count, but none of the breakups ever stuck. I guessed we enjoyed hurting each other too much—and making up.

Our on-again, off-again relationship continued through college, when I graduated and officially took over as head vintner at the winery. Things seemed to get more serious then. We had more frequent conversations about the future, what we wanted from our lives, settling down in Portland and having a family. Even so, for years, something held me back from proposing, from taking that next step to making things permanent.

"I should've known it was all too good to be true. I think, deep down, I *did*, even if I hadn't wanted to admit it to myself," I told Ella wryly.

"What happened?"

"I caught her fucking my brother in her office one night. She'd been working late, so I showed up with dinner from her favorite Thai takeout place to surprise her, and I walked in on them together."

"Fuck," Ella hissed. "I hate her."

I smiled, dragging her into my arms. "The worst part about it is, after I left, *they* got together—but then Sammy started cheating on her with her sister. And now...he's marrying Mellie's sister, Char."

"That's seriously fucked up," Ella said. "And I thought Delia hooking up with Owen after Amara had been bad enough."

"At least Amara and Owen had been done for years at that point," I reminded her.

"And it didn't affect our family dynamic one bit."

"My problems with my brother started long before that day, but...yeah, that was kind of the final nail in the coffin of us ever having a relationship."

Ella didn't respond to that, only pulled me down the hall to the bedroom. As soon as we crossed the threshold, she shut the door behind us and unceremoniously stripped her cardigan and sundress off. That left her standing before me in nothing but a set of lacy underthings, the fabric covered in florals and sheer enough that I could see both her pussy lips and nipples beneath.

As she reached behind her to unhook her bra, she nodded at me, silently urging me to get naked as well. My shirt floated to the floor as she released the clasp, but her hands cupped her breasts, keeping it on for the moment as the straps slipped down her arms.

"So tell me, Wills..." she began, fingertips drawing distracting circles around her nipples, "you got a boss's daughter kink?"

I grinned wickedly as I stalked toward her, kicking out of my pants and boxers as I went until I was completely naked in front of her. Ella backpedaled until the backs of her knees hit the edge of the mattress and she collapsed backward.

She looked like a fucking angel, hair fanned out around her on the soft beige comforter, all that golden, tatted skin on display.

She was, without a doubt, my exact version of heaven given human form, wrapped in this perfectly fierce and feminine package.

I crawled between her legs and hovered over her, my mouth inches from hers.

"Nah, Wildflower. Just a *you* kink."

chapter 27
Ella

THE NEXT MORNING, WHILE Liam was still passed out after having given me another orgasm barely an hour before, I carefully and silently slipped out of bed, dressed, and headed out to the kitchen. After I got coffee brewing, I stepped out onto the porch to call my sisters.

"Well, well, well," Delia, who was naturally the first to answer, said. "If it isn't the wayward sister."

I rolled my eyes. "You're annoying."

"You love me," she said, blowing me a kiss. "But really, you've been MIA. Where the hell have you been, *loca*?"

"Fucking hell," Amara grumbled as she joined the call, adjusting sleeping baby Cora in her arms. "Have you been marathoning *Twilight* again?"

"Hey," Brie said when her face appeared in the corner of the screen. "Don't be a hater. *Twilight* is a cult classic."

"Thank you, Baby Brie," Delia said happily, then noisily slurping from her coffee mug.

At last, Chloe appeared, baby Aleah propped up against her shoulder.

"Why are we always talking about *Twilight*?" she sighed.

"At least it's not Anne Hathaway marathons," Brie supplied. "We've moved past those, right, Ella?"

"Oh, we're *way* beyond Anne Hathaway."

There was enough suggestion in my tone that my sisters immediately perked up. Chloe even went so far as to call for Logan and hand Aleah off to him and, almost in sync, Cal stole Cora away from Amara so they could give me their full attention.

"Spill. The. Fucking. Tea. Sis," Delia said, punctuating each word with a clap of her hands.

"The first thing you guys should know," I started, pausing for dramatic effect, "is that I'm in love with Liam Danvers."

"Holy shit," Amara breathed.

Brie and Chloe merely squealed, and Delia cut right to the heart of the matter by saying, "Tell us *everything*."

So I did. I filled them in on everything that had happened since I called them that first night in South Dakota. Somehow, that had only been five days ago, but it felt like a lifetime.

"This is crazy, isn't it?" I asked, shaking my head. "To fall in love in less than two weeks?"

Brie shook her head. "I knew Ezra was the one the first time I laid eyes on him. So no, I don't think it's crazy at all."

My other sisters hummed in agreement, though I knew it had taken each of them longer to come around to the ideal of a lifetime with their partners.

"Do you guys...approve? Of him?"

"You're grinning, El," Delia said. "We haven't seen you this happy in *years*. If he's the person responsible, it doesn't really matter what we think, does it?"

"Of course it matters!" I protested. "You're my sisters, and if I'm bringing this guy into the family, I want you and the guys to like him."

Amara, who worked closest with him, shrugged. "He's a great guy. And as we told you before, you could do a lot worse than Liam Danvers."

"Actually," I started. "I don't think I could do any better. He's...yeah. He's it for me, I think."

Brie's voice sounded a little watery when she said, "You deserve this, sissy. After everything, more than anyone, *you deserve this*."

And finally, I believed her.

❧ ❦

"I can't believe you talked me into this," Liam grumbled as we stumbled out of Dusk Valley's only tattoo shop later that morning. Thanks to the fact that all of the Lawless brothers were heavily tattooed and frequented the place, one of the artists was willing to squeeze us in.

I was now the proud owner of a majestic purple Volkswagen van tattoo. It sat just above the crease of my right elbow, and Liam's same arm spotted a matching one. I made him pause outside the shop with me, arms extended, so I could snap a picture and share it on my Instagram.

"You love it," I told him as we walked hand-in-hand behind West, who had been all for the impromptu tattoo session. While we'd been getting ours, he'd added a little bird to the piece that took up most of his back in honor of his mom.

"I love *you*," Liam amended, dropping a kiss to my forehead.

"So much you got my name tatted on you too," I teased, reaching out to tap the space next to the blue butterfly where he'd added my initials.

"I told you days ago not to tempt me," he replied.

Fuck, that was sexy. To be branded on his skin as a physical representation of the way I was branded on his heart and soul.

"Just think," I said. "One day, our grandchildren will ask us about them and we can tell them about this trip where we fell in love."

Liam softened at that. "Well, when you put it that way..."

Raising onto the balls of my feet, I gave him a quick peck. "I knew you'd see things my way."

"I don't know about you guys," West said, turning to face us but continuing to walk backward, "but I'm fucking starving. How about we swing into the deli for lunch?"

At that moment, my stomach let out a low growl, and I nodded emphatically.

West led us inside, making small talk with every single person we passed, and I almost felt like I was back home. There was nothing that beat the familiarity of small town life.

After lunch—where I consumed the best grilled cheese and homemade tomato soup I'd ever had in life, though I'd never tell Ezra that—we wandered the main drag of Dusk Valley, popping in and out of shops and letting West tell us stories about the history and growing up there.

We spent the remainder of the afternoon, before the sun went down, on a horseback ride through the rolling hills and fields that made up a small portion of ranch land. I was mesmerized and deeply contented by the simplicity of it all, the mighty creature beneath me, surprisingly gentle despite its size. Minus the horses and the drastic differences in landscape, the whole vibe reminded me of home.

That night, we had another boisterous dinner at the Lawless family table before Finn and West decided they wanted to take us to the local watering hole. Once that idea was floated, the entire family decided they'd be joining us, save Birdie, who said she was too old to hang with us young guns. I kissed her on the cheek as we all filed out, thanking her for another amazing meal, and followed Liam back to our cabin.

I was in the middle of changing when a light knock came at the door, and Liam disappeared to see who it was. Voices floated back to me as I donned my dress, rushing to do up the buttons running from between my boobs all the way to the hem, which hit me at mid-calf, before Liam returned. I didn't do up all of them, loving the way the ones I left opened at the bottom created a little slit that offered tantalizing glimpses of my thigh tattoo. With my arms exposed, the bulk of my ink was on full display, and once I put my black cowboy boots on, I felt like a badass.

I'd gone a little heavier on the makeup than I had in recent months, but still lighter than anything I'd worn when I'd been with Alfie, hooked delicate silver hoops and studs into my ears, and slipped on a few of my favorite rings.

During that time, makeup had been armor for me. Hiding the dark circles under my eyes from lack of sleep when we'd gotten in yet another fight and I couldn't relax until it was solved.

Spoiler alert: they rarely ever were. We fought about stupid shit, frequently, that never saw any sort of resolution.

That wore on a girl after a while.

I supposed, if you wanted to get technical, I started dressing and making myself up to look emo, mostly because I was so fucking depressed and, maybe, somewhere deep down, silently screaming for someone to notice and help me.

Shaking my head, I threw away those thoughts. That was all ancient history, and deserved to remain in the past.

Liam was my present—and, if I was really goddamn lucky, my future.

As though I'd conjured him, I heard Liam's footsteps as he came back down the hall, and said, "Who was—"

"Holy fuck," he breathed, cutting me off. I turned to him, finding him stalled in the doorway, those bright blue eyes darkened as they raked my body head to toe.

I did a little twirl. "You like?"

"I'd *like*," he growled, stalking toward me and slipping his hand along the outside of my thigh and beneath the dress, finding I wasn't wearing panties, "to strip you out of it and have my wicked way with you."

I gasped as he slid a finger through my slit, toying with me. Fuck, his hands were magic. Even that single touch had my legs weak and shaking. Gathering my wits, I placed a hand on his chest and pushed him away—or tried, but the man was a wall of muscle and didn't move until he planted a kiss on the side of my neck—then wagged a finger at him. "Down boy. We have somewhere to be. And you know someone will come looking for us if we don't show up."

"Damn nosy Lawlesses."

Ignoring the comment, I nodded at the box in his hands. "What's that? Who was at the door?"

"West was bringing me something to wear tonight."

I frowned. "You're already dressed."

Unintentionally, we'd decided to match tonight, with him in his dark wash jeans and black button down shirt, and brown work boots, me in my little black dress and the cowboy boots I'd bought in Deadwood. Without answering me, he set the box on our bed and removed the lid.

The cowboy hat he withdrew was also black, the hatband a shiny strip of dark leather. Gingerly, he removed the hat from the box and set it atop his head, adjusting it until it was comfortable.

Sheepishly, he looked at me. "What do you think?"

The uncertainty in his eyes almost sent me to my knees, the knowledge that this man wasn't always as sure of himself as he'd like me to believe—and that made him even more loveable in my eyes.

Slowly, I approached him and pressed my palms to his chest, digging my nails into his shirt and dragging him closer until we were both shielded by the brim of his hat.

"You're giving me major Rip vibes right now."

Liam's eyes flared with heat. "Does that make you my Beth?"

"If that's what you want," I said, tilting my face and offering up my mouth.

"I want anything that ends with us together forever," he said, leaning in, a breath away from my lips.

"Deal," I replied, then kissed him.

chapter 28

Ella

THE SWALLOW WAS EXACTLY the kind of bar you'd expect to find in a small western town like Dusk Valley. The floors were sticky, tables were a mixture of short squares and circular high tops, crammed together in the free space surrounding a large dance floor, the bar itself dominating the back wall. They didn't serve food, and smoking indoors had been outlawed ages ago, but the scent of cigarette smoke still clung to the place. They also didn't serve any specialty drinks that required a blender or any other frilly accouterments. They had beer, boxed wine, and the standard, staple liquors you'd find anywhere in America.

We followed West and Finn inside and toward a far corner where the rest of the Lawless men and Aria were set up. The table was already full of empty bottles and watery glasses. Liam kept me close to his side as we pushed through the crowd and gathered around the edge.

"See you got started without us," West said, socking Trey on the shoulder.

"Punch me again and my fist is going through your face," Trey promised his younger brother, providing a smile that was all teeth to match.

West raised his hands in surrender. "Whatever you say, Fed."

"Don't call me that," Trey growled.

Liam and I shared a look, and I shrugged before he disappeared with West to get us drinks.

Aria tugged me onto the chair next to her and said, "God, it's so nice to have another girl around."

I snorted. "I've got four sisters," I reminded her. "This is...uncharted territory."

Aria sighed heavily, leaning closer so I could hear her over the music but no one else could. "They mean well, and I love them so much, but...sometimes, it's a lot."

"I can imagine."

If there was one thing I'd picked up about the Lawless men since we'd arrived in Dusk Valley the day before, it was that they were unfailingly loyal to and extremely protective of each other. In Aria's case, it was surely more *over*protective than the kind they asserted over each other, and I could see how exhausting that would be.

"They're...overbearing," Aria continued, "but they're the best and my favorite people on the planet."

"Even Owen?"

"*Especially* Owen," she confirmed. "Even though he's not here, he's been taking care of all of us since Daddy died."

My heart squeezed painfully at the reminder of this family's loss, how their Dad had died when Owen was a junior in college. I did the mental calculations and realized Aria couldn't have been more than six at the time.

"What do you mean, taking care of you?"

Aria smiled, almost sadly, and I saw so much of my sister's boyfriend in that expression. The genes in the Lawless family were strong.

"You know he gave up his final year of college eligibility to go pro, right?" I nodded. "Most people think that was because it's what Daddy would've wanted, but one thing I've learned about my dad—and my brothers, for that matter—is that not a single one of them can be told what to do. Owen left college a year early because Mama was barely holding it together without Dad, and he didn't want us struggling. Trey was in college, Lane about to graduate high school. The twins and Crew were always getting into trouble, and I was this little girl, so young I didn't know up from down in the world, especially not one with my father suddenly missing from it. I'm sure Mama would've figured it all out eventually, but Owen gave us money that kept us afloat those first few years. He paid for college for those of us that went, covered ranch expenses when times were tight, made sure we had clothes on our backs and food on the table." Aria's eyes went misty, and she sniffled loudly and blinked rapidly before any could fall. "My oldest brother is the best man I've ever known. Your sister got a really, really good one."

Before I could respond—honestly, I was struck stupid and into silence anyway—the band ended their song, the bar going quiet until someone called into the mic, "Ariiiiiiiiiiiii."

The girl next to me jumped to her feet and grinned. "That's my cue."

West and Liam returned then, but I looked at Trey and said,

"Where is she going?"

He only smiled, crossed his arms over his chest, and leaned back in his chair. "Watch."

After accepting my bourbon from Liam, I swiveled on my chair to face the stage, where Aria now stood behind the mic.

"Good evening, beautiful people," she grinned, and a raucous greeting rang out from the crowd. "What do y'all wanna hear tonight?"

Someone shouted, "Carrie Underwood!" into the silence that followed her question, and Aria turned to look at the band.

"What do you think, boys?"

In answer, the opening notes of "Before He Cheats" rang out, and the cheers grew in volume.

And when Aria started singing, I was transfixed, entirely mesmerized by how such a powerful voice came out of such a petite package. How the girl who'd been sitting beside me not long ago, getting emotional over her family, morphed into this badass singer in the span of a few minutes.

"Holy shit," Liam breathed next to me.

I only nodded. "She's amazing."

Swiveling my head, I glanced around at Aria's brothers, who were each singing along proudly as the youngest of them entertained the crowd.

When the song ended, West hopped up on a chair and shouted, "That's my baby sister!"

The entire crowd cheered along with him, but the bright lights on Aria did nothing to hide the blush that crept up her neck and over her cheeks. Still, she remained nothing but professional as she launched into another country song, this one a Megan

Moroney tune that had everyone in the bar screaming the words right back at her.

Aria strutted up and down the stage, twirling and dancing and singing her heart out.

To witness such a thing was nothing short of incredible. Each of her brothers may have been talented in their own rights, but the baby of the family had definitely taken her fair share of the pot.

After a few more numbers, she told everyone she was taking a break—to numerous groans—and made her way back to us. The entire band appeared to be breaking as well, grabbing a drink, a smoke, or disappearing down a long hall toward the back with a woman on their arms. In their place, top forty began piping into the room from the sound system.

When Aria reached us, I threw my arms around her and squeezed her tightly, then held her out in front of you.

"You are incredible!" I squealed.

Aria blushed again. "It's just for fun."

"No, Aria. You are insanely talented. Don't sell yourself short."

She reached out and clasped my hands. "You really mean it?"

I nodded emphatically. "Of course I do."

She grinned, letting go of me as Lane wrapped one of his heavily muscled and tattooed arms around her neck and kissed the top of her head.

"Killed it as usual, my girl."

Aria glanced up at her brother, eyes shining with joy. "Thanks."

"There's our girl!" West shouted, having just come back from the bar. While I was entranced by Aria and her performance, it seemed West was getting turned up.

I'd been so focused on the Lawless family that I was caught entirely off guard when a hand slipped around my waist from behind, sprawling possessively over my abdomen and pulling me back against his body.

"Hey baby," Liam said low in my ear.

"Hey, handsome. Having fun?"

"Not really my scene," he admitted. "I'd much rather make good on my threat to strip you out of that dress."

I turned in his arms and looped mine around his neck. "You think that was a threat? Baby, I'd strip myself out of this dress if you asked nicely."

"That's all it takes, huh?" He took his hat off so he could nuzzle my neck. In one smooth move, I grabbed it from him and stepped back, running my finger along the brim.

"Remember the cowboy hat rule?" I asked him, peeking up at him through my lashes.

Liam's eyes flared. "You gonna ride me later, Wildflower?"

I lifted the hat over his head and set it back atop his dark hair. "Only one way to find out."

Liam grinned, remembering the scene I'd painted for us as we left Wyoming.

The song changed, and it seemed the entire female population of the bar let out a simultaneous squeal of excitement. Before I could react, to search out the source of the fuss, Aria rushed up to my side, threw an apology at Liam, and towed me out to the dance floor.

"Do you know how to line dance?" she shouted at me as

someone cranked the tune louder, filling my very soul with the sounds of "Shiver" by Ed Sheeran.

I winked at her. "I think I can keep up."

Aria's brows raised in surprise, but she didn't get a chance to say anything else because the crowd began to move, us right along with it.

Losing myself in the beat, in the steps, in the sense of camaraderie I'd found with this family that wasn't mine but *felt* like it on the other side of the country—it was the most free I'd been in a long time.

Liam had a lot to do with it too, and I couldn't help the girlish giggle that escaped me every time our eyes connected across the room. He wasn't even pretending to converse with the guys, wasn't pretending to let me have my fun until he got to have his later. He simply stood there at the edge of the dance floor, arms crossed, beer bottle dangling carelessly from one of the beautiful tattooed hands, watching me. Anyone who looked at him, looked at me, looked at *us*...they just *knew*. Knew we were together. That I belonged to him, and he to me.

When the song ended, I bent over, hands on my knees, to catch my breath. A hand landed between my shoulder blades, and Aria's face appeared in my periphery.

"You weren't lying!" she said excitedly. "You can more than keep up."

I straightened with a laugh. "Delia is crazy popular on TikTok, right? And she got this bug up her ass a few summers ago about us learning the dance to that song. That's literally the only one I could've pulled that off for."

Aria's glee morphed to melancholy in a heartbeat. "I wish we lived closer. I could use some sisters."

"You've always got us, Aria," I told her. "We're only a phone call away."

"All of you?"

I nodded, confident in speaking for my sisters in this moment. "All of us."

She grinned, squeezing my hands, then pulling me to the center of the floor as another song kicked up—a Morgan Wallen banger that had us swaying our hips and screaming the lyrics at the top of our lungs.

Halfway through, a set of hands found their way to my hips, and I stiffened, knowing instantly they didn't belong to my boyfriend.

"You new in town?" a gruff voice asked as I attempted to pull away.

I looked to Aria for help and found her in the arms of a different guy, forgetting about me for the moment. "Just passing through," I told him, trying to back away, searching over his shoulder for Liam. But his spot at the edge of the dance floor was empty.

"Even better," the guy said with a grin, exposing his too-white teeth. "I'm—"

"She doesn't give a fuck what your name is," a new voice said, and Liam appeared from behind him, shoving him back and putting his big body between us.

"Why don't you let her decide that?" the guy said, giving me a smarmy grin. "You wanna come home with me, don't you?"

My upper lip curled, a disgusted sound leaving me. "Fuck no."

"C'mon now," he said. "You don't mean that "

"I definitely do."

Liam turned his head to look at me. With that wicked gleam in his eyes I loved so much, he took his hat off his head and set it on mine. "What about me, baby? You wanna come home with me?"

I grinned, making a show of looking him up and down, fingering the brim of the hat coyly. "I don't know…" I trailed off.

"Hey man!" the new guy protested. "You can't do that."

Liam barely spared him a glance. "My hat, my woman. Now fuck off."

"How about we take this outside and settle it like real men?"

"I don't think that'll be—"

The expression on Liam's face cut me off as he fully put his back to the new guy. Then he hauled me up over his shoulder like a sack of potatoes, one hand planted firmly across the backs of my thighs to keep my dress down. The guy who made a pass at me shouted for someone to help me, but I was laughing so hard, it was obvious I wasn't in danger. The Lawless family, finally recognizing the commotion, hooted and hollered at Liam as he walked me down that long hallway toward the back.

We pushed outside, finding the small parking lot entirely abandoned, the streetlight that normally would've illuminated the area burned out. Liam set me on my feet slowly, my body gliding down his as he did, his hands settling low on my hips and pushing me backward until my spine met the side of the building.

"Impressive display," I told him. All I could see was the way his eyes captured the light of the moon—dark, endless pools I wanted to sink into and stay there forever.

"He was touching what's mine."

"Yours, huh?" I said playfully.

I knew the answer—hadn't needed to ask. I was his in every way, shape, and form. Mind, body, soul. In all the ways he'd already had me and all the ways he wanted me in the future.

But as surely as I belonged to him, Liam Danvers belonged to me, and I couldn't say for certain I wouldn't have reacted similarly had another woman put her hands on him.

Liam merely tapped my head. "You're wearing my hat, Wildflower. Tell me, what was that rule again?"

"Technically, it's West's hat."

"Ella," Liam growled.

Tipping my head back, I let loose a laugh, and the hat fell from my head.

Liam's mouth was on mine in a heartbeat, hands in my hair, clutching me tightly, fusing our lips together until there wasn't a millimeter of space between us. We came together fervently, sloppily, like we couldn't survive going a second longer without being together like this. I moaned when his tongue swept inside, caressing mine, and the sound seemed to slow things down. Liam moved more intentionally, sucking on my tongue, pulling at my lips with his teeth, peppering my cheeks and jaw with kisses.

When he pulled away, I chased after him with a sound of protest, and he obliged me with another kiss—chaste, closed-mouthed, and entirely too short.

"Why'd you stop?" I asked.

Liam reached down and tangled our fingers together, bending first to pick up the hat before pulling me around the building to where the van waited in the full parking lot. The band had kicked up again, and Aria's full, gorgeous voice floated out into the night, the neon sign flashing, attempting to lure us in.

Instead, we got in the van, and Liam finally answered my question, sending shivers skittering across my skin.

"I'm taking you home, Wildflower, where no one but the trees will hear you scream for me."

chapter 29
Liam

THE DRESS, THE HAT, the cowboy boots, and the hour or so of watching her line dance and shake her ass on the floor at the Swallow with Aria had me damn near coming out of my skin.

I was fucking ravenous for her as I roughly pushed us through the door of the cabin, tossed West's hat off to the side, and backed Ella into the nearest hard surface, which happened to be the wall.

Perfect. It gave us just enough leverage for me to stick my thigh between her legs so she could grind down on it while I plunged my tongue into her mouth.

She tasted like a heady combination of beer and bourbon, and I sucked on her tongue, wringing every drop I could free from her.

My hands were everywhere, moving up and down her sides, to her hips and ass, roughly palming her breasts and groaning against her when those damn sexy piercings dug into my palms.

"You're driving me insane," I growled as I pulled away an inch. "This fucking dress, Ella. My god. I've been thinking all night about how you're not wearing underwear, and how easy it would be to slide my hand between your thighs and toy with you."

Her chest heaved wildly as she stared at me, gaze heavily lidded.

"Now would be a good time to test that theory."

I withdrew my leg from between hers, grinning at the wet spot on my jeans.

"You're soaked for me, aren't you, Wildflower?"

"One way to find out."

Instead of bunching her dress up around her hips like I'd fantasized about earlier, I gripped the seam and tore it open, those tiny, infernal buttons that kept her presentable all night flying free and pinging against the floors and walls.

Ella frowned as it gaped open, baring her front to me from her tits all the way down to her cunt. "I liked that dress."

"I'll buy you a new one," I assured her as my fingers slipped through her slit, lazily twirling around her clit. Ella gasped, and I chuckled darkly. "Don't care so much about the dress now, do you, baby? You only care about the way I play with my perfect pussy."

"Yours," she replied.

It wasn't a question because we both knew the truth.

Every part of her belonged to me.

Without warning, I shoved two fingers inside her, and her head dropped to my shoulder. Fuck, she was so tight, so wet and warm, and she whimpered as I withdrew and slowly pushed back in, her nails digging into my biceps.

"So responsive," I murmured as her legs began to shake.

"Liam," she whispered, my name a plea. "Please."

I moved my hand faster, thumb circling her clit, and shifted so

I could press my cock into her thigh, desperate for some friction of my own.

"Ella," I breathed, feeling her walls clamp tighter around my fingers, telling me she was close. "Tell me you love me."

She lifted her head, eyes clearing momentarily as she gave me a smile brighter than the sun—and pressed her thigh harder against me. Fuck. I was seconds away from coming, my release gathering at my spine and threatening to burst free.

"I love you," she said. "More than I ever thought possible."

As though the words were a detonator, Ella fell apart, collapsing against me as she did. Her entire body quivered as her release rolled through her.

And I followed her down with a shout, both my hand and my hips jerking almost clumsily against her as the edges of my vision darkened.

When we both stilled, Ella said, "Did you just..."

"Yeah," I grinned, not a hint of shame to be found. "I just came in my pants."

Ella reached for my belt and fly, deftly undoing them and pulling my jeans and boxers down.

"Fuck," she whispered when my cock sprang free, coated in cum. "You're a mess."

I only grinned. "And what a damn fine mess it is."

There was a wild edge to Ella's answering smile.

I kicked off my boots and stepped out of them as she circled her hand around me, coaxing me back to life while she lowered her mouth and licked me clean.

"I fucking love you messy, baby. Knowing you only get like this with me? Fuck, it makes me so wet."

"Goddamnit, woman," I ground out. On her knees, her dress hanging open, skin flushed from her orgasm—I'd never seen anything more fucking beautiful in my life.

When she returned to her feet after toying with me some more, she walked backward a few steps, crooking a finger at me as she said, "C'mon, Wills." She turned and started down the hall, but over her shoulder added, "Bring the hat."

I hurried after her, grabbing the hat and stripping the rest of the way before I met her in our bedroom.

Ella had shed her dress and flicked on one of the bedside lamps, standing naked in the center of the room, the low light setting her skin glowing. I'd had her numerous times in the last few days, in numerous ways, but I doubted the shine would ever wear off. I didn't think I'd ever get used to the knowledge that this woman was *mine*.

Mine to keep.

Mine to love and cherish and worship.

Mine to fuck.

And damn, did I love fucking my girl.

"Give me the hat," she directed, "and get on the bed."

I rushed to obey, practically throwing the hat at her before I climbed on the mattress and settled on my back in the center.

Still with her back to me, I took a moment to trace her curves with my eyes, mesmerized by her hips and ass and the way they dipped and flared to give her that perfect hourglass shape.

Ella settled the hat on her head, then turned to face me, grinning wickedly.

As she crawled onto the bed between my thighs, I said, "Wear the hat..."

"Ride the cowboy," she finished.

"I'm not a cowboy," I reminded her.

Straddling my lap, she rocked her hips, my cock sliding through her slit in a tease of what was to come.

Her hands came up to cup her breasts while she moved, and she smiled down at me. "I think you'll do just fine. Feel how wet I am? That's all for you, baby."

Bucking my hips up into her, making her gasp, I said, "Get on then."

Ella lifted slightly off me and reached between us, gripping me at the base and notching my head at her entrance.

With aching, torturous slowness, she sank down, taking me inch by inch until I bottomed out, until her ass rested on my thighs. Wriggling atop me experimentally, she adjusted until she found that perfect angle. I knew when she did because I sank even deeper into her, deeper than we'd ever gotten in any other position. Ella threw her head back, hand flying up to hold the hat in place, and moaned loudly.

"Ella," I breathed, my hands skating up her sides, thumbs brushing almost absently over her nipples until they came up to cup her cheeks. I tilted her head down, and she bent over me, changing to angle in the way that had me cursing under my breath.

"You feel so good."

"There's nothing better," I agreed. "You are...god, Wildflower. You're everything to me. A fucking goddess, and I'll spend the rest of my days worshiping you just like this."

Leaning forward, she gently kissed me before saying, "Promises, promises."

And then she began to move.

Tentative at first, slow, back-arching rolls of her hips that had me withdrawing only slightly before pushing back in. She leaned back and placed her palms on my thighs, shifting onto the balls of her feet so she could bounce.

I'd be damned if it wasn't the hottest thing I'd ever seen. Her pussy spread open, pink and swollen, my cock disappearing inside her with each downward shift. Her skin flushed and glowing, her eyes open but slitted, like she wanted to watch but wanted to savor it all too.

And that fucking hat. I'd never be able to look at a cowboy hat the same again, not after this. I'd forever remember her moving over me, undulating her hips, resting her hands on my chest instead of my legs for a different angle—one that had her clit rubbing against me.

Across the room, I caught sight of us in the giant mirror that rested on the floor near the closet. She was gorgeous from every angle, but seeing her from the back, writhing on my cock, her tattoos waving as she moved—I think it unlocked a kink I didn't know I had.

Reaching up, I pinched her nipples between my fingers, tweaking one of those piercings in a way that had her crying out.

"Sensitive, are we?" I chuckled.

"I need more," was all she said.

Without giving either of us time to think, I sat upright, lifted her off of me, and scrambled around behind her, shoving home forcefully. Now, we faced the mirror, and I grinned at the blissed out expression Ella wore.

"Oh fuck," she gasped, head dropping forward, that hat finally falling off.

Unceremoniously, I picked it up and flung it across the room. After all, as she'd so helpfully reminded me earlier, it *was* West's hat, and the only man allowed in bed with my girl was *me*.

"That better, baby?" I asked, punctuating the words with a thrust that sent her ass rippling. *Fuck*. I'd fantasized about it so many times, but my imagination could never have done it justice.

Ella made some unintelligible sound, but now *I* was the one who needed more.

Gripping her upper arms, I pulled her backward, her spine arching, head falling against my shoulder.

Ella swore, squeezing her eyes shut, mouth popped open. "So fucking deep."

"Open your eyes, baby," I commanded. "Watch us."

Her eyes flew open, locking on mine in the mirror.

"Arms around my neck," I instructed. "And hold on."

"Or what?"

"You let go, I stop. Understood?"

"Yes, daddy," she quipped.

I blinked slowly, skin tightening as Ella gauged my reaction.

"Liam?" she asked, her blissed out expression morphing to concern and...embarrassment? "Sorry, it slipped. It won't—"

Against her ear, I murmured, "Say it again."

Before she could, her arms came up around my neck like I'd asked, and my fingers slipped between her legs, thrumming her clit.

"Say it again," I repeated, damn near growling at her. "Tell me how that feels."

"It feels—" she gasped. "*Sooooo* good, daddy."

"Goddamnit, Ella," I gritted out. "How do you keep getting better?"

She huffed out a laugh. "I could ask you the same thing."

I bucked my hips into her, and her fingers tightened at my nape, tugging on my hair, nails digging into my flesh.

"Remember what I told you."

"Hold on," she confirmed. "And watch."

"Good girl."

"Anything for you, daddy."

There was no mercy in my thrusts as I slammed into her, retreating and advancing so quickly, the springs of the bed squeaked ominously beneath us. Over and over I powered into her, circling my fingers around her clit, roughly and rapidly. Ella's moans built in volume until she was practically screaming.

Just as I'd intended.

"You take me so fucking good, Wildflower," I grumbled, moving my free hand from her hip to her tit, squeezing it probably tighter than I should.

But I was unleashed, feral, that beast normally dormant in my chest set free, knowing it had finally met its match. Not even a freight train could've stopped me then.

I *was* the train. Destination? Making my girl come.

"Liam," she gasped.

I knew she was close, by how tightly her pussy gripped my cock, by how she bore down on my fingers with every upward thrust, by how tightly she held onto me, fingers pressing into my scalp, heeding my warning that I'd stop if she let go.

But there was no fucking way I was stopping now.

"You gonna come for me, baby?"

Giving up the fight of watching us at last, her eyes fluttered closed, head lolling to the side as I worked her over.

"It's okay," I murmured. "You can let go. Scream as loud as you want, Wildflower. Soak my cock. *Please*. I need it."

I'd resorted to begging by the end. I wasn't coming until she did, and my self-control was fraying rapidly, the strings holding me together no more substantial than cobwebs.

Still she held out. The stubbornness of this one was going to kill us both.

"Ella," I commanded. "Let go."

And then I did something wild.

I bent my face, sealed my lips over that delicate, sensitive spot where her shoulder curved up to her neck, and bit down.

At last, she broke, screaming and clawing at me as I fucked and rubbed her through it, shaking violently in my arms as the orgasm crested and rolled through her, endless and powerful.

Moments later, the pulsing of her pussy milked my own, and I released with a shout, my entire body going rigid, my movements turning jerky as I spilled long and hot inside her.

When I'd completely emptied myself, still buried inside her, I collapsed backward, taking her with me.

The only sound in the room was our labored breaths—until Ella let out a rough laugh.

"What's so funny?" I asked, pulling out of her at last and rolling us so I hovered over her. I glanced down, deeply pleased to see my cum dripping from her pussy. While I waited for her to answer, I collected it on my finger and shoved it back in. She twitched against the intrusion, but heaved a deep, satisfied sigh.

"Your self-control is fucking superhuman," she said finally, shaking her head in disbelief.

"That's another rule," I said simply, leaning up to kiss her softly. "I don't come unless you do."

"Trust me, Wills. I'm not complaining."

I grinned, gesturing to my body. "What's there to complain about?"

Ella responded by grabbing a pillow and smacking me with it.

I ripped from her hands, gathered her into an embrace, and reclined against them.

She snuggled against me, and soon, her breaths evened out. Gently so as to not wake her, I shifted and rolled us until I could free the comforter and pull it up over our bodies.

And then, with a smile on my face and my girl sated in my arms, I fell asleep.

chapter 30
Liam

THE ENTIRE LAWLESS FAMILY waited outside the main house the next morning when Ella and I pulled up to say goodbye. In truth, I had zero desire to leave, would've been content to make that little cabin Ella and I had spent the last two nights in our new home and forget all about the final leg—and ultimate destination—of this trip.

The Lawlesses passed us around with hugs and claps on the back, exchanged phone numbers, promises to keep their brother in line—a task no one could accomplish save maybe Delia; Owen did what he wanted, when he wanted—and plans to come back and visit soon.

These people were warm and welcoming, a real family, and it made leaving and heading toward my own broken one that much harder.

I was quiet on the drive, my mind whirring a thousand miles a minute. This stretch was the longest of our trip thus far, eight hours that seemed to pass slowly and far too quickly all at once.

The only saving grace was that I had Ella at my side. She had no idea what she was doing for me, simply holding my hand, letting me sit in my silence because she knew it was what I needed. Allowing me to play an entire audiobook from start to finish without interrupting to ask questions or make me rewind it like she usually did.

She was just...there. A steady presence, an anchor holding me down when I felt like I was going to float away.

Too soon, we were driving through Portland, headed toward the outskirts where Mellie's family winery was.

I'd spent the first eleven days of this trip relaxing, unspooling myself and giving everything I could to Ella and making it memorable for her. But the moment that sign came into view, everything I thought I'd let go of came rushing back, my entire body going taut once again.

Ella must've noticed the change, because she said, "It's okay, Wills. I'm here."

I glanced at her, trying to give her a smile that I was afraid looked more like a grimace. "I know, baby. It's the only reason I'm not turning the fucking van around and giving the whole thing the middle finger."

She squeezed my hand tighter. "It's going to be okay."

"You don't know my family," I grumbled.

"If they're as bad as you say, we'll just disappear. Just say the word, Wills, and we make a run for it."

I didn't have the heart to tell her they were worse than I could've conveyed with words, and only firsthand experience would prove it.

When we pulled into the lot in front of the resort attached to the winery, I was damn near crushed by a wave of déjà vu. Instead of getting out of the van right away, I merely turned it off and sat in silence, letting my eyes sweep over the buildings and the vineyards beyond.

It looked exactly the same, yet felt entirely different. Or maybe it was just me that was different, seeing this place through fresh eyes, through vision cleared over the course of the last five years.

"So this is it, huh," Ella said. I shifted to face her, unable to stop my chuckle at her wrinkled nose. "Bit gaudy, don't you think?"

The chuckle became full, booming laughter.

"Careful, Wildflower. Don't let any of them hear you say that."

Ella shrugged. "I guess I just prefer something with a bit more history. Don't you?"

I clasped her hand between both of mine and brought it to my mouth, pressing a kiss to her knuckles. "If I had to choose between this place and Chateau Delatou...well, it's not really a choice at all."

By the way her face softened, I knew she understood what I was telling her.

I'd choose Michigan over Oregon.

Chateau Delatou over Renault Vineyards.

Ella Delatou over Merlot Renault.

It wasn't even a fucking contest.

"Let's get this over with."

Ella nodded, let go of me, and got out of the van. Reluctantly, I followed, feeling for all the world like I was walking toward my death.

As we unloaded our bags, a bellhop appeared with a cart,

greeting us brightly.

"Welcome to Renault Vineyards! May I ask what the name on the reservation is?"

"Danvers," I said.

"Ahh, wonderful! Here for the wedding, I presume?" he asked, though he didn't wait for my response as he clicked the side button on a radio and relayed my name to presumably the front desk.

"Unfortunately," I told him under my breath.

"Excellent!" he said, clearly not having heard me. "How are you related to the happy couple?"

"I'm the groom's brother."

"Wonderful, wonderful," he said cheerily as the last of our luggage was loaded. "Well, if you'll follow me, we'll get you all checked in and settled in your suite. The rest of your party arrived a few days ago, and I'm sure they'll be pleased to know you made it safely."

"I doubt—"

Ella elbowed me hard in the side and said, "Yes, I'm sure they will."

The bellhop hummed the entire way into the gilded lobby, wearing my patience dangerously thin. As I looked around, returning for the first time in a half a decade to this building I'd once spent so much time in, I could see what Ella meant.

It *was* gaudy. Ostentatious and cold and sterile despite all the gold accents and rich fabrics.

I barely paid attention as the woman behind the desk checked us in, handing over two antique-looking keys that I knew were actually less than twenty years old.

"Pierre will bring your bags up," the desk attendant said, gesturing to the bellhop. "We hope you enjoy your stay!"

"Not fucking likely," I mumbled as we turned away.

"Deep breath," Ella said as we walked away.

"Sorry. I just...being back here—it's hard."

"I know," she assured me. "But you've got me, and we're going to make the most of this weekend, just like we have every other moment of this trip. Okay?"

I couldn't argue with her, not with that determined glint in her eyes or her vehement words and how deeply I knew she believed them.

"Okay, baby," I said, hauling her in and pressing a kiss to her temple. "Whatever you say."

"I love you," she reminded me. "That's the only thing that matters."

"Yeah," I said, stopping right there in the middle of a narrow hallway, guest rooms branching off from each side, and spun her to face me so I could kiss her properly. "But I love you more."

Ella grinned. "C'mon. Let's go freshen up and find something to eat. I'm fucking starving. Breakfast feels like years ago."

I smiled in response, grateful that she was picking up the slack at a moment when I desperately needed stability, when my level-headedness seemed to be failing me for the first time since...well, since the last time I'd been in this place.

There had been days, in the aftermath of the implosion of my and Mellie's relationship, where I genuinely believed I'd never find the woman meant for me. The one who was my equal in all the ways that mattered, but who loved me just as much for our differences as for our similarities.

And then I met Ella Delatou, and that was the day my life changed forever.

Those four years apart were worth it to have her pressed against me now, by my side as we navigated this next adventure.

⁂

Ella and I spent the bulk of the following morning and afternoon in bed, tangled in each other, pausing only to eat or use the restroom. She knew I was trying to lose myself in her, doing whatever I could to avoid facing my family, and was all too happy to oblige. I loved her even more for it—that she wasn't pushing me to do something I wasn't ready to do.

Then again, I'd never be ready.

Finally, we couldn't avoid it any longer, though I did give her another orgasm in the shower before we peeled ourselves away from each other to get ready.

I'd chosen a suit for tonight so dark blue it was nearly black, a stark white shirt beneath, a maroon tie and pocket square. I'd received strict instructions that my tattoos were not allowed to be on display, and though everything in me balked at the idea of buttoning myself up and pretending to be someone I wasn't, ultimately, I decided it wasn't a fight worth having.

Besides, Ella would scandalize my family enough for the both of us.

She must've had an endless supply of black dresses tucked away in what little luggage she'd brought with her, because while it was the same color, this one was entirely different from the one of the night before.

I swear to god, the thing must've been custom made for her. That was the only explanation for the way it perfectly formed to each curve and dip of her body, leaving absolutely nothing about her figure to the imagination.

Words completely eluded me, my mind blissfully blank. All I could do was twirl a finger in the air, urging her to spin in a circle. She happily obliged me, even going so far as to pop her booty out and shoot me a wink over her shoulder before facing forward again.

"Where the hell did you get this?" I asked, approaching her and running my hands over her hips, the satin catching against my callouses.

"Aria," she said simply.

"Remind me to send her a thank you card. My *god*, woman."

The front draped into sort of a cowl that offered a perfect view of the upper curves of her breasts, thin straps arcing over her shoulders and tying behind her neck. The entire back was exposed, as were the bulk of her tattoos—just the way I liked them.

I leaned in, pressing my face into the crook of her neck and inhaling deeply. I'd never be able to smell jasmine again without thinking of her, without being reminded of this trip.

As if sensing I had every intention of latching onto her skin like a goddamn vampire, then traveling south and repeating the process on her pussy, Ella pushed me away and gave me a pointed glare.

Turning me toward the door, she patted my ass and said, "Let's go or we'll be late."

I sighed, knowing she was right.

It was time to face the firing squad.

The first person to see us when we arrived in the bar downstairs, which had been closed to the public for this weekend, was my mother, and I was grateful for the opportunity to ease Ella into things before she'd be thrown to the wolves. I'd do whatever I could to protect her, but my father and brother were assholes, and there weren't many ways to shield someone from the words they tended to dole out like pointed barbs.

"Oh, my baby boy," my mom said as she approached, her hands coming to my face, simply resting there as her blue eyes—*my* eyes—darted across my face. "It's been too long."

"I know," I whispered, leaning in to hug her. "I'm sorry."

In the same way that Ella's scent now reminded me of the happiness and joy we'd found on this trip, my mother's warm vanilla one would forever bring me back to the only fond memories I had from childhood.

After lingering a little longer in that embrace, simply because I hadn't seen her in so long, I let go and stepped to the side, ushering Ella forward.

"Mom, this is my girlfriend, Ella. Ella, this is mom, Andrea."

"Girlfriend?" Mom said, blinking in surprise a moment before her mouth tipped up in a grin and holding a hand out for Ella. "It's a pleasure to meet you, Ella. And please, call me Drea."

I quirked a brow. She *never* allowed anyone save close friends to call her by her nickname. In that motherly way of hers, she must've sensed Ella was a good one—and that this relationship was going to stick forever if I had anything to say about it.

Before conversation could continue, a voice boomed out behind us, and I audibly groaned.

"William, my boy!" my father boomed as he approached our little circle, forcing himself into the space between me and my mom. "About time you showed up. We thought you were getting in yesterday."

"We did," I said coolly and without elaboration.

"Well, nice of you to show your face, then."

"Good to see you as well, Dad," I said through gritted teeth.

"And I see you've dragged someone in off the street," he said, his upper lip curling.

"This is Ella, Will. Liam's new girlfriend."

My dad huffed out a disgusted sound, not even bothering to pretend for the sake of keeping up appearances.

"Pleasure to meet you, Mr. Danvers," Ella said sweetly, though we all heard it for the lie it was. She had a death grip on my upper arm, nails damn near puncturing through my sport coat and shirt beneath, barely holding back from launching herself at him.

"How did you two meet?" Dad asked me, pointedly ignoring Ella.

She clearly didn't like being dismissed like that, so before I could, she replied, "He works for my family's winery."

Dad's eyes narrowed. "*You*'re a Delatou?"

My girl stuck her hand out. "Ella Delatou, at your service."

Dad merely stared at her, trying to figure out how to use this knowledge to his advantage—or maybe just trying to figure out how to get rid of her.

"Your family has been so wonderful to Liam," Mom said, saving Ella from the awkwardness of my dad ignoring her handshake. "We're thrilled he found a home in Michigan, doing what he loves."

Dad snorted, but wisely kept his mouth shut.

Something in me eased then. My father would likely never approve of Ella—not the tattoos nor the purple hair—in the same way he never approved of me. But my mother loved her, and as long as Gramps did as well, I was set.

The rest of my family could get fucked, my baby brother most of all.

And as if I'd summoned him, there was a commotion at the door as Sammy and his bride, Char, appeared. A thundering applause went up from their gathered guests, each of them preening under the attention.

God, they truly were a match made in hell. I was more thankful than ever that I lived on the other side of the country.

My brother and I looked so little alike it was a wonder we were born of the same two parents. I heavily favored my mother's side of the family with my dark hair, height, and broad build, though Mom was the exception to the rule as far as size went. Sammy, on the other hand, took after Dad. He was several inches shorter than me, not even six foot, fair-haired and skinned, and more delicately built. He was what I'd call a pretty boy.

I watched him offer his too-white smile to everyone he passed, shaking hands, leaving his bride in his dust as he practically beelined for our little grouping once he set eyes on me.

"Well, well, well," he said when he reached us. "The prodigal son has returned."

"I don't think you know what that term actually means, Sammy."

My brother stiffened. "Don't call me that."

"Why not?"

Sam straightened, spine going ramrod as he attempted to level me with a glare. His shoulders drew back, chin raised, eyes narrowed. "My name is *Samuel*. I'm no longer that stupid little boy who used to idolize you even when you made my life a living hell," he spat.

I couldn't help but bark out a laugh. "If that's the way you remember our childhood, you're even more brainwashed than I thought."

"Just because *you* pissed on tradition—" my little brother hissed, but Dad put a hand on his chest, stalling him.

"Fight nice, boys. There are too many eyes on us."

"And all you've ever cared about is your image," I gritted through the fakest smile I could manage.

Ella hovered nearby, pulled into conversation with my mom, and I was grateful for it. Grateful she was missing this trainwreck, that someone who genuinely cared about me was welcoming her into the fold.

I was tall enough that I could see over practically every head in the room, my gaze swiveling around as I searched for a way out, and I knew it the moment Mellie appeared.

Bracing myself, I waited for the gut punch.

It never came.

I grinned, ignoring whatever my dad and Sammy were saying in favor of returning to Ella's side. Having her tucked against me, I could fully relax—into the knowledge that I was fully over Mellie, that I was fully wrapped around Ella's little finger, that *this* was the love I was meant to find and keep forever.

Without breaking her stride in conversation with my mom,

Ella only shot me a quick wink and snuggled deeper into me.

Mellie must've been scanning the crowd for me, because when I looked up to track her progress, I was unsurprised to find her coming toward me, a wide, excited grin on her face. When she reached us, she gave my parents kisses on their cheeks, said a polite hello to Sammy, then whirled on me.

"William," she said in that sultry tone of hers I'd once loved so much; now, it only grated on my ears. "Good to see you. It's been, what...four years?"

"Five," I corrected.

"Too long regardless. How have you been? How's that little job in Michigan?"

"That *little* job is great," I gritted out. She could take pot shots at me and my character all day. That I could handle. But I wouldn't stand for her insulting my job, nor the family that had given it to me—especially not with one of those people standing next to me. "Recently released a line of canned cocktails in collaboration with the CEO, curated a menu for a new distillery that opened locally, and orchestrated construction on a community garden. Plus the grapes are off to a great start this season. I think our 2026 vintage will be our best yet, don't you, Wildflower?"

"Couldn't agree more," Ella said, one corner of her lips twisted up in a subtle smirk.

"Oh!" Mellie gasped, bringing a hand to her chest as she acknowledged Ella for the first time. "Forgive my rudeness. I'm Merlot Renault, but you can call me Mellie."

"Pleasure," Ella said. "I'm Ella Delatou."

"Delatou?" Mellie cut a look to me. "Isn't that the family you work for?"

"Sure is," I said proudly.

"Well..." she trailed off, brown eyes darting between me and Ella. "Seems some things haven't changed after all."

I knew the barb would come when she learned who Ella was, and I was glad I'd had the foresight to warn Ella about Mellie's attitude. Neither of us reacted, though internally, I was deeply annoyed with Mellie for saying such a thing.

The situations could not be more different. Mellie and I had been so young when we got together. Punch drunk in lust, experiencing puppy love. Inconsequential in the grand scheme of things, ultimately only serving to show me what I didn't want.

What Ella and I had was...everything. She was my soulmate. The woman I'd move heaven and earth for if she asked. The one I wanted by my side for the rest of my days.

"Actually," I told Mellie, "everything has changed."

An emotion I couldn't name flitted across her eyes, there and gone in a flash, but I knew it only meant one thing: trouble.

"We'll see about that."

In response, Ella shifted toward me so she could wrap her arm around my waist, her heels making it as simple as leaning in to press a kiss to my bearded cheek.

"C'mon, Wills," she said, running a hand up my torso and gripping my tie. "I think it's about time you buy me a drink."

Anything to get the fuck away from these people.

chapter 31
Ella

LIAM'S GRIP ON MY hand was borderline painful as I led us through the crowd toward the bar, unapologetically pushing my way past people to reach it as soon as possible. I needed some alcohol in my system, something to take the edge off the rage coursing through me.

I understood, in a sort of detached way, that my family wasn't exactly the norm. My parents were disgustingly obsessed with each other, even after over thirty years of marriage, and my sisters were my best—and, let's be real, *only*—friends.

But to see people who shared the same blood flowing through their veins be so blatantly cruel and cold toward each other had me wanting to start tearing limbs from bodies in Liam's honor. I'd never felt this way about anyone—never imagined I could kill a person with my bare hands.

For Liam, I'd do it, though. I'd do anything I could to never have to see that pain flash across his eyes again.

At last, we bellied up to the polished wood bar, and I raised a hand to flag the bartender down. His eyes landed on me quickly, and I recognized the perks of having a great set of tits. No bartender could resist serving me immediately, much to the annoyance of those around us, who shot me dirty looks and whispered unkind remarks behind their hands.

"Helloooooo gorgeous," the bartender said when he approached. "What can I get you?"

"Baby?" I said to Liam, who appeared at my side. I grinned as the bartender stumbled back a step.

"Buffalo Trace," Liam said. "Neat."

The bartender nodded, eyes shifting to me, though much less appreciatively now. "And for you?"

"I'll have the same."

When he disappeared to do his thing, I glanced up at Liam, whose brow was raised.

"Bourbon?" he asked.

"You think I'm drinking any of the swill they call wine in this place?"

Liam barked out a laugh and pressed a kiss to my hair. "Fuck, I love you. I couldn't survive this without you."

"Stick with me, Wills. I'll protect you."

"Three!" someone shouted from nearby, and Liam's head whipped toward the sound, his smirk blooming into a full blown, face-splitting grin.

"Gramps!" Liam yelled back, sounding like a little boy being reunited with one of his favorite people after a long time away.

And I supposed, in a way, that was exactly what was happening.

"There's my favorite grandson!" Liam's grandpa boomed as

he waded through the crowd, quite literally shoving people out of the way to wrap his grandson in a hug. After clasping him for probably longer than was proprietary for two grown men to do, Liam pulled away and studied him, giving me a chance to do the same. Though he had to be in his late-seventies or early eighties, he'd somehow maintained a youthful appearance. It must've been the smile, which was downright gleeful as he looked at Liam. His hair was shock white and full, eyes a paler blue than Liam's. Where his son and other grandson were stockier built, William Danvers the first was taller and narrower, though slightly curved from age.

"Gramps, I'd like you to meet someone."

His grandpa held up a hand before Liam could continue, his eyes shrewdly darting between us, then widening in surprise.

"You're in love."

It wasn't a question, and though Liam's cheeks turned pink, he said, "This is my girlfriend, Ella. Ella, this is Gramps."

I extended my hand, but Liam's grandpa waved it away and pulled me into his chest. He smelled of Old Spice and cigar smoke, a homey, comforting scent that had me relaxing against him.

"It's great to finally meet you, Mr. Danvers," I told him when we parted. "I've heard so much about you from Liam."

"Please, call me Bill," he said, eyes going a little misty as he placed a hand on Liam's shoulder. "And I hope Three only shared the good things."

Liam chuckled, but my eyebrows drew together in confusion. "Three?"

"Because he's the third," Bill explained.

I hummed. "I like that. Maybe I'll have to replace your nick-name."

Liam leaned closer, his lips brushing the shell of my ear as he whispered, "You can call me 'Three' after I make you come that many times later."

A shiver wracked my body, and heat pooled in my core.

"Promises, promises," I replied.

"Baby, you know I'll make good on them."

He would too, and I looked forward to it.

Bill awkwardly cleared his throat, but before he could say anything else, a bell rang out, followed by someone shouting over the din, "Dinner is served!"

In a mass exodus, the crowd shifted in a single direction like the flow of a river, and Liam, Bill, and I were swept up in it, shuffled through a set of doors on the far end of the bar and into a spacious dining room. There were maybe fifty people, and we were all directed to the tables on the far side of the room, where a lone two-seater sat on a raised platform, Sam and his fiancée already seated.

"Wait," I said to Liam, placing a hand on his arm and yielding his progress toward a table near the back. Bill continued and snagged us seats in his stead.

"What's wrong?"

"Nothing. It's just...are you in the wedding? I can't believe I hadn't thought to ask before now."

"Yeah," he sighed. "Best man."

"What the fuck. You don't even like each other."

"Dad forced it on us. Said we had to keep up appearances."

"That's...horrible."

Liam gave me a wry smile, hand on the small of my back as we resumed our path to the table. "That's life as a Danvers."

"Maybe you should take my last name when we get married," I mumbled.

Liam pulled up short, jerking me to stop. "Absolutely not. You'll take my last name, and you'll like it." He nodded at his grandpa. "Besides, Danvers is his last name too, and for him and him alone, I'm proud to have it."

With a mock salute, I murmured, "Yes, daddy."

Like the gentleman he was, Liam pulled out a chair for me at the small circular table, then took one of the two remaining seats, sandwiching me between him and Bill.

Once everyone had settled, an impressive gathering of waiters appeared, each carrying two dishes, moving around the room in a well-choreographed dance to pass them out to guests.

I barely paid attention to what I was eating as each course came and went, too intent on charming the pants off Liam's grandfather. And it seemed, by the end of the meal, when dessert was cleared away and guests rose from the chairs to dance, mingle, or refill their cocktails, that I'd done my job perfectly.

With a wide grin, Bill looked at his grandson and said, "Don't let this one go. You remind me so much of me and your grandma."

My heart softened, and Liam gripped my hand. I knew he'd lost his grandma shortly before he'd left Portland, and that the loss had precipitated the downfall of him and Mellie. That he'd pulled away in those final few months as he struggled mentally with the hole his grandma had left in his life.

"Don't worry," Liam said to Bill, though his eyes remained

locked on mine, "she's stuck with me forever."

I leaned in for a kiss, whispered, "Forever sounds good to me."

⁂

Liam's hands seemed to be everywhere at once as we pushed into the room after bidding his grandfather good night. He was downright greedy in the way he caressed and squeezed, pulling me against him, the thick ridge of his cock digging into my stomach. Sealing his mouth to mine and plunging his tongue inside. I met him with equal fervor, desperate for him, my clit throbbing, begging for attention, my core clenching around nothing, aching to be filled.

"Are you okay?" I asked when he peeled his mouth from mine in favor of sucking on the skin of my neck as he tugged on the tie of my dress. It released but caught on the tips of my breasts, and Liam eagerly pulled it free, rolling it over my hips until it fell to the floor.

He didn't return to his feet, merely remained on his knees, staring at my exposed pussy like he was a man starved and only my taste would satisfy him.

"I'm fine, Wildflower," he said, leaning in to nudge me with his nose, inhaling deeply. God, that shouldn't be so sexy, the simple act of him sniffing my most intimate place. But I wanted him to do it again and again, then follow that inhale with a taste. "But...this is what I come from. You and your family...you're lucky. That your enterprise is self-contained. That the small town is so good to you. That you haven't ever had to experience a moment of the shit I've had to deal with my entire life. And not only that..." He trailed off, glancing up at me. There was so much worry in his eyes, and before I could question it, he continued. "Your family genuinely loves and cares for each other. I never really had that. Just Gramps and Gram and mom."

"They're amazing people," I reminded him. "And they were enough. They raised you right."

"Dad is an only child," he said, his hands coming up to cup my ass, face resting against my stomach. "And Gram and Gramps...they knew they went wrong somewhere with him."

"I don't necessarily think it was all their fault. They both had a hand in raising you, and you turned out wonderfully."

"I don't want you to think less of me," he whispered against my skin. "Those people—my dad, my brother, Mellie's family—they're awful. But they aren't me. I'm not sure I ever belonged here."

Reaching down, I threaded my fingers through his hair, tugging until he looked at me. "You're right," I told him plainly. "Because you belong to me."

Liam softened, his troubled expression clearing away as quickly as it appeared. "I love you."

"I love you too, baby. Now be a good boy"—I brought my fingers to my pussy and spread it open for him—"and give it a taste."

"Yes, ma'am," he said, his tongue darting out and tracing the edges of my fingers, around and around my clit. My legs nearly gave out at that first drag. I'd never get over how fucking perfectly he ate me, lapping at me like he wanted to savor me, like I was the most exquisite thing he'd ever tasted.

Hand still gripping his hair, I stepped out of my dress and

retreated to the bed, sitting on the end and hooking my heels on the edge. Baring myself completely, giving him full access to torment me with that beautiful mouth.

"Prettiest goddamn pussy I've ever seen," he breathed, the air puffing against my slick, swollen flesh, raising goosebumps on my arms and legs.

I leaned back, unable to hold myself upright any longer, wanting to simply enjoy the sensations of this moment. Liam spread me open wider, hands high on my thighs, keeping me bared for his consumption.

And then he did something that had me yelping in surprise—though I didn't entirely hate it.

"You like that?" he asked, chuckling.

"Do it again and find out."

A low groan rumbled through him, and he lowered his mouth to my back entrance, tentatively licking at the hole before sweeping forward over my entire pussy. I moaned.

"Fuck, that's...different."

"Good or bad?" he asked, thumbing at my clit.

"Good."

"I wanna fuck you here, Wildflower," he said, finger toying with me, lightly brushing against that spot.

"Have you ever?" I asked, lifting onto my elbows so I could look down at him. I fucking loved him all wrecked like this, hair a tousled mess from my fingers, irises stormy with desire, my arousal in his beard.

Liam shook his head. "Have *you*?"

"No," I whispered, unsure why I was suddenly nervous. "Can we...work our way up to it?"

"Of course," Liam said. "Guess I'll just have to content myself with eating this pussy for now."

He didn't give me any warning save those words as he dove back in, staying away from my ass as he focused on the things he knew I did like. That torturous drag of his teeth over my clit, when he stiffened his tongue and shoved it into my entrance, fucking me with it while he worked my clit with his fingers.

And then, finally, when he filled me with three fingers, even though it wasn't quite as good as his cock, it still drove me higher and higher, that pressure in me coiling tighter with every advance and retreat.

I was a fucking goner when he sealed his mouth over my clit and sucked it into his mouth, fingers moving as rapidly as his tongue until I shattered.

Each orgasm Liam brought me to was nothing short of mind-blowing, wiping my thoughts deliciously blank until there was nothing but him and the pleasure he gave me. I felt like I was floating on a cloud, high above my body. Nothing had ever felt as good.

When my shakes and shivers ceased, Liam stood, shucked his clothes, and hovered over me.

"One," he said against my lips.

I huffed out a breathless laugh. "Oh, we're counting now?"

"I told you downstairs. You're coming three times tonight, or I'm going to die trying."

"What a way to go," I murmured as he kissed me, moaning as my taste combined with the bourbon he'd pounded all night exploded on my tongue. "Fuck, you taste good."

"Not as good as you, Wildflower."

Reaching down, I gripped his cock at the base and worked upward, swiping my thumb over the head, then lifting it to my mouth and sucking off the precum I'd collected.

"Debatable."

"Wicked, filthy girl. You ready for this cock now?"

"I'm *always* ready for your cock."

Instead of crawling between my thighs, Liam moved around to the side of the bed and reclined on the pillows.

"Ride it then," he said, his big hand flexing along his length.

"You got a thing for me on top?"

"Baby, have you *seen* your tits?" he asked in response.

I merely giggled, collecting them in my hands and shaking them at him. He groaned, biting down on his lower lip, and I returned my attention to his cock.

God, he was huge. Everything about Liam was large, and his cock was no exception. Thick, long, with a broad, blunt head that managed to brand that perfect spot inside me every time he slammed home, a vein crawling up the underside.

Turning and crawling over to him, I settled between his legs, my tongue darting out for a taste.

"You wanna suck me off first? You'll get no objection from me. You suck that cock like such a good little slut."

Such filthy fucking words that only served to crank up my desire. Forced me to squeeze my thighs together for some temporary relief. Closing my mouth around him, I took him as deep as I could, gagging as he bumped against the back of my throat. Breathing through my nose, I swallowed, fighting off the reflex, relishing the way he groaned and bucked into me.

"Goddamnit, woman. You're good at that." He fisted his hand

in my hair and pulled me off. "But I need to feel you."

I obliged, straddling his hips and rocking back and forth, his cock sliding through my lips, coating him in my wetness. His tip brushed against my clit, the sensation so heavenly I could get off just like this.

"How is it you feel so good every time?" I asked absently, resting my hands on his chest but still slowly rolling against him.

"I was made for you," he said simply. "You gonna get off like that?"

"Thinking about it."

"Use me however you need, baby."

Sprawled out the way he was, hands resting beneath his head, looking for all the world like a sexy wet dream come to life with the beard, the blue eyes, the muscles and tattoos—I'd never understand how I got so lucky to find a man who was both easy on the eyes with the most stunning insides to match.

I wanted him to fill me, but this slippery slide of our bodies, the tempting way his broad head pressed into my clit with each shift of my hips—another orgasm coiled tighter and tighter until I was bucking roughly against him. Nothing could've stopped me as I worked myself over, Liam's palms splayed across my thighs, holding me down. The friction, the fit, the feel—it was too much.

As if sensing what I needed, Liam reached up and tweaked a nipple, and I fell apart once again, collapsing against his chest as I trembled.

"Ella," he breathed. "That was..."

"Yeah," I sighed. "Just give me a second."

His hands brushed up and down my spine until I came back

to myself fully.

When I sat up at last, he grinned.

"Two," he said, and I couldn't help my eyeroll.

Then my eyes flicked to the wrought iron bed frame and the four posts at each corner, and an idea sparked. Instead of sinking down onto him like I craved, I got off the bed on shaky legs and padded toward the bathroom, returning a moment later with the straps from fluffy bathrobes, grateful there had been four.

Liam's eyes widened in curiosity.

"Do you trust me?" I asked.

He grinned. "Fuck yeah, I do."

I started at his ankles, looping the strap around one then the other, securing them to the posts at the bottom corners. Liam tugged experimentally against them, and I smiled proudly when they didn't budge. Then I repeated the process on his wrists before once again joining him on the bed.

Tapping my chin contemplatively, I stared down at him, eyes raking over every inch of his body.

"Where should I start?" I asked rhetorically.

"Thought you wanted my cock."

"Oh, I do," I said, reaching out to grab it, loving how the silky flesh felt against my palm as I worked it up and down.

"I didn't know this side of you existed," he admitted.

"Honestly? Neither did I." Shifting so I was between those thick thighs, I leaned in and ran my tongue along the tattoo stretching up the left side of his torso, pausing to flick one nipple then the other before heading back down. I sank back on my knees and said, "Thank you for letting me explore it."

"Thank you for trusting me."

I reached for his cock again, and his hips jumped, his length pulsing in my hand.

"How close are you right now?" I asked.

"Put that mouth on me and I'm coming down your throat in seconds."

I grinned wickedly, bending only to roll my tongue around his head. Then I collected all the saliva I could muster and spit it on his cock, using my hand to work it up and down until he was coated, aiding the endeavor with some of my own cum. Fuck, this was hot. The way he just let me use him like this, the sexy scene he presented all restrained, eyes hooded, chest rapidly rising and falling in anticipation as he waited for my next move.

I shifted until my chest was over his groin, and Liam realized what I was doing a moment before I pressed my boobs together around his shaft, because his eyes flared with excitement.

"Oh fuck," he breathed as I began to move. The most Liam could do was jerkily circle his hips, searching for friction, and I moved faster, wanting him to come undone quickly so I could put us both out of our misery and ride him until we were both screaming. "Oh, fuck, Ella. God, that feels incredible. You want me to come on your tits?"

"Yes please." I pressed my boobs in harder, increasing the pressure, and Liam swore creatively.

"Oh god, oh fuck, okay, I'm gonna come."

His rambling was adorable and sexy in equal measure. I loved how his eyes squeezed shut and fingers wrapped tightly around the robe straps as ropes of cum left him, painting my chest, my face, and his stomach. Guttural, unintelligible noises left him as he continued to spill, his limbs shaking against his restraints.

Before he could fully collect himself, not even bothering to clean myself up save swiping a splash of his cum off my nipple and sucking it into my mouth, I sat up, straddled him, and impaled myself on his cock.

We both groaned as he filled me completely, my head dropping back, hands resting on his thighs for leverage.

"You're trying to kill me," he breathed when I began to undulate my hips.

"Nah, baby," I told him, my breath picking up as I rocked faster, so goddamn desperate for him that I couldn't take it slow.

"You're right," he said, jerking up into me. "Let's see how fast we can get you to orgasm number three."

Pretty damn fast, if the pressure at my clit was any indication. "Besides," I murmured. "I can't kill you. I'm not done with you yet."

And I didn't think I ever would be.

WHEN I WOKE UP the next morning, the morning of my brother's wedding day, I was surprisingly...refreshed.

Considering the lack of sleep Ella and I had gotten the night before, I should've been exhausted and sore, but all I felt was energized.

Once today was over, Ella and I could return to Michigan and never look back. Except to see Mom and Gramps, I'd never have to come out west again save on the road trips Ella and I would inevitably take. There was peace in that.

The ceremony was at noon, and Ella and I had accidentally slept until ten, so we rose and quickly got ready. Since I'd refused to come out here for tux fittings and generally anything that had to do with today but the actual ceremony itself, I'd sent my mom my measurements and she took care of making sure I had something to wear that matched the rest of the groomsmen, a group of which consisted of a bunch of my brother's equally as entitled frat bros.

But my bespoke, cream-colored tux paled in comparison to Ella's outfit. Today, she wore a pink slip dress that fell to her ankles. The fabric was delicate and adorned with numerous wildflowers. With her hair curled and pinned to one side, makeup subdued, and delicate gold jewelry, she was a fucking vision.

Ella was wealthy, but she didn't feel the need to flaunt it, something I'd always admired. Hell the entire Delatou family was wealthy—richer than even my family—but you'd never know it from the way they acted. I wondered how different my life would be if I'd been raised by people more like Leon and Lena instead of my own parents. Mom did what she could but my father was a tyrant.

"Once again," I said, shaking myself from my thoughts and pressing a quick, soft kiss to her lips to avoid smearing her lipstick, "we have to get out of here before I take you back to bed."

"I've grown quite fond of that bed," she said, giving the mattress a little pat as she walked by it. "In fact, I think we should get a four post bed just like it."

I paused at the promise in those words, at the plans for a future she'd supplied in such an off-handed comment.

I pointed a finger at her, then gripped her hand. "We will be discussing that further at a later date. For now, let's go get this wedding over with so we can get the fuck out of here."

"Lead the way, Wills."

When we reached the main lobby of the hotel, we were greeted by my mom at the foot of the stairs.

"Oh, finally," she breathed when she saw me. "We were beginning to think you'd run away or something."

I laughed, kissing her cheek. "I definitely considered it."

"Well thank you for being here," she said, smiling up at me. "If not for *them*, then at least for me and your grandfather."

"You and Gramps are the *only* reasons I'm here."

My mom's expression softened, and as I had many times over the course of my life, I once again wondered why she continued to remain shackled to a man who was no better than a piece of chewed up gum stuck to the bottom of her shoe. More than anything, I wanted my mom to be happy, and I just didn't think she was. She'd gotten really fucking good at pretending, though.

Sammy appeared in the doorway of a room off to the side, and I could practically see the steam pouring from his ears as he waved me over. After squeezing Ella's hand a final time, I reluctantly walked to him.

"About fucking time," he grumbled, though he pasted on a fake smile and made a show of hugging me for the photographer stationed nearby, capturing every moment of this *joyous* occasion. "We have to be out there like...now."

"Then I'm right on time," I grinned as I pulled away, though my cheeks felt brittle and liable to crack under the force of it.

"Whatever," Sammy said with an eye roll. "Follow me so we can line up."

I did as I was told, walking behind him and his buddies through a door on the far side of the room, which opened onto a receiving area at the back of the atrium where the ceremony was being held.

Yeah, as if this place wasn't pretentious enough as it was, there was a fucking *atrium* on the grounds.

The Delatous would *never*.

The groomsmen quickly paired off with the bridesmaids, assumingly having been alerted ahead of time who they were walking down the aisle with. With a jolt, I realized as best man and maid of honor, I would be stuck next to Mellie for much of the formal parts of the evening.

Fuck me.

"Hello, William," Mellie said as she sidled up to me. Though the silhouette of each was different, all the bridesmaids wore dresses in a burgundy color that, with Mellie's pale coloring, didn't do her any favors. Nor did the heavy eyeshadow I thought was meant to be a smokey eye but missed the mark.

I squared my shoulders, resolving to be cordial, and said, "I actually go by Liam."

Okay, so much for cordial.

"Apologies," she said. "I haven't seen you in so long. You could've changed your whole name by now. Your last name is still Danvers, isn't it?"

"Yes," I gritted out, trying my damnedest to hold it together.

I didn't understand how I hadn't seen it before everything fell apart. How I hadn't caught onto her scheming and underhandedness. How like my father and Sammy and other players in this world she was. Fuck, was I glad I had gotten out. Before, everything Mellie did was magical to me, and I'd thought myself lucky that she was even giving me the time of day.

Now, it took all my self-control not to shrug her off when she slipped her hand through my proffered elbow.

Sammy walked down the aisle with Mom, Dad, and Mellie's mom, kissing both of the women on their cheeks before taking his position at the altar.

The harpist began strumming, and the procession began, four

pairings going before it was my and Mellie's turn.

I did my best to smile and appear happy as we made our way toward the altar, but I could tell I was failing miserably. Mellie, meanwhile, was eating up the attention, a bright grin on her face, offering little waves to the friends and family we passed. Almost as if she was saying, "See? Liam and I look so good together." As though she was trying to convince me.

She must've read my mind, because she said, "This should've been us," through her smile. "It still can be."

We reached the end of the aisle, and a moment before we parted, I whispered, "Never."

I took up my spot next to Sammy as Mellie did the same on Char's side, her lower lip jutting out in a pout briefly before she schooled her expression into that of happiness and excitement for her younger sister.

The harpist launched into the wedding march, and the guests rose to their feet, turning to watch as Char and her father came down the aisle.

I didn't give a fuck about her, or this whole charade.

Instead, my eyes found Ella's in the second row, and everything in me that had been whipped up in the last twenty minutes settled. I knew without a doubt I was looking at my forever, and while Mellie had serious delusions if she thought she and I would ever find ourselves wed, I could easily picture the day when I vowed myself to the second youngest Delatou daughter.

Hell, I'd marry her right this second if she'd let me. Shove my brother and his bride to the side and commandeer the entire affair, simply so I could forever call her mine in every sense of the word.

But if I knew Ella as well as I thought I did, she'd want something small and intimate. On the vineyard, probably. With a big floral arch that she designed herself, her sisters standing next to her. Funnily enough, when I imagined who would be by my side, I envisioned each of the partners of the Delatou women. Logan, Cal, Owen, and Ezra had been more like brothers to me than my own ever had.

I tried to pay attention to the ceremony, I really did, but it was difficult with Ella so close, her presence drawing my attention in like a lodestone. Rings and vows were exchanged, the officiant read that cliche 1 Corinthians Bible verse, Sammy and Char kissed, and just like that—it was over.

"We should talk later," Mellie said as we moved back up the aisle.

"There's nothing left to say," I assured her.

"Please, Will—Liam," she corrected. "Just give me a chance to explain myself."

I'd never considered the possibility that she might owe me an apology, that I might *deserve* one, and suddenly, I found myself wanting it.

"Fine."

⚘ ⚘

Photos were interminable, mostly because my cheeks were fucking aching from faking a smile, and my entire body, every nerve ending, begged me to get Ella back in my arms.

At last, we entered the reception, and though I knew it would piss my father and brother off and raise all kinds of questions from the guests, I left my seat at the head table empty in favor of joining Ella and Gramps at theirs once again.

Before she could utter a single word, I hauled her against my body and crashed my mouth to hers.

It wasn't an overly explicit kiss. There was no tongue, only an extended length of time where my lips remained pressed to hers, breathing her in, drinking in the sensations of being with her.

When I let her go, Ella swayed a little on her feet, but I steadied her with my hands on her hips.

"Hi," I grinned.

"Hello to you too," she said.

"That was some greeting," Gramps said from behind me, and I turned to him, giving him a sheepish apology.

Now that the hard part was over, I could sit back and enjoy my time with my girl and Gramps. We chatted all through dinner, and when the speeches were out of the way—Dad gave one in my place because there was no way in fuck I was getting up there and saying anything nice about Sammy and Char—the DJ got the music going.

I was surprised by the selection—namely that it was all music from this century.

A slow song came on, and I pulled Ella to her feet, walking us to the center of the dance floor and wrapping her in my arms.

"I have to ask," she said, though the way she gnawed on her lower lip told me she was nervous about the question she had.

"Yes?" I prompted.

"Did you and Mellie—" She stopped, shook her head, and started again. "Were you ever close to...*this*?"

I shook my head, lifting my hands to cup her cheeks. "No,

baby. We were—" I thought about the best way to phrase it without hurting Ella. Then again, I knew she'd understand. Knew she felt the rarity of what we had exactly as I did. "We were off more than we were on, and though I thought we were getting more serious at the end there, it wasn't ever like this. Believe me when I say I have never felt for anyone the way I feel for you. And maybe it's crazy to say, but I know without a doubt that the only woman I ever want to marry is *you*."

Ella nodded, tears welling in those gorgeous green eyes, making them sparkle even brighter than normal.

"Happy tears?" I asked.

"Happy tears," she confirmed.

The song ended, and something neither of us had any interest in dancing to began playing, so I led her off the floor.

"I'm going to go get us more drinks," I told her. "Go hang out with Gramps and rest."

"Rest?" she asked, quirking a brow. "For what, exactly?"

"Oh, I think you know, my dear. Let's call it a repeat of last night. But this time"—I leaned in to whisper in her ear—"*I'm* tying *you* up."

"Promises, promises," she said, winking and disappearing into the crowd.

I made my way toward the bar, but I pulled up short when I caught my parents in my periphery, having what appeared to be a whispered argument. Dad was red in the face, visibly pissed off. That wasn't shocking. What was, however, was the fact that my mom was shaking. With anger or fear, I couldn't tell, and when my dad gripped her upper arm tightly and didn't let go when she tried to pull away, I frankly didn't give a fuck.

Before I reached them, Dad finally released her and disappeared.

"Mom," I said, careful not to touch her when I reached her side. "Are you okay?"

Mom rested her hand against my cheek—against the beard I'd refused to shave simply on principle when Sam asked me to—and gave me a soft smile. "I'm leaving him, sweetheart. I've never been better."

Any normal person probably would've been blindsided and hurt by the news that their parents were getting divorced, but not me. All I could do was grin at my mom and wrap her in my arms, whispering into her raven hair how proud of her I was.

"You can move to Michigan," I whispered when we broke apart.

"I'll consider it," she said. "Depends if you're giving me grandchildren anytime soon."

She glanced pointedly over my shoulder, at where Ella and Gramps chatted at the table, as he tipped his head back and laughed loudly, Ella giggling behind her margarita glass.

"Maybe."

"You love her."

It wasn't a question, but it was the second time in as many days that she'd brought it up.

"More than I ever thought possible."

Mom nodded, and rose to kiss my cheek. "I love you, my boy. You've done beautifully, and I'm so proud of you."

My nose stung with emotion and I croaked, "I love you too."

"I think I might like Apple Blossom Bay," she said almost absently as she wandered away. "We'll talk more tomorrow."

As I continued my trip to the bar, I felt like I was floating. Everything was so...good. Perfect. Exactly as it should be.

Until Mellie stepped into my path and rained all over my parade.

chapter 33
Ella

"So tell me about yourself, Ella," Bill Danvers said when we were seated at our table.

"What do you want to know?"

He leaned forward conspiratorially. "Everything."

A chuckle burst free, but if that's what he wanted, that's what he'd get.

I told him about growing up in Traverse City and spending our summers on the peninsula. How my sisters and I were raised on the vineyard, running rampant through the vines and generally giving our parents grey hair.

"That can't have been easy for your dad," he said. "Raising five girls."

"I actually think it was easier on him than we were on Mom," I admitted with a grimace. "That man...he'd do anything for us. And I mean *anything*, if you catch my drift."

Bill nodded knowingly. "I'd do the same for my grandsons."

I raised a brow. "Even Sam?" I blurted, then clapped a hand

over my mouth. "Sorry, that was rude."

He just waved me off. "Yes, even Sam. I don't think people are inherently bad. I just think they're a product of their circumstances. Three has always been a much kinder, gentler soul who wanted absolutely nothing to do with the family business, and unfortunately, when Will realized that, Sam was the next best thing to take up the mantle when he eventually retires. But I've seen good in that boy, and despite the, shall we say, *messy* way in which he and Chardonnay—"

"Wait, her name is *Chardonnay*?"

Bill sighed heavily as though he was annoyed, even going so far as to pinch the bridge of his nose before saying, "Yes. Awful, isn't it?"

"It's definitely a choice," I said as diplomatically as I could. "Damn, I'm glad my parents hadn't named *us* after wine varietals."

Bill nodded sagely. "The point I'm trying to make," he said, steering us back to the matter at hand, "is that despite the messy way they got together, they do actually love each other, and that sort of bond can go a long way for changing people for the better."

For their sake, I hoped he was right. That this marriage union would make Sam a better person who maybe wouldn't blindly follow in his father's footsteps. Who, maybe one day, would be able to build a better relationship with his big brother.

I drained the rest of the marg and set the glass down, scanning the room in search of Liam. I found him talking to his mom, hugging her, and my heart expanded in my chest. I hated for him that his brother and father were such shitty people, but I was so grateful he'd at least had his mother and grandfather to pick up the slack, to remind him that he was loved no matter what anyone else might say.

I had them to thank for the man *I* got to love.

He let his mom go and turned toward the bar, and I couldn't look away as he walked, forever mesmerized by the way that big body so fluidly ate up space. How he moved with such grace, each movement intentional. Everything about Liam was intentional, from his words to his actions to his clothes, his home, the people he chose to surround himself with.

It would forever be a gift that I was the person he'd chosen *forever* with.

He was maybe ten feet from the end of the line snaking toward the bar when a woman stepped in front of him—Mellie.

They exchanged words before she put a hand on his arm and gestured for him to follow her out of the room.

I saw red with that touch.

I'd never considered myself a possessive woman. Even watching fans throw themselves at Alfie after shows hadn't done much to raise my blood pressure.

That right there should've been a sign I wasn't as invested in the relationship as I should've been.

But everything was different with Liam, and I didn't appreciate *his* ex putting her hands on what belonged to me.

"I'm sorry, Bill," I said, rising from my chair. "If you'll excuse me, I'll be right back."

"No worries, Ella," Bill said, patting my hand. "Just bring my grandson back with you."

I gave his shoulder a squeeze as I moved past him, rushing

across the room in the direction I'd seen them disappear, as quickly as I could on my stilettos. Eventually, I gave up, leaned against a wall to slip them off, then continued on my way.

Beyond the ballroom where the reception was held, hallways bobbed and weaved like a maze with numerous doors leading in all directions. On near-silent feet, I walked slowly, ears straining for any sound to alert me to where they went.

"So, 'Liam,' huh?" I heard someone ask faintly.

Coming to another corner, I peeked around it and into the room on the other side, finding Liam and Mellie standing in the middle of it.

Liam had his arms crossed over his chest, really testing the limits of that shirt as it strained against his arms and shoulders, looking entirely unimpressed and unwilling to be standing there.

"I've always gone by Liam," he told her. "You just refused to call me that."

"Because it sounds so...common."

"Yet you allow people to call you Mellie."

She snorted. "Touché. I'm just saying...you're not common, Liam. You were destined for more than that girl you brought with you and being some vintner at some shitty little place in Michigan. Come home," she implored him. "Take over this place with me. Let's begin our dynasty."

"No."

I grinned at the absolute certainty in that word.

Mellie remained unperturbed and stepped closer, tiptoeing her finger up Liam's tie, wrapping all five of them around it just below the knot.

I waited—waited for him to push her away, to step out of her reach.

Instead, I watched in horror as Mellie leaned in and pressed her mouth to his.

All the air left my lungs, and I swore my heart stopped in my chest.

Not again. Not again. Not again.

Tears blurred my vision, and I didn't wait to see what happened next. I merely turned and ran, groping through my clutch for my phone, dialing my sisters before I was even safely ensconced in my room.

Our room.

God, it smelled like him.

I smelled like him. Every part of me was marked in some way by him. He was branded deep on my bones in a way I'd never be rid of.

Fuck, I thought this was it.

I thought I was done looking.

I was openly sobbing by the time Delia answered.

It was always Delia who picked up first, and that realization comforted me. When everything was spiraling out of control, it was nice to know some things would never change.

"Ella?" she asked. "What happened? Are you okay?"

"He-he-he—" I tried to force the words out around my choked sobs, but I kept getting caught on the next word. "*Kissed*," I spat at last. "He kissed her."

The proclamation was followed by a wail, and I collapsed to the floor, throwing my shoes angrily across the room, narrowly missing the TV and instead punching a small hole in the wall, the heel lodging itself there and staying.

"What the fuck is going on?" Amara asked when she joined the call.

Through my tears, I glanced at my phone screen, too distraught to pick it up, to see all four of them were there. With me when my world was falling apart.

The only goddamn people I could ever count on.

"Apparently, *he* kissed someone," Delia explained. "I'm assuming *he* is Liam, but that doesn't make much sense. That man is a fucking simp if I ever saw one."

"What's a simp?" a male voice asked, but Delia shushed him.

"Not now, QB. The grownups are talking."

I choked on a laugh. "I don't know why he puts up with you."

"Me either!" Owen shouted from the background.

"Are you sure you saw what you think you did?" Chloe asked. "I mean, I agree with Delia. That's very unlike him."

"I know what I saw!" I snapped.

"Okay," Brie said placatingly. She'd been doing that since she was old enough to talk, always playing referee amongst her four older sisters. "Okay, El. We believe you. Did you talk to him?"

"No. I ran."

"Classic," Chloe said.

"What's *that* supposed to mean?"

Chloe looked chastened as she said, "Sorry. Just a book thing."

"This isn't a fucking *book*, Coco. This is my *life*."

And it was once again in shambles around me.

"We know, sissy," Amara said softly. "What do you need from us?"

"A flight," I said quickly. "Get me a fucking flight. And a car. Get me out of here."

"Are you sure that's the best idea?" Delia asked.

"I just want to be home," I told her.

"So you're going to leave without giving him a chance to explain," Chloe said.

"I love him," I wailed, angrily swiping at my eyes. "And he fucking *cheated*. I'm not fucking doing this again."

The reminder that I'd done this kind of breakup once before was a bucket of ice water over my head, and I rose to my feet, stripping off my dress and rolling it into a tight ball. I dug through my duffels until I found some comfy clothes I could wear to travel in.

The problem was...then, it hadn't meant nearly as much as it did now.

"What're you doing?" Brie asked.

"Packing," I said, first heading into the bathroom where I unceremoniously swept all of my toiletries into a plastic bag and tied the handles, not even bothering to find the case. Then I stomped around the suite, haphazardly tossing the rest of my shit in my canvas duffels, leaving anything that was replaceable.

All of it was replaceable.

Apparently, even me.

God, when would I ever learn?

Certain relationships could change you.

Being with Alfie changed me in a negative way. He brought out all of my worst qualities and exacerbated them until I became unrecognizable to even myself. I became small, weak-willed, a welcome mat for him to step all over.

But being with Liam?

With Liam, I was...me.

The girl who loved pulling over on the side of the road in the middle of nowhere Wyoming to drop seeds that would hopefully lead to pretty wildflowers sprouting up at the edge of an endless field.

The girl who wore ultra-feminine dresses and floppy sun hats because they made her feel pretty.

The girl who loved a man because he deserved it, not because he'd guilted her into it.

And damn, did I love William Danvers.

I loved him for all the small things, like how he didn't feel compelled to fill silences with idle chit chat. How he quickly learned my coffee order and got it for me every time we managed to stop for the night in a town with a cafe. How he walked behind me on our first hike in South Dakota, content to move at my pace, never making me feel like a burden for our slow progress because he was more worried about my safety and enjoyment than his own.

And I loved him for the big things too. The way he allowed me to come on this road trip, offering a hand to me when he saw I was struggling. The way he never belittled my dreams when I was brave enough to voice them. How he made me brave enough to voice them. The way he held me in his arms until my anxiety calmed that first night in the tent.

I loved the way he said my name like it was something to be savored. How, after the last of our physical walls fell, he was comfortable enough with me to initiate passing contact, like reaching over the center console in the van for my hand and giving it a quick squeeze. The gentle kisses he pressed to the hair at my temples when we stood side by side in line at a store or waiting to be seated at a restaurant.

How he made love to me, worshiping me like I was the goddess he prayed to every night—like loving me was his religion, and my body his church.

And the thing I loved most?

That he loved me for me, jagged edges, thorns, sharp words and all.

I was heading back to Michigan differently than the woman who'd embarked on this journey. I had changed, for the better, and it was all thanks to him.

It was just a shame we weren't going back together. That he'd taken something so beautiful. So pure and perfect and rare and magical...and shit on it.

My sisters were silent while I packed, but just as I drew the zipper closed on the final duffel, two things happened at once.

First, Amara said, "Your car and flight are booked. Be downstairs waiting in ten minutes to head to the airport. Your itinerary is in your email."

I relaxed a fraction. "Thank you, Mar."

But as soon as I finished speaking, the door flew open, and Liam rushed inside.

Fuck, this was going to be harder than I thought.

"I gotta go," I told my sisters and ended the call.

Liam and I merely stared at each other, his face stricken, mine surely red and splotchy from anger and tears.

"Wildflower," he breathed. "What the fuck is going on?"

THE MOMENT MELLIE PRESSED her lips to mine, I gripped her upper arms and shoved her away. I'd made it a rule my entire life to never take a rough hand with a woman, but when she refused to take no for an answer, drastic measures had to be taken.

"I told you no!" I shouted.

That was another of my rules: never raise my voice to a woman.

It seemed I was breaking all of them where Mellie was concerned. I should've known better than to follow her back here, to let her get me alone. I should've known she'd pull some shit like this.

"So you're really happy with that...tattooed freak? You can't be serious, William. There's no way someone so common could be enough for you. She's not good enough. And we were always so good together. Remember how perfect everything was? How good the sex was?"

I blinked at her slowly, then couldn't stop myself from barking out a laugh, even though my skin was crawling at the memory that I'd ever been inside this woman. God, I'd been such a fucking moron. And I wish I could chalk it up to being a dumb kid, but I'd spent the better part of my twenties with this person, and I'd never recognized how...rotten she was. Right to her very core.

"You know what your problem is, Mellie?" I said, removing my cufflinks and stuffing them in my pocket. Her attention remained on my forearms as I slowly rolled up one sleeve then the other, revealing *my* tattoos—way more than I'd ever had when we were together. I relished the way her eyes widened. "You think because you have money, you're better than everyone else on the planet who is beneath your tax bracket." I stepped into her space, glaring down at her. Mellie was so much shorter than Ella, I was nearly folded in half over her. "But let me tell you something, *Merlot.* That 'tattooed freak,' who also happens to be my girlfriend and the love of my life, has more money than you could ever dream of, and she's a thousand times the woman you could ever hope to be."

Mellie's mouth opened and closed like a fish out of water, searching for something to say, but I held up a hand.

"Now here's what's going to happen. I'm going out there to find my girl, and you're going to stay the fuck away from us the rest of the night. Got it?"

She only nodded, and I chuckled. The woman who always had something to say was finally silent for the first time in her life, and the quiet was pure bliss.

Without a backward glance, I stalked from the room and made my way back to the reception hall, beelining for the table where Gramps sat alone.

"Where is Ella?" I asked him. Her empty margarita glass, filled with half-melted ice, sat on the table in front of her chair. It appeared she'd been gone a while.

"She went to look for you," Gramps said, lifting the sleeve of his shirt to check his watch. "She's been gone maybe twenty minutes?"

"What the fuck," I breathed, turning away from Gramps and sweeping the room, searching for purple hair and a pink dress.

But my girl was nowhere to be found.

"Do you know…did she see anything?"

"Do you mean did she see you leave with Merlot? Yes, she did."

Fuck. Could she have found us? Had she heard the awful things Mellie was saying about her? Had she seen that kiss?

Fuck, I had to find her.

Pulling my phone out of my pocket, I clicked on her contact, but it went straight to voicemail.

Not a good sign.

I was frantic now, yanking at my hair as I willed myself to slow down and *think*. Mom crossed my path then, and I pulled her to a stop.

"Have you seen Ella?"

"No, sweetheart. Not for a while. Why, what's wrong?"

"Nothing," I said, waving her off. "Everything is fine."

"Okay…" She definitely didn't believe me, but I didn't care much, tuning her out as she sat down next to Gramps and told him she was divorcing his son.

"About damn time!" Gramps cheered, and though a smile tugged at my lips, it was quickly wiped away by the panic seizing my chest.

"I'm sorry, you guys," I told them. "I have to go find Ella."

"Sure thing," Gramps said. "Go get your girl. I'm going to tell your mom all the ways to milk your father for all he's worth in the divorce."

I shook my head, that smile threatening again, and raced from the room.

Please be here, please be here, I silently chanted the entire way up to our floor. With shaking hands, I inserted the key in the door and pushed it open.

"I gotta go," Ella said into her phone, then ended the call.

I couldn't make sense of what I was seeing. Of the sweats. Of the makeup smeared across her face. Of the complete lack of clothes and shoes strewn about the room like they had been when we left for the wedding.

Then I noticed her bags on the bed.

Fully packed.

She was leaving.

But why?

"Wildflower," I breathed. "What the fuck is going on?"

I chanced a step toward her, but she held up her hands.

"Don't come any closer. And don't call me that. That was a nickname from a man who loved me, and you very obviously *don't.*"

"What are you talking about?"

"I saw you, Liam," she said. Her voice was flat. Entirely void of emotion. "I saw you with Mellie."

Fuck. Fucking fuck.

"Ella, please. You have to let me explain."

"No!" she shouted, face coming alive with anger in an instant. "I *saw* you. There's no talking your way out of this. No feeding me some lie to get out of it."

"Goddamnit woman," I said, rushing her and gripping her arms before she could dart away from me. "Did it ever occur to you that *she* kissed *me*? And that I pushed her away immediately after? And that, after she insulted you, I told her you were the love of my life, a thousand times the woman she could ever hope to be, and to stay the fuck away from me?"

Ella stilled, her gaze fixed on a point somewhere in the middle of my chest. I had to admit, she was making a valiant effort not to look at me. Probably because she knew the second she did, she'd see the truth in my eyes.

Misunderstandings were embarrassing for the person who got it all wrong, but I understood why she'd reacted the way she did.

"Baby," I sighed. "All the things we've said, all the moments we've shared...the *love* we've made—it was all real. I promised you I'm not like him, and I meant it. I would never do anything to jeopardize what we have."

"You still let her kiss you."

"I pushed her away immediately, which you would've seen had you stuck around."

Ella's shoulders relaxed, and at last, she looked at me.

The pain shining in her eyes fucking gutted me, and I hated that, inadvertently, I was the reason for it.

"I can't do it again, Liam."

"I know, baby. *I know*. I've been there too, remember?"

"It's really over between you two?" she asked. "This weekend didn't drag up any old feelings?"

"*No*," I promised. "It's been over for years. Since before you and I ever met. And then I laid eyes on this stunning, tattooed, purple-haired beauty, and I knew there'd never be anyone else. There is only you, Wildflower. There will ever only be you."

Several tears overflowed from the well in her eyes, and I leaned in, kissing them from her cheeks.

"I'm sorry," she said softly, voice watery. "I...overreacted."

"I know why you did, and I'm not begrudging you your feelings. But you can't run away from me, Ella. If this is going to work, you have to talk to me. Stay. Be here with me. Believe me, and trust me. That's what you were doing, right? Running?"

She nodded. "My car is supposed to be here..." She grabbed her phone from where she'd tossed it on the bed and tapped the screen. "Now."

I shook my head, a soft chuckle escaping me. "You Delatou women work fast."

Ella finally smiled, and it was the same as the sun coming out on a cloudy day. A welcome, warming appearance.

"Think we could get a second seat on that flight?"

She held up a finger, as if to say *hold please*, then began tapping away at her screen. A moment later, she glanced up at me. "I'll do you one better, Wills. I upgraded us to first class."

The anxiety that had been holding my chest in a vice grip since I rushed back into the reception and realized she was missing loosened its hold, and I gathered her into my arms.

"I love you, Ella Delatou. Promise me you'll talk to me the next time something sets you off like this."

"I promise," she assured me. "And I love you, William Danvers. What do you say we head home?"

Home.

Damn, I loved the sound of that.

FOUR MONTHS AFTER THE TRIP

THE CASUAL WAY I strolled into Blossom's that crisp September afternoon completely belied the nerves that had taken root in my gut. I was about to do something categorically insane, but...well, I'd never exactly been in my right mind where Ella Delatou was concerned.

"Just a moment!" Fanny called from the back when the bell over the door tinkled with my entrance.

Hands shoved deep in my pockets, I wandered around the room, running over my plan in my head while I waited.

At last, Fanny appeared. "What can I—oh. Hi, Liam. Ella's not here. She's—"

"At the winery," I smiled. "I know. I'm actually here to see you."

"Okay..." Fanny had every right to be suspicious. I'd never spent much one-on-one time with the woman, not in the five years I'd lived in Apple Blossom Bay, and certainly not in the four months since Ella and I had returned from our trip.

"I need to buy some flowers."

Her forehead creased in confusion. "Why couldn't this be taken care of when Ella was here?"

"Because they're for Ella."

"Okay..." she said again, stepping deeper into the showroom floor. "Which ones do you want to buy?"

I grinned. "All of them."

"All...of them?"

"Yes, Fanny," I confirmed. "Everything you've got. And then, if you wouldn't mind, the guys will be here shortly to help me bring them all upstairs."

Fanny's gaze narrowed. "What are you up to, Liam Danvers?"

I shrugged, affecting a nonchalance I certainly didn't feel. "I'm proposing."

"You're *what*?" Fanny gasped. "Oh my god. Let me see!"

I knew what she meant without her elaborating, so I withdrew my right hand from my pants' pocket, the velvet ring box clutched there, and held it out to her.

She gasped again when she opened it. "Liam..." she said, glancing up at me. "You did good, boy."

"I had help."

She grinned. "You were smart to go to them."

I'd had an idea in mind ever since I got a bug up my ass about proposing—which, for the record, was quite literally the second we returned from our road trip. It had only taken me this long to work up the courage. And I knew I wasn't buying a ring she was meant to wear forever without her sisters' input.

I wasn't even worried she'd say no, because I knew without

a doubt she loved me as much as I loved her. It was more...we were moving really fast, and I'd been terrified of what her family would say.

I'd worried needlessly. All seven of them were on board from the moment the words left my lips—yes, even Leon, who clapped me on the back heartily and welcomed me to the family.

"Take them," Fanny said suddenly.

"What?"

"Take them," she repeated, sweeping her arms out. "Take them all. Consider this my going out of business sale, and everything is free."

"Fanny, you can't—"

The only woman leveled a finger in my face. "Don't tell me what I can and can't do, boy. I love that girl like she's my own, and as long as this business is still in my name, what I say goes. Since today is my last day as owner of Blossom's, this seems like the perfect send off."

I couldn't help but chuckle. "She's going to be pissed."

"Oh, for a number of reasons, surely. But think of it this way: you two can start your lives together with an entirely fresh slate. It'll be good problem solving practice for her," Fanny added with a wink.

"Baptism by fire," I grinned. "I like it."

"You're a good man, Liam. And she's lucky to have you."

"Nah," I waved her off. "I'm the lucky one."

"I better be invited to the wedding!" she said as she disappeared down the hall after a knock came at the back door.

A moment later, the cavalry arrived, Delia leading the charge. I shook my head; I should've known she wouldn't be able to stay away, even though I specifically requested all the sisters keep Ella occupied.

"How'd you get away from her?" I asked Delia as she led Logan, Cal, Owen, and Ezra in.

"Told her there was an emergency at the distillery that QB couldn't handle by himself."

"Whiskey," Owen groaned. "Quit making me look bad in front of the boys."

Delia merely shrugged. "Just reminding them who wears the pants in this relationship."

We all glanced down at her legs, which were bare beneath the hem of her dress.

"Metaphorically speaking," she added with an eye roll.

Fanny joined us, clapping her hands together and shouting, "Chop, chop! We haven't got all day!"

Like being ordered around by a drill sergeant, we all hopped to attention, gathering arrangements in our hands and following Delia up the stairs.

⚜ ⚜

Three hours later, the stage was set.

Ella's apartment was small enough that there wasn't really a free inch of flat surface to be found save the path from the doorway to where I stood in the center of the kitchen/living spaces. My hands were so clammy I couldn't stop wiping them on my pants.

I'd briefly considered dressing up for the occasion, but I didn't want to tip Ella off by having her also dress up, so I opted for my typical uniform of jeans and a black cotton tee.

While I waited for the text to come through telling me Ella had arrived, I popped the ring box open and studied it one final time before I'd be able to slip it onto Ella's finger.

I'd wound up sourcing it from a boutique jeweler in Detroit who specialized in custom rings, and it had been worth every penny. The band twisted around like vines, ultimately rising up to four little leaves that held a large, square-cut amethyst at their center. I'd already purchased her wedding band, too, which was more of the same vines, little leaves branching off with a much smaller amethyst stone in their centers.

The ring was one-of-a-kind and wholly perfect for my girl.

I couldn't wait to see her wearing it every day for the rest of our lives.

Just as I snapped the box closed and dropped it back in my pocket, my phone buzzed in the other, and I withdrew it to find a message from Delia.

Delia Delatou: She just pulled up! Good luck!

"Fuck," I breathed into the empty room.

There was no reason to be this nervous, but I couldn't quell the anxiety squeezing my chest. Couldn't quiet that little voice in my brain saying, "What if she says no?"

I'd never survive.

"No," I said, shaking out my limbs. "No. She's going to say *yes.*"

Footsteps on the stairs had me straightening and making a last-ditch effort to pull myself together.

Her key slid into the lock, and I watched the handle turn as she opened it and pushed inside.

Then came to a stop in the doorway, hand flying to her mouth as she took in the scene.

When her eyes landed on me, widened in shock, she said, "What the fuck?"

I chuckled, all the nerves and anxiety leaving in an instant.

"Hi, Wildflower."

"Hey, Wills," she replied. "What's all this?"

"Come here and I'll tell you."

She dropped her bag in the entry and walked slowly toward me, her head swiveling as she attempted to process the flowers, the petals, the candles.

Me, waiting for her.

"Is this like a birthday surprise or something?"

"Or something," I grinned, hauling her against me when she was within reach. "Happy birthday, baby."

"Thank you," she whispered, rising to give me a kiss—which I ended before it could get too heated.

Ella frowned. "What's going on?"

I didn't respond, just stepped away from her and dropped to a knee.

"No," she breathed.

I only smiled, turning the ring box over in my hands as I stared up at her.

Even in her ripped jeans and Delatou & Danvers tee—the one she'd stolen from me all those months ago and refused to give back—she was a goddess. I'd happily stay in this position for the rest of my life, worshiping at her feet.

"Ella Jane Delatou," I began. "You are...everything. The most breathtaking woman I've ever had the pleasure of knowing, both inside and out. I knew from the very first second I laid eyes on you in the flower shop downstairs that you were meant for me, and while it took us a while to get here, I don't regret any of it. This time with you has been the sweetest and most joyful of my life, and I'm hoping, exactly as you've given me every day of the past four and a half months, you'll give me the rest of your years too." With shaky hands, I opened the box, the ring sparkling in the flickering candlelight, and Ella gasped again, tears instantly filling and spilling free from her eyes.

"Wills..."

"Will you marry me, Wildflower? Will you make me the happiest, luckiest goddamn man in the world and be my wife?"

I'd barely had the words out before she was tackling me, both of us landing in a heap on the floor with her on top of me. Thankfully, the candles were battery operated, or we surely would've lit the place on fire.

"Yes, yes, YES!" she chanted, peppering my face with kisses. "Fuck, I love you. Yes, I'll marry you."

I sat up, hauling her with me, and she straddled my lap as I slid the ring on her delicate finger. Then I lifted us both to our feet, bending her backward and kissing her soundly.

When we straightened, Ella held her hand in front of her, mesmerized by her new piece of jewelry.

"Do you like it?" I asked, almost shyly. "If you don't, we can get something different. You're stuck with it forever, so I want you to love it."

"Liam...it's perfect." She smiled up at me, eyes shining with so much love it took my breath away. The fact that she reserved that look for *me*? I'd never take it for granted. "I love it so much. I'm literally never taking it off."

I gave her another kiss. "That's the point."

"Come here," she said, feeling around in my pockets until she found my phone. Then she grabbed my hand and took a couple steps away. "Remember that picture you took of me in the hot springs?"

I grinned. "You wanna recreate it?" I asked, wiggling my brows.

"Not like that! I'll be keeping my clothes on this time, but the idea is the same."

I pretended to pout, but directed her where I wanted her, holding her hand as that gorgeous ring refracted rainbows to the ceiling. Once I'd snapped it, she opened my texts, started a group chat with her entire family—partners included—and sent it.

Once that was taken care of, I said, "I have another question."

"Anything."

"Will you move in with me?"

Ella frowned. "What's wrong with my place?"

I glared down at her, then without a word, lifted my hands over my head...and easily touched the ceiling, elbows still bent and everything.

Ella giggled. "Okay, we need somewhere with higher than seven foot ceilings. Got it."

"Is that a yes?"

She threw herself into my arms, and I caught her easily, swinging her around in a circle.

"That's a hell yes."

I grinned and captured her mouth, letting my tongue sweep against her bottom lip and gently pulling it. "Thank god. I'd have been willing to find a new place, but I fucking hate moving."

"Speaking of," she said, pulling away and turning her head side to side. "How quickly do you think we can pack my shit?"

Before I could answer, a thundering sounded on the stairs, like a herd of wild animals racing toward us. Ella and I merely turned toward the open door, grinning widely as the first of her sisters—Delia, of course; it was always Delia—rushed us.

The second before they reached us, before we got swept away in the excitement of her family—*my* family now too—I kissed her one last time.

"I love you, Wildflower."

"And I love you more."

ONE YEAR AFTER THE TRIP

"I CAN'T BELIEVE THE big day is already tomorrow," Mom said, leaning back in her chair and resting a hand on her stomach. My and Liam's rehearsal dinner had, of course, been catered by Ezra and Brie, and we'd had more food than we knew what to do with. Each of us girls and my parents would be eating leftovers for the next several weeks.

And that was saying nothing of the feast they'd curated for tomorrow. Even though they were both in the wedding party, they'd been very adamant about having a hand in what we served, saying it was their gift to us, and Liam and I weren't about to turn that down.

Brie, however, refused to allow anyone else to make my cake, and I was grateful for that. That, even though she'd be standing next to me along with Chloe, Amara, and Delia, someone so special to me had created the cake Liam and I would ceremonially cut.

After we'd finished eating, and had shared a nightcap of Dela-tou & Danvers Lena's Best Sangria, the wait staff—which Owen had brought in from Birdie's—handled the cleanup while we prepared to part for the night.

Tonight marked the first time since we'd set off on our road trip a year ago that Liam and I had spent apart. I hated the thought of sleeping without him, but my sisters insisted it was tradition, and I couldn't argue with that.

It also marked the first night in a long time that I was truly off work, leaving the reins of the flower shop to my lone employee. I'd taken over Blossom's last fall, after Fanny settled all of her affairs in Michigan and went to Arizona for the winter, only to never come back save this weekend. I'd been royally pissed when I realized she'd given all of my inventory to Liam for our proposal, but I couldn't stay mad for long. I was, after all, getting the love of my life and a wedding out of the deal.

The guys were spending the night at Cal and Amara's while us girls were staying here. Tomorrow, we'd get ready at the Villa before the ceremony was held at the winery—exactly as I'd envisioned since I was a little girl.

The guys rushed outside toward Owen's truck, piling inside, but Liam remained in the doorway with me, as unwilling to leave me as I was to let him go.

"I love you," he murmured, bending to kiss me, one of those slow, gentle ones he knew really got me going. But now wasn't the time or place for that, especially not when Logan rolled down the window to the truck and shouted.

"Let's go, lovebirds! Save the kissing for tomorrow."

"Your brother-in-law is a pain in my ass," he grumbled against my lips.

"You love him."

"I do," he agreed. "I love all of them, but not nearly as much as I love you."

"Well I would certainly hope not," I teased. "After all, you're not fucking any of them. Or are you?" I tapped my pointer to my chin contemplatively. "I've always thought your and Ezra's bromance skewed a little more *romance* than bro…"

Liam pinched my sides and leaned in to nip at my neck. "Wicked girl. You know there's only one person in the world for me."

"She must be incredible to have snagged a catch like you."

"Incredible doesn't even begin to cover it."

My cheeks heated, and I pushed him away before I could give into my urge to drag him upstairs and have my way with him.

"I love you," he said as he bounded down the steps.

"And I love you."

"See you tomorrow."

I grinned. "I'll be the one in white."

Actually, my dress was more cream than white, and adorned with wildflowers that started on the base of the bodice and flowed all the way down the full skirt. I'd be changing into something easier to move in for the reception, but I figured since I was only getting married once, I was going full send on the dress for the ceremony.

"I can't believe you're getting married before me," Amara pouted as she wove delicate purple flowers into my hair.

I snorted. "It's literally two weeks, *Princess*," I said, emphasizing Cal's nickname for her. "I think you'll survive."

Amara sighed. "I suppose you're right," she said, stepping back to survey her work, her hand immediately falling to her stomach and the bump growing there. "As long as we get married before this little one arrives, I don't really care when it happens."

"But sooner rather than later," Delia said as she approached us, holding my earrings in one hand and necklace in the other. She handed the necklace off to Chloe, who went around behind me while Delia hooked the teardrop amethysts into my ears. "You don't want to be a cow on your wedding day."

Amara smacked her. "Don't call pregnant women cows, Lia. Frankly, it's fucking rude. I can't wait to see how big you get when you and Owen eventually have kids."

"Seriously," Brie snorted as she joined us as well, having just put on her dress. "Have you seen that man? He's huge. And his brothers are just as big."

"Aria is tall as hell too," I reminded them. "And we're not exactly...petite."

Delia sighed. "Fuck. I'm going to have monster, ten-pound babies, aren't I?"

We all devolved into laughter, but quickly sobered. I reached for the two nearest to me—Chloe and Delia—linking my hands with theirs. Around we went until we were all connected.

While Brie and Chloe were both already married, Amara and Cal had only gotten engaged a few months before on their daughter's first birthday. Owen had proposed to Delia last November, and they were planning a ceremony for the upcoming October, right before Delia's birthday.

"I couldn't do life without you guys," I said to them, sniffing and tipping my head back to avoid any tears spilling free and ruining the makeup Delia had painstakingly applied.

Seriously, she threatened bodily harm if I ruined it.

"Ditto," Brie said, and we squeezed each other's hands. "But this is just the beginning for us. The guys...they've only made things better, haven't they?"

"They have," Chloe agreed. "And the babies."

I grinned as I thought of my nieces—Aleah, Cora, and Brie and Ezra's daughter, Harley. They were the lights of our lives, and I was seriously looking forward to the day when Liam and I welcomed our first into the family.

"Our last names are changing," I said, trying to smile through the tears, "but we're Delatous forever."

"Forever," they agreed. I don't know which of us moved first, but suddenly, we were pulled into a group hug, each of us sobbing noisily.

"What the hell is going on in here?" someone asked, and we broke apart to find Mom standing in the doorway, hands on her hips, glaring at us. "I mean, seriously? Can't you guys hold it together for like...I don't know. An hour?"

"No," we all blurted at once, then immediately started laughing.

"Well, figure it out," Mom said, moving toward the bed and gathering two of the bouquets—which I'd designed and Fanny arranged when she'd arrived a few days ago from Arizona—and handed them to Brie and Delia. "The ceremony starts in ten minutes."

My sisters and I all shared a shocked and horrified look, then burst into motion. Delia quickly touched up everyone's make-up, Chloe and Amara made sure the girls were ready to walk down the aisle with their flower baskets, and Brie called Ezra to make sure he had the rings.

It was pure chaos, but I wouldn't have it any other way.

All the nervous and excited butterflies I'd been feeling up to that point flew away as I stood before the closed patio doors of the winery, Dad on my right. This was finally the moment all my dreams came true, and I couldn't wait to get down the aisle, marry Liam, and start our forever together.

"You're happy?" he asked me.

"More than I've ever been before."

He pressed a kiss to the top of my head. "That's all I've ever wanted for you five. These men...I couldn't have asked for better for my babies."

"Stop it," I hissed, taking the hanky from his hand and dabbing at my eyes. "If you make me cry, Delia will kill you."

Dad scoffed. "I can take your sister."

One by one, my sisters disappeared with their partners until all that stood between me and Liam were Aleah, Cora, and baby Harley, who the older two towed behind them in a little red wagon.

I could hear my guest's laughter and coos of happiness and excitement as the girls made their way down, and I waited for my cue, the moment the song I'd chosen to walk down the aisle to would kick on.

The opening strings of "God Bless the Broken Road" filtered through the doors, and Dad glanced at me.

"Ready?"

"Let's do this."

Any hope I had of not crying evaporated the moment I laid eyes on Liam, who was the most gorgeous man I'd ever seen, standing beneath the archway I'd spent hours on in his cream-colored suit, almost the same shade as my dress. And the second he saw me walking toward him, he choked out a sob, doing his best to keep his eyes on me and hold it together. Ezra, who was his best man, settled a hand on his shoulder and whispered something that had Liam laughing and swiping at his eyes.

At last, we reached the end of the aisle, and while I'd given the officiant strict instructions not to ask the archaic "who gives this woman to be wedded to this man" question, Dad still approached Liam and shook his hand, then joined our hands before letting go.

"I love you, my girl," he whispered as he kissed my cheek, then went to take his place next to Mom.

"Hi, Wildflower," Liam mouthed.

"Hey, Wills," I grinned.

As we'd opted for traditional vows, the ceremony passed in a blur, though it felt as though Liam and I were the only two people on the planet as we exchanged them and placed rings on fingers. The ceremony wasn't the important part, anyway.

Everything that came after was.

And when the officiant pronounced us husband and wife, I didn't even wait for him to give the instruction to Liam to kiss me before I threw myself into his arms and did it myself.

I pulled away, Liam wearing a grin that rivaled my own in size, and I wiped some gloss from his lips as we turned to our guests.

"And now, for the first time," the officiant began, "I am

pleased to announce Mr. and Mrs. Danvers!"

To cheers and bubbles and the bass-heavy opening of "Let's Get Married" by Jagged Edge, Liam and I sauntered back up the aisle and into the winery, where we'd take a breather before heading out to the vineyard to take pictures.

Liam pulled me against him the second we were alone, and I yelped in surprise as the thick length of him pressed into my stomach.

"Have you had that the whole time?" I asked, curious how he'd managed to hide it.

"Nah," he said, leaning in to nuzzle my neck. "Only popped up when that guy said 'Mr. and Mrs. Danvers.'"

"You liked that, huh?"

He pulled away to look at me. "Baby, I've been dying to give you my last name since the day I met you."

"Well, Mr. Danvers," I said, tugging on his tie until his mouth was a breath away from mine. "What do you say we get in some trouble before we have to greet our guests?"

Liam's grin was positively feral as he took my hand and said, "Lead the way, Mrs. Danvers."

❧❧❧❧❧ ❧❧❧❧❧

As had the ceremony, the rest of the day—photos, guests congratulating us, cocktail hour, and dinner—sped by in a blur.

My sisters had us all crying and laughing as they stood up and made speeches, particularly Chloe, who used her gift with words and experience as a married woman and now mother to offer us some advice. I was grateful in that moment that we'd elected to hire a videographer, because once the Chateau Delatou bubbly started flowing, and we hit the dance floor, I had no hope of remembering anything but how alive I felt, how fucking happy I was, and how amazing it was to have all of my favorite people in one place, celebrating me and the love of my life.

We shared our first dance to "Cover Me Up" by Morgan Wallen, which I let Liam pick and ultimately decided was pretty perfect for us. We cut the gorgeous chocolate cake made by my sister, and took a million photos. We danced until our feet hurt, until the DJ announced it was time for our guests to head outside for our sendoff.

Liam and I changed once again, this time into comfy travel clothes. It was late, and we were only heading as far as our house, but I wanted our photographer to catch us leaving, looking like we were heading off to some tropical locale instead of just to our cabin on the outskirts of town.

The true star of the show wasn't even me and Liam.

No, it was the purple VW van waiting for us outside the entrance to the winery. After the road trip, neither of us could stand to part with it, so we'd purchased it from the company Liam had rented it from for a pretty penny. It was worth it, though. I smiled every time I looked at it, stored safely in our garage to protect it from the elements, and I couldn't wait to take more adventures in it alongside my *husband*.

When we pushed out onto the walkway, we were greeted by all of our guests twirling sparklers in the air, cheering and offering us congratulations one final time.

At last, we were settled in the van—me behind the wheel and Liam in the passenger seat—both of us hanging out the windows shouting thank yous to everyone for coming.

And then it was time to go, the engine sounding like music to my ears when I turned it over. Riley Green played softly from the speakers, the soundtrack to the rest of our lives.

I turned to Liam, and my world narrowed to that point. To his face, to those blue eyes and his pearly white smile. To his entire person. Straight to the heart of the man beneath, the heart that belonged to me.

"What do you say, Wills? You ready for our next adventure?"

Liam leaned back in his seat and tapped the dash.

"Take me away, Wildflower."

acknowledgements

I FEEL LIKE THE list of people to thank gets longer with every book.

First, and foremost, Mom, Dad, and Sissy. Thank you for believing in me, for supporting me, and for always encouraging me to chase this silly little dream. I wouldn't be the woman I am without you three, and I'm grateful you're mine.

To Granny J, who reads every book cover to cover—even the spicy scenes that I should be embarrassed about my grandma reading but am somehow not. I always look forward to your text messages after you finish. Thank you for being my biggest cheerleader. And, of course, thank you to Grandpa Vic, who is always asking after my writing. I may have named Vic after you, but you couldn't be more opposite if you tried. "Teacher" will always be my favorite nickname.

To my angels, Grammy and Grumpy. It breaks my heart that you never got to be here to watch me achieve this lifelong dream of mine, but I feel you with me every day. Every time I find a random coin around my house or the office that I know wasn't there before. Every sunny day, every time the Packers win, and every birthday, holiday, and random Tuesday. I know you're with me. I love you and miss you so much.

To Mer, who at this point doesn't even need a paragraph because there isn't anything I can say that I haven't already. For always having my back, for putting up with my crazy plans for my career—even when you have to tell me to chill out because ideas come to me faster than I could ever write them. For loving me and supporting me and being the best goddamn long-distance bestie in the world. I love you more than TikTok loves Joey B thirst traps.

To Jenn Chipman, Jenn McMahon, Karley Brenna, Erin MacKenzie, Ava Hunter, Sarah Bailey, Michaela Jean Taylor, and Chelsea Curto: I fucking hit the jackpot with author friends like y'all. I'll forever be grateful to have you in my corner, and to say I'm proud to know each one of you is the understatement of the century. I know there are so many more of you to name, but just know if you're reading this, I appreciate you so much more than I could ever say.

To Sav, Emma, and Kait, for jumping into this one in the eleventh hour and being the best beta readers ever. Your enthusiasm for my stories means the most, and it's something I will never take for granted.

To Sarah Lassen, who has been the most avid and one of my loudest supporters from the moment that random ERWB TikTok went viral.

To Samantha, for sending this series out with a bang by creating the most stunning, perfect cover for Ella and Liam. You never cease to amaze me, and I am forever thankful to have had you with me on this crazy ride with me from the beginning.

And last but certainly not least, to my readers. Can you believe we're here? Ten months and four books later, this series is complete. You have changed my life with Love on the Vine and the Delatou sisters. Every edit, every reel or TikTok, every comment, like, share. Every recommendation and DM. All of it. I'll never be able to accurately express just how fucking grateful I am for every single one of you, whether you've only read a single page or all eight books—even FTB and OTL!—cover to cover. It'll never stop being surreal that there are people out there who consider me an auto-buy author, who impatiently wait for my next story. THANK YOU THANK YOU THANK YOU.

AMANDA CHAPERON REALIZED HER passion for books, and for writing, at a young age. Growing up, she was rarely found without a book in her hands, a hobby she carried into adulthood. She writes what she loves to read: messy, relatable characters, lots of steam, and always a happily ever after.

She currently lives in Michigan with Gryffin, her Golden Retriever. She loves all things romance, fantasy, young adult, and thrillers that keep her up at night.

Dicktionary

My dear sweet reader, please use this guide to avoid (or seek out) the spicy scenes, which can be found in the following chapters:

Chapter 19
Chapter 20
Chapter 22
Chapter 23
Chapter 29
Chapter 31

Spread those pages, my friend.